C000178282

The confederate a
knew where the an
payment in gold w
was short in the S

Belle Boyd, beautiful confederate spy,
knew how to get the gold but needed help if
her plan was to succeed.

Fate threw her in with a certain captain in
the Texas Light Infantry – a young man
who was already spoken of in the same
breath as the legendary leaders of the
South.

His name was Dusty Fog.

*Title awaiting publication

# J.T. EDSON OMNIBUS
## Volume 8

THE COLT AND THE SABRE
THE REBEL SPY
TO ARMS! TO ARMS!
IN DIXIE

**CORGI BOOKS**

# J.T. EDSON OMNIBUS VOLUME 8
A CORGI BOOK o 552 13609 3

THE COLT AND THE SABRE originally published in Great
Britain by Brown Watson Ltd.

PRINTING HISTORY – THE COLT AND THE SABRE
Corgi edition published 1968
Corgi edition reprinted 1971
Corgi edition reprinted 1975

PRINTING HISTORY – THE REBEL SPY
Corgi edition published 1968
Corgi edition reprinted 1968
Corgi edition reprinted 1971
Corgi edition reprinted 1974

PRINTING HISTORY – TO ARMS! TO ARMS IN DIXIE!
Corgi edition published 1972

Corgi Omnibus edition published 1991

Corgi Books are published by Transworld Publishers
Ltd., 61–63 Uxbridge Road, Ealing, London W5 5SA, in
Australia by Transworld Publishers (Australia) Pty. Ltd.,
15–23 Helles Avenue, Moorebank, NSW 2170, and in New
Zealand by Transworld Publishers (N.Z.) Ltd., Cnr. Moselle
and Waipareira Avenues, Henderson, Auckland.

Printed and bound in Great Britain by
Cox & Wyman Ltd., Reading, Berks.

# The Colt and the Sabre

## CHAPTER ONE

## MISS BOYD PREPARES TO LEAVE

Up at the big house, taken over by the 6th New Jersey Dragoons' officers as their mess, a ball was in progress. Music, laughter, the hum of conversation, clink of glasses and clatter of plates came faintly and annoyingly to Private Hooley's ears as he stood guard on the stables which housed the pick of the officers' horses. After over an hour on the duty, Hooley found the noise growing increasingly more distasteful. More so when he knew that all but the essential men on guard detail celebrated news of a United States Army victory over the rebels back east.

When Hooley enlisted in the Dragoons, filled with patriotic fervour, he expected to spend all his time alternating between charging and routing the grey-clad enemy and being fêted by an adoring civilian population. Instead he found himself sent to Arkansas, where he learned foot-drill, how to ride a horse in a mighty uncomfortable fashion, dismount and prepare to fight on foot, perform the essential military task of kitchen-police and stand guard duty. None of them pleasant or attractive to a man who looked for high adventure; and of them all, he cared least for standing guard. A two-hour stretch on the stable post could stretch on and on until it felt more like two hundred. Especially when, like tonight, the brass could be heard celebrating and being fêted by what passed in the Bear State for an adoring civilian population.

A shape approached the stables, coming from the rear of the big house. From the white cap, black dress, white apron and the fact that the approaching woman carried two travelling bags, Hooley deduced that she must be a servant to one of the fancy, high-toned gals attending the ball. He could tell little about the woman's figure or face, for a maid's uniform did not tend to emphasize its wearer's shape and so far she had not entered the limited area of light from the stable door.

'Howdy, gal,' he greeted, it sounding better than lining his Springfield carbine and calling the formal 'Halt, who goes there?'

'Howdy, you-all,' answered the girl, her voice husky and holding a hint of a southern drawl. 'Just bringing these bags down for my mistress. She's going to have Captain Haxley take her home. Only the good Lord knows when that'll be. And I've got to stay here and wait for her.'

At that moment the girl entered the patch of light. She stood maybe five feet seven in height and, despite the limitations of her clothes, gave the impression that she could show a mighty pretty figure dressed more suitably. The white cap hid all her hair, but Hooley did not give a damn for that as he studied her face. Hooley prided himself on his judgment of women, and he decided that the girl before him was about as beautiful as he had ever seen. Taking in the almost faultless features, the long-lashed dark eyes, the slightly upturned nose, Hooley's main attention rested on the full lips and their warm, inviting smile. If Hooley knew anything about women – and he would modestly admit that he knew plenty – that girl wanted company real bad.

'Got to wait down here?' he asked.

'Sure have,' she agreed, halting by the door and setting down the bags. They were made of good leather and designed to strap on to a saddle; not the usual kind of luggage a lady of quality used when travelling, although Hooley ignored the point.

'Could get mighty lonesome,' he remarked, glancing around to make sure that nobody observed him.

'It surely does,' answered the girl. 'Say, does this stable have a golden horseshoe nail?'

Knowing what the girl meant, Hooley fought down an anticipatory gulp. Even after only a year in the Army, he knew the legend of the golden horseshoe nail and its use in luring members of the opposite sex into the privacy of a stable.

'Sure it does,' he said and hoped his voice did not sound as husky to her ears as it came to his.

'Sergeant Papas was going to show it to me,' the girl explained, 'but he's not been around to see me.'

That figured, thought Hooley, for Papas held post as

8

sergeant of the guard. No love being lost between Hooley and Papas, the private figured showing his sergeant's prospective prey the 'golden horseshoe nail' might be highly diverting. Having made a study of such matters, Hooley knew that the officer of the day would be most unlikely to make rounds while the dance ran its course and, without prodding by his superiors, Papas never left the guard house when on duty.

'Come on inside,' he grinned. 'I'll show it to you.'

Entering the stable, lit by a solitary lantern hanging over the door, Hooley rested his carbine against the door and looked around him. Some twenty horses stood in the line of loose stalls around the walls. A rack supported McClellan army saddles at one side of the room. Hooley ignored both sights, his attention being on the ladder which led up to the hay loft. Did he have time to take the girl up there, or should he show her the 'golden horseshoe nail' in the less comfortable confines of an empty stall?

While Hooley pondered on that important problem, the girl opened the vanity bag which had hung from her wrist and been obscured by the travelling bag in her hand. Taking out a silver hip-flask, she threw a dazzling smile at the soldier. As she came towards him, he caught a whiff of perfume. Not the brash, cheap kind poorer girls mostly used, but something more subtle and expensive. If Hooley thought of the matter at all, he put the aroma down to the maid helping herself to her employer's perfume. Such a trivial detail never entered Hooley's mind, it being fully occupied with thoughts of forthcoming pleasure and interest in the contents of the flask the girl offered to him.

'I sneaked this out of the house,' she told him. 'Got it filled up with some of the best I could find.'

Taking the flask, Hooley removed its stopper and sniffed at an aroma even sweeter to his nostrils than the perfume the girl used. He had never come across so fine a smelling whisky and forgot his manners. Tilting the flask, he drank deeply, making no attempt to let the girl precede him. The whisky bit his throat and burned warmly as he sucked off what would have been a good four-fingers drink in the post sutler's store – and better whisky than that shrewd trader ever offered the enlisted men at that. Having drunk, his thoughts turned to other matters. Gallantly he rubbed the top of the flask and offered it to the girl.

9

'How about you?' he inquired as she replaced the stopper.

'Shuckens, a girl doesn't drink strong liquor,' the girl giggled. 'I only brought it out in case I met a handsome gentleman who looked thirsty.'

'You've got a real kind heart, gal,' Hooley declared, feeling his spirits rise as the whisky sank warmingly into his belly.

'I sure have,' she agreed, placing the flask back into her bag. With her hand still inside the bag, she suddenly stiffened and stared in a horrified manner at something behind him. 'Look out!' she gasped.

Hooley spun around, not knowing what might be waiting for him. Even as he began to turn, he saw a change come to the girl's face. No longer did it hold either warm invitation or startled fear, but a cold, determined expression transformed her beautiful features. Before the change could register in Hooley's mind, he had completed his turn. A sudden dizziness whirled up inside Hooley, although it did not last for many seconds.

Holding a short, lead-loaded, leather-encased billie, the girl's hand emerged from her bag and whipped around in the direction of Hooley's head. While many regiments of the U.S. Army now tended to standardize their equipment, the New Jersey Dragoons retained their traditional uniform. The buff-coloured trimmings of the uniform, differing from the more general cavalry yellow, made a handy conversational piece in a bar; and the peaked, soft-crowned cap was claimed to be far more comfortable than the 'Jeff Davis' or Burnside hat now issued to other regiments. However, the cap offered no protection against the sun or an attack on the base of the skull. Coming around with a snappy flick of the wrist, the billie caught Hooley's head just under the rim of the hat and he crumpled forward, collapsing to the floor without a sound.

'Sorry, soldier,' the girl said, her voice still husky and 'deep south,' but bearing the accent of an educated, cultured upbringing. 'They do say showing the golden horseshoe nail to a girl weakens a man. And I reckon you'd rather have your brass think you'd been jumped from behind than know you'd taken a drugged drink.'

Even while speaking, the girl returned her billie to the vanity bag, bent and gripped Hooley's ankles to drag him aside so he would not be visible from the door. Leaving the soldier, she went straight to the stall housing the colonel's favourite horse, a big, fine-looking bay gelding noted for its stamina and speed. Collecting a saddle from the rack, the girl carried it to the bay's stall. There she removed her cap, exposing almost boyishly short hair so black that it seemed to shine blue in the lamp's light. Next she unfastened and wriggled out of the maid's dress. Even had Hooley been conscious to witness the disrobing, he would have met with disappointment. Instead of emerging dressed in underwear, the girl proved to be clad in a man's dark blue shirt, tight-legged black riding breeches and high-heeled riding boots with spurs on their heels. An opportunity to caress her hips while she wore the maid's dress would have handed Hooley a surprise, for she wore a gunbelt with an ivory-handled Dance Brothers Navy revolver butt forward in the open-topped holster at her left side.

Leaving her discarded clothing on the floor of the bay's stall, the girl began to saddle the horse. She worked fast, handling the bay deftly despite its reputation for being awkward and mean. With her chosen mount saddled, she led it to the barn's door and fastened it just inside. Collecting another saddle from the rack, she went again to the stalls. This time she selected and saddled a powerful roan, the pride of the major commanding Company D, leading it to the side of the bay.

For a moment the girl stood by the barn's door, listening to the sounds of revelry which came from various parts of the camp. She saw nothing to disturb her, no sign of approaching authority; which did not entirely surprise her as she had been at the ball and seen the officer of the day enjoying himself in a manner which made his attending to duty an unlikely possibility.

'I hope the boys do their part,' she mused, returning to release the remaining horses.

On being freed, each horse made its way towards the door of the barn and passed out into the darkness. Outside they began to bunch, uncertain of what course to follow. After turning loose the last horse, the girl went and dragged Hooley outside. Her blow had stunned him, but the laudanum in the drink she gave him served to keep him quiet long after the effects of the blow wore off. Another quick glance around and the girl entered the barn once more.

Taking down the lantern, the girl carried it to the stall where her clothing lay. She hurled the lantern against the wall. Glass shattered, oil sprayed out and flames licked up, bounding across the straw. Calmly the girl waited until she felt certain that her discarded clothing would be consumed by the spreading flames, then she ran to the two saddled horses. Already the roan's reins were secured to the bay's McClellan saddle. The horses moved restlessly as the flames began to lick up and grow in fury. Showing considerable skill, the girl swung astride the bay and urged it out into the night, the roan following, obedient to the gentle pull of the reins.

Drawing her revolver, the girl rode towards the freed horses. 'Yeeah!' The ringing yell of the Confederate cavalry burst from her lips and she fired a shot into the air.

Startled by the yell and shot, the horses began to run. Letting out another wild yell, the girl urged her mounts after the departing animals, hazing them away from the house and towards the open Arkansas range land. Even as the horses' hooves drummed out loud in the night, from various points about the Dragoons' camp came more rebel yells, shots and flickering flames as hay and straw piles took fire. Disturbed horses snorted and moved restlessly, voices shouted questions, curses and orders, the whole punctuated by the wild ringing rebel war yells and occasional shots.

Up at the big house, the band came to a discordant halt in the middle of a Virginia reel. The more sober officers reacted first. Leaving their partners, they led the rush from the building. Outside all was pandemonium. A bugler sounded assembly, blowing lustily but without effect. Celebrating men poured from the sutler's building, most of them too drunk to make any logical deductions. The sound of shooting increased, yells went up as horses were freed from two company picket lines to add to the confusion.

One of the first people from the officers' mess was Colonel Verncombe, commanding the Dragoons. Halting, he stood glaring around him at the confusion. Fires blazed from three different points, men dashed about wildly and without any co-ordination while a flurry of revolver shots down by A Company's picket lines merged into the noise of stampeding horses.

'What the hell?' yelped a major, cannoning into his colonel.

12

'It's a full-scale attack!' Verncombe answered. 'Get down and start organizing your—'

'Look there!' yelled a lieutenant, pointing to where flames licked up the walls of the officers' stables.

'Get men down to it!' Verncombe barked back. 'Save our horses and gear if you can. Where the hell's the sergeant of the guard. Officer of the day! Find the guard. The rest of you, to your companies. On the double!'

'Can we help, Vic?' asked an infantry colonel, who, along with several of his officers, had been a guest at the ball.

'Keep the civilians and womenfolk inside and from under foot, Paul,' Verncombe replied, watching his officers scatter to their companies.

Long before any defence could be organized the firing died down and the sound of hooves faded into the distance. Cursing non-coms restrained their excited men and prevented them, wasting ammunition shooting at shadows. Sweating officers started to check on the damage inflicted by the raiders and asked questions with regard to the strength of the force which attacked them.

An hour later a glowering Verncombe watched his company commanders gathering around. Face almost black with controlled fury, he waited to hear their reports. A smoke-blackened lieutenant came first, after an abortive attempt to douse the fire at the officers' stables.

'We couldn't save anything, sir,' he said. 'But at least the rebels took all the horses out before firing it.'

'That figures,' grunted Verncombe. 'How about the sentry?'

'We found him stretched out on the ground, clear of the building. Been struck from behind. I've sent him to the surgeon.'

'Good. How about it, Major Klieg?'

'They destroyed our hay supply and the corn stored by Company C, sir,' answered the major. 'Cut the picket lines, but my men managed to drive them off before they could do more than scatter the horses. Horses ran back into the camp and I've a detail rounding them up.'

'And casualties?' asked Verncombe.

'Not in my company, sir. I don't think we got any of them; or if we did, the rebs carried them off.'

Other reports came in. Company A had lost all its horses and half of Company E's mounts had gone, while the rest scattered through the disturbed camp. Three fodder stacks were either burned out or so badly damaged that they would be of no use in feeding the regiment's horses. While there had been some stiff fighting, casualties proved to be light. A few slight wounds and no deaths came as a result of the raid, although various claims were made as to the number of the enemy killed.

'Sounds like an entire regiment jumped us,' said Verncombe dryly as he listened to his company commanders' reports.

Naturally no soldier wanted to say a small force caused such havoc in his camp and so most of the claims would be exaggerated. Knowing this, Verncombe decided that a company – a well-trained and organized company – of Confederate cavalry had made the attack.

'Who do you reckon it was?' he asked the senior major.

'Texas Light Cavalry, sir,' the other answered without any hesitation.

'That's Captain Dusty Fog's company, sir,' another officer broke in. 'One of my men claims to have seen him before. Said he couldn't miss knowing Fog. Great, big, bearded feller on a black stallion eighteen hands high if it's an inch. The soldier claims to have seen Fog leading one party and thinks he might have hit him.'

'What's amusing you, Major Pearce?' growled Verncombe, glaring at the commander of Company D as that worthy let out a low guffaw of laughter.

'Remarkable feller that Captain Fog, sir,' Pearce replied. 'One of my sergeants claims that he saw Fog and helped drive him off before he could free our mounts. Says he's sure he put a .44 ball in Fog before the rebs pulled back.'

'An attack like this would be typical Texas Light Cavalry work though, sir,' one of the other officers pointed out.

'They've never struck in this area,' another objected.

'A thing like that wouldn't worry Fog,' Verncombe put in.

Over the past year the name of Captain Dusty Fog, Texas Light Cavalry, had risen to almost legendary heights. To the Union troops in Arkansas the name meant more than that of the South's other two top raiders, John Singleton Mosby and Turner Ashby. At the head of a company of hard-riding Texans, Dusty Fog struck like a tornado, coming unexpectedly and creating havoc, then disappearing again. His men could out-ride and out-shoot any Union outfit;

although no Yankee cared to even think it, much less **admit** such an unpalatable fact.

A raid of the kind which just struck the Dragoons would be typical Dusty Fog tactics. Yet Verncombe wondered about certain aspects of the attack. The stunning of the stable guard and the freeing of the officers' horses did not strike him as being unusual. Dusty Fog fought in a chivalrous manner and would not kill unless in battle, if he could avoid doing so. Nor would he leave horses to burn, especially good quality mounts his own side could use against the Yankees. No, those two points did not worry Verncombe. The colonel felt surprised at the minor, comparatively speaking, damage inflicted on his surprised and disrupted camp. Under such conditions, he might have expected far greater losses of horses at least.

Suddenly a chilling thought struck Verncombe, one that drove all others from his head. One of his companies was at that moment acting as escort to a visiting general, taking him to Fort Smith in the Indian Nations. Grabbing senior Union officers and whisking them off behind the Confederate lines had long been a prime activity of Dixie's raiding trio. If Dusty Fog should hear of the general he might easily strike in that direction.

On giving the matter further thought, Verncombe decided his fears were unfounded. The route taken by the general lay to the north of Russelville. With such useful booty as almost a hundred head of prime horses in his hands, Dusty Fog would be highly unlikely to go further north. In Fog's place, Verncombe knew he would head straight back towards the Ouachita River and the safety of Confederate-held territory.

'Best get back to the guests some of you,' he told his officers. 'The rest start getting things cleared up.'

'Do we take after them, sir?' asked the commander of Company A, seething with rage at the loss of all his horses.

'By the time we could, they'll have too much of a head start,' Verncombe replied bitterly. 'All right. Let's make a start.'

The ball had come to an end, but the infantry colonel succeeded in keeping the civilian guests from bothering the hard-pressed Dragoons. After a time, the visitors began to prepare to leave.

In the confusion following the attack, nobody missed a

15

very beautiful blonde girl who had been present earlier in the evening. The Dragoon officers had too much on their minds to pay much attention to their departing guests. If either the infantry officers or the civilians missed the girl, they said nothing, thinking she was a member of a Dragoon family. During the evening, she had mingled with the other people present; pleasant, witty and yet never staying with one group for any length of time, so nobody missed her. However, it was an indisputable fact that she neither went with the Dragoon families to their quarters, nor left with the other guests.

## CHAPTER TWO

## MISS BOYD IN DISTRESS

A MILE from the Dragoons' camp, the girl slowed her two horses and allowed the officers' mounts she had driven before her to stream off into the night. Twisting around in her saddle, she looked back to where flickering fires and some noise marked the camp's site. By now the shooting had died down, but she could guess at the confusion it caused among the Dragoons.

After ensuring that she was not being followed, the girl started her horses moving once more. She rode through the darkness for a short time until coming to the bank of a small stream. Turning her mounts downstream, she continued along its bank until reaching a wagon road and ford. There she went into some bushes, slipped from the saddle and let the horses graze.

Time passed and hooves drummed as a rider came down the road. Instantly the girl drew her Dance, cocking it and handling it in a manner which showed she knew how to use it. Moving to her horses' heads, she peered through the bushes to where a rider approached. The darkness prevented her from being able to identify the approaching man, or even tell if he be civilian or soldier. Hefting her Dance with the right hand and gripping the bay's reins with her left, the girl began to whistle a tune. At the first sound, the rider's hand dropped hipwards and lifted holding a gun.

'Southrons, hear your country call you,' he said in a low voice.

'Up, lest worse than death befall you,' answered the girl, holstering her Dance in the certainty that the other be friend.

The whistling of 'Dixie' might have been done by a Yankee, but the rider knew few Union supporters would know the fiercely patriotic words put by General Albert

Miles to Daniel D. Emmet's tune. So he holstered his gun and rode closer.

'How did it go?' asked the girl, coming from cover.

'Smooth as a snake's belly, Miss Boyd,' the man replied.
'Were any of your men hurt?'

'Nary a one. We did just like you said, moved in and waited. The Yankees were all whooping it up, or in their beds. Didn't hardly see as much as a sentry. Got away with a fair bunch of hosses. What'll we do with 'em?'

'Send them west. If you meet a Confederate Army outfit hand them over. If not push them into the Indian Nations.'

Either way the horses would be lost to the Yankees for no Indian would return a bunch of prime horses to the Union Army.

'You sure planned things slick, Miss Boyd,' enthused the man. 'Me and the boys didn't fire more than a dozen shots at most. Those Yankees made up for it. Did any of 'em shoot each other?'

'It's possible,' Belle Boyd agreed. 'Say, I had to destroy those maid's clothes you brought to me.'

'That's all right, ma'am,' the man replied. 'Can we do anything more for you-all?'

'No. Scatter to your homes like you usually do, after you've got rid of the horses. And thanks for your help.'

'It's been a real pleasure, ma'am,' answered the man, watching the girl mount the bay and ride off leading the roan. He gave an admiring grin and rubbed the neck of his horse. 'Yes, sir, hoss. That Belle Boyd's sure some gal. Wonder what brought her out this ways.'

Holding her horse at a steady, mile-eating trot, Belle Boyd rode south-east along the trail. While the man she had just left, and his band of Southern patriots, had proved to be of the greatest help to her, she knew that she must have the aid of a larger, better armed force to make use of the information gathered since her return from Europe. A dozen men, no matter how brave or loyal, could not handle the next part in Belle's plan. On the next occasion Belle organized a raid on a Union force, she wanted to really have a strong Confederate Army outfit at her back.

All she had to do was ride across about sixty miles of hostile territory, ford the Ouachita without being caught, and report to the nearest Confederate force to be granted the aid she needed. That her request would receive immediate

18

attention she did not for a moment doubt, for Belle possessed an almost legendary fame among the grey-clad soldiers of the South.

Born into a rich Southern family, Belle grew up with every advantage and luxury, yet had a restless spirit which prevented her from becoming a pampered milk-sop. As a child she always preferred boys' games to girlish pastimes and her indulgent father, who wanted a son, taught her to ride, shoot and other male accomplishments. Nor did she ever forget them, and continued to defy conventions through her teens. The clouds of strife grew in the South and Belle's father had been an out-spoken champion of every sovereign state's right to secede from the Union if its policies and interests came into conflict with the remainder – one of the main causes of the Civil War, although the Union supporters used the slavery issue as being more suited to induce their people to fight.

One night, shortly before the start of the War, a bunch of Union supporters attacked Belle's home. Belle's mother and father were killed in the attack and the girl received a wound, being helped to escape by some of her family's 'down-trodden and abused' slaves. By the time Belle recovered from her wound, the War had started, and she put her newly-developed hatred of the Yankees to good use by becoming a spy. Without formal training, Belle still became a very useful agent for the Confederacy. She gathered and passed on information, often delivering her own messages instead of relying on a courier. Old Stonewall Jackson himself often referred to Belle as his best courier and admitted that she and the South's other lady spy, Rose Greenhow – Rose gathering the information and Belle delivering it – made the defeat of the Yankees at the first battle of Bull Run possible.

With such a solid recommendation as that at her back, Belle knew she could rely upon the aid of the Confederate troops in Arkansas, once she found them.

Keeping up a steady seven-miles-an-hour trot, and changing horses frequently, Belle followed the trail to the southeast. One talent developed since the start of the War, an invaluable one in her chosen line of work, was the ability to carry the memory of a map in her head. Thinking on what she had seen at the Dragoons' camp, while searching Colonel Verncombe's office for the information she required, Belle knew that she must cross the Coon Fork of the Arkan-

sas River. Her discussion with the Southern patriots warned
her that the Coon Fork ran fast and deep for many miles
and could only be crossed by a bridge – and every bridge
carried a strong Union guard. With that knowledge in mind,
Belle continued to follow the trail and lay her plans for
crossing the river when she reached it.

Dawn began to creep up, a faint but ever-growing grey
forcing out the blackness of the eastern sky. Halting her
horses, Belle slipped from the saddle and looked around
her. Not a half-mile ahead, although still hidden from sight,
lay the Coon Fork, and the trail she followed crossed the
river over a bridge.

Opening one of her travelling bags, which hung strapped
to the bay's saddle, Belle took out a carefully folded white
satin ball gown. The gown, made to her own design, had
been much admired at the Dragoons' camp and packed
when Belle changed ready for departure. Two other boxes
lay in the bag, one containing her blonde, red and black
wigs, all so carefully made that only a *very* close inspection
could differentiate between them and a real head of hair
when Belle wore one or the other. The second box carried a
dark blue Union officers' fatigue cap with gold braid decor-
ating it. Taking out the cap, Belle donned it at a rakish angle
which served to partially hide her face under the peak's
shadow. She repacked and secured the bag and then un-
strapped the overcoat which hung militarily neat on the
cantle of the roan's saddle.

Although the 'cloak coat' proved to be somewhat large,
Belle found no difficulty in donning it or fastening the frog
buttons to keep it in place. She decided to leave the sleeve-
length cloak in position as it helped to further disguise her
shape. Having used a similar bluff on more than one occasion, Belle felt no great anxiety as she mounted the roan,
gripped the bay's reins in her left hand, and started to ride
towards the bridge.

Despite her cool appearance, Belle felt a momentary
twinge of doubt and concern as she came into sight of the
bridge. Fear of Confederate raids led the Union forces to
maintain a strong guard on every important bridge, and the
nature of the Coon's flow made it imperative that the bridge
she approached stayed in use. So a force of almost company
strength had been camped by the bridge.

Belle based her arrival on coming in with the dawn, at a

time when human energy was at its lowest ebb. From the look of the lines of pup tents and lack of burning fires, most of the guard detail lay in their blankets. No crew manned the squat, evil-looking Vandenburg Volley gun which covered the further approaches to the bridge, but she did not doubt that its crew slept in the pup tent close by it, or that it stood with all eighty-five .50 calibre barrels loaded ready to discharge at any hostile force foolish enough to try to rush from the other side of the river.

Only one sentry stood watch, leaning against the upright support of the bridge and, from all appearances, not more than half asleep. However, a disturbing sight to Belle's eyes were the half dozen or so men saddling their horses beyond the line of tents.

Sucking in a breath, Belle continued to ride, apparently unconcerned, down the trail towards the bridge. Hearing the hoof-beats, the sentry turned his attention towards the approaching figure. He studied the two fine-looking horses and could identify an officer's fatigue cap and overcoat. Having seen numerous officers cross the bridge, the sentry regarded the approaching rider with no great concern nor suspicion.

In addition to possessing a naturally husky contralto voice, Belle was a good mimic. Approaching the sentry, she slowed down her horse. By keeping her head down, she prevented him from making out too much of her features as she growled, 'Lieutenant Murray, 6th New Jersey Dragoons, riding dispatch.'

A formal enough announcement and one the soldier might have taken at its face value. However, the man was an old soldier, the kind who took his duty seriously and stayed alert even after a long spell on his post. His eyes took in the two horses, noting their excellent condition and breeding. Such animals would belong to an officer and attracted no suspicion. Then his gaze ran up the booted legs. The cloak-coat trailed down far enough to hide Belle's breeches and her boots gave no sign of anything being wrong. Nor did the cloak-coat – until the man's eyes reached the cuffs of the sleeves. For a moment he studied the decorative knot formed by three silk braids and suspicion clicked in his head. The rider claimed to be a lieutenant in the Dragoons, yet those triple braids announced the wearer held rank as major.

One did not spend twenty years in the Army without learning caution when handling officers. There were a number of explanations, most of them innocent, why a shavetail should be wearing a major's cloak-coat.

'Do you have anything to identify yourself, mis—' he began, looking up at Belle as he moved closer. The words trailed off as he realized that the face did not belong to a man. 'Who the—'

Jerking her foot from the stirrup iron, Belle delivered a stamping kick full into the sentry's face. The impact rocked the man backwards, sending him stumbling clear of the horse. Involuntarily his finger closed on the trigger of his Springfield carbine and the gun crashed as he fell over backwards.

Even as the man reeled away from her, Belle set the two horses running across the bridge. Behind her, she heard yells and knew the shot had roused the camp. A glance to one side showed her the group of men at the horse lines were hurriedly completing their saddling and would very soon be giving pursuit. Mounted on fresh horses against her own which had been working all night, the men would give her a hard run for her money.

At which point Belle remembered the Vandenburg gun and realized the deadly menace it posed to her life as she raced her horse across the bridge. Already the more capable members of its crew had left their tent and hurled themselves towards their cumbersome but deadly weapon. Cumbersome it might be, but Belle knew its full potential under the present conditions and doing the work for which it had been designed. The Vandenburg could be likened to a shotgun in that all its bullets left the barrels at the same moment, fired by a central charge. In a test, a 191-barrel model Vandenburg put ninety per cent of its balls into a six-foot square at one hundred yards and Belle doubted if the smaller type behind her would prove any less accurate. The eighty-five bullets would sweep the bridge like a death-dealing broom; nothing on the wooden confines could escape them.

Although freshly wakened from sleep, the gunner reached his weapon with commendable speed. Throwing himself to the firing position, he took aim through the square, three-inch aperture of the rear sight. Specially designed to cover the spread of the bullets, the sight showed him the speeding rider had almost reached the end of the bridge. While being a fine weapon for defending a restricted area such as a bridge, the gun possessed one serious disadvantage. It took time to unscrew and open the breech, reload the eighty-five separate chambers of the barrels, replace the central charge and percussion cap, then close and lock the breech into place again. If the gun missed its mark, the escaping rider would be well out of range long before another discharge could be fired.

Expecting at any moment to feel the crashing impact of the Vandenburg's volley tear into her, Belle watched the end of the bridge rushing closer. She started to turn the roan, drawing the bay after her and blessing it for being so obedient to control that it followed without fuss. She felt the end post of the bridge brush her leg in passing and the bay drew slightly forward on its loaded roan companion. Each racing stride carried her closer and closer to being beyond the area of the Vandenburg's spreading charge and still the gun did not fire.

Then it came, a roaring bellow that shattered the dawn, drowning out every other noise. The gun bucked and slammed back hard with its terrible recoil and its volley of lead hissed forth along the bridge. Even as he fired, the gunner realized he had left things a shade too late to catch the rider in the centre of the bullets' pattern. Maybe too late for a hit even.

Belle heard the 'splat!' of a close-passing bullet splitting the air by her head. Then there came a soggy thud, a jarring sensation just behind her leg. The roan screamed, lurched and started to go down, caught by a chance ball after the main charge missed by inches.

Charging through the disturbed camp, the six-man detail, who had been preparing to ride escort on a supply wagon to their regiment's camp, let out wild yells of triumph as they saw the roan going down. They had been unable to cross the bridge until the Vandenburg bellowed, but now could do so and pick up the rider. Or so they believed. Almost as soon as the gun fired, the leading riders reached the end of the bridge. Startled by the noise and flame, one of the horses shied violently, throwing its rider before stampeding wildly. The remaining four men, a sergeant and three privates, managed to keep control of their mounts and headed across the bridge at a gallop.

23

Feeling the roan going down, Belle kicked her feet from the stirrups. She clung on to the bay's reins, swinging the horse round as it tried to run on. Praying that the bay's bit and bridle held firm, Belle kicked her left leg over the roan's saddle and jumped clear. From the moment her feet touched the ground, she started to run, fighting desperately to keep her balance. A wild grab closed her fingers on the bay's saddle, gripping the pommel and clinging on desperately. The bay slid on its haunches as it tried to obey the orders of its reins. In doing so, it presented Belle with a chance to get a foot in the stirrup. Hampered by the cloak-coat, Belle could not make a flying mount. In fact she found difficulty in swinging herself afork the bay at all. After a momentary pause, the bay started moving again, going along the trail at a run. Belle's free foot stamped down once and she clung to the saddle grimly. With a desperate heave, she managed to raise herself, throw a leg across the saddle and dig a toe into the security of the stirrup iron to keep herself astride the bay. Doing so cost her valuable time which she could not spare.

Better mounted than the others, the sergeant drew ahead during the dash over the bridge. On reaching the other side, he charged after the fleeing girl and drew his Colt to fire a shot. On hearing the bullet hiss by her head, Belle glanced back and saw her danger. A keen judge of horse-flesh, she knew the sergeant's mount ought to be able to run down the bay, being more fresh than the animal Belle sat. That shot had been mighty lucky to come so close when fired from the unstable platform offered by a racing horse. Lucky maybe, but Belle knew a lucky shot killed just as dead as one taken with the most careful aim.

Belle knew she must do something to prevent the sergeant drawing any nearer. Remembering how the overcoat impeded her, Belle saw a way. Keeping the bay running at a slow gallop, Belle started to wriggle from the coat. In this the garment's extra size proved advantageous. Unhooking the frog buttons, Belle freed the coat and, working carefully, wriggled her arms from the sleeves. The left arm came free as another shot narrowly missed her. Grabbing down, she caught the reins in her left hand and jerked the right out of the sleeve. Instantly the coat whisked behind her.

Too late the sergeant saw his danger. Dropping his Colt, he tried to check his horse's forward rush as the coat came fluttering down before him. The coat struck the horse's fore-legs, tangling them and bringing the animal crashing down. Pitching over the horse's head, the sergeant tried to break his fall. He was only partially successful, landing rolling but breaking his shoulder. Ignoring their fallen non-com, the remainder of the party charged on after the fleeing girl.

Having ridden since early childhood, Belle knew the dangers of galloping a horse over a hard-packed surface like the trail. Due to the jarring impact on the iron-hard earth, the hooves or legs might easily be damaged, in which case Belle would fall a victim to the pursuing Yankees. Another point she considered was that she stood a better chance of escape while riding over rough ground, being willing to gamble her skill on a horse against that of the following soldiers.

Turning the horse, she headed it from the trail and out across the rolling country. Underfoot the springy grass and loose soil served as a cushion for the racing hooves and lessened the danger of injury. Belle used all her skill to ease the horse's task in what she knew must be a long, hard race for freedom. Had the bay been fresh, she could ride the soldiers out of sight in a couple of miles. With it tired from a long journey, she knew she must aid it all she could.

Throwing her weight forward to be taken on the knees and stirrups, Belle lifted herself clear of the seat of the saddle and bent forward at the waist. Riding in that fashion offered as little interference as possible to the thrust and stride of the bay's hind legs and acted as an aid to speed. To increase her control and give a better feel of the horse's mouth, Belle took a shorter grip on the reins. Her whole arms gave to the movements of the horse's head, but she maintained her control over the animal. Under such conditions a horse's natural instinct for self-preservation tended to make it rush wildly along, so Belle knew the need for control.

Behind her one of the men did not understand the danger. His horse careered along, its reins flapping. Losing his hat, the soldier panicked and had no idea of collecting, regaining control of the racing animal. He drew ahead of the others, but found the horse running off to one side at an angle which grew more acute to the direction of his quarry. Grabbing a firm hold of the reins, the soldier tried to correct this. Feeling the savage tug at its mouth, the horse tried to fight against the pressure, lost its footing and went down.

The rider went flying, struck the ground and scraped along in the dirt before coming to a moaning, barely conscious halt.

Not knowing that her pursuers now numbered only three, Belle kept her horse running. Luck more than good horsemanship kept the remainder of the Yankees in their saddles and their fresher horses lost no ground. On they went and a mile fell behind them. Sliding down slopes in a rump-scraping churning of dust and flying stones, fighting upwards when necessary, tearing along level ground, the bay ran like a creature possessed. Belle gave up her entire attention to controlling and handling the horse, never daring to relax for a moment. Sweat poured down her face, trickling into and stinging her eyes.

Ahead lay a slope, steeper and higher than any other so far climbed. Under Belle, the bay showed signs of distress. She estimated they had now covered almost two miles from the bridge. If the bay made it to the top of the slope, she stood a chance of escaping. By that time the Yankees' horses must be almost as leg-weary as her own mount. Glances taken to the rear during the chase had told her of the following men's abilities and she knew their horses must be suffering. The slope ought to prove their breaking point.

Through the sweat-mist in her eyes Belle saw shapes on the slope above her. A trio of riders appeared on the top and started down. Though blurred, her eyes still picked out enough to tell that the men wore uniforms.

Desperately she tried to turn the horse. It staggered, lost its footing and came to a churning halt. Belle gave a groan as her hand dropped towards the butt of her Dance. This area lay well within the sphere of Union control and the men above her cut off her escape. It seemed that Belle's mission would come to a sudden end.

CHAPTER THREE

## MISS BOYD MAKES HER POINT

'Kiowa's wig-wagging, Cousin Dusty.'

Almost before Lieutenant Red Blaze finished speaking, Captain Dustine Edward Marsden Fog raised his right hand in a signal which brought Company C's V-shaped formation to a halt. The tanned, grey-clad riders sat their horses like statues, making no chatter as they scanned the range around them or looked ahead to where their outfit's forward scout stood by his mount looking in their direction and signalling to the column.

How close did the Dragoon's description fit the man who had carved himself such a name throughout the war-torn country?

The black stallion between Dusty Fog's knees stood only seventeen hands high, but a matter of four inches could be overlooked. However, Dusty could hardly be described as a great, big feller when he stood a mere five feet six inches in his Jefferson boots. Not that he was puny with the small size. His shoulders had width that hinted at strength, he tapered down to a lean, fighting man's middle, with straight, powerful legs. A white Jeff Davis hat rode his dusty blond hair, its broad brim offering shade for his tanned, intelligent, handsome young face. Cut of good quality material, the uniform he wore emphasized his physique although it did not entirely conform with the Confederate States Army's *Manual of Dress Regulations*. True the stand-up collar bore the required triple three-inch long, half-inch wide gold braid bars of his rank, but he did not wear the black cravat at his throat. Instead a scarlet silk bandana, tight rolled and knotted, trailed its long ends down over the cadet-grey of the jacket. While the double row of buttons, seven to the row, ran up his double-breasted jacket and its sleeves bore the double strand gold braid decoration of a captain, it lacked the skirt 'extending half-way between hip and knee'

27

expected by a strict adherent to regulations. His tight-legged breeches conformed to regulations, the yellow cavalry stripe running down the outer seam. His weapon belt did not conform, for instead of a single revolver in a close-topped holster and a sabre, the wide brown belt, worn lower than normal military fashion, supported a matched brace of bone-handled 1860 Army Colts butt forward in open-topped holsters. Not that Dusty ignored the *arme blanche* of the true cavalryman. He sat in a range saddle, low of horn and with double cinches; a long Manila rope strapped to one side of the horn, and at the other hung a Haiman Brothers sabre, made to his own specifications by one of the finest companies in the world.

The Yankee Dragoon did not come very close in his description of Dusty Fog. Not a great, big, black-bearded feller, but a youngster of eighteen – yet one full grown in the arts of war.

'Hold up the company, Cousin Red,' he ordered. 'Let's go, Billy Jack.'

Red Blaze, a pugnaciously handsome, freckle-faced youngster with a fiery thatch of hair that showed from under his pushed-back hat, nodded. Dressed in a similar manner to his illustrious cousin, he topped Dusty by a good six inches and had a powerful frame. Yet he never gave a thought to his superior size when Dusty gave him an order. Like most people, maybe more so as he grew up with Dusty, Red never thought of the other in mere feet and inches. To the admiring Red, that small Texan stood the tallest of them all and he felt no envy or jealousy at his cousin's fame.

Tall, gangling, his mournful-featured face and prominent Adam's apple giving him a hang-dog, care-worn appearance, Sergeant-major Billy Jack followed his captain as the other rode towards the lead-scout.

Despite the strangulation of the Union blockade upon Confederate ports, the men under Dusty's command all appeared to be well mounted, dressed and armed. They relied upon the Yankee army for most of the necessities of life, raiding to replenish their supply of arms, powder and lead, or whatever commodity happened to be needed. Although few of them had heard of it, they were by birth, up-bringing and training ideally suited to follow the Napoleonic way of making war support war.

Organized and financed by rich men of the Lone Star

State, the Texas Light Cavalry was commanded by officers who knew the rudiments and refinements of horseback fighting through much personal experience against exponents of the art such as Mexican *banditos* and *Comancheros* or the various hostile Indian tribes who roamed their State's vast area. Every man in the regiment had been reared with a horse as a means of survival instead of a mere method of transport. Skilled almost from teeth-cutting days in the use of firearms, they came to war with at least as much experience as a regular Union Army outfit and far more than any of the volunteer regiments the Yankees used to maintain their hold on the north-east land beyond the Arkansas River.

Kiowa, a tall, lean, Indian-dark man in the uniform of a sergeant, had halted his horse back from the edge of a slope and stood looking down. While nobody, except possibly his mother, would call him handsome, he possessed all the keen senses and knowledge of an Indian brave-heart warrior and made an ideal scout upon whom Dusty never failed to trust the safety of the company.

'Yankees chasing a gal,' Kiowa remarked, an unusually long speech for him.

Which, while not gabby, explained everything happening below. Moving forward cautiously, Dusty and Billy Jack looked down the slope and witnessed the final stages of the chase. They saw Belle Boyd start her lathered, leg-weary horse on the difficult climb up the slope.

'She'll not make it,' Dusty remarked. 'Let's go help her.'

Returning to their waiting horses, the three men made rapid mounts and urged the animals down the slope. All showed their considerable riding skill in staying afork their horses on ground most people would either have ignored or walked down. Seeing the girl look up, Dusty expected her to make further efforts to reach them. Instead she reined the horse in a turn and only succeeded in bringing it to a sliding halt. Her right hand went down and drew the revolver she wore. Guessing that sweat blinded her, or at least prevented her from recognizing the cadet-grey of his uniform, Dusty let out a ringing rebel yell.

Never had any sound come so sweetly to Belle's ears than did that wild 'Yeeah!' Dusty let forth. Two shots crackled from below, but the bullets went wild. Having ridden hard, fast and far, the Yankee soldiers were in no shape for fancy revolver shooting. Apparently they realized that and saw their danger, for they turned their leg-weary horses and started to gallop back towards the safety of the Coon Fork bridge.

'Take after them!' Dusty ordered. 'We don't want them stirring up the whole damned country.'

'Yo!' answered Billy Jack, throwing an admiring glance at the girl as he and Kiowa passed her in their reckless ride down the slope.

Belle thrust away her Dance and gave her full attention to regaining control of her horse. With that done, she raised a hand to rub the sweat from her eyes. Being in good physical condition, the girl soon had her breath back and could think clearly once more. Studying Dusty, she reached rapid, and correct, conclusions. The uniform told her some of it, but not quite as much as the insignia on his hat. One did not need to be a student of military matters to recognize that silver star in a circle as the badge of the Texas Light Cavalry.

From Dusty, the girl turned her attention to where Billy Jack and Kiowa had reached the foot of the slope and now urged their horses after the fleeing Yankees.

'Can your men handle it?' she asked.

'Unless there's a whole lot more Yankees close up they can,' Dusty replied.

'The nearest are almost two-mile off.'

'Then the boys'll have caught up with those three before they reach help.'

Watching the expert manner in which the two Texans handled their racing horses, Belle could understand her rescuer's quiet confidence. Even mounted on fresh animals, the Yankees would be hard put to out-ride the pursuing Texans. She turned her eyes to Dusty.

'I suppose you are wondering who I am and why the Yankees were after me.'

'The thought had hit me,' Dusty admitted.

'May I ask who you are, sir?'

'The name's Fog.'

Belle glanced at Dusty's collar bars and then looked him over. Being a shrewd judge of human nature, she saw beyond his youth and small size to the real man underneath. However, it did take some believing that he really was—

'Captain *Dusty* Fog?'

'I've been called that at times.'

Shots sounded from the foot of the slope and ended any more conversation for a few moments. Turning, Belle and Dusty looked down to see how the two non-coms fared against the trio of Yankees. It seemed that the Texans had managed pretty well. Even as Belle looked down, she saw one of the blue-clad soldiers slide sideways from his horse and crash to the ground. By all appearances the Yankees decided flight would not save them and turned to make a fight. Fighting offered them little better chance when matched by a couple of highly skilled horse-back warriors like Kiowa and Billy Jack. When the second soldier took lead in his shoulders, the third decided to yell 'calf rope' and surrender. Throwing aside his revolver, he jerked his arms into the air – just in time to stop Kiowa cutting him down.

'They didn't get far,' Belle remarked.

'I never figured they would,' Dusty replied. 'Let's get back to my company.'

Although Belle could hardly hide her delight at learning that the fates threw her in with the very aid she needed, she managed to conceal her emotions. 'What will you do with the Yankees?' she asked as they turned their horses up the slope.

'Take them with us until we get where we're going.'

'May I ask where that would be?'

A smile flickered on Dusty's face. 'May *I* ask what you said your name was?' he countered.

'Would you believe me if I told you that I'm Belle Boyd?'

'A Southern gentleman never doubts a lady's word, ma'am,' Dusty replied, 'but I'm a soldier – and they like proof.'

'When we get to your company, I'll give you proof,' Belle promised.

On reaching the company, Belle found that she would not be given an immediate chance to prove her identity. Dusty showed a commendable reluctance to staying out in such an exposed position and prepared to move on. Although he could see his cousin seething with unasked questions, Dusty let Red stew for a time.

'We'll be making a long halt at the foot of the slope, ma'am,' Dusty told the girl. 'I reckon your horse'll make that far. When we move on, you can use one of our reserve horses – if you can handle it.'

31

'If it has hair and the usual number of legs on each corner, I can handle it,' Belle answered.

Although Belle's arrival and appearance caused something of a stir among the soldiers, discipline remained and they kept their comments down to low mutters while moving off. Belle had long since stopped feeling embarrassed at the attention her revealing riding clothes attracted among members of both sexes.

At the foot of the slope Billy Jack and Kiowa stood by their horses and guarded two dejected prisoners, one tending to the other's shoulder. A still, blue-uniformed shape sprawled on the ground beyond them.

'Had to kill that one, Cap'n Dusty,' Billy Jack reported.

'It happens,' Dusty replied. 'Take a point, Kiowa. We'll make our long halt by that stream down there.'

'Yo!' Kiowa answered, going to his horse.

During her dash for freedom Belle had barely noticed the small stream. Surrounded by a force of skilled fighting men, she could allow her tired horse to drink in safety. She noticed that the two prisoners were in no way mistreated, but that an escort surrounded them and prevented any chance of escape.

Much as Belle wanted to lay her suggestions before Dusty, she set about attending to her horse first. To fail in such an elementary precaution was foreign to her nature, and she knew failure would lower her standing in Dusty's eyes. While stripping off the bay's saddle, she felt Dusty's eyes on her. Belle Boyd had a reputation for being real good with horses and she had to prove it to an acknowledged master in that line.

After the bay had drunk its fill and indulged in a good roll, Belle accepted the loan of a feed bag from one of the Texans, collected some grain from the supply carried on a pack horse and fed her mount. All around her men carried out the same tasks, working with the minimum of supervision. Not until every horse had been cared for did the men prepare their own meal. Nor did the Texans relax and grow careless. On each side, far from the column but in sight of it, keen-eyed pickets kept watch for any sign of the enemy.

Opening one of her bags, Belle took out a pair of black silk stockings. She slipped a hand into the top of one and drew a slip of paper from where it had been concealed in a pocket carefully and cunningly built into the upper section.

Handing the paper to Dusty, she watched him open and read it.

'It is genuine,' she remarked.

'I know old Stonewall's signature. Nobody else could write that bad,' Dusty replied, looking again at the message identifying Belle Boyd and requesting all C.S.A. personnel to render her every assistance. 'You'd get this from Colonel Cope in Atlanta, I reckon.'

'There's no Colonel Cope in our Secret Service,' Belle answered, pleased that the other did not take the document entirely for granted. 'I don't often have orders but when I do, I get them from General Mandeville.'

'Pleased to meet you, Miss Boyd,' Dusty smiled. 'May I present my second-in-command, Mr. Blaze. Red, meet Miss Belle Boyd.'

'Right pleased to know you, ma'am,' Red greeted.

'My pleasure, sir,' she replied. 'Now may I ask what you're doing here, Captain Fog?'

'General Hardin sent me up this way to create a diversion. Stir up the Yankees and draw some of their men out this way. He's sending Company A in to destroy a Union supply depot near Little Rock. I figured on wrecking a bridge up there on the Coon Fork of the Arkansas.'

'That's where I came from and picked up my escort,' Belle warned. 'There's a company and a Vandenburg volley gun guarding it.'

'We figured on at least that much,' Red put in. 'Dusty's taken better guarded things than that.'

'Would you be interested in hitting at an even more important target?' Belle inquired, smiling a little at Red's open admiration for his smaller cousin.

'If it's worth while,' Dusty agreed.

'Would you say raiding a U.S. Army paymaster with fifty thousands dollars in gold is worth while?' asked the girl.

Dusty and Red exchanged glances and Belle could see she had their interest.

'I can think of less important things,' Dusty finally said. 'Let's hear about it, Miss Boyd.'

'It began after I returned from Europe a few days back,' Belle explained. 'I went to Washington and picked up some information from one of our agents. The U.S. Government is sending fifty thousand dollars in gold to the Indian Nations. It's partly payment for troops there and the rest to

33

be divided among the chiefs of the Osage, Pawnee, Cow and Arikara tribes as an inducement for them to keep the peace and resist the suggestions of the Cherokee Nation to take sides in the War. So I came straight out here and finished at the Dragoons' camp near Russelville. I learned all I could, then headed for our territory. It would have been tight if I'd had to cross the Ouachita and find a Confederate outfit, but meeting you here gives us plenty of time. I know the route they'll take with the shipment and the other details.'

'How big an escort will it have?' asked Dusty.

'The Yankees don't want to attract too much attention to the shipment for obvious reasons. So ostensibly it will be merely guarding the carriage of a general on a tour of inspection. The escort will consist, in this area, of a large company of Dragoons, between fifty and sixty men.'

'A fair number,' Dusty remarked, thinking that his force numbered only forty and that at least six of them would be needed to guard the reserve and pack horses.

'Only Dragoons though,' grinned Red, his eyes glinting with the light of battle. 'Comes to a fight, we've damned nigh got that many outnumbered.'

'That depends,' Dusty drawled, eyeing his impetuous cousin tolerantly.

'On what?' asked Belle.

'Whether we take them on under our terms and on our ground, or theirs,' Dusty answered. 'Tell me about your activities. Everything you've done since you came out here.'

Speaking concisely and leaving out only the names of her helpers, a precaution Dusty admired, Belle gave the Texans a clear picture of everything she had done including her escape and how she covered her tracks.

'I'm sure nobody missed me in the excitement. And I reckon the sentry will insist he doesn't know who hit him,' she concluded – which proved to be correct, for at that moment Private Hooley stood before his colonel and stoutly affirmed how he had been struck from behind by a person or persons unknown – 'And if I know soldiers, they'll none of them be willing to admit they don't know how few men jumped them. In fact, I'd take money that they swear to seeing a Confederate company, probably your own, Captain Fog, jump them.'

Dusty accepted the tribute to his face without any comment, being more concerned with the practical side of the

34

matter. 'Then the Dragoons may be out looking for us,' he pointed out.

'It's possible,' admitted Belle. 'However, I'd guess that Colonel Verncombe won't bother. He'll believe that, having over fifty of his horses, you'll have made a fast run for the Ouachita, and will get right to clearing up the damage rather than waste time.'

'Only thing to do is find out where the Yankee general will be travelling then,' Dusty commented and walked to where his saddle lay on its side. Opening one of the pouches, he took out a folded map and returned to the others. Spreading the map, Dusty looked at the girl. 'Any suggestions, ma'am?'

'You might try calling me "Belle", "ma'am" makes me feel old,' she smiled. 'They'll be going over the Crossland Trace.'

Examining the map, Dusty ran his finger along a line marking the Crossland Trace, a wagon route running to the north of Russelville and communicating with the Indian Nations' forts. The map, looted from a Union Army camp, was good and carried enough detail for Dusty to be able to visualize the land through which the shipment travelled. For almost five minutes he sat studying the map, while Red and Belle left him to his thoughts. At last he looked at the other two.

'How long before the shipment comes through?' he asked.

'I'll send a man to relieve Kiowa,' Red remarked, and rose to give the order.

'Red appears to know you,' Belle said and then answered Dusty's question. 'Captain Christie met it this morning and will be started out now. I'd say that we might pick it up the day after tomorrow. An escort and carriage won't be travelling at any speed.'

'Reckon it won't,' agreed Dusty. 'All non-coms, Mr. Blaze.'

Knowing his cousin, as Belle said, Red had already given the order which brought the company's sergeants and corporals gathering about their leader. Dusty told them their mission and eager rumbles went up among the half-circle of tanned, tough-looking men. Then he proceeded to explain his plan in detail, after scraping clear a piece of earth on which to draw a large-scale map.

Belle watched everything and her original relief at being

35

rescued by Dusty grew to delight at her good fortune. Already she had made an estimation of Dusty's capabilities and knew her judgment was correct. Not only was the small Texan a top-grade fighting man, but he also possessed a shrewd, calculating brain – and used it. If attention to detail guaranteed success, then their mission must be a success. However, Dusty's plan surprised her in one respect and, when he finished talking, she brought up the point.

'I thought you might make your move further west.'

'And I would,' agreed Dusty, 'if I could find a place so well suited to my idea. You'll stay with the reserve mounts' detail when we make our attack, Belle.'

'With your permission, I'd rather go with your party,' she objected.

'You, ma'am,' grinned a burly corporal. 'It'll be no place for a woman.'

Sighing resignedly, Belle came to her feet in a swift, graceful move and faced the man, but looked towards Dusty. 'I have this trouble every time,' she remarked. 'Well, it may as well be now as later.'

'You've left me behind, Belle,' Dusty answered.

'Every time I offer to take a hand in a fight, some big, strong man decides that it's no place for a woman and I have to prove my point,' she explained, taking out her Dance and removing the percussion caps from its chamber. 'Unload your gun, Corporal.'

After glancing to Dusty for permission, and receiving it, the grinning corporal followed Belle's lead in rendering his right side Colt safe. Holstering his gun, he faced the girl from a distance of about four feet. Belle's right hand lifted to hover over the butt of her Dance.

Watching the girl, Dusty smiled a little, although his gaze directed at her feet instead of her hand. Instead of the normal stance for drawing and shooting, Belle's feet formed a T position about her shoulders' width apart, the left pointed at the corporal, the right's heel aimed at the centre of the left, and both knees slightly bent.

Down stabbed the corporal's hand in a smooth, fast move, fingers closing on and lifting the Colt. Even as his gun came clear, the corporal realized that Belle had not even attempted to draw her Dance. Instead she drew back her right leg, maintaining her balance with grace and agility. Straightening out her left leg, she raised herself on to her

toes so as to gain added power to the right as it swung forward and up. Her toes caught the corporal's hand just as
the Colt came out. Giving a yelp of surprise and pain, he
lost his hold on the gun. His troubles did not end there.

In a continuation of the kick, Belle came down to both
feet, rotated her body in a swift pivot and delivered a rear
stamping kick to the man's stomach. Although she used less
than her full strength, Belle doubled the startled soldier
over. Again Belle pivoted, her right hand raising, clenched
into a fist, and driving down so its heel struck the back of
the man's neck and sent him to his knees. Stepping back,
Belle drew and cocked her Dance.

'Well?' she asked.

Roars of laughter greeted her actions and the corporal
looked up with a rueful grin. 'Reckon this's no place for a
*man*,' he said. 'You wouldn't've fooled Cap'n Dusty that
way, I bet, ma'am.'

'Not being fooled is why he's the captain and you're only
a corporal,' Billy Jack pointed out.

'How about it, Dusty?' asked Belle.

'You've made your point,' Dusty answered with a grin.
'You ride with my party. Now if you've finished fooling
about, we'll go through the plan again.'

## CHAPTER FOUR

# CAPTAIN FOG'S PLAN

EVEN though he approached the section of the Crossland Trace known as the Funnel, Captain Christie of the 6th New Jersey Dragoons felt neither concern nor apprehension for the safety of the visiting general entrusted to his care.

Some freak of nature had left a curious land formation at that point of the Trace. The gash carved into the land by innumerable wagon wheels and horses' hooves passed along the bottom of a valley towards a high, sheer cliff to wind through a narrow gorge which alone gave access to the land beyond the cliff. The valley itself had wooded slopes, but a good hundred yards of clear, open land separated the woods from the trail and, in Christie's considered opinion, rendered unlikely the chances of a successful ambush.

Riding slightly to the rear of the general's wagon, in a position which kept himself under the view of the senior officer while giving the appearance of being entirely occupied with the work of ensuring his charge's safety, Christie looked back at his command. A large company, sixty in strength, armed with Springfield carbines and Army Colts, strung out behind the general's carriage made an impressive and comforting sight. Only a good-sized Confederate force would risk attacking so many men, Christie decided, and he doubted if a rebel outfit of any size could come so far north into Union-held territory. So he kept all his command riding in four smart, military-looking columns which ought to please the general, and ignored the suggestion his sergeant-major made about sending scouts ahead or putting flanking details out to search the wooded slopes.

Christie was one of a new breed of officer the War brought into the Union Army. Before the outbreak of hostilities, the South provided the majority of officers for the army, but most of them left to join their seceding states when the War began. Faced with a shortage of officers, the

Union had to accept many men who would never have made the grade in the strict days before the War. Christie was one of them. Not that he originally intended to become a soldier. An interest in politics and a hatred for anyone who did not blindly conform to his beliefs made a patriot out of him. Having a prominent member of the Radical Republican Party for a father, Christie received acceptance and faster promotion than his talents merited. However, one needed to come into the eye of senior authority to rise higher than a captain, even in war-time. Coming into the eye could be done in two ways, by courage and endeavour on the battlefield, or by showing to good advantage in some general's presence. Not wishing to risk his valuable neck in action, Christie chose the latter. By waving his father's influence, he gained command of the escort for General Main, and to prevent anyone sharing the limelight, he left his second-in-command at the regiment's headquarters.

Day-dreaming of a rosy future when, on Main's recommendation, he reached field rank, Christie rode towards the opening of the gorge. Suddenly his pleasant thoughts were shattered by a series of wild, ringing yells and a scattering of shots from the rear. Turning in his saddle, he saw something which sent a shock of apprehension through him. Having a firm belief that he was destined to do great things in the improvement of his country, Christie avoided taking risks and had never been in action. For a moment his numbed mind failed to function as he watched the grey-clad riders burst from the left side of the trail some distance behind the end of his column.

Fortunately for Christie, his sergeant-major was an old soldier. Christie always regarded the non-com as a semi-illiterate fool who came into the army because he could not hold down any other work, but at that moment the captain could have fallen on the other's neck in joy.

'Driver, move that carriage on the gallop!' the sergeant-major roared. 'First three files follow it. Remainder form line. Dismount. Prepare to fight on foot.'

Although Christie had laid down instructions for action in case of an attack, he could not collect his thoughts in time to give them. Even the sergeant-major might have failed had the rebels come in with a silent rush instead of yelling and firing shots prematurely.

Typical of his type of mentality, Christie had been a martinet who drove the men under him rather than leading them. In this instance the driving bore fruit. Long hours of drill had taught the men in the escort to react almost instinctively on hearing commands. The carriage's driver swung his whip and urged his four-horse team forward at an increasing pace into the mouth of the gorge, followed by a sergeant and the first three files of four men from the column. The remainder of the escort worked fast, swinging their horses into line across the mouth of the gorge. On dismounting, one man in six grabbed hold of the reins of the other five's horses to leave the five free to fight. That had become standard U.S. Army tactics, although Christie trained his men in what he regarded as an improvement on normal procedure.

Most cavalry outfits had one man in four holding the horses. Christie decided that one in six would give him more men to fight and trained his company accordingly, putting the sergeant-major's tentative objections down to the stagnated thinking of a limited military mentality. Certainly the system showed its merit as the horse-holders grabbed their companions' reins and backed off to leave five, not three, men facing the enemy.

Standing in the centre of his men, Christie gave a superior smile as he watched the rebel cavalry mill uncertainly just beyond pistol range. To Christie that only went to prove his theories. It was so like the decadent Southerners to botch a good chance, then show cowardice in the face of a determined enemy. So thought Christie, nerve coming back as he saw the danger diminish. All he needed to do was keep his men in position and hold the rebels back until the carriage gained a good lead, then mount up and follow.

At Christie's side, the sergeant-major watched the rebels also, but felt very disturbed at what he saw. Unlike his officer, the non-com had seen action and knew a thing or two. So he wondered why such a troop as the one facing them would make a damned fool mistake like spoiling what would have been a first-class surprise attack by premature yelling and shooting. Although about half the size of the Yankee escort, that many men would still need to know their business to penetrate so far into Union territory undetected. Such skill did not mix with blundering incompetence or reluctance to fight, both of which the rebels had apparently showed.

Even as the sergeant-major opened his mouth to mention his fears to Christie, he heard the crack of a rifle shot from the right side of the slope almost level with his escort. A croaking gasp came from behind the sergeant-major and he twisted around to see one of the horse-holders collapse, bullet in head and hand opening to release the reins it held.

More shots crackled from the trees and the non-com estimated that at least five rifles covered them. A small force, until he realized what the riflemen's position and purpose meant. The shooting of the horse-holder had been no accident. Another two of the men holding the horses took lead, releasing their charges. More bullets screamed down, the loose horses began to mill and scatter, making their riders forget fighting and try to catch them.

Seeing the danger, the sergeant-major yelled orders for a party of men to make an attack on the attackers among the trees. As he started to move forward to give direction to the counter measures, a bullet caught him in the chest, spun him around and dropped him to the ground. Another horse-holder screamed an instant later, fell and allowed a further six animals to add to the confusion.

Up among the trees, Kiowa swung his rifle down after dropping the sergeant-major. The lean scout and his four-man detail – selected as being the best rifle-shots in the company and armed with Sharps, Henry or Spencer long guns 'borrowed' from the Yankees – worked with deadly precision, following Dusty's orders.

On their arrival at the Funnel that morning, Dusty's men had been put into their positions and given a final run-through of their orders. On examining the area in which he would operate, Kiowa added a touch of his own to his leader's plans. After dropping the sergeant-major, Kiowa prepared to put his own touch into action.

Near where Kiowa knelt in the shelter and concealment of a slippery elm, a couple of springy young saplings had been bent over, their upper foliage stripped away and the tops secured by ropes. Balanced upon forks at the upper end of each sapling rested a Katchum four-pounder hand grenade, its percussion-cap fuse ready in place. Kiowa threw a glance at the saplings, rested his Henry against the elm and yelled:

'Now!'

Drawing his sheathed bowie knife, Kiowa sprang to the

41

nearer sapling and one of his men leapt to the other. Razor-sharp steel sliced through the retaining ropes. While the spring of the saplings' rise to an upright position did not have the force to hurl the grenades the hundred yards or so which separated the rebels from the Trace, it flung the missile far farther than any human hand could. Downwards curved first one, then the other grenade. The firing mechanism, a tube of soft metal with a flange at its outer end and a percussion cap at the other, drove into the ground. A dull roar shattered the air, drowning any other sound for a moment, then a second explosion heralded the arrival of the other grenade.

Already spooked by the shooting and noise around them and disturbed by seeing others of their kind milling about, the horses still held by the remaining men assigned to that duty began to fight to escape. At that moment the sense of the Army's methods showed. One man could just about handle four horses during the heat of action; he had no chance of restraining six battle-scared animals, especially when under fire directed at him.

Struck by a careering horse, two men staggered and dropped their carbines. Other men forgot their duties as they tried to grab at passing animals. Complete chaos, of a kind only a real efficient leader could halt, reigned among the Dragoons, and Christie found his theories of how to handle men completely inadequate faced with the grim realities of war. The remaining horse-holders, realizing that their fellow workers had not been shot by accident, discarded their duty and turned free the struggling, terrified horses.

At which moment, following on the heels of the grenades' explosion, Red Blaze gave the order to his party to attack. Cutting through the wild, rebel yells, came the music of the bugle sounding the charge. Like puppets when the handler works the strings, every Texan's horse sprang forward in a disciplined rush at the disorganized Dragoons. And this time the Texans came on, determined to force home their charge. Reins looped around saddlehorns, leaving the riders' hands free to handle weapons, guiding their horses by knee-pressure, the Texans came down shooting and adding to the confusion already rampant among their enemies.

Even then a good commander might have rallied his men and saved the situation, for the Dragoons still outnumbered the Texans by almost two to one. Christie never even gave the matter a thought as panic gripped him. All his superiority over the common herd left him; his bombast about the damned cowardly rebel scum forgotten as he watched the wave of grey-clad riders pouring down towards him. Thrusting away his revolver, he sprang for and managed to catch the reins of a passing horse. Once in the saddle, he deserted his men and knocked down a corporal who was trying to rally a defence against the Texans' charge.

While Red Blaze might be a reckless young cuss with a penchant for becoming involved in any fight he might witness, he possessed one prime virtue which few people, himself included, knew about. Dusty knew it and was aware that given a responsible task Red became the coolest, steadiest hand a man could ask for. So even in the heady excitement of the charge, Red did not forget Dusty's orders.

'Stop that officer escaping, Bucky!' he yelled.

'Yo!' whooped a corporal at the end of the line and swung his horse away so that it charged up the slope at an angle which brought it towards the fleeing Christie.

Shock and terror came to Christie's face as he saw the Texan boiling up the slope towards him. Then the courage of a cornered rat sent Christie's hand to his holstered Colt. Twice the Texan's revolver spat, but the lead missed and Christie brought up his weapon. The courses of the two horses converged rapidly and Christie fired wildly, to make the fatal mistake of missing. Again the Texan squeezed his Army Colt's trigger, and at a range from which he stood little or no chance of missing. Searing agony ripped into Christie as he felt the shocking impact of striking lead. The gun fell from his hand and he slid from his horse to crash to the ground. On raced Christie's mount, heading up the slope at a gallop, but the Texan let it go. Having done his part in halting the officer's escape, the Texan swung his mount and rejoined his command.

A condition of wild confusion reigned among the Dragoons as they made an attempt to fight back against the on-rushing rebels. Men yelled, tried to use their guns, but were hampered by others of their party trying to capture mounts, or by the horses scattering through their ranks in wild stampede.

Demoralized by the loss of any guiding force – Red's men knew their business and cut down any Yankee who

43

showed signs of organizing a defence against them – the Dragoons needed only the sight of Christie deserting them to save his own neck to make them decide that they had had enough of war. Unfortunately escaping did not prove easy for the Yankees as Kiowa's party had performed their assigned duty very well. So well that not a single horse-holder still retained a grip of any of his comrades' mounts, although a few did keep a grip of their own animals. Not that the possession would do any good for them. Following Dusty's orders and Red's reminders, the Texans cut down any man who tried to escape.

'Don't shoot!' yelled one of the Dragoons, throwing aside his unfired Springfield carbine. 'I quit!'

Such action in a command as badly shaken as Christie's company was certain to prove infectious. Guns rained to the ground and arms shot into the air in surrender. A few of the harder souls, long-term soldiers who saw battle in Indian campaigns, might have fought in out, but most of them had already taken lead and the remainder recognized the futility of continuing the uneven struggle.

'Hold your fire!' Red's voice boomed out like a clarion call.

Bringing his men to a halt, Red wasted no time in self-congratulation at a very well handled piece of work. Yet he might have taken pride in his achievement, for he brought about the capture of an enemy force almost twice as large as his command, inflicting heavy casualties on the Yankees, without the loss or wounding of a single Texan. True the plan had been out of Dusty's fertile brain, but carrying it to its successful conclusion fell upon Red.

With the wild, heady excitement of the charge still throbbing through him, Red still retained enough command of himself to know what must be done. While the Yankees had shown every sign of surrender, giving them time to re-gain their senses or recover from their shock might have disastrous results. Even now Red's command was outnumbered by the enemy and up close could be badly mauled if some leader managed to rally the dispirited Yankees.

'Line them up, disarm them!' Red ordered.

Moving swiftly, yet with skilled precision that told of long practice, the Texans formed up the Dragoons in small parties and separated them from their weapons. Although the Springfield carbines were smashed beyond repair by beating against the ground, the Army Colts suffered no damage. To a rebel no piece of enemy property had so much attraction as those latest products from the Hartford factory of Colonel Samuel Colt and, while unwilling to weigh their mounts down with single-shot Springfield carbines, the Texans willingly added the burden of the Dragoon's revolvers.

While the disarming took place, Red recalled another section of the company.

'Kiowa!' he yelled.

'Yo!' came back the answer from the trees.

'You can come out now, we've done got them all hawg-tied down.'

'That Red sure is a fighting son,' grinned one of Kiowa's party as they went to collect their horses.

'He sure is,' agreed another and threw a look at the captured Dragoons. 'Man oh man, Cap'n Dusty's plan worked out real well.'

'Now me,' put in Kiowa dryly. 'I'd've been more surprised if it *hadn't*.'

## CHAPTER FIVE

## CAPTAIN FOG ACQUIRES WEALTH

FROM the front, the small knot of bushes looked natural enough, although the only growth of its kind anywhere nearer than a hundred yards from the trail at the western mouth of the Funnel. In fact until less than an hour before even that clump of bushes did not grow so close to the trail, having been cut higher up the left slope of the valley and replaced in the position Dusty Fog selected as best for his purpose. Lying behind the bushes, hidden from sight of anyone on the trail, Dusty watched the mouth of the Funnel for the first sight of the paymaster's carriage. Already he could hear shots in the distance and knew the first part of his plan had begun. Everything now depended on how well Belle Boyd had been able to learn about the character of the man commanding the paymaster's escort; and also on whether Dusty called the play right about how the Yankee commander would react to Red's attack.

Would the Yankee play into Dusty's hands by making a fight on foot across the eastern mouth of the Funnel, allowing the paymaster's carriage to build up a good start on any pursuit by the Texans? If the Yankee halted, might he not keep the carriage close at hand? If he sent it, how many men were likely to be in its escort?

On the answer to those questions hinged the success or failure of Dusty's strategy. Probably even more so than it rested upon his ability to hit a one-inch round mark at fifty yards with a borrowed Spencer carbine. Should the first part of his plans fail for any reason, Dusty would have no need to demonstrate his skill with a shoulder arm by hitting the detonator flange of the six-pounder Ketchum grenade facing him on the far side of the trail.

Every instinct Dusty possessed told him that the Yankee commander would act in the required manner. Even the crack U.S. Army outfits like Custer's 7th Michigan Cavalry only rarely fought in the saddle. By virtue of their training and traditions, the Dragoons always fought dismounted. Once the Yankees left their horses, Dusty knew he could rely on Red and Kiowa to handle their parts of the plan. Which left only Dusty and Belle to perform their assigned tasks for the affair to be brought to a successful conclusion.

For a moment Dusty wondered if he had done the correct thing in allowing Belle to take such an active part in what would be a dangerous business. Then he grinned as he decided that he had been given little or no choice in the matter. Taken all in all, that beautiful girl spy had a mighty persuasive way about her. More than that, his men admired her and regarded her as being lucky for them. During the long ride north to the Crossland Trace they had seen no sign of Yankees, even though the route they took led them within two miles of the Dragoons' camp at Russelville. Even the crossing of the Coon Fork of the Arkansas gave them no trouble due to Kiowa finding a shallows with a firm gravel bottom that offered good footing for the horses. Belle had proved herself capable and as good as any of the men at handling her horse, a thing which raised her even higher in the estimation of the Texans. So Dusty found that the men in the party he told Belle to join not only accepted her presence but appeared to let her take command in the place of a non-com.

Including Belle in one party had been caused by necessity. Three men guarded the two Yankee prisoners and the company's reserve horses some distance away in a valley bottom. Taking them away from the company as well as Kiowa's detail and the ten men Dusty required did not leave Red with many guns for his part of the plan. However, it had been amusing to see those five leathery soldiers, bone-tough fighting men all, show pleasure at having Belle with them and accepting her as their leader – or did it? One of the prime qualities of any fighting man was the ability to recognize a leader; and the Texans saw those qualities in Belle just as they recognized leadership in Dusty or Red.

Anyway, Dusty mused, it was long gone too late for him to think of changing his force around and sending the girl to the safety of the prisoner-guarding detail.

As if giving definite proof that it was indeed too late for a change, Dusty heard the growing rumble of hooves and steel-rimmed wheels upon confined hard rock. He still could not see the paymaster's carriage, nor, due to the deflection and distortion caused by the Funnel's walls, form any kind of guess how many horses approached. Not that Dusty wasted time in idle conjecture.

On hearing the sound, Dusty eased forward the Spencer carbine and rested its barrel upon the crown of his hat which lay ready for that purpose upon a rock before him. So carefully had he selected his position and arranged the cover that, although he could take a good aim at the trail, no part of himself or the carbine showed beyond the bushes. Closing his left eye, Dusty took careful aim at the triangle of light-coloured rocks which showed plainly at the far side of the trail. Slowly he moved down the tip of the foresight so that centred on the black circle of the Ketchum's detonator flange in the middle of the triangle. While the Spencer could not be classed with the latest model Sharps rifle in the accuracy line, Dusty figured that its twenty-inch barrel ought to send a four-hundred-grain .56 calibre bullet right where aimed at fifty yards, even if the propellant power be only fifty grains of powder.

A quick glance showed Dusty that the carriage had burst into sight at the mouth of the Funnel. On its box the driver swung his whip and yelled encouraging curses at the four-horse team while a second soldier, riding as guard, lent a hand by pitching rocks at the team and added his quota of verbal inducement. Close behind the rocking, lurching coach came the escort: a sergeant and twelve men. Big odds against Dusty's party happen he failed to make good his shot at the Ketchum's detonator flange.

From the way it continued to race along, the carriage and escort did not intend to halt and await word of how the main body fared. That figured, knowing the consignment the Yankee general carried in the carriage. He would want to build up as good a lead as possible in case the Texans broke through the rearguard defence of the main body. Well, maybe he would not want to desert his companions, but clearly intended to do his duty by keeping moving.

Dusty settled down, cuddling the stock of the Spencer against his shoulder and caylng the carbine, setting the tip of the foresight's blade exactly in the centre of the back sight's V notch and aligning them carefully on the black dot at which he aimed. For a moment the team horses and carriage hid his mark from sight and the dust churned up by hooves and wheels masked it. Holding his fire, Dusty did not panic even though he knew what depended on his making a hit. The escort did not ride right up to the carriage, but stayed far enough back to keep an uninterrupted view of the trail and valley ahead. Brief though the gap might be, it gave Dusty just enough time. The dust cleared and he saw his mark, finding as he hoped that his aim still held on it. Without fluster he squeezed the trigger. The Spencer barked, belched flame and sent its bullet hurtling out.

An instant later, with a dull roar and burst of flame, scattering fragments of metal casing and surrounding rocks in a deadly fountain, the Ketchum exploded. Dusty's bullet must have almost touched the sergeant's horse in passing, for the animal caught the full force of the explosion, both it and its rider going down in a hideously torn mass of lacerated flesh and spurting blood. The blast swept the nearer two men of the leading file from their horses, tumbled the third out of his saddle and threw the remainder of the escort into confusion. Reining in desperately, trying to regain control of their plunging, terrified horses, the second file ploughed into the first, horses going down. One of the final file crashed into the jumble, a second pitched over his horse's head as it came to a sudden halt.

'Yeeah!'

Acting on their orders, five of Dusty's men burst into sight on the right side of the valley, making all the noise they could manage. Guns in hand, they tore down the slope towards the disorganized escort.

Only two of the escort avoided the tangled jumble, and they more through luck than by good management. Wild with terror inspired by the explosions, screams and stench of spilled blood, the horses reared, fought and finally bolted to the left, headed in Dusty's direction.

On firing his shot, Dusty started to work the Spencer's loading lever and at the same moment thrust himself rapidly out of his cover. He knew that none of the Dragoons must be allowed to escape, but could not handle the Spencer freely enough from his hiding place to rely on taking his share in bottling in the Yankees. Both the approaching Dragoons appeared to be good horsemen and were already gaining control of their mounts. Seeing Dusty, and guessing that it was he who detonated the explosion, they charged in his direction. One of the pair drew his Army Colt and fired at Dusty, but thirty yards was too great a range for a man to perform accurate shooting with a handgun when astride a racing horse. Drawing back the Spencer's side-hammer, Dusty threw the carbine to his shoulder, took aim and and touched off a shot in return. Caught in the shoulder by the heavy bullet, the eager Dragoon pitched out of the saddle, his gun dropping from his hand.

Ignoring his fallen comrade, the second man continued his charge and drew his gun. From all appearances he was an old soldier and well-versed in his business. Not for him to open fire wildly at a range where luck alone might guide home the bullet. Instead he headed straight for Dusty, meaning to ride the other down and end the affair at a distance from which he could hardly miss.

Dusty worked the lever of the Spencer, feeling the breach start to open, stick for an instant, then came back – only no empty cartridge case flicked into the air. Metal cartridge manufacture had not yet developed to a stage where reliable cases were the rule rather than the exception and accidents frequently happened. Even without looking, Dusty guessed that the case had stuck tighter than usual in the chamber and the withdrawing ejector tore its head off, leaving the remainder of the brass cyclinder inside the gun and effectively preventing the insertion of a replacement bullet.

Nearer rushed the Dragoon, still holding his fire. Dusty's right hand left the Spencer, driving down and across his body in a move almost too fast for the eye to follow. Trained fingers curled around the waiting white handle of the left-side Colt and its streamlined length flowed from the holster. Back drew the hammer under Dusty's thumb and his fore-finger slipped into the triggerguard. He did not offer to raise the gun shoulder high and take sight in the formal manner; with the Dragoon rushing closer by the second there would not have been time. Not that Dusty needed to use a fancy duelling stance. He had been trained to handle his Colts in the manner of the Texas range country and down there if a man needed a gun, he mostly did not have time to adopt a fancy stance before using his weapon. Even as the Dragoon fired his opening shot, Dusty's Colt roared from waist high and aimed by instinctive alignment. Like Dusty figured, the Dragoon knew how to handle a gun. Only the fact that the man fired from a mighty unsteady platform saved Dusty; and at that the Dragoon's bullet stirred the Texan's hair in passing.

For his part, Dusty shot back the only way he dared under the circumstances – for a kill. There was no time for taking a careful aim and sending a bullet into the man's shoulder, not when faced with an enemy so skilled in use of a gun. So Dusty sent his bullet into the Dragoon's chest as offering the easiest target under the prevailing conditions. Jerking under the impact of the lead, the Dragoon let his gun drop and slid off his horse. So close had it been that Dusty was forced to throw himself aside to avoid being run down by the horse.

Down on the trail, the Dragoons had been too dazed and shocked to offer any resistance and, even as Dusty shot down the second man, were surrendering to his five Texans. One of the five, Dusty's company guidon carrier, wheeled away from the rest. Leading Dusty's stallion, as was his duty at such times, the guidon carrier loped over to where his captain waited. Dusty took the black's reins, mounted and turned his attention to where Belle's party intercepted the fleeing carriage.

'Steady!' Belle breathed as she watched the carriage hurl by the point where the Ketchum grenade awaited Dusty's bullet.

Around her, concealed among a clump of bushes, the five men assigned to take the carriage held their restive mounts in check. At Belle's side, the burly corporal whose challenge had brought a lesson in *savate*, gave the girl a grin. He volunteered to ride in her party with the express intention of showing Belle how it was done. Yet he, like the others, willingly accepted her as the leader.

All heard the crack of Dusty's Spencer followed by the roar as the Ketchum exploded.

'Charge!' Belle ordered, her voice low but urgent.

Setting her spurs to the flanks of her mount, she sent it leaping out of cover and down the slope. Dance in hand, she led the men towards the wagon in a fast and deadly rush. Yet they went in silence, without as much as a cowhand yell to give warning of their presence. Lack of cover caused Dusty to station the party farther from the trail than he wanted, but he tried to ease their task as much as possible.

Racing their horses downwards, Belle and the Texans

watched the carriage for the first sign that its occupants noticed them. Seventy-five yards, fifty, thirty; still the driver and guard, watching the ambush of the remainder of their escort, failed to see or hear their danger. The hooves of their team and the rumbling of the wheels on the trail drowned out the grass-muffled drumming of the Texans' mounts. Even General Main stared back at the havoc Dusty's grenade caused among the Dragoons during the first, dangerous moments of the charge.

Suddenly the driver became aware that his team careered along the Trace without guidance from him. Twisting around, he prepared to handle the reins and saw the charging group. His warning yell, garbled though it came out, served to bring the guard's attention to the front. The warning came just too early for Belle's party to make a safe contact with the enemy.

Belle had chosen to wear her Union Army fatigue cap and taken with her dark blue shirt and black breeches it gave her the appearance of a Yankee soldier. Under the stress and excitement of the moment, the guard completely overlooked certain aspects of Belle's appearance which ought to have told him that he did not look at a man. To his eyes a member of his own army rode with the rebels: a traitor; a lousy, stinking renegade who had sold out to the enemy and brought death or injury to a good few Union soldiers that day. Fury boiled inside the guard and he swore to himself that he would get the damned traitor or want to know why not.

Although she saw the guard's eyes riveted on her, Belle felt no great anxiety at first. The Springfield carbine issued to the Union Army's enlisted man had never been a weapon noted for accuracy and she reckoned she could take a chance on the guard shooting at her from the swaying box of the racing carriage.

Only the guard did not hold an inaccurate Springfield carbine.

Apprehension ripped through Belle as she realized that the guard's weapon had two barrels. No matter how the box rocked, a ten-gauge shot-gun at that range would be unlikely to miss if its handler knew his business. From the smooth way the guard started to raise his shot-gun, Belle figured he knew enough to make things all-fired dangerous for anybody he aimed to hit.

At Belle's side, the burly corporal saw the raising of the shot-gun and with something of a shock realized that the guard aimed to cut the girl down. Swinging his horse, the corporal rammed it into Belle's racing bay and staggered the other animal aside. Flame tore from the shot-gun's right barrel as nine buckshot balls lashed from its muzzle in a spreading pattern of death. At twenty-five yards the balls had spread enough so that a human body would catch most of them – and the corporal had ridden into the place he knocked Belle from. Seven of the .32 calibre balls tore into his body. He jerked backwards, striking the cantle of his saddle. The army Colt slid from his fingers and he fell sideways to the ground. His four male companions fired back at the guard, but missed.

Only Belle's superb riding skill kept her in the saddle as her horse reeled under the impact of the corporal's charge. Not only did she retain her seat, but collected and brought the bay under control. At the same moment her brain screamed a warning that she must do something or take the shot-gun's left barrel's charge. The guard saw his first shot miss the girl and wavered between which of the attackers he ought to try at next.

Much as she hated what she must do, that pause gave Belle her chance. Bringing up the Dance, she threw a shot at the nearest of the carriage's team. Even from the back of the racing bay, Belle could hardly miss so large a target. Screaming as the .36 ball hit it, the horse stumbled and went down, bringing the other leader with it. Instantly the carriage lurched to a violent halt. The guard's shot-gun boomed, but as an involuntary measure as his finger tightened on the trigger when he was thrown forward. He hit nothing and before he recovered took a bullet from one of the Texans.

The driver could do nothing beyond trying to keep himself from being thrown off the box and also prevent his team from killing each other or themselves in their wild panic. Inside the coach General Main had been pitched forward, his head smashing into the side. Blackness welled over him and he collapsed to the floor.

Leaving the men to handle the carriage's driver and occupant, Belle whirled her bay around in a rump-scraping turn and left the saddle before the animal stopped. She holstered her Dance as she ran to where the corporal lay sprawled on the ground. Dropping to her knees beside the stricken man, she gently raised his head and pillowed it upon her knees. For a moment she thought he was dead, then his eyes opened and he looked at her. A pain-wracked grin twisted his lips.

'Reckon I put one over on – you – this – time – ma'am!' he gasped.

Before Belle could make any reply, she saw his body stiffen, blood oozed out of his mouth and his eyes glazed over, then the body went limp. For the first time in three or more years Belle felt the impact of death. She knew that she owed the corporal her life. If he had not knocked her horse aside, it would be she who lay on the ground. Tears trickled down Belle's cheeks and she remained on her knees, cradling the soldier's dead head in her hands.

Hooves drummed behind Belle but she did not look up to see who approached.

'How is he?' asked Dusty's voice.

Turning, Belle looked up at the small Texan. Grief showed plainly on her face and she replied, 'He's dead. Died saving me.'

'Poor old Mike,' Dusty said, his voice gentle. 'He was a good soldier.'

The corporal had also been a good friend in the days before the War, companion on more than one schoolboy escapade. However, Dusty had long since learned that friends died in battle, but that life must go on. The lives of the rest of the company depended on Dusty, so he must hold down his sorrow at losing a friend and force himself to go ahead with the work at hand.

'I'll send somebody to tend to him,' Dusty told Belle. 'Come and help me find the money.'

Gently Belle laid the still form on the ground and came to her feet. Looking around, she found everything under control. Already Dusty's party had joined the men who rode with her. The Yankee prisoners stood to one side under guard and attended to their wounded. On Dusty's orders, two of the Texans came forward to load the dead corporal on his horse. Back at the reserve horses, one of the packs, carried a couple of shovels with which a grave could be dug. At the carriage, the driver, now disarmed, and a Texan helped a dazed, bloody-scalped, groaning General Main from inside.

54

'Have you pulled the General's teeth?' asked Dusty.

'Sure have, Cap'n,' grinned the Texan and held up one of the small, metal-cartridge Smith and Wesson revolvers which had become popular with members of the U.S. Army assigned to more sedentary duties. 'Ain't this the fiercest gun you ever did see though.'

The hoots of derisive laughter which rose from the other Texans, firm .44 calibre addicts who regarded even the .36 Navy bullets as being a mite small for *serious* work, did nothing to make them relax their vigilance or control of their prisoners. Although Dusty held the same views as his men, he stopped their comments with a low growled word.

'Rider coming fast, Cap'n Dusty,' announced one of the men.

'It's Kiowa,' another went on.

Bringing his horse to a halt by the carriage, Kiowa threw a quick glance around, nodded with satisfaction, then reported to Dusty.

'Went off right as right could be. Red's marching the Yankees through the Funnel right now.'

'Any casualties—' asked Dusty.

'None. Leastways, not on our side.'

'Good,' Dusty said and turned to look in the direction of the Funnel. Then he swung back and watched two of his men, under Belle's urgings, removing a large box from the carriage.

'This's what I wanted, Dusty,' the girl breathed.

Something in her attitude drew Dusty's eyes to Belle. Mere lust for money did not give her the air of excitement. True she would probably receive a percentage of the consignment as a reward for her efforts, but he knew patriotism and not profit had been her motive.

Drawing his right-hand Colt, he sent a bullet into the lock, shattering it. Belle threw back the lid and looked at the canvas bags. Taking one out, she borrowed Kiowa's knife and slit it open. Gold coins glinted in her hands and she raised her eyes to Dusty's.

'How do we transport the money?' she asked. 'The carriage won't help us.'

'Never aimed to use it,' Dusty replied. We'll make up the money into loads for two pack-horses. Then I'll sent Kiowa and Red to escort you back to our headquarters. Reckon

Uncle Devil'll see that you get where you want to go after that.'

'Can't you come with me?'

'Reckon not. I don't know how soon the Yankees will learn about this raid, but I do know it'll make them pot-boiling wild when they hear. So I figured to keep my boys in this area, stir things up just like I was sent to do.'

'That'll be risky,' Belle pointed out.

'Sure,' Dusty agreed. 'But maybe they'll figure I've still got the money with me and give you an easy trip through. Anyways, I've got to try to draw as much of the Yankee strength as possible up here so that Cousin Buck has a better chance of taking that supply depot and getting Company A out alive.'

Much as Belle wanted to ask Dusty to come back with her, she did not. She knew the dangers of her own task and needed help, but a whole company of the Texas Light Cavalry might be wiped out if Dusty failed to do his part in a large plan. Making a swift calculation, Belle decided that she had a few days to spare even allowing for travelling time.

'How long will you be out?' she asked.

'Two days, should be back at headquarters in four,' Dusty replied, wondering at her questions.

'I may see you there then,' Belle smiled.

'Likely,' agreed Dusty and turned back to attend to preparations for joining Red and pulling out.

## CHAPTER SIX

# A FURLOUGH FOR CAPTAIN FOG

'Lawsy me, Cap'n Dusty, sah,' greeted the fat, jovial-looking Negro butler as he opened the front doors of the big house taken over by the Texas Light Cavalry for their officers' mess. 'You-all looks all peaked, gaunt and tired.'

'I feel a mite that way, Oscar,' Dusty replied.

Since parting from Red, Belle and Kiowa, Dusty had been constantly on the move. By pushing his men and horses to the very limits of their endurance, he stirred up a hornet's nest in north-west Arkansas and left the Yankees feeling that they had been hit by a raging Texas-twister in all its fury. An unexpected evening rush took the reinforced guard at the Coon Fork bridge by surprise, coming as it did from the northern bank of the river. After destroying the Vandenburg gun – the horses were too tired and in no shape to haul such a valuable piece of booty back to the Confederate lines – Dusty's men crossed the bridge and destroyed it behind them. The rest had been fairly easy. Walking more than they rode their leg-weary horses, the men made for and crossed the Ouachita, then passed through Confederate-held territory to their regiment's headquarters.

Already the men had attended to their horses and saddles, cleaned their weapons, ate a good meal and now prepared to catch up on some badly needed sleep. Dusty knew that before he could think of resting he still had to make his reports, write at least one of the letters to the parents of the seven men who died on the mission, and clean his Colts. No man who lived as Dusty did ever failed to take *that* precaution.

'I'll want some boiling water sent up to my room after I've seen Colonel Blaze, Oscar,' he told the butler.

'If it am boiling, it ain't for washing,' the Negro answered. 'And if it's for cleaning your guns, I'd sure admire for you-all to do it outside. It sure makes the room smell something wild if you-all does it indoors.'

'Reckon you're right at that,' Dusty smiled. 'Have it out back of the kitchen in fifteen minutes.'

Big, burly, yet hard-fleshed and capable-looking, Colonel Blaze saw Dusty immediately. One glance told Blaze that his nephew had been hard-travelled and looked in need of sleep.

'Make it short, boy,' Blaze ordered. 'I'll have the full story later.'

Taking the chair brought up by the sergeant who showed him into the room, Dusty sank down with a low sigh of contentment. Then he shook off the lethargy and said, 'You'll know about the gold consignment, sir?'

'Red brought it in two days ago. They had to lay up north of the Ouachita for a day because of Yankee activity stopping them crossing.'

'Pleased they made it. Where's Red now?'

'I sent him out of a foraging expedition, we need meat and the next shipment of beef hasn't come in from home yet,' Blaze grinned. 'Had to give him something to do or he'd've been heading back across the Ouachita to look for you. Damned short on discipline that boy. Takes after his pappy.'

Dusty grinned and let the statement ride, knowing that the Colonel had high regard for Red's sterling qualities and meant nothing by his growled-out tirade. Wanting to get through so that he could finish his other work and catch some sleep, Dusty told his uncle of his company's activities after separating from Red. At last Blaze nodded with satisfaction. From what Dusty told him, the stirring-up process had worked real well.

'I expect Major Amesley'll want your report in writing, Dustine,' he said. 'But see to it after you've had some sleep.'

'Yo!' Dusty replied, rising and saluting.

On leaving the colonel's office, Dusty went through the rear of the building and found, as he expected, a bowl of boiling water waiting for him. Already his striker had taken his saddle to his room and brought down the box with cleaning gear for the guns.

Normally Dusty would not have thought of emptying both his guns at the same time, but he figured that in the safety of his regimental headquarters he could dispense with the precaution of always keeping one weapon ready for use. Unbuckling his gunbelt, he removed and laid it on the small table by the wall. After taking off his hat and jacket, he put them with the belt. He drew the two revolvers from their holsters and carried them to the table in the centre of the yard, putting one down by the steaming bowl of water while he prepared to clean the other.

While the 1860 Army Colt could truthfully claim to be the finest fighting handgun of its day, hard-hitting, accurate, robust and well-constructed, it only functioned correctly when given proper care and attention. Since the correct functioning of his guns could mean the difference between life and death, Dusty always devoted time to their maintenance. After a prolonged period of regular use, like the past few days had called for, more than a mere cleansing of the barrel and cylinder's chambers was necessary.

After setting the right-hand Colt at half cock, Dusty took the basic precaution of removing the percussion caps from the cylinder nipples. Not until he had guarded against accidental discharge did he drive out the wedge which held the barrel and cylinder on the lock frame's base pin. Turning the cylinder slightly, he worked the ramming lever under the barrel so that its head pressed against the partition between two of the chambers and so forced the barrel free from the base pin. Next he removed the cylinder from the base pin and carefully worked the bullets out of the chambers. Although the base of each paper cartridge had been torn on loading, to facilitate the ignition of the enclosed charge, the powder could be used again and the lead remoulded into fresh bullets; so Dusty made sure he drew each load correctly and set them where they would be safe from splashing water. Placing the barrel and empty cylinder into the water, he turned his attention to the lock frame.

Pieces of exploding percussion caps often worked down into the mechanism of the gun, and a careful man removed them regularly. It said much for the ingenuity of the Army Colt's designer that the mechanism was so simple an ordinary user could strip and assemble it without needing to call upon the service of a trained gunsmith. Using the screwdriver which came in the case with his guns, Dusty removed the three screws holding the butt grips in place. He then unfastened the screw which connected the main spring to the triggerguard and turned the spring from under the hammer's tumbler. Removing three more screws allowed him to

59

take off the triggerguard and he twisted away another to gain access to the double spring which bore on the trigger and bolt. Next he removed the trigger and bolt by unfastening two screw-pins. Lastly he released the screw-pin which allowed him to withdraw the hammer, its hand still attached, downwards through the lock frame.

With that done, Dusty set to work on the second Colt, repeating the process and finally started to give every part a thorough cleaning. While working, he heard footsteps approaching and looked up at a man and a girl who came towards him. For a moment he hardly recognized Belle Boyd, as she wore a stylish grey dress and a large-brimmed hat from under which hung long red hair. At her side strode General Ole Devil Hardin. Tall, ramrod straight, immaculate in his uniform of a full general of the Confederate States Army, Hardin's lean, tanned face had the look of a hard disciplinarian tempered with a sense of humour. His face showed no expression, but relief glinted in his usually hard black eyes as he studied his illustrious nephew.

'Carry on with your work, Dustine,' Hardin greeted as Dusty lowered the lock-frame in preparation to render military courtesy by coming to attention and saluting. 'Pleased to see you back, boy.'

'So am I, Dusty,' Belle went on, trying to sound formal but belying the effort with her warm smile.

'Which same makes three of us,' Dusty answered with a faint grin.

'Rough trip, boy?' asked Ole Devil.

The grin died away and Dusty nodded his head. 'Rough enough, sir, I lost seven men when we tangled with a battalion of Yankee cavalry. Had to run near on four miles before we lost them. I think they were the 8th Pennsylvania Regiment.'

Which, as Hardin knew, meant that the Yankees did belong to the regiment named. Dusty was well enough schooled in his work to know the need for accurate identification of an enemy force.

'Good,' Hardin growled. 'The 8th are based to the east. You've pulled out at least some of them and will have everybody's attention on the west.'

'I hope so, sir,' Dusty replied. 'Cousin Buck will have it hard enough on his assignment. Anything I could do will help him a mite.' He paused for a moment, giving his attention to cleaning the lock-frame, then went on, 'What's next for me, sir?'

'How's your company?'

'Horses are about done, but a few days will see them right, or we can draw from the regiment's remounts.'

'It's time your men came off active duties for a time,' Old Devil stated, having already seen the condition of the horses Dusty brought back from the patrol. 'How'd you like a furlough, boy?'

'Back home in Texas, sir?' asked Dusty, trying hard to hide the eagerness in his voice.

' 'Fraid not. In Matamoros.'

Using a rod, Dusty fished one of the barrels from the water. His eyes went first to the girl, then swung back to Ole Devil. 'Matamoros in Mexico, sir?'

'If there's another, we're not interested in it,' Ole Devil replied, watching Dusty start to clean the barrel. 'It's a right lively place for a young feller to spend a furlough in, or so they tell me.'

'And if it's any inducement, Dusty,' Belle put in. 'I'll be going there with you.'

'Why not tell me the *assignment*, sir,' Dusty suggested

Turning his grim face towards Belle, Old Devil smiled one of his rare smiles, 'I told you we might as well lay our cards straight on the table, Miss Boyd.'

'It's usually the best,' she agreed. 'Only in my line one gets used to taking the long way around.' She turned back to Dusty and watched him thrusting the cleaning rod through the Colt's barrel while its heat dried the moisture from it, 'You see, Dusty, 'I'm taking that Yankee gold to Matamoros and I'd naturally prefer to have a reliable escort along with me.'

'The town's lively all right, Dustine,' Old Devil continued, 'A lot of our people went down there when the Yankees took over Brownsville. Then deserters from both sides began to trickle in. All the usual type of riff-raff and adventurers have moved there, it serves as a handy point for smuggling blockade-run goods into Texas and that game doesn't attract many saints. Then there's the French garrison and most likely a fair amount of Mexicans who are getting ready for the big rebellion that's brewing down there against Maximilian . . .'

'You're forgetting somebody, General,' Belle stated.

'Who, ma'am?'

'Yankee spies. Pinkerton runs a mighty efficient organization and won't have overlooked a good bet like Matamoros.'

'He'll likely have them there,' Dusty agreed, 'and in touch with the U.S. Navy ships on blockade service along the Texas coast. All in all, I can think of a whole heap safer places to take the gold.'

'That's why Miss Boyd wants an escort, Dustine,' Ole Devil said.

'Preferably you, Dusty,' Belle went on.

'I'm game, if that's the way you want it, sir,' Dusty answered.

'Damn it, that's *not* the way I want it. But with a shipment of arms due to arrive at Matamoros in the near future, I'd like to see the South lay its hands on them.'

'So that's it,' Dusty breathed, then raised the barrel and looked through its now shining bore.

'The shipment is one I arranged for in England just before I left,' Belle explained. 'The man gathering it is not one of our supporters, but a merchant captain with a shady reputation. Normally when he insisted on payment in gold, I would have ignored the offer, especially with the conditions he laid down. But I saw the consignment. New Enfield rifles—'

'Which are as good guns as a man could ask for,' Dusty interrupted. 'For infantrymen that is.'

'Better than anything we have from our own sources,' Belle replied. 'He is also supplying a large quantity of ammunition and British powder is the best in the world. The consignment is worth the money.'

'You saw the consignment?' asked Dusty.

'And had it checked by a gunsmith.'

'Why is there such a delay in his arriving at Matamoros, and why go there instead of running the blockade to bring the guns into a Southern port?'

On hearing Dusty's questions, Belle felt certain she had done the right thing in requesting that the small Texan be appointed her escort for what she knew must be a dangerous mission. Clearly he aimed to take nothing, not even her loyalty, to chance; and she admired him for his caution.

'Captain Smee, the owner of the consignment, is no supporter of the Confederate States, which is why he says he will deliver to Matamoros rather than risk running the blockade. As for the delay, his ship is in dry-dock receiving a thorough re-fit after damage gained, I feel sure, in some illegal enterprise. He is quite willing to sell his arms to us, but only if we come to Matamoros for them. In Matamoros he can find other customers. The Mexicans fighting to establish one of their own in command as *Presidente* could use those arms. So could the French army of occupation. Even the Yankees would buy the consignment rather than see it fall into our hands.'

'I think of the four, that jasper Smee would rather sell to us,' Ole Devil commented. 'The Mexicans might like the arms, but I doubt if they've the kind of money to pay for it. As the French can have arms shipped from France at less cost, they won't go so high. Maybe the Yankees would buy the shipment. In fact they're certain to try. They can use those arms just as well as we could. So I want that shipment in our hands, Dustine.'

'That figures, sir,' Dusty said quietly, for he knew the situation well.

'Smee has done this sort of thing before, though not dealing with us,' Belle continued. 'The arms are packed in boxes marked "Farm Machinery" or something equally innocent. Not that he needs to go to any great lengths.'

'The Yankees control Brownsville and can cover the mouth of the Rio Grande,' Dusty warned. 'And they've blockade-ships in the area.'

'But Smee sails under the British flag,' Belle pointed out.

At that time Britain was still *the* major world power and sane heads in the Federal Government fought shy of antagonizing the great country across the Atlantic. Opinion in Britain still remained sharply divided on whether to give active support to North or South in the War. A chance insult, an affront against the Union Jack, would give added weight to the arguments of the interests favouring the South. Earlier in the War, a Yankee naval ship's interference with British merchantmen on the high seas caused a diplomatic storm that only considerable tact and some concessions prevented from developing into anything worse. So while under the laws of war ships of a blockading squadron had the right to search neutral vessels trying to enter an enemy port, Matamoros lay in the territory of a neutral nation and the Yankees had no right to interfere with a British ship making for it.

'Which means the Yankees will either have to stop us buying the consignment,' said Ole Devil, 'or prevent us from receiving it after the purchase. Miss Boyd will handle the purchase, Dustine. But it will fall on you to ensure its safe delivery. I won't tell you how to accomplish that. It will depend on conditions in Matamoros.'

'It won't be easy, sir,' Dusty replied.

'I know. That's why I'm allowing you to take Mr. Blaze with you.'

'Red?'

'He was christened Charles William Henry,' Ole Devil growled dryly.

'Reckon *he* remembers that, sir?' grinned Dusty. 'Who'll be commanding the Company while we're away?'

Due to their considerable successes in the field and the fact that they handled most of the difficult raiding chores for the regiment, Company C regarded themselves as the élite of the élite; a crack fighting outfit with pride of achievement to boost them. Such men regarded their officers as being only one shade lower than God and would never take to following any other leaders without considerable fuss. Any officer placed in command of Company C, even temporarily, would have a restive outfit to control until he won their respect. Another point Ole Devil had to remember was that all the men capable of taking over Company C, and making a go of it, already ran their own companies and would not care to change. However, the General knew the only way out of his difficulty.

'I'm putting your father in command,' he replied.

Dusty's father, Hondo Fog, held rank of major and acted as second-in-command of the Texas Light Cavalry. With his forceful personality he could take over Dusty's company and maintain it as the small Texan would wish.

'It's time Company C came off active duty anyway,' Ole Devil went on. 'I'll keep them around the camp. A spell of guard detail, drill and work here won't hurt them.'

It would also give the outfit time to catch up on their rest and allow the horses to regain that peak of condition so necessary in the work Company C handled. Dusty felt relieved to know that his men would not be out on patrol while he went on the assignment to Matamoros.

'How do we get there, sir?' he asked.

At that moment Hardin saw the fatigue-lines on Dusty's

face. 'Damn it, boy!' he barked. 'Leave it until tomorrow. Finish cleaning your guns and then go get some sleep. That's an order.'

Dusty nodded in agreement. That was one order he intended to carry out.

## CHAPTER SEVEN

## DISTURBING NEWS FOR MISS BOYD

*'AND in conclusion, I say again how deeply grieved I am at having to send you this news, and how I sympathize with you in your loss; but I repeat that your son died gallantly while performing his duty and in so doing helped to save the lives of his comrades.*

*Yours sincerely,*

*Dustine Edward Marsden Fog,*
*Captain, Texas Light Cavalry.'*

Laying down his pen, Dusty looked at the letter before him and wondered if he could have expressed himself any better, or maybe lessened the blow of having to tell parents that their son would never come back from the War. A feeling of anger and frustration hit him at the thought. How the hell could one soften such a blow? However, he knew that he must write the letter. Hating the task bitterly, he still did it to the best of his ability and, although he never learned of it, his letters did in some small measure help the grieving parents.

Seven letters lay on the table before him, six of them already sealed in the addressed envelopes ready for dispatch. One of the letters bulked larger than the rest. Belle Boyd had written to the parents of the corporal who gave his life for her and added her condolences to Dusty's message.

Coming to his feet, Dusty stretched himself and grunted as his muscles protested at the strain. However, his young frame had become hardened to strain and he felt refreshed by a long night's sleep. Actually it had been closer to a full evening, night and morning's sleep, for he went to bed as soon as he completed cleaning and reassembling his Colts and did not waken until almost nine in the morning. A bath and shave, although that latter had not yet become a daily necessity in his case, refreshed him. After eating breakfast alone in the dining room, the rest of the officers already being about their duty, Dusty returned to his room on the upper floor and set to work at writing his reports and the letters to his dead men's parents.

Like any outdoorsman, Dusty hated to be cooped up in a room. Having completed his paper-work, he decided to take a stroll around the camp. He wanted to see Belle Boyd and discuss the assignment, but he also wished to make sure that his men were all right and that the horses received correct care and attention.

A faint smile flickered across his face as he took up the jacket, now cleaned, pressed and with the metal work gleaming, from where it hung behind the door. His striker, a man with some thirty years' army service behind him, looked ominous and muttered about the *Manual of Dress Regulations* every time he handled the skirtless jacket. In fact, since a certain Lieutenant Mark Counter, something of a Beau Brummel although a man of considerable courage and ability, introduced the skirtless jacket which became popular with the younger bloods of the C.S.A., considerable controversy raged around the propriety of an officer wearing such a garment. The older set, always inclined to damn anything modern, made rumbling noises at the flouting of dress regulations, but many of the younger officers wore and found the jacket comfortable. At that time Dusty and Mark had not yet met,* but the small Texan figured the other to be a shrewd judge of what a *fighting* cavalry officer should wear. The hanging skirt of the regulation jacket was an infernal nuisance and also a serious hazard when forced to make a rapid mount over the rump of a horse, while the skirtless jacket gave greater freedom of movement under all conditions; and, to Dusty's way of thinking, looked even smarter than the old style.

Dusty and Red shared a room on the upper floor of the building, although expecting to be evicted to live with the other junior officers in the tented lines if senior members of the C.S.A. came on an extended visit. Knowing that Dusty needed rest, Red had left early and not returned. So Dusty donned his jacket ready to go out in search of his second-in-command.

* Dusty and Mark's first meeting is recorded in THE YSABEL KID by J. T. Edson.

Swinging his gunbelt around his waist, Dusty fastened the buckle and then secured the thongs which held the holster tips down. He took up the two Colts. Checked that each nipple had a percussion cap firmly seated upon it and that the hammer of each gun rested on a safety notch between two of the nipples. Taking precautions like that came naturally to Dusty. He knew that even in his regiment's camp he might need his guns, and if he did need them, there would be no time to start checking on and replacing any percussion caps not in place. Making sure the Colts' hammers rode safely was another simple, but necessary precaution. No man with any brains in his head carried a loaded revolver with its hammer resting on a capped nipple.

The door of the room opened and Dusty's striker entered, having heard his officer moving about and guessing that the letter-writing session had ended. Knowing Dusty's views on writing, the striker kept out of the way until the distasteful business had been concluded.

'Take the letters to the orderly room, Dick,' Dusty ordered.

'Yo!' the striker answered. 'And don't you go tearing about neither. Take it easy for a spell. That danged company of your'n won't fall apart if you leave it for a spell.'

'You know it, and I know it,' Dusty grinned, 'but I don't want Uncle Devil to know it or I'll be looking for a fresh command.'

'Hope it's one where they make you wear the right jacket,' sniffed the striker, sealing the last envelope and taking up the others.

'If they do, I'm going home to mother.' Dusty told his striker and left the room before the other could make any adequate reply.

Dusty walked from the house and made his way through the neat tented lines to his company's area. Visiting Billy Jack's quarters, he heard his sergeant-major's report on the welfare of his men. From there Dusty and the lean non-com passed on to the horse lines where the regiment veterinarian and stables sergeant waited. After checking that the welfare of his horses was well in hand, Dusty gave Billy Jack the good news. Relief showed on the lean sergeant-major's face as he heard that the company would be able to relax and reform before making any more sorties against the Yankees.

'Red and I are going on an assignment,' Dusty went on. 'Only if anybody asks, we're on furlough. Pappy'll be running the Company until I get back.'

'That'll be all right,' Billy Jack answered. 'If there's no more, Cap'n Dusty, it's Saturday and I've a card game waiting.'

'Gambling'll be your downfall,' Dusty warned.

Grinning, the lean non-com saluted and ambled away. Dusty watched the other go and smiled. There went a real good man, one in whom a feller could trust his life. Turning, Dusty walked towards the big house. To get there he had to pass a large storehouse which had been emptied and converted into a fencing school for the Regiment. Hearing the unmistakable sound of swords in action, he walked towards the open door of the building and looked inside.

A fencing match was in progress, watched by the *maitre d'armes* and seven or so of the younger officers of the Regiment. Remaining outside, Dusty studied the contestants and noted the high standard of skill both showed. The skill did not surprise him really, for Major Amesley, the *maitre d'armes* – he also acted as the Regiment's adjutant – had been a fencing instructor in New Orleans, and taught the junior officers all he could. Pete Blaze, Red's older brother, could claim to be the best sabre fighter in the Regiment and, although using an *epee de salle* instead of the *arme blanche* of the cavalry, performed with skill. So did his opponent. Clad in her Union army kepi, dark blue shirt, black breeches and light shoes, Belle Boyd handled her *epee* to such effect that Pete could not make a hit on her. Nor could she get through to him. Suddenly she jerked off her kepi, tossed it into Pete's face and went into a lunge. Blinded by the hat, Pete failed to recover in time and he felt the *epee*'s button touch him in the belly.

'I always say if you can't lick 'em, trick 'em,' Belle stated, avoiding Amesley's accusing eye.

Laughing, the rest of the officers gathered around the girl. Not having been reared under the strict rules of the *code duello,* they regarded the girl's breach of fencing etiquette as amusing. Requests to try a few passes against Belle came from all sides, but as the girl was about to accept one challenge she saw Dusty enter the building. One of the others turned to look at the new arrival.

69

'Hey, Dusty,' he greeted. 'Come on in and give Belle a whirl. This gal's a living wonder with an *epee*.'

Eagerly the other officers joined in the appeal for Dusty to try his hand in a bout with the girl. Belle regarded the small Texan with expectant eyes and hoped he would agree to face her. Since her arrival at the Regiment's headquarters, she had heard many tales of Dusty's blinding speed and deadly accuracy when using his Colts and also of his ability at unarmed fighting, but little had been said of his knowledge of fencing. She wanted to gauge his ability in that line.

'Loan me an *epee*,' Dusty said. 'I'll learn how it's done.'

Taking the offered *epee* after removing his hat, jacket and gunbelt, he stepped into the centre of the hall. Belle had recovered her hat and moved into place before him, smiling as she studied the relaxed ease with which he handled the *epee*.

A faint smile came to Amesley's face and he moved forward. Nothing could quite compare, in his opinion, to watching the interplay between two skilled users of the *epee*. While he taught the Regiment how to handle their sabres, at heart he clung to the belief that the *epee* was the only true gentleman's weapon and hoped the girl would not spoil what promised to be a fine bout by using any trickery.

Gracefully Belle raised her *epee* in the salute and watched the relaxed, casual manner with which Dusty replied to the courtesy. If the way he handled his *epee* proved anything, he knew at least the basic rudiments of fencing. From what Belle had seen so far among the Texans, that did not surprise her. She wanted to see how much further his knowledge went.

'*En garde!*' Amesley ordered. 'Engage.'

The blade touched and Belle attacked with a covered thrust but felt Dusty's *epee* deflect her own slightly and parried his counter-attack with a deft wrist twist which gladdened Amesley's heart as he watched. While the opening moves told Belle that Dusty knew more than a little about handling an *epee*, before many seconds passed Belle began to realize just how good he was with that weapon. Yet for all his skill, Dusty found that the girl could handle his attacks and prevented him from making a hit on her.

Steel glinted, hissed and clashed as the bout went on.

Attacks on arm and body, thrusts at low or high angulation, *froisse* attacks, *prises de fer*, were made and parried; even beats at the blade, most difficult of all moves to accomplish with an *epee* were tried without the one attempting the beat taking the point of the blade so far out of line that it left the forearm uncovered for a counter thrust. Even the stern old master, Amesley, could not resist joining in the applause when Belle, in the course of her attack, carried her left foot as far back as possible, dropped her left hand to the floor while extending her right arm with the hand high and thumb downward so as to direct her sword towards Dusty in the low line. Only by a very rapid retreat did Dusty avoid being taken by Belle's *passata sotto* and her low lunge, a classic and entirely legal move, carried her body under his blade.

For over a minute the duel went on fast and furiously. Sweat trickled down Belle's face and she had never found a moment when she might chance getting off balance to repeat the trick which beat Pete Blaze. However, she saw her chance as they came in close. Just as Dusty wondered if he ought to call off the contest, for the girl had already taken on Pete in a long bout, he caught a warning glint in her eyes.

Up drove Belle's left foot, aimed at his middle. She gave only that one very faint hint of her plan, but against a man with Dusty's lightning fast reactions such a hint was enough. From the raised balance position, Dusty's left hand sped down and his fingers closed on her leg before the foot reached him. Belle gave a startled yelp as she felt his strength. Then he twisted on the ankle, turning the foot inward and raising it higher than Belle meant it to go. This caused Belle to turn her body away from him and, losing her *epee,* she went down to land on her hands, face to the floor. Still gripping the ankle in his hand, Dusty, placed his right foot between her legs and dropped to his knee so as to bend the trapped limb across his. The move came so swiftly that Belle could not even think of countering it. Pain knifed into her knee and she gasped. Instantly Dusty released his hold and came to his feet.

'I'm sorry, Belle,' he said, bending to help her rise. 'I just went on with the move without thinking.'

A wry smile came to Belle's face. 'Mike was right. I wouldn't have fooled you with my *savate.*'

71

'You sure can handle a sword,' Dusty commented.

'I had a good teacher,' Belle replied and in an attempt to make amends for spoiling Amesley's enjoyment of the bout by her attempt at trickery, went on, 'almost as good as the man who taught you.'

'I'd like to see you matched against Dusty when you are fresh, Miss Boyd,' Amesley put in, accepting the compliment with a slight bow.

'We'll see what we can do, sir,' Dusty promised. 'And now, how about coming riding with me, Belle?'

'My pleasure, sir,' Belle answered with as near a curtsy as she could manage while slightly winded and wearing breeches instead of a skirt. 'If the other gentlemen will excuse me.'

Jumping to the wall, Pete Blaze took down one of the *epees* from the rack and returned to block the way to the door. 'We won't,' he warned. 'You'll have to fight your way out.'

Eagerly the seven other young officers grabbed training weapons and aligned themselves with Pete.

'Two against eight?' asked Belle with a smile. 'How about it, Dusty?'

'Danged if we haven't all but got them outnumbered,' Dusty replied and winked at her. 'Let's follow the Boyd family motto.'

Dropping his *epee*, Dusty went forward in a fast, rolling dive that carried him under the blades of the waiting swords. His hands shot out to grab the inner ankle of the man on either side of Pete and his body struck and knocked his cousin over backwards. Coming erect at the end of his roll, Dusty retained his grip on the ankles, jerking them into the air. Taken by surprise, the trapped men tipped over, to land in a tangled heap upon Pete.

Keeping her *epee* in her hand, Belle bounded forward and into the air in a *savate* leaping high kick. Drawing up her legs, she shot them out, one foot striking each of the central of her four opponents in the chest and flinging them backwards. Rebounding from her attack, which carried her body over their swords, Belle landed on her feet once more. With a swift, deft bound, she twisted the amazed third man's sabre from his grasp. Whirling, Belle lunged at the fourth and passed his guard long before he thought to make it.

'You're dead!' she announced as the *epee* bowed gracefully from hand to chest.

'And so are you, Stan,' declared Dusty, scooping up a sabre and delivering a cut at the body of the last of their attackers while that worthy stood open-mouth and amazed.

Whether any of the eight would have accepted their 'deaths' was not to be discovered. A soldier appeared at the door of the building even as Dusty spoke.

'Company A is back!' the man yelled.

Instantly all thought of carrying on with the fun departed and the discomfited attackers untangled themselves to rise and leave the room. Dusty returned his *epee* and sabre to the wall rack, collected his hat, jacket and gunbelt, and joined the others outside to watch the returning company.

'Buck's all right,' Pete breathed in relief as he watched his twin brother riding at the head of the approaching column.

Leaving his men, Buck Blaze rode towards the others and halted. Although his face showed fatigue, he managed a grin as his eyes rested on Dusty.

'We got it, Dusty,' Buck said. 'Hardly saw a Yankee all the way, thanks to you. Prisoner we took at the depot allowed most of the men had been sent west after your boys. You sure riled the Yankees this time out.'

'Pleased to hear it,' Dusty replied. 'Did you lose many men?'

'Four. It'd been a damned sight harder happen you hadn't drawn so many of the Yankee troops to the west.'

On a previous attempt at destroying the depot, with less forethought or planning, half a company of a Virginia cavalry regiment were killed or captured. That had been during the period when Ole Devil found himself fully occupied with assuming office as commanding general of the Army of Arkansas.

Dusty watched Buck ride away after Company A. Somehow his cousin's news made him feel better. There had been a big saving of lives through his actions.

'Well, Dusty,' Belle remarked after Buck left, 'we've fought our way out. Let's take that ride, shall we?'

'I reckon we can,' he answered.

Borrowing two horses from the Regiment's remount pool, Belle and Dusty rode from the camp and along the forest-lined trail towards Hope City. At first they talked of Dusty's fighting skills and he described the deadly ju jitsu and karate techniques taught to him by Ole Devil's servant, a smiling Oriental who claimed to hail from some country called Nippon. At last, about a mile from the camp, Dusty brought up the subject which interested him most.

'When do we leave?'

'As soon as authorization to purchase the guns is telegraphed to me from my headquarters. The Government may have some other plans for using the money, or may not want to deal with Smee.'

'How'd you figure we'll get to the coast and reach Matamoros?'

'Pick up a riverboat at Fulton and go down the Red, but swing off along the Atchafalaya River instead of joining the Mississippi. Go through Grand Lake to Morgan City and join a fast blockade-runner there, use it to reach Matamoros.'

'And how do we go up the Rio Grande to Matamoros?' asked Dusty. 'A Confederate blockade-runner won't be flying the British flag.'

'I'm not sure how,' Belle admitted. 'I think we'll be put ashore south of Matamoros and make our way overland.'

'That'll mean taking horses with us,' Dusty remarked.

A red-headed woodpecker flitted from the trees ahead of the horses, made a rapid change of direction and sped off towards the thick bushes flanking the other side of the trail. Then it seemed to be trying to halt in mid-air and its chattering cry burst loud as it swung away from the bushes to speed off and disappear into the trees again.

Watching the bird's appearance, Dusty followed its flight until it made the second hurried change of direction. His eyes caught a sight of something blue in colour and at odds with the greens or browns of the surrounding bushes. In a flickering blur of movement, his left hand crossed to draw the right side Colt.

'Come out with your hands raised high!' he ordered, cocking the Colt. 'Do it slow and real easy.'

Belle halted her horse and for once just sat staring instead of reacting with her usual speed. While she carried her Dance in an open-topped holster, she had never mastered the knack of drawing it really fast. So far little publicity had been given to the deadly techniques of the Western gun fighter and few people in the more pampered East had any conception of just how swiftly a frontier-trained man could draw his weapon. To Belle, who had been engaged in her own business and failed to see Dusty shoot the Dragoon at the mouth of the Funnel, it seemed that the Army Colt just appeared in Dusty's left hand; and for no reason that she could discern.

Hands in the air and moving slowly, a bearded man stepped from the bushes. He had the appearance of a poorer class manual worker and did not appear to be armed. Although blue, his shirt was a lighter shade than that worn by the Yankee army; which was fortunate for him, as Dusty would have shot without challenging otherwise.

'Don't shoot, sir,' he said. 'Maybe the lady knows what comes after "Southrons, hear your country call you".'

'Up, lest worse than death befall you,' Belle answered. 'He's a friend, Dusty. You won't need your gun.'

'*My* friends don't hide out when they see me coming,' Dusty commented.

'*Mine* do,' Belle countered. 'Do you have a message for me?'

'Yes, ma'am,' the man answered, throwing a glance at Dusty and making no attempt to pass on the message.

'Will you wait here, please, Dusty?' asked Belle, knowing that the man did not wish to speak in front of the small Texan.

'It's your deal,' Dusty replied.

Belle and the man walked up the trail, the girl sitting her horse and leaning down to speak. A few moments passed and Belle turned her horse to ride back towards Dusty while the man disappeared into the bushes. Even before Belle reached him, Dusty knew something troubled her.

'We'd better go back to the camp, Dusty,' she said. 'I've just had some disturbing news.'

## CHAPTER EIGHT

# PROMOTION FOR MAJOR AMESLEY

THE short, smiling Oriental servant showed Belle and Dusty into Ole Devil Hardin's office. Seated at his desk, the General shoved aside a pile of papers on which he had been working and then came to his feet.

'You wish to see me, Miss Boyd?' he asked.

'I do, General,' Belle replied.

'Was just going to send for you anyway. Your authorization to take the money and buy the arms has just come in.'

Belle and Dusty exchanged glances and despite their being accustomed to living in danger, both felt a faint tingle of anticipation run through them.

'Give Miss Boyd a chair, Tommy,' Ole Devil ordered, for, despite his inborn objections to a young lady wearing men's clothing and indulging in such an unfeminine business as spying, he never forgot the social graces. When the girl had been seated at the desk, he continued, 'What did you want to see me about, Miss Boyd?'

'I can't go into details such as who the man was, or how he came by his information, of course,' Belle answered, 'but I can assure you that the word he brought is genuine and accurate.'

'Maybe you'd better tell me which man you refer to,' growled the General.

Quickly Belle told of the meeting with the agent and Ole Devil sat stiff-backed in his chair, taking in every word. Moving on silent feet, Tommy Okasi handed his employer a cigar and rasped a match for it. Through the smoke, Ole Devil studied Belle's face.

'The gist of the message is that one of Pinkerton's best men has been on my trail almost ever since I landed in New York. Strogoff, the agent, arrived in Russelville on the day after the gold raid. He investigated it and is sure that I was responsible for it. More than that, my information is that the Yankees guess at the use to which we intend to put the gold – and where.'

For the first time Belle saw Dusty and Ole Devil come close to showing emotion. A flicker of expression crossed Ole Devil's face, almost mirrored by the glint that appeared in Dusty's eyes. Watching them, Belle saw how Dusty reacted in much the same manner as his uncle and realized that the small young Texan tried to model himself on the tall, grim-faced warrior who commanded him.

'How the hell did they learn about the Matamoros?' Dusty asked when Ole Devil failed to raise the point.

'Pinkerton runs an efficient organization; never sell him or his men short on that,' Belle warned. 'I was probably under observation most of the time I was in England. If so, they know about my meetings with Smee, and he isn't the most loyal of men.'

'Do you think this Smee jasper sold you out?' growled Ole Devil.

'It's possible,' Belle admitted.

'That's not going to make our work any easier,' Dusty remarked.

'I know. The U.S. Secret Service don't like Rose Greenhow or me, we've made them look fools too many times. Pinkerton's crowd swore they would get me after I escaped from the Old Capitol Prison after they put me there.'

'I never did learn how you pulled that,' Dusty said.

'Some other time, Dustine,' Ole Devil ordered and looked at Belle. 'In the face of what you've told me, I think you had best stay in the South. Dustine and Red – Damn it, Dustine, you've got *me* calling him "Red" now – Anyhow, they can make the purchase and delivery.'

'I'm afraid that's not so easy, General,' Belle smiled. 'Dusty and Red are both good fighting men, but they haven't played *my* game long enough to know it.'

'How do you mean?' asked Ole Devil.

'I'm not selling Dusty or Red short on any counts,' Belle assured him, noting the anger-furrow which came between his eyes. 'But you wouldn't send one of your companies out under the command of a civilian – would you?'

From what she had already seen of Ole Devil, Belle figured that line would be the one he understood the best. Her judgment proved correct and an admiring glint crept into the hard black eyes as Ole Devil sat back in his chair.

'I see now how you've stayed alive so long, Miss Boyd,' he stated.

Dusty frowned and put his doubts to words. 'Belle's a valuable spy and the South needs her, sir.' His eyes turned to Belle and he went on, 'and I'm not saying that just because you're a woman. But the Pinkerton bunch want you and I've heard they aren't particular how they go about getting somebody they're after. You'll be mighty conspicuous down there.'

'I agree, Miss Boyd,' Ole Devil put in. 'Even though you're a pretty fair hand at disguising yourself, any American girl down there will stick out like a nigger on a snowdrift. Unless you plan to go there as a Mexican.'

'My Spanish is non-existent,' Belle smiled. 'There are some white girls down there, working in the *cantinas* or on the streets, but going as one of them would limit my usefulness.'

'Yes,' agreed Ole Devil. 'There'd be too many places in Matamoros closed to that kind of woman; and I wouldn't want you to go into the kind of hell-holes there are in Matamoros.'

'I can take care of myself pretty well, General,' Belle replied. 'But a *cantina* worker would not serve my purpose.'

'We're assuming that the Yankees in Matamoros hear that we're coming,' Dusty reminded the others.

'I've told you that Pinkerton's crowd are thorough,' Belle answered. 'Strogoff had already telegraphed news of the raid to Washington. From there, word can be passed to New York and a fast Navy boat sent off. Even starting today, we could hardly be in Matamoros before word reaches the Yankee spies there.'

'We'll lose nothing by assuming that's already happened, Dustine,' Ole Devil pointed out.

'Yes, sir,' Dusty answered in a disinterested manner which drew Ole Devil's eyes sharply towards him.

Seeing that Dusty did not intend to say more, and knowing his nephew *very* well, Ole Devil turned back to Belle. 'Could you pass yourself off as a French girl?'

'Possibly, although my French is of the Creole variety. There can't be so many French girls in Matamoros that the sudden appearance of another would go unnoticed. Of course, it is a thought.'

Glancing at Dusty, Belle waited for him to make a comment, but he sat back in his chair, a blank expression on his face. For almost a minute nobody spoke. Then Dusty sat forward in his chair. While he tried to keep his features free from expression, a faint glint of eagerness showed on them.

'What is it, Dustine?' asked Ole Devil.

'Just a fool notion, sir.'

'Go ahead,' the General ordered, thinking of other occasions on which Dusty came out with a 'fool notion' that proved to be a very sound piece of planning and brought success.

'Like we figure, Belle's arrival in Matamoros is bound to attract some attention – no matter what she wears or how she tries to hide.'

'We'd already assumed *that*,' growled Ole Devil.

'Then why hide her at all? Let her arrive in plain view and with conspicuous company.'

'Such as?' asked Belle.

'Let her go into town as the wife, or *amie* – is that the word I want?—'

'It'll do,' grunted Ole Devil. 'I have heard of even Confederate officers having such things.'

'But why would a Confederate officer be in Matamoros?' smiled Belle.

'He could have come in from Texas on an official visit to the French authorities, to discuss—'

Dusty's voice trailed off at that point, for he had not been able to think of a convincing reason for the visit.

'He's come to discuss an exchange of deserters. Quite a few French soldiers have gone over the hill, jumped the Rio Grande and settled in Texas. There are some of our own down below the border. The visit could be to arrange for an exchange – with more serious undertones, such as a closer association between our Government and the French.'

'That's a really good idea, General,' Belle breathed. 'The French would be only too pleased to give us co-operation if they thought their cause in Mexico might benefit by it.'

'Only it won't work,' Ole Devil answered.

'Why not, sir?' asked Dusty.

'Such a mission would not be handled by a captain, no matter how distinguished his record, and a first lieutenant.'

'That's true enough,' Belle agreed. 'But I still like the idea.'

'We need a field, or staff officer with us, sir,' Dusty stated.

'I could appoint you temporary rank, Dustine, but you're too young.'

'Yes, sir. But it sounds like the kind of trip Pappy would like.'

'You know I can't spare an active officer,' Ole Devil pointed out. 'I can't spare you and R—Mr. Blaze if it comes to that.'

Although Ole Devil held the Yankees in Arkansas and had inflicted some heavy losses on them, he did so by superior tactics and fighting ability. Outnumbered by the enemy, only keeping every man fully employed prevented the Confederate Army from being swept back to the borders of Texas and held them firm beyond the Ouachita. Taking Dusty's company out of the field would mean cancelling, or postponing several projects as Ole Devil well knew. He could not spare both Hondo and Dusty at one time.

'Major Amesley could come, sir,' Dusty suggested. 'His orderly room staff do most of his work anyway, and he's champing on the bit to see some action.'

'You could be right at that,' smiled Ole Devil. 'Wouldn't need to put too much strain on his leg and he's got the way with him to carry the affair off.'

'There would be no objection on age grounds to Major Amesley receiving promotion, General,' Belle remarked.

'How do you mean, ma'am?' asked Ole Devil. 'You think I should appoint him a lieutenant or full colonel for the trip?'

'A brigadier general would be even better,' she replied calmly.

'A *general*!' Ole Devil barked.

'Yes. The French Army officers are either members of the *ancien regime*, or, as they say, of the people. The former respect a man for his breeding, which we know the Major has, and his rank. The latter, like most of their type, are arrant snobs and are more likely to show deference to a general than to a major or colonel. One other point to remember is that a general would be more likely than a colonel to have a captain and first lieutenant on his staff.'

'That's true,' conceded Ole Devil, then smiled. 'So's everything you said. However, promotion from major to brigadier general might be construed as straining the powers of even the commanding general of the Army of Arkansas.'

'My department would back you on it,' Belle promised. 'Put it down to the necessity of the situation. And the promotion would only be temporary – and unpaid.'

'You can be certain of the last,' Ole Devil informed her definitely.

'And all the expenses will be defrayed from the Yankee gold,' she went on.

'I should think so too,' he replied, and for a moment his face softened in a smile.

In that moment Belle saw the kindly man hidden under the hard mask of discipline and façade of irascible nature. The mask did not stay broken for long and the old, cold face returned.

'My compliments to Major Amesley, Dustine,' he said. 'Ask him to come to see me as soon as it's convenient. Which means right now, convenient or not.'

'Yo!' Dusty replied, rising and crossing to the door.

Five minutes later, Dusty returned with Major Amesley at his side. For the first time Belle noticed the slight limp which told that the wound received in the early days of the War had left its mark. While waiting for Amesley to appear, Ole Devil had told the girl how the major received the wound and also mentioned his age. Belle could hardly believe that tanned, sprightly man had sixty years on his shoulders and would have put his age at the most in the very early fifties.

Emotion played on Amesley's face, although only one who knew him as well as did Ole Devil Hardin could have noticed it, as he approached the general's desk. Being a well-educated man, Amesley could easily add together two and two to make the correct answer. He knew Belle's identity and guessed that something important kept her in the area. Nor had Dusty's excitement – again only observable to one who knew the signs – gone unnoticed. Amesley hoped against hope that the call to Ole Devil's office meant a chance to get away from dull routine and perform some useful fighting task for his country. The old wound stiffened his leg to the point where continued strenuous exercise rendered it unable to move with the speed necessary to keep a combat soldier alive. So he did duty as adjutant and trained the young bloods to handle their swords, much as the tasks galled him. Watching Ole Devil, Amesley prayed that there would be a change in the air.

'Sit down, Beau,' Ole Devil said, waving a hand towards the chair Tommy Okasi brought to him. 'Do you know the Mexican port of Matamoros?'

'Can't say I do, sir.'

Ole Devil proceeded to run through the situation, with Amesley listening attentively and casting occasional glances at Belle or Dusty. At the end, he nodded his head.

'I can handle my part of it, sir,' he stated.

'Well, be cagey with it,' Ole Devil warned. 'Nobody in our Government will come out with a definite official statement about siding either the French or the Mexicans, not wanting to antagonize either side. You'll probably find the French brass mighty interested. Particularly those so close to the border. Feel them out, learn all you can about their sentiments, but don't make any promises that our Government will have to stand by or refute later.'

'May I say something, sir?' Dusty put in.

'Feel free,' Ole Devil answered.

'The Yankees are going to be real interested in our reason for being in Matamoros.'

'I'd say so.'

'And they'll probably put it down to our trying to organize an alliance with the French.'

'Probably.'

'Then they'll be watching us all the time.'

'No, Dustine,' Belle interrupted. 'They'll be watching "General" Amesley. He has to hold their attention and leave you and I free to arrange for the shipment of arms when Smee arrives.'

'That may be,' Dusty replied doubtfully. 'But while the Yankees are watching Major Amesley, they're going to see him spending a whole load of their gold.'

'So?' asked Ole Devil.

'Aren't they going to think that just a little mite strange? A Confederate "General" spending Yankee gold.'

'I think I can answer that, General,' Belle stated. 'Going from what I saw in Europe – and I can't see Matamoros being any different – there'll be considerable reluctance to accept paper money issued by either side.'

'That figures,' Ole Devil answered. 'Whichever side wins won't uphold the other's currency. Foreigners would fight shy of taking something that may wind up by being just so much paper after the end of the War.'

'Then you don't reckon the Yankees'll be suspicious when they see us spending U.S. minted coins?'

'Not if we use coins with pre-war dates on them,' Belle asserted.

'Are any of the coins dated before the War?' asked Ole Devil.

Nobody replied for a moment, then Dusty looked across the desk. 'I don't reckon any of us thought to look, sir,' he admitted.

'Then somebody had better look,' growled Ole Devil. 'And soon.'

'I'll see to it, sir,' Dusty promised. 'Sure hope that it's all in double eagles though, or I'll be checking it all day.'

'You've maybe got something better to do?' asked Ole Devil with a grin, then turned his attention to the rest of the occupants of the room. 'Anything more before we break this off, Miss Boyd?'

'I'd like somebody to arrange our passage down river,' Belle answered.

'Have your orderly room sergeant see to it, Beau. Have you anything you want?'

'Only my stars and sleeve insignia,' Amesley replied. 'How about my staff?'

'You'll have Dustine and Red Blaze as your aides and Miss Boyd will be your *amie*. I'll leave it to you how you arrange *that*.'

'Servants, sir?' Amesley continued.

No Confederate general would travel without at least one servant to minister to his needs and all present knew that everything must appear normal if their mission was to succeed.

'Any suggestions, Dustine?' asked Ole Devil.

'My striker, he's a cool hand and can be trusted to keep his mouth shut. And I reckon Billy Jack'd go to private to act as Major Amesley's striker.'

'A brigadier general could run to a sergeant-major for striker, sergeant at least,' Ole Devil countered. 'But why Billy Jack?'

'Dick's a mite long in the tooth for rough games and this might turn out to be real rough,' Dusty replied. 'Anyways it's time Billy Jack had a furlough.'

'Will he volunteer to go along?' Belle inquired.

'I'll order him to volunteer,' grinned Dusty. 'How about a maid for you?'

'We'd best hire one down there, say mine quit before we left Texas,' Belle answered.

'Which brings up another point,' Dusty went on. 'You'll be travelling as a lady—'

'Why thank you 'most to death, kind sir,' smiled Belle.

'You know what I mean,' Dusty answered. 'That means you can't ride into Matamoros dressed like you are today. Which also means that you going in afork a horse is out.'

'Well, Dustine?' queried Ole Devil.

'We need a carriage of some kind, sir. And we can't hope to be lucky enough to pick one up in some deserted bay on the Mexican coast.'

'Take one with you,' Ole Devil suggested. 'Pick it up either in Alexandria or Morgan City. You'll need something to carry the gold on and pack horses wouldn't be the best answer.'

Watching the men, Belle was struck by the attention they paid to small details. Many Army men she knew would never have thought to discuss the matter, but send her out to fend for herself. Belle felt gratified and pleased with the way her luck placed her in the way of such helpful and competent men.

'Anything more?' asked Ole Devil.

'Only how we're going to handle the transportation of the money, and I reckon I can handle that, sir,' Dusty answered.

'Miss Boyd?' Ole Devil went on.

'Nothing that I can think of off-hand.'

'Beau?'

'I'll take up anything I think of with Dusty, sir.'

'Then that's all, Miss Boyd, gentlemen.'

Rising, Dusty and Amesley saluted their general and left the office with Belle on their heels. At the door Amesley halted and looked down at his sleeves.

'Brigadier General,' he smiled. 'Now there's a promotion for you, Dusty.'

'Yes, sir, General,' Dusty answered, grinning back. 'It sure is – even if you don't get paid for the rank.'

## CHAPTER NINE

# CAPTAIN FOG ENCOUNTERS
# A TRAVEL HAZARD

BEFORE the War, the *Rosebud* had made the big run along the Mississippi from St. Louis to New Orleans and competed for trade with the many other side-wheeler steamboats which carried passengers and freight at speeds no other form of transport could equal. However, the War disrupted the river-boat trade, for the Yankees controlled the Mississippi's lower reaches and their gunboats raided far up-stream in a manner which rendered peaceful trading decidedly risky. Only a few of the boats remained in business and the *Rosebud* found a useful route lay between Fulton on the Red River in Arkansas and Morgan City down at the mouth of the Atchafalaya.

What with shortages of freight and passengers, word that a brigadier general, his niece – being a man of the world, Captain Boynes of the *Rosebud* accepted that the young woman accompanying 'General' Amesley *might* be his niece – and staff wished to make the full trip was something of a windfall. In accordance with the *Rosebud*'s tradition of hospitality and luxury, Boynes and his clerk stood on the boiler deck at the point where the double stairway from the main deck curved together, and waited to greet their distinguished passenger. There were no boilers on the 'boiler' deck, it being given over to the big main cabin which served as lounge, dining room, bar and general gathering place for the first class passengers. Lining the main cabin on its two outer sides were the passengers' accommodation; known as staterooms due to the early-day practice of naming each room after a State of the Union. Each stateroom had one door opening into the lounge and another gave access to the promenade-deck which surrounded the superstructure.

The *Rosebud*'s reputation for luxury and good service had been honestly made and even with the War in progress some of the old standards remained. Stewards in clean white clothing darted along the main deck to collect and carry the newly arrived party's baggage aboard and to the boiler deck. At one side the mate stood glowering at the delay and waiting to set his roustabouts to work at preparing to haul in the gangplank and cast off.

'Who is this General Amesley, Rube?' Boynes asked of his clerk, a man with an almost encyclopaedic knowledge of who was who in Arkansas.

'Never heard of him, Cap'n. Them buff facings on his uniform mean he's in either the Adjutant General, Quartermaster General Commissary or Engineer's Department. A desk-warmer most likely.'

'Those two with him aren't desk warmers though,' Boynes stated, nodding to Dusty and Red as they followed Belle and Amesley up the stairs. 'That's the Texas Light Cavalry uniform and arms belts.'

After some discussion at Regimental headquarters it had been decided that Amesley travelled down to the coast in his new rank so as to become accustomed to answering to his temporary title of 'general'; a minor consideration some folks might have thought, but Belle insisted on it and Ole Devil backed up her superior knowledge of the deadly game they played. They must take no chances, for the Yankee spy organization did not employ fools and a mistake might ruin the entire assignment. Again following Belle's recommendations, the Regimental tailors had worked all night to remove the cavalry yellow stripes from the legs of Amesley's trousers and replace them with the double row of buff-coloured cloth as became a general officer of one of the non-combatant departments – all generals wore buff facings on their jackets no matter to which branch of the Army they belonged.

Using her knowledge, Belle suggested that Amesley posed as a member of the Adjutant General's Department. Being concerned with the legal aspects of the Army's organization, such an officer would be the most likely choice to handle negotiations for the exchange and return of deserters. In addition, the Adjutant General's Department rarely came into the public's eye, which would explain why Amesley's name was not familiar to any Yankee spy. Finally, a member of the non-combatant Adjutant General's Department on such a mission might be expected to have along a couple of combat soldiers as his escort; which explained away Dusty and Red's presence.

Stepping forward, Boynes raised a hand to the peak of his hat. 'Pleased to have you aboard, General,' he said. 'My clerk here will escort you to the Number One stateroom.'

'Thank you, sir,' Amesley replied. 'And what of my staff?'

'Your niece is in the next stateroom, the captain and lieutenant beyond her and I've put your strikers in a cabin on the Texas deck.'

'My thanks sir,' boomed Amesley. 'Come along, Clarissa, my dear.'

'Will there be any danger from the Yankees, Cap'n?' Belle asked.

Only it was not the calm, competent Belle Boyd who organized the raid on the Dragoons' camp and helped plan the present assignment; but a fluttery, naïve, not too bright young thing just asking for a big, strong man to protect her. The change went far beyond merely donning a stylish travelling dress – purchased in Hope the previous evening – hat, blonde wig and parasol. If Dusty had not known the real Belle, he would have taken her for what she pretended to be. Certainly the *Rosebud*'s captain did not doubt her character.

'Land-sakes no, ma'am,' he answered, glowing with protective manhood. 'You'll be as safe aboard the *Rosebud* as if you were at home. Now if you'll excuse me, I have to get us under way.'

'If you'll come this way, General Amesley, sir,' the clerk said, bowing and waving a hand towards the double doors of the lounge.

Although the stewards handled most of the baggage, Dusty and Red insisted on carrying their own saddles. Each of them had his range-rig slung over one shoulder and a Henry rifle swung in his other hand. Dusty decided to take along the fifteen-shot Henrys rather than the Spencer carbines so as to have extra fire-power should it become necessary to make a fight.

The other passengers, Army officers going on furlough, civilians travelling about their business, and a few women, studied the new arrivals with varying degrees of interest. Taking in the buff facings and leg stripes, the Army men knew Amesley belonged to a non-combatant department; they also noticed the fine *epee de combat* which hung in his

87

belt slings instead of the usual general officer's sword. Nor did the soldiers fail to observe his fighting man's carriage and decided that his slight limp prevented him from commanding a fighting outfit.

'At ease, gentlemen,' Amesley said, breathing a little easier as he looked around and failed to see anyone who might recognize him as the adjutant of the Texas Light Cavalry.

While Amesley might go unrecognized, the same did not apply to Dusty and Red.

'I tell you that's Captain Fog,' an infantry major said to the artillery officer at his side as they watched Amesley being escorted to the best stateroom on the boat. 'I saw him lead a charge at Mark's Hill that turned the course of the battle.'

'Him?' scoffed the other. 'That small kid—'

'He didn't look small to me and my company that day,' the major growled.

Other eyes studied Dusty and Red. A couple of young lieutenants from the major's regiment exchanged glances.

'Texas Light Cavalry,' one said. 'Look at those gunbelts. They must think they pickle their nuts in salt-brine.'

'And those damned Yankee rifles that you can load on Sunday and shoot all the week,' the second answered. 'I wonder if they've any ammunition for them, or if they just tote them to look big.'

'We'll see before we reach Shreveport,' grinned the first. 'Wonder what they're doing going down the river?'

'On furlough most likely. Who's the general?'

'Some shiny-butt from back east most likely. Reckon we'll meet him later.'

'We'll meet those two horse-soldiers while we're at it,' stated the second.

Fortunately for their future well-being, the *Rosebud* started moving before the two shavetails managed to meet Dusty and Red with the object of proving an infantryman's superiority over the cavalry. Just as fortunate, the infantry officers met their major and learned Dusty's identity before the small Texan made another appearance in public.

While comfortable, Dusty and Red's stateroom could not be described as spacious. It contained a couple of narrow, though well-padded bunks, a washstand and a small, curtained-off area just large enough to hang a few clothes in. When the two saddles and the bulky pouches carrying spare clothing and ammunition had been laid on the floor, little space remained for walking about the room. Being hardened veterans, even though so young, neither Dusty nor Red worried unduly about their surroundings. Both had lived considerably rougher than at present during their time in the Army.

'Let's go see how the others are getting on,' Dusty suggested after the boat churned away from the Fulton docks.

After visiting Belle and Amesley, and finding both settled in comfortably, Dusty and Red went up one of the flights of stairs leading to the Texas deck. This perched on top of the boiler deck and, in addition to housing second class passengers, the senior members of the boat's crew, clerk's office and barber's shop, offered a larger area than the promenade deck below on which travellers might take exercise. Set on top of the Texas deck was the wheelhouse, its large glass windows offering the pilot and captain an unrestricted view of the river and surrounding country.

Dusty and Red did not go up to the wheelhouse deck, figuring that the pilot and captain would not want visitors underfoot at that time. Instead their attention was drawn to a small bunch of the younger passengers who gathered at the rear of the Texas deck cabins to watch a display of pistol shooting. The shooter, a tall, slim, well-dressed young man in civilian clothing, held a magnificent percussion-fired single-shot duelling pistol in each hand. Taking sight with his right-hand weapon, he fired and severed the neck of an empty bottle standing on the guard rail at the end of the deck.

Moving forward, the Texans saw a pretty, stylishly-attired young woman with the two infantry shavetails.

'Of course, my brother wanted to join the Army,' she was telling the officers, her voice warm, friendly and inviting. 'But the Government asked him to continue running the family business. We manufacture firearms, you know. You, being serving officers, can imagine how he felt about that.'

'A man has to do his duty where he must, Miss Dimsdale,' the taller shavetail replied, although he might not have taken so lenient and tolerant a view of an able-bodied man who failed to answer the country's call to arms if the man did not possess such a charming sister.

'Poor Paul,' the girl sighed. 'He's such a fine shot and a wizard with a sword. He would have made a good soldier. As it is – well, you must be our guests at dinner tonight.'

89

'We'd be right proud to, Miss Dimsdale,' agreed the second officer.

While listening to the by-play between the girl and officers, Dusty and Red paid little attention to it, being more interested in the shooting. As good shots themselves, Dusty and Red could admire another skilled performer, and the slim civilian proved to be all of that. At twenty-five feet the neck of a bottle did not make a large target, even when armed with the ultimate of handgun precision, a duelling pistol.

'He's some shot,' Red remarked as the second bottle's neck burst under the impact of a bullet. 'Those are straight-shooting guns, too. I reckon you can take him though, Dusty.'

'Well, don't you go flapping off your mouth about it,' Dusty answered.

At the moment Belle appeared on the deck and walked along to join the two Texans. Although she still looked as when she boarded the *Rosebud,* Belle sounded her old, competent self.

'I heard the shooting,' she remarked in a low voice, her eyes going to the good looking girl who still stood with the two officers.

'There's nothing to worry about,' Red replied with a grin.

Again Belle threw a glance towards the other girl. 'Isn't there?'

Glancing at Belle Dusty wondered what she had seen to put a burr under her saddle. He knew Belle too well to put the dislike she showed towards the other girl down as mere feminine jealousy and hoped she would enlighten him. Before Belle could do so, Captain Boynes came down from the wheel-house deck, saw his most important passenger's 'niece' and strolled over to greet her. Instantly Belle reverted to her new character and Dusty did not find an opportunity to ask her about her dislike.

Time dragged by, with the *Rosebud* continuing to make good speed with the Red River's current pushing under her and aiding the turning of the big side-wheels. Dusty and Red found little chance to speak with either Belle or Amesley alone all day, but being interested in the novelty of their new surroundings did not let that worry them. Night came and the dinner gong drew passengers to the main lounge. Amesley was joining a party of senior officers at the captain's table but Belle came to sit with the two Texans. Even with the War on, the *Rosebud* offered a very good menu, although much of the meat would be from wild animals rather than beef.

'Brother Buck and brother Pete never had it this good,' Red stated.

Thinking back to the antics Red's brothers brought off on her final night with the Texas light Cavalry, Belle smiled. 'Buck and Pete don't deserve it this good,' she declared, then turned her head to look across the room as a burst of laughter rose from a table where the two infantry officers sat with the Dimsdales. 'Now there're a couple of young men looking for trouble.'

'A lot of folk entertain soldiers these days,' Dusty answered. 'Folks who wouldn't look at a man in uniform other times get all friendly when the shooting starts.'

'You're a cynic, Dusty,' Belle smiled. 'And I've a suspicious mind. I *could* be doing those two an injustice, but I doubt it. Did you ever hear of a firearms company called Dimsdale?'

'Nope – not that that means anything. There're a lot of small companies making arms for us on contract to the bigger concerns.'

'Reckon they're Yankee spies, Belle?' Red asked when Dusty stopped speaking.

A faint smile crept across Belle's face. 'I doubt if they're anything as dramatic as that. Look at the "General". He appears to be enjoying his new rank.'

Realizing that Belle had said all she meant to on the subject of the Dimsdales, Dusty and Red turned their attention to eating. Almost three years' service in the Army had given them a fatalistic outlook and they now tended to live for the moment. So, given an opportunity like at the moment, they always ate well; a man never knew when he would be on short rations.

Through the meal Belle watched the Dimsdales' party and noticed that while the soldiers drank frequently neither their host nor his sister attempted to keep up with their consumption. Once the meal ended, Belle found herself the centre of a party of young officers and reverted to the part she played, which prevented her from being able to pass on her theories to the Texans.

Never really happy in a crowd of older men who held

lower rank than themselves, Dusty and Red backed out of the group surrounding Belle and went out on to the deck. Deciding to make the most of their opportunity while aboard the *Rosebud*, Dusty and Red strolled around the promenade deck and then went down the stairs to the bows of the main deck. Up forward, on either side of the bows, an iron cresset held a brightly glowing fire of knotty pine chunks and the flames illuminated some of the river's surface and left side shore line. In times of peace there would have been far more cargo stacked forward, but the War had an adverse effect on trade. However, a few large packing cases lined the sides and one very large box stood up in the bows, a clear passage running through the rest of the cargo to it.

Behind the cargo came a storage of cut wood ready for use and then lay the furnaces, boilers and engines which drove the paddlewheels and propelled the *Rosebud* through the water. Coloured firemen fed the flames of the furnaces and the engineer, a bulky, grimy-faced white man, supervised everything. At the stern, the Negro roustabouts threw dice, talked, or slept in the knowledge that they had no more work to do until they reached the next town.

Although not a man who encouraged passengers to loaf around his domain the engineer raised no objections in Dusty's case. Having heard the small Texan's name, the engineer decided that a young man with such a reputation for fighting Yankees had earned the right to be treated as an equal. Leaving his post for a time knowing he could rely on his crew of firemen, the engineer greeted the Texans. The War was discussed, with much profanity on the engineer's part. Then a question from Red brought the subject around to riverboat work. Sitting on the rail so he could keep an eye on the working of his engines, the engineer began to talk about the good days before the War when the *Rosebud* ran the Mississippi. He told of wrecks, explosions of boilers due to over-pressure, races and cargoes which almost set the decks awash with their bulk and weight. For a man who punctuated almost every sentence with blistering invective, the engineer painted a vivid picture of life on the riverboats. At last, after mentioning river pirates, he turned to the fabulous gambling for which the boats had become notorious. Listening to the latter reminiscences, Dusty began to see the reason for Belle's suspicions of the Dimsdales.

'Don't get so much of it now, though,' the engineer concluded. 'Folks don't tote that much money with 'em. Not that we ever had much on the *Rosebud*. Cap'n Boynes stopped it when he could.'

At that moment Red pointed ahead, along the side of the boat and towards the illuminated shore. 'Whooee, Cousin Dusty. Look there!'

Turning, Dusty followed the direction of his cousin's pointing finger. A low whistle of admiration left the small Texan's lips at what he saw. Standing at the edge of the water, its head thrown back proudly and its great spread of antlers rising high, as fine a bull elk as Dusty had ever seen stood watching them. Then it gave a quick, explosive snort, whirled and bounded off into the blackness beyond the fire's glow.

'See a lot of 'em,' remarked the engineer. 'Deer, bear, cougar even. The old *Rosebud* don't scare 'em until she gets real close. Happen you feel like sport, bring a couple of rifles down here some night.'

'I never took to shooting something just to see it fall,' Dusty replied. 'Nor me,' admitted the engineer, 'But happen you shoot anything, we can put off one of the boats we're towing and the roustabouts'll fetch it aboard. The cook can use the meat.'

'We'll see about it,' Dusty promised.

'Well, I'll be getting back to work,' the engineer said.

'Sure. I reckon we'll go back to the lounge, don't you, Cousin Red?'

'I'm ready when you are,' Red agreed.

On their return to the lounge, Dusty and Red felt amazed to discover they had been away for over two hours. Several card games were in progress, including one in which Amesley played oblivious of distractions. Dusty saw that Dimsdale sat at a table in the middle of the lounge and close to the passage which led between two staterooms and on to the promenade deck. Watched by his sister, Dimsdale played twenty-card stud poker with the two officers and a bluff, hearty-looking man who wore the dress of a prosperous farmer. Dusty saw that although the girl kept the soldiers supplied with drinks, she treated her brother and the farmer less generously.

Standing with a couple of young artillery officers, Belle was in a position to keep her eye on the game. Catching

Dusty's attention, Belle excused herself and moved around the Dimsdales' table to meet him.

'It looks straight enough so far, Dusty,' she said in a low voice.

'How's it going?' he replied.

'Evenly so far, no exceptional wins or losses. I could be wrong about them. Do you know the game?'

Dusty nodded. Twenty-card stud, with only the aces down to tens of each suit used, had a reputation for being a real fast gambling game. Each of the four players received his first card face down and bet blind on it, then played with the remainder of the cards face up. With so few cards and every one in play, a man needed a clear mind to follow the game correctly and it needed following if one wished to avoid substantial losses. From what Dusty could see, liquor had dulled the two soldiers' judgment.

'You say that they're not losing much?' he asked.

'Not yet,' Belle answered.

At that moment the Dimsdale girl yawned, in a ladylike manner, and stirred uneasily in her chair. Turning, her brother smiled at her. 'Tired, honey?'

'A little. Will you be long, Paul?'

'How about it gentlemen, will we?'

'I don't want to keep a *lady* from her bed, Paul,' the farmer replied, laying great emphasis on the word 'lady'.

Drunk they might be, but the two young officers were Southern gentlemen and raised in a tradition of chivalry towards the opposite sex.

'Nor me,' the taller declared.

'We'll finish now,' his companion went on. 'Unless you want to chance playing without Miss Maudie sat there to bring you luck, Paul.'

'Oh, I'll be all right, gentlemen,' Maudie cooed.

'No, ma'am,' the taller shavetail insisted, reaching towards his money. 'We're calling the game off right now.'

'Just have one more hand,' Maudie suggested quickly – maybe a shade too quickly the listening Dusty thought, and a glance at Belle told him her mind ran on the same general lines.

Both soldiers appeared to be reluctant to keep Maudie any longer from her bed and Dimsdale shrugged. 'All right. Hey, though, it's my turn to buy the drinks. One more hand while we drink them, then win or lose we break up the game for the night.'

'I'll go and fetch them,' Maudie suggested. 'I need to walk, my – limbs – are stiff from sitting so long.'

Before any of the men could comment on the propriety of a young lady doing such a menial thing as fetching a tray of drinks, the girl rose and walked towards the bar. Handing the deck to the taller soldier, Dimsdale requested that he prepare to deal.

'Give 'em a real good riffle this time, Jefferson,' the farmer suggested with a grin. 'I've not seen a good hand all night.'

Taking the cards, the soldier started to give them a thorough riffle. However the farmer interrupted the game to tell a story and the riffling continued after the joke's conclusion. Maudie came towards the table, a tray of drinks in her hands, as the soldier set the deck down before the farmer to be cut. In doing so, Maudie had to pass where Belle stood in apparently earnest conversation with Dusty.

'Why I tell you-all, Captain Fog,' Belle said, 'that Simmerton girl wore a hat with a brim this size—'

And to illustrate her point, Belle spread her arms wide apart. In doing so, the left slapped upwards under the edge of Maudie's tray and knocked it from her grasp. Tray, glasses, liquor, all went tipping into the air and drew every eye in the room towards the noise. However, most people's attention went not to the tray or the enraged face of Maudie as whisky spread over her dress – but to a deck of cards, identical to those in use at her brother's table, that fluttered out of the girl's fingers which had held them concealed under the tray.

## CHAPTER TEN

## MISS BOYD AROUSES SUSPICIONS

A SILENCE that might almost be felt dropped upon the room at the sight of the cards and knowledge of their implications.

'Your – sister – dropped something, *hombre*,' Dusty remarked.

Dimsdale's eyes went to the scattered cards, then lifted to Dusty's face. Snarling out a curse, the man started to thrust back his chair and rise. His right hand moved towards his left sleeve's cuff – and froze inches from the concealed butt of a Derringer pistol as he found himself looking into the barrel of Dusty's left-hand Colt. Never had Dimsdale seen such speed and he could hardly believe that he looked into the .44 calibre muzzle of the long barrelled revolver which less than a second before rested in its holster at Dusty's right side.

Although not as fast as his illustrious cousin, Red took the farmer out of the game as that worthy began to rise and reach in the direction of his inside pocket. Twisting his right-hand palm out, Red closed his fingers around the butt of his off-side Colt and slid it from leather to end such hostile moves and gestures.

'Now just sit there easy, *hombre*,' Red ordered and the click of his gun coming to full cock added force to his words.

Leaving the card game he played with the senior officers, Boynes crossed the lounge fast. 'That's a whole lot of card for a game of stud,' he said. 'Reckon this is where you asked to get off, Mr. Dimsdale.'

'I don't know what you mean,' Dimsdale answered suddenly.

'You want for me to search your baggage?' countered Boynes.

Knowing that such a search would produce even more damning evidence against him, and cause the loss of a lot of gambling equipment of a highly specialized nature, Dimsdale surrendered.

'We'd like to be put ashore here,' he gritted through his teeth.

Turning to the gaping infantrymen, Boynes asked, 'Did you lose much?'

'I'm a hundred down,' the taller replied. 'Say, did he – were they—'

'Sit down, mister!' Dusty barked as the soldier began to rise and, despite the amount of liquor the infantryman held, he knew better than to disobey.

'You boys split out what's on the table between you,' Boynes suggested and Dimsdale raised no objections.

All the time the men spoke, Maudie had been glaring with almost animal fury at Belle. 'You caused all this!' she screeched and threw herself at the Southron girl with fingers crooked ready to grab hair.

Not wishing to show her talents in the art of self-defence before the passengers, Belle retreated hurriedly and backed down the passage towards the door to the promenade deck. She kept ahead of and clear from Maudie's fingers, thrust open the door with her rump and backed out. Still shouting unladylike curses, Maudie followed and the door swung closed behind her. Nobody moved, the fury on Maudie's face had been enough to halt the men. A crack like two billiard balls connecting sounded on the promenade deck. The door burst inwards and Maudie entered, moving backwards. Spinning around, she hit first one wall then the other before falling into the lounge and landing face down upon its floor. A moment later Belle appeared, looking the same naïve, fluttery blonde.

'Oh my!' she gasped, looking down at Maudie's recumbent body with well-simulated horror. 'The door swung back and hit her. I *do* hope she isn't hurt.'

Possibly only Dusty and Boynes had been in a position to see what happened along the passage and neither of them intended to mention that the door had closed *behind* Maudie before the crack of fist against chin sounded.

Watched over by the mate and Red Blaze, Dimsdale and the 'farmer' stood at the side of the lounge while Boynes examined the cards. Not that he needed any further proof than the presence of the second deck. However, he found the deck in use on the table to be marked.

97

'It's an old game,' he told Dusty. 'The gambler lets his victims hold their own most of the evening, then rings in a cold deck by some trick. This time the girl would have held the tray out so it hid the deck on the table and the farmer would have made the switch unseen. Then the officer, believing it to be the deck he riffled, deals out good hands, the betting is forced up, and either Dimsdale or the farmer wins it. That way, if the victims don't want to play the next night, the sharp has made some profit.'

'What'll you do with them?' Dusty asked.

'Put them ashore. They know what to expect.'

'Not the girl,' Dusty objected, nodding to where Maudie sat on the floor, holding her jaw and with tears trickling down her face.

'She was in on it,' Boynes growled.

Having been raised with a belief that no man could meet with a worse fate than being set afoot, Dusty pleaded for the girl. He spared no sympathy for the men, but stated frankly that he would not countenance the girl being put ashore and forced to walk the fifty or more miles to the next town.

'Have it your way,' Boynes grinned. 'Take those two to the main deck, Mr. Hogan, and see that they go ashore as soon as possible.'

'Aye, aye, sir!' boomed the mate. 'Let's have yez, buckoes. Make one wrong move and I'll be busting your hands.'

'No rough stuff, friend,' Dimsdale purred. Then his eyes went to where Dusty and Belle stood watching him. Shrewd judge of human character though he might be, the gambler could not decide whether Belle's intervention had been pure accident or done deliberately and with knowledge of the forthcoming switching-in of the cold deck. Then his eyes went to Dusty again and saw a real *big* man. 'Maybe we'll meet again some time, Captain Fog.'

'Maybe,' Dusty replied.

'Let's go,' the mate ordered, and the gamblers passed out of the lounge.

Crossing to where Maudie rose, Boyne ordered her to go to her stateroom and stay in it until they reached the next town. Obediently Maudie left the lounge and from that moment maintained silence on what happened when she followed Belle through the promenade deck door. Maudie had her pride and hated to think that a feather-brained girl like

98

the blonde could flatten her with such ease. Not until much later did Maudie start to wonder if maybe that blonde had been quite so naïve as she pretended. Naïve or not, the blonde certainly knew how to throw a punch. It was a long time before the aching throb left Maudie's jaw.

While Maudie retained her silence about the attack, at least one person in the lounge felt very interested in the way she came to make such a dramatic re-entrance. Events brought every game of cards in the room to a halt, including one involving three field rank army officers and a trio of civilians; only one of whom is of any interest. Manny Engels, plump, prosperous-looking, sat staring across the room and trying to reconcile Belle's handling of Maudie with what he had seen of her so far. After giving Belle's face a long, searching glance, Engels dropped his eyes to the recumbent Maudie, swivelled them to where Dusty stood covering Dimsdale and finally turned his gaze to Belle once more. In the silence which followed the dramatic happenings, Engels heard Belle's explanation for Maudie's condition, but did not find it convincing. There was more to the affair than met the eye, Engels felt sure of that.

'Let's get on with the game, shall we?' asked one of the players as the gamblers left the room.

'Deal me out,' Engels replied. 'I'm tired and want to take a turn around the promenade deck before I turn in for the night.'

None of the other players raised any objections, so he collected his money and left the table. On the promenade deck, he walked along until he could see the two gamblers and their baggage put ashore. However, after the boat started moving again, he did not follow his proposed course of going to bed. Instead he found a shadowy corner of the deck and remained in hiding. Time dragged by, but Engels showed patience. At last a light glowed in one of the staterooms as its lamp was brightened. A moment later he saw Dusty Fog emerge from the next room, walk along the deck, take a stealthy, cautious look around and then enter the newly-lit door.

On silent feet Engels moved towards the stateroom. Apart from Captain Boynes, nobody on the *Rosebud* knew of Dusty and Red's connection with Amesley and Belle. If any of the other passengers thought of the matter at all, they assumed that the Texans were grabbing an opportunity to make a trip down-river while on a furlough. However, during the trip, Engels had noticed that Belle spent some time in private conversation with Dusty and showed reluctance to be seen doing so. Being of an inquiring nature, Engels decided that the matter might prove worth investigating. A clandestine association between a junior officer and the *amie* of a general – Engels discounted the idea of her being Amesley's niece – offered possibilities handled properly.

On silent feet Engels advanced towards the door of Belle's stateroom and cocked his head towards it, listening to the conversation within. Due to the nature of its design and construction, the upper portions of a riverboat was of necessity made of light and flimsy material. Being thin, the walls of the stateroom allowed Engels to listen without approaching too close.

'That was close, Dusty,' Belle remarked as the small Texan slipped into her room through the promenade door shortly after she entered from the lounge after pleading that the excitement had given her a headache.

'Sure was, Belle,' Dusty agreed. 'Happen she'd laid hold of that wig, the folks would have thought she'd hand-scalped you.'

'Likely,' Belle answered and smiled as she realized how she now slipped into using the laconic terms her Texas friends employed. 'I don't think anybody was on the promenade deck to see me hit her as she came through the door. She did look surprised when I stopped and let her have it.'

'Yeah,' Dusty drawled and, keeping his voice at the same easy drawl, made his way cautiously towards the promenade deck door. 'I wonder what the folks in the lounge are making of it?'

Even as he spoke, Dusty twisted the handle of the door and wrenched it open. Fast though Dusty had moved, Engels licked him to it. On the first movement of the door's knob, Engels started to walk away along the deck. Although he had not gone far, the man put himself beyond any chance of Dusty proving that he had been eavesdropping on a private conversation.

'What was it?' Belle asked, joining Dusty at the door.

'I'm not sure,' Dusty replied. 'Just got the feeling that somebody was out there, but he'd passed by when I got the door open.'

'Do you think he was listening?'

'I don't know. Reckon he might have been though.'

'Do you recognize him?' the girl asked.

'It's a travelling man, seen him around the boat, but I don't know his name.'

'We'd best stay away from each other until he leaves the boat,' Belle suggested. 'And I'll keep my eyes on him.'

'Be best. You know this game better than I do,' Dusty agreed. 'I'll get out of here while there's nobody watching. If any of the womenfolk aboard see me leaving your stateroom it might cause talk.'

'Not only women gossip,' Belle smiled.

'Nope,' Dusty replied. 'But they do more of it than we do.'

With that Dusty stepped through the door and walked along the promenade deck. Smiling still, Belle closed the door behind him and went to prepare for bed.

Engels continued his stroll around the deck, guessing that Dusty watched him. Showing no sign that he had been listening, he turned the corner of the promenade deck and circled around until he reached his own stateroom. Inside, he started to undress and while removing his shirt came to a sudden halt. One of the necessities of a man in his line of work was the ability to remember conversations, and he turned the words he had heard over in his mind. Why had the Texan addressed the girl as 'Belle,' and what did the reference to her wig mean? When Engels first saw Belle, he marked her down as the beautiful but brainless *amie* of an elderly man. Now he wondered if there might be something deeper than that about the blonde beauty.

Sitting on his bunk, and leaving his undressing as thoughts began to churn through his head, Engels tried to remember if he had ever heard of a General Amesley. No such name came to his mind, although he felt inclined to put the fact down to Amesley belonging to the non-combatant Adjutant General's Department – or had been inclined to think that at first. Maybe Amesley only pretended to be on the Adjutant General's staff. Perhaps he held an appointment in another Department which tried to keep its activities out of the public's eye. Amesley might be one of the powers of the South's efficent Secret Service. In which case the girl most probably was not Amesley's *amie*.

Belle! The name bounced back into Engels' mind almost as if powered by a blinding light. When one thought of the Confederate States' Secret Service and heard the name Belle, one immediately coupled the name with Boyd. Excitement ripped into Engels at the thought. Belle Boyd; one of the South's top two female spies. If the girl on the boat should be Belle Boyd, that accounted for why she wore a wig. Never had such important information come Engels' way and he hoped he could make the most of his discovery. He wondered if he might learn what mission took Belle Boyd and Captain Dusty Fog down the Red River. Being aware of Dusty's reputation and having a fair idea of Ole Devil's shortage of men, Engels knew only a matter of the greatest importance would take the Texan from the firing line. Discovering the nature of the assignment could greatly add to the profit his information about Belle Boyd brought in.

With the idea of confirming his suspicions in mind, Engels entered the lounge at breakfast time the following morning and looked for the objects of his interest. Belle and Amesley shared their table with a couple of the top-class families while Dusty and Red sat among the younger officers. In passing, Engels halted at Belle's side and, in the pretence of inquiring after her health after the excitement of the previous evening, studied the girl. Sharp though he might be, he saw nothing in her answer or appearance to suggest that she might be other than what she appeared on the surface. Although he studied it carefully, he could find no proof that the neatly coiffured blonde curls might be a wig. However, he did notice a change in Amesley's attitude towards Belle. The 'General' now showed some interest in Belle that had been lacking the previous day. After seeing Engels bedded down for the night, Dusty had visited Amesley and warned that they might be under observation, offering the suggestion that more interest in his 'niece' might not come amiss.

During the remainder of the trip down to Shreveport, Engels continued his surveillance of the party. After some thought, he decided that Red might prove the most fruitful of the quartet to pump. However, Red had been primed for such a move and his answer told Engels only that he and Dusty had taken a furlough and aimed to see what pleasures Alexandria or Morgan City might offer. Nothing Engels learned from Red gave any hint that other than a pleasure trip brought the two Texans from Arkansas. However, Engels learned, from hints Red dropped, that the two young men travelled as Amesley's aides so that their expenses might be defrayed against the taxpayer; the 'General' being an old friend of the family and not averse to doing a good turn for an influential person like Ole Devil Hardin.

On the second night Engels kept a close watch, but saw nothing to help him. Dusty and Red spent the early part of the evening on the main deck, where Red's Henry rifle brought down a prime young whitetail deer buck which would be of use to the boat's cook. After that the Texans returned to the lounge where they joined the other young officers in a rowdy, low-stake game of *Vingt-Un*. Amesley and Belle spent their evening in the company of the senior passengers and Engels decided to keep watch in case of another visit by Dusty to the girl's cabin.

In stateroom after stateroom the lamps were extinguised and Engels stayed patiently in his position at the stern end of the promenade deck. Midnight came and just as the man decided he would go to his room, he heard a door open along the deck. The promenade deck was illuminated by a couple of small lamps and Engels could see that Amesley, not Dusty Fog left his room and entered the girl's quarters. Stealthily the watcher moved forward and halted outside the door of Belle's stateroom. He heard only what one might expect from such a visitation and after a short time decided that his suspicions might have been wrong. Assuming that nothing further would happen that night, Engels went to his bed. He did not know that while he watched Amesley, Dusty kept an eye on him; nor that after his departure Amesley returned to his own stateroom to spend the night.

'What do you think, Dusty?' asked Belle, as they met while strolling on the hurricane deck the next morning.

'He watched you last night,' Dusty replied, leaning on the protective rail and watching the shore slip by. 'I don't know if we've got him fooled or not. Seeing a Confederate 'General' go into your cabin wearing just his shirt, pants and socks ought to have convinced him.'

'If he heard what we said, it could,' Belle said, and smiled in recollection of an incident in her cabin. 'Poor Major Amesley looked real embarrassed at entering a lady's room that way. He— I sure won't be sorry to get to Morgan City, Captain Fog. I do declare this itty-bitty cabin's plumb ruinous— Oh, good morning, Mr. Engels. How are you-all on this beautiful morning?'

In a flash, on seeing Engels approach, Belle Boyd disappeared to be replaced by Clarissa, Amesley's 'niece'. Having seen the girl in earnest conversation with Dusty, he attempted to get close enough to hear what was being said; but Belle proved too quick for him.

After making small talk with Dusty and the girl for a time, Engels passed on. Nor had he reached any decision when the boat pulled into Shreveport. Watching Maudie Dimsdale take her departure, Engels decided that he might possibly learn something of use from her. He knew the boat would not be departing for two hours at least and so went ashore. Following Maudie, Engels found no difficulty in striking up an acquaintance. Her 'brother' had left the *Rosebud* without providing any money for her well-being and over a meal she told Engels what had happened when she followed Belle out on the promenade deck.

While listening to the girl's description of how an amazing change came over the blonde, turning her from a scared little milk-sop to a cold, deadly female who used her fist like she knew what it had been given her for, Engels happened to look around the room. A feeling of cold shock hit him as he saw a tall, gangling sergeant-major of the Texas Light Cavalry seated at a nearby table and apparently engrossed in eating a meal.

Engels felt sure that the 'blonde' on the boat must really be Belle Boyd, and also guessed that she and her escort must be suspicious of him. Slipping some money under the table to Maudie, Engels made the usual suggestion and she agreed.

'I'll just have to go out back first,' he told the girl and thrust back his chair. 'Wait for me.'

While walking towards the door marked 'MEN'S,' he figured she would have a long wait.

## CHAPTER ELEVEN

# THE INVENTIVE GENIUS OF MR. HENRY AND CAPTAIN WILLIAMS

'AND there I was, just a-sitting and waiting,' Billy Jack admitted as he stood on the hurricane deck of the *Rosebud* with Dusty. 'Comes fifteen minutes, I got to figuring that happen it took him *that* long, he should be told how good croton oil works. So I went to tell him and, dog-my-cats, if there's not another door out of the room. It led to the street, but time I got 'round to figuring *that*, he'd up and was long gone.'

Looking at his sergeant-major's miserable expression, Dusty had difficulty in holding down a grin. Billy Jack knew Dusty's attitude when somebody reported a failure through lack of foresight, and expected an explosion. However, Dusty realized that the lean non-com had not been trained in the business of following a suspected person and so made a mistake which lost Engels.

'It can't be helped,' Dusty declared. 'I'll go down and see if he's come back on board.'

'You reckon he's a Yankee spy, Cap'n Dusty?' asked Billy Jack.

'I'm keeping an open mind,' Dusty answered. 'He did meet up with that Maudie gal and buy her a meal. But that doesn't mean he wanted to learn anything from her.'

'Nope,' agreed Billy Jack. 'Happen he's come back, what say we lay hold of him tonight and ask him a few questions?'

'He might not want to answer,' Dusty pointed out.

'Maybe he'd change his mind after he'd been dragged head down for a spell behind the boat.'

Unfortunately for Billy Jack's plan, one essential item was missing. On visiting the clerk's office, Dusty learned that Engels had sent a messenger to the boat with instructions to collect his baggage. Knowing that travelling salesmen often made unscheduled departures should business come their way, the clerk raised no objections and could offer no suggestion as to where the baggage went after leaving the boat. Nor did he connect Engels' departure with a letter brought aboard for delivery to an address in Alexandria; although both the baggage collector and the man who brought the letter had been hired by the departed Engels.

While Dusty would have liked to make an immediate start to a search for Engels, the *Rosebud* was due to leave Shreveport before he could do so. Allowing Billy Jack to return to the card game which went on pretty continuously in the barber's shop, Dusty went down to the boiler deck and located Belle, Red and Amesley.

'Billy Jack lost him,' Dusty told them after making sure he would not be overheard by any of the passengers other than his party. 'He followed Engels into town and saw him meet up with that Maudie girl. Engels took the gal into an eating house, bought her a meal and then started talking quiet to her. She did some answering but Billy Jack couldn't hear what they were saying.'

'Could have been asking her what happened on the promenade deck,' Amesley commented. 'Most likely was; if he's a Yankee spy and suspicious of Miss Boyd.'

'Reckon he is a Yankee spy, Dusty?' asked Red.

'Could be. Or maybe he's just the kind of sneak who'd listen at a stateroom door for fun.'

'The riverboats have always been good sources of information.' Belle put in. 'A soldier going on or coming off furlough tends to talk more than when he's with his outfit. There's a chance that Engels was aboard to learn anything he could.'

'What'll we do about him?' Red growled.

'There's not much we can do,' Belle replied. 'We can't delay our trip while we go back and look for him. Even if we could persuade Captain Boynes to turn around without telling him far too much. When we reach Alexandria, I'll see a friend and arrange for a very close watch to be kept on Mr. Engels.'

'Happen he's decided that you aren't what you seem, maybe even guessed that you're Belle Boyd,' Dusty said quietly. 'Can he pass on the news to the Yankees?'

'I'd be surprised if he couldn't,' Belle answered. 'There's no telegraph to them, of course, but he could pass the message verbally, or written and concealed on a courier.'

106

'Which same the feller couldn't reach the Yankees until long too late to find us,' Red stated, sounding a mixture of relief and disappointment. Red always craved for excitement and had so far found the trip boring.

'Unless Engels decided his information is so important that he sends it by carrier-pigeon,' Belle warned.

'Do you reckon he might do that?' Amesley inquired. 'Would he have access to the pigeons, I mean?'

'Don't sell the U.S. Secret Service short, Major,' Belle replied. 'I'd bet that every major town along the river has its spy set-up including pigeons hid away somewhere.'

'Of course it could be that we're blowing this thing up out of all proportion,' Amesley said. 'Engels might be no more than a venal sneak who wanted to know something bad about a young man who's gained the fame he can never achieve. The kind of man who's a failure himself and wants to bring everybody down to his level.'

'We *could* hope for that, sir,' Dusty admitted. 'But I'd hate like hell to rely on it. I figure we should work on the assumption that Engels is a spy and that he'll send word about us to the Yankees on the lower Mississippi.'

'And what will they do?' asked Amesley.

'Was I the Yankee commander, I'd make a stab at stopping us,' Dusty stated. 'Reckon they could do it, Belle?'

'I'm not sure,' she replied. 'Why not go ask Captain Boynes? He knows the river better than any of us.'

The men adopted Belle's suggestion and took their problem for solution to Captain Boynes. Having seen his boat safely on her way out of the harbour, the Captain welcomed 'General' Amesley and Dusty to the wheelhouse deck. Amesley followed the plan arranged as they came up to the topmost deck, by explaining that he was on an important mission with Dusty as his escort. Without going into too much detail, Amesley went on to say that he feared the Yankees might make an attempt to intercept him and prevent his arrival at Morgan City.

'What're their chances of doing it, Captain?' Dusty asked when Amesley finished speaking.

'How do you mean?' Boynes inquired.

'Could the U.S. Navy's Mississippi Squadron get through and attack the *Rosebud*?'

'With their iron-clads or gunboats?'

'Something like that.'

A grin came to Boynes' lips. 'The Yankees might control the lower river, but we own everything for a good way below the Atchafalaya. We've batteries of guns that nothing short of a full-scale battle *might* break through. And if there's a sign of a break-through, there's a fast side-wheeler kept fuelled and ready to run up river like the devil after a yearling to raise the alarm.'

'How about them slipping through at night?' Dusty went on.

'Not with iron-clads or gunboats. Going upstream they'd have to use their engines, which means noise and flames glowing from the smoke-stacks.'

'Could they run through in one of those submarine things I've heard about?' Amesley wanted to know. 'We've used them and I reckon the Yankees could have them.'

'Maybe they have,' admitted Boynes. 'But the biggest only carried six or eight men.'

'That'd be enough if they got in close and planted their explosives,' Dusty pointed out.

'They'd have to get close enough to do it,' Boynes answered. 'Even underwater that'd take some doing. Don't forget that my pilot's used to spotting things under the river's surface even in the darkness. If he could see a snag* in flood-water mud, he'd not miss anything as large as a submarine.'

That figured as Dusty admitted to himself when thinking of the skill every successful river pilot must possess if he hoped to keep his boat out of danger.

'There's nothing to worry about then,' Amesley commented.

'Not too much,' Boynes agreed. 'But I'll make sure that we keep an extra careful watch, General.'

'My thanks, sir. And, of course, I don't need to ask you not to mention my mission to anybody.'

'You don't,' Boynes replied. 'I don't want my other passengers worrying, and they sure as hell would if I let them know about your mission.'

Returning to the boiler deck, Amesley found Belle surrounded by a bunch of junior officers. A scowl from the 'General' caused a hurried scattering of the shavetails and Amesley sat at the girl's side to tell her of the meeting with Boynes.

* Snag: Tree which has fallen into the river and is embedded in the bottom.

'We don't have much to worry about then,' she said. 'I didn't expect any trouble until we're beyond Alexandria anyway. Of course, we may have nothing to fear even then.'

While Belle did not sound any too certain as she spoke, she would have been even less so had she been in a position to see a carrier-pigeon rise from the wooded country about a mile to the east of Shreveport. Circling twice until it got its bearings, the bird struck off in a south-easterly direction, headed down river in the direction of Yankee-held territory.

The journey went on without incident. Mile after mile fell behind the *Rosebud* and Dusty's party settled down to the tedium of travelling. Each night Dusty and Red took their Henry rifles to the main deck where they kept watch for some suitable addition to the boat's larder.

On arrival at Alexandria, Belle and Dusty went ashore and the girl made arrangements for a watch to be kept on Engels. From the same source she made the arrangements, she learned the latest news concerning her mission. Clearly the Yankee Secret Service knew, or guessed, where the gold taken in Arkansas was going and that meant they would try to stop its arrival. Just how far the Yankees might have gone with their plans Belle could not learn. While hoping for the best, she prepared to handle the worst.

After loading up a good-sized cargo of cotton which would be run through the Yankee blockade and sold in Europe to help finance the Confederate war effort, the *Rosebud* pulled out of Alexandria on the final leg of its journey to the town of Morgan City.

'There's not much chance of getting anything tonight, Cap'n Dusty,' said the mate, Hogan, as he stood at Dusty's side. 'This's 'gator country.'

Earlier that day, the *Rosebud* had left the main river to follow the narrower but still navigable reaches of the Atchafalaya. Thick wooded country closed in on either bank, ideal territory for animals had it not been for the menace of the big Mississippi alligators which Dusty had seen sprawling on sandbars or diving hurriedly from the banks as the boat approached. Living in fear of alligator attacks made the local game far more alert, watchful and suspicious than the creatures of the upper river. However, the cook needed meat, so Dusty and Red had agreed to try their luck that night.

Accompanied by the mate and the pilot's cub – assistant – the two Texans stood partially concealed behind the big wooden crate which still rested forward in the bows and clear of the piles of cotton bales which now covered most of the free space on the main deck. The cressets glowed brightly, lighting the river ahead and flickering upon the shoreline at both sides, giving the waiting men a clear sight of any animal which might be risking the dangers by coming to the river's edge for a drink.

'We'll give it a bit longer,' Dusty stated.

Time dragged by slowly and the men scanned the banks for any sign of life. Up in the wheelhouse, the pilot stood at the big wheel and his eyes never left the dull ribbon which glowed ahead as what little light filtered down from above reflected on the river's surface. Long practice had trained him to look beyond the area illuminated by the cressets and pierce the blackness of the night in a never-ending search for signs of danger ahead.

'Cap'n!' he said.

Turning from the door of the wheelhouse where he had been standing and talking with a few passengers, Boynes stepped to the pilot's side.

'What's up, Marse?'

'Up ahead there,' the pilot answered. 'I saw the loom of some— Yes. There it is. By cracky! It's—'

He stopped speaking and his right hand stabbed up to close on the whistle's cord, jerk at it and send a series of piercing blasts ripping through the night.

At about the same moment that the pilot called to Boynes, Red Blaze peered along the river, squinted his eyes and then he pointed. 'What's that ahead there, Dusty? Up the river.'

The rest of the meat-hunting party followed the direction of Red's pointing finger. All could see the dark shapes, blacker than the surrounding area and contrasting with the dull ribbon of water, one near each bank of the river. Being more used to such sights than the Texans, Hogan recognized the dark bulks first; and did not like what he saw.

'Boats!' he growled. 'Trouble ahead.'

Loud in the night rang a series of blasts from the *Rosebud*'s whistle. In echo to it came a spurt of flame from the right side boat, the crack of exploding powder, and an instant later Dusty felt something strike the side of the *Rosebud* under the level of the main deck. Following the shot from the boat cannon, oars dipped down and tore apart the river's surface as powerful arms propelled two big naval launches forward and on a course to converge with the approaching riverboat.

Raising his leg, Hogan delivered a powerful kick to the big box they had used for cover. It appeared to be of poor construction, for the sides burst open and fell outwards. Grabbing quickly, the pilot's cub caught the falling top of the box and flung it aside. In less time than it took to tell, the box had gone and its contents stood revealed. Mounted on a swivel instead of the usual artillery carriage, a box of ammunition by its side, stood a Williams rapid-fire cannon, its one-pounder barrel pointing ahead.

Dusty and Red might have felt surprised, or delighted, to see such an effective weapon at that moment, but neither had time. Long used to reacting swiftly in an emergency, they wasted no time in idle speculation. That shot meant the approaching boats did not bear welcoming friends and so they took the appropriate action. Two Henry rifles raised swiftly, their butts snuggling against shoulders and their barrels lining on the boats. Trained fingers squeezed triggers and worked loading levers, firing bullets, ejecting empty cases and replacing them with loaded rounds so the cycle could be repeated and a hail of lead sweep into the oncoming boats.

Nor did Hogan and the cub react with any less speed or decision. Jerking open the lid of the ammunition box, the cub took out a self-consuming paper cartridge. The gun already held a charge as was proved by Hogan not operating the mechanism so that loading could take place. Standing behind the gun, he gripped the firing handle with his right hand, while his left took hold of the weapon's reloading crank. Hogan knew that the left-hand launch, not having fired the four-pounder boat cannon in the eye of its bows, offered the greater menace at that moment, so he gave it his attention. Turning the Williams on its swivel, he took sight and his thumb depressed the lever on the side which served as a trigger.

The whip-like crack of the Williams merged with the rapid beating of the two Henry rifles. Muzzle-blast flames stabbed out and a one-pound, 1.75 inch ball tore from the Williams. At so short a range, even a light ball could inflict damage on the timbers of a launch. The ball struck the boat just over the water-line, burst through and ripped into the leg of the ensign who prepared to open fire with his own cannon. A scream burst from the young officer's lips. His hands jerked convulsively, one tugging the firing lanyard and the other swinging the gun so it pointed away from the *Rosebud* when it fired. As a result the four-pounder's ball missed the river-boat.

On firing, Hogan twirled forward the cranking handle and the breech opened. The cub dropped in the charge he held and bent to scoop another from the box. Around went the handle, the breech closed and sheared the end from the cartridge to expose the powder to the percussion cap's spurt of flame – said cap being automatically fed on to its nipple from a spring-loaded container. Long before either cannon in the launches could complete the tedious process of muzzle-loading, the Williams fired again and a third time; each ball hammering into the boat.

Voices yelled, women screamed and feet pounded on the boiler and promenade decks as the passengers heard the sounds of the fight. However, the pilot and men on the bows refused to be distracted, knowing that the safety of the boat and all aboard her depended on their attention to duty.

The Yankee attack had been well-planned. Two big launches – each with a crew of twenty men armed with cutlasses and either Navy Colts or Spencer carbines – had come up the Mississippi under oars, slipping by the shore batteries and guard boats during the night. On reaching the point where the Atchafalaya cut off from the main river, the launches turned south and laid in wait for the *Rosebud* to make her appearance. Given surprise and the backing of the four-pounder boat cannon each launch carried, the Yankee force should have been able to sink the big side-wheeler; and might have succeeded but for the alertness of the pilot and Red Blaze – and the inventive genius of Mr. Tyler B. Henry and Captain Williams, C.S.A.

Handled by two men skilled in their use, the Henry rifles caused havoc and confusion out of all proportion to their size. Lead raked the two launches, striking down the men at the oars and throwing the others off their stroke. Equally deadly, perhaps even more so, the Williams added its quota to the rout of the enemy. Time after time, working at almost the full sixty-five rounds per minute maximum speed, the rapid-fire cannon drove its balls into the side of the launch on the left side of the river. As the number of holes grew, so water began to pour into the rocking launch. Then the weight of the cannon took the bows down and the crew plunged into the water.

Caught in the repeated hail from Dusty's Henry, the right-hand launch swerved violently into the path of the approaching *Rosebud*. Swinging the tiller, the coxswain tried to steer his charge out of danger; but he only partially succeeded. The *Rosebud* caught the launch a glancing blow, hesitated for a moment, then the thrust of the paddles drove it on. Jolted by the impact, the nearest cresset tipped over and dumped its flaming contents into the passing launch. Yells rose as the Yankee sailors tried to avoid the downpouring fire. A man, his shirt blazing, screamed and dived into the river. Then the launch capsized and its crew found themselves floundering in the water.

With the safety of his passengers to consider, Boynes did not hesitate in his actions. Behind him men struggled in the water, some wounded and bleeding in a manner likely to attract the attention of any hunting alligator which caught the taste of gore, but he could not stop to render aid. Already some of the attacking party had reached the shore and their metal cartridge carbines cracked. Calmly Boynes dabbed his cheek where glass from a breaking wheelhouse window splintered it and then he rang up full speed ahead. On the main deck, the cursing engineer, riled at missing what sounded like a real good fight, laid hold of the controls and increased the pace of the turning paddle-wheels.

Lowering their hot, smoking rifles Dusty and Red looked back down the river. A few spurts of flame showed where the Yankee sailors on shore took final shots at the departing *Rosebud*, but neither Texan wasted lead in replying.

'That was close,' Dusty said.

'Real close,' agreed the mate and slapped a hand fondly on the breach of the Williams gun. 'But we sure showed them how the old *Rosebud* can fight.'

'Wonder what those Yankees were after?' the cub put in.

'Figured to stop this load of cotton getting down to Morgan City,' Hogan answered. 'What else?'

While Dusty and Red would have given the mate a good answer to his question, neither offered to do so. The small Texan took one final look back along the river before going to the boiler deck in search of Belle and Amesley.

After passing through a congratulatory crowd, he entered the lounge and went to where Belle stood alone.

'Major Amesley's up with the captain,' she explained. 'What do you think, Dusty, was the attack by chance?'

'Could be, but I doubt it,' he replied. 'Anyway, we're through them now.'

'We're through the Mississippi Squadron's effort,' the girl corrected. 'Next time it will be the Yankee Secret Service. I'll bet they're watching for us in Morgan City in case the sailors failed to stop us.'

CHAPTER TWELVE

# MISS BOYD SEES A SNAKE FIGHT

BEFORE the War, and the Yankee blockade increased its importance, Morgan City had been such a small place that it hardly rated the second portion of its name. Even now, though vastly grown due to the sudden increase of trade and prosperity, there was little sign of permanent settlement, as the majority of the new buildings appeared to be of a flimsy nature, hurriedly erected and made of whatever materials came to hand.

Although three ocean-going ships lay at the docks or just off-shore in Atchafalaya Bay, the arrival of the riverboat *Rosebud* still drew a crowd of loafers. Mingling with the crowd and looking no different from many of its members, two agents of the U.S. Secret Service gave the approaching *Rosebud* a careful examination.

'Looks like she's seen some fuss,' Joe Riegel, tall, heavily built, and dressed like a waterfront idler, remarked, nodding to the raw plug in the cannonball hole under the *Rosebud's* bows.

'She got through though,' Murt Fanning, also tall, lean and wearing cheaply elegant clothes that looked much too good for him, answered.

They watched as the riverboat came alongside the dock, its two side-wheels giving a manoeuvrability no screw-driven vessel her size could equal. Down came the gangplank with a rush almost as soon as the boat came to a halt. Urged on by a mate, roustabouts darted about their tasks and soon the passengers began to come ashore. In accordance with tradition, the most socially prominent passengers left first. The Yankee spies studied Amesley and Belle as Boynes saw them off his ship.

'Reckon that's her?' Fanning inquired.

'Can't see any other blonde gal with a reb general, can you?'

'Nary a sign. What now?'

'We follow 'em, that's what. Most likely they'll be putting up at the Dixie Plaza, but Flora'll want to know if they don't.'

The mention of their superior's name brought a wry twist to Fanning's lips. 'Can't say that I go a whole lot on taking orders from a woman.'

'You tell it to her then,' grinned Riegal. 'Only make your will afore you do it. Come on, let's get clear and along the street towards the Plaza.'

On leaving the boat, Amesley and Belle waited for Dusty to join them and spent their time saying their good-byes to various people or avoiding invitations to visit. A general, even one in a non-combatant outfit, could expect good service and a two-horse open carriage rolled up, its driver seeking business.

'Have the bags put aboard, Mr. Blaze,' Amesley ordered. 'We'll go to the hotel and you can follow us with the men.'

'Yo!' Red replied, glancing at the crowd and feeling pleased that he would not be responsible for the safe keeping of the money.

While the loading of her and Amesley's baggage went on, Belle sat in the carriage looking about her with interest. Her eyes went to the three ships, passing from one to the next, estimating their readiness for sailing. Not until the bags, with the money hidden in false bottoms, had been safely stowed and the carriage began to move off did she mention her conclusions. She sat at Amesley's side, facing the driver, while Dusty took the opposite seat.

'How well do you know Morgan City?' he asked, keeping his voice low.

'I shipped out of here on my way to Europe,' Belle replied. 'We're in luck, Dusty, the *Snow Queen*'s in.'

'Which ship was that?' Amesley asked.

'The three-masted, screw-propeller craft painted lead-grey, laying off-shore. She's a fast sailer, used to run ice to the south before the War.'

A vessel employed in the business of transporting ice from the northern states to countries which never saw snow had need of great speed. Such a quality also was of use to a block-ade-runner.

'Will she do for us?' asked Dusty.

'I know her captain. Stacey Millbanks is a loyal Southron

and a good man. I wouldn't care to trust the gold aboard the *Dora* and the *South Star*'s only just arrived, she's still taking off her cargo.'

'Then it's the *Snow Queen* for us,' Amesley stated. 'How do we find Captain Millbanks?'

'We'll do it after we've been to the hotel and settled in,' Belle replied.

After following Belle's party to the Dixie Plaza Hotel, the two Yankee spies prepared to deliver their information to the controller of the U.S. Secret Service ring in Morgan City. They walked along the main business street of the town and passed through a side alley to enter an area of tents and wooden buildings all devoted in one way or another to entertaining visitors to the city. Set back in a clump of trees, the small house attracted little attention; nor did its owner wish it to, for anybody who wanted to use its amenities could easily learn of its whereabouts and needed no help in finding it.

'Where's Flora?' Fanning asked the bulky man in the loud check suit as he came towards them on their entrance.

'In her office. You don't reckon she'd be laying with one of the sports, now do you?'

Scowling, Fanning shoved by the bouncer and walked across the comfortable lounge. A few scantily-dressed girls who sat around the room gave Fanning and Riegel hardly a glance, for neither were of any use in the business way, being employed, or so the girls imagined, by the madam of the house as touts to steer in customers.

'They've arrived, Flora,' Riegal announced. 'The *Rosebud* pulled in with a hole in her. It looks like the Mississippi Squadron tried to stop her.'

'And failed,' Flora hissed, coming to her feet. 'Is the girl Belle Boyd?'

'We've never seen her,' Fanning pointed out.

'Nor have I, that I know of,' Flora said, her voice a low, hate-filled hiss. 'But she exposed one of my friends in Richmond and broke up a good spy-ring. I want her stopping, you two. Don't forget, if it's Boyd, she has fifty thousand dollars of our money.'

'She's at the Dixie Plaza now,' Fanning put in.

'As it's the only decent hotel in this God-forsaken town, she would be,' answered Flora. 'But she'll be wanting to contact Captain Millbanks as quickly as she can.'

'Why Millbanks?' asked Fanning. 'There's three boats in—'

'You don't think she'd be fool enough to trust herself and *our* fifty thousand in gold, to Duprez of the *Dora,* and the *South Star* won't be ready to sail for at least three days. No. The *Snow Queen*'s our ship.'

'Do we get word to the blockade ships?' asked Riegel.

'And have them bungle it again?' Flora spat out. 'No. We settle Boyd here in town. I don't know what she aims to do with that gold, the pigeon message didn't say. But whatever it is, those soldiers will be lost without her. Get rid of Boyd first and the rest will be easy.'

'How do we get rid of her?'

'How the hell would I know, Fanning?' Flora spat out. 'Watch for a chance. It— Wait though. If I know Millbanks, he'll be at the snake fights all this afternoon. And if I know Boyd, that's where she'll go looking for him. Get over there, you pair. If you can arrange an 'accident' to her – do it.'

'*Snake*-fights!' Dusty said as he and Belle walked towards where an excited, shouting crowd of men and women gathered at the foot of a slope on the edge of town. 'I've seen dog-fights, cock-fights, even bull-fights. But I've never heard of snake-fights before.'

'You soon will have,' Belle smiled back. 'Don't ask me what the fascination of them is, but they're very popular down here.' While speaking, she and Dusty mingled with the people surrounding a twenty-foot wide, five-foot deep pit dug in the ground, its sides lined with shiny metal sheets. Pointing to a slim, handsome man in the peaked hat and uniform frockcoat of a sea captain, Belle continued. 'There's our man, Dusty.'

However, Dusty's attention was riveted on the bottom of the pit, and the two snakes which had just been tipped into it. Harsh and menacing came the warning burr from the big, thick-bodied snake on the far side's tail rattles as it landed in the pit, slithered a few feet and then coiled itself defiantly. Up raised the flat, triangular-looking head, jaws opening to show the hideous fangs and the flickering forked tongue. The big diamond rattlesnake lay in the pit, evil as sin and a whole heap more deadly.

Showing much less caution than when he unloaded the rattlesnake, the promoter of the snake-fights tipped the second contestant into the pit. Four feet long to the diamond-back's five and a half, and nowhere near as bulky, the round-headed, somehow pop-eyed challenger did not appear to have a chance of survival. For a moment it darted at the sides of the pit, trying without success to climb the metal-sheathed walls. Then it became aware of the diamondback's presence. Instantly it stopped trying to escape. The slim body curved into an elongated 'S' and the small head raised high as it studied the coiled horror in the centre of the pit.

Silence dropped on the watching crowd. Only the in-cessant buzz of the rattler's warning call sounded. Wriggling forward fast, the slim snake avoided a strike by the diamond-back's powerful, poison-backed jaws. Like a flash the thin body began to curl around the thick, harsh-scaled length of the other snake. The diamondback began to throw itself wildly around the pit, thrashing and struggling to break the steadily-tightening hold laid upon. Again and again the diamondback slashed and drove its head at the other. Slowly but surely, the slim snake's coils tightened and it moved nearer and nearer the spade-shaped, evil head. From a long tangle the two snakes became a knot, then a ball of pulsat-ing movement. For almost fifteen minutes the struggle raged, beginning with fast movement and slowing gradually until at last all movement ceased.

'Well, I'll be damned if that skinny ole snake ain't killed the rattler,' said a soldier at Dusty's side.

'He for sure has,' grinned the civilian standing next to the private. 'Reckon that's five dollars you owe me.'

A faint grin came to Dusty's face at the words. That 'skinny' killer belonged to the *Lampropeltis Getulus* family, the king snake, which lived exclusively on other snakes, kill-ing their prey by constriction and to a certain extent being immune to the other's poison. Apparently the soldier did not know that in such an affair the king snake almost invariably won the fight.

Before Dusty could enlighten the soldier, Belle tugged gently on his arm and led him to where Captain Millbanks stood holding a wooden box that had small holes drilled into its top.

'May I speak with you on a business matter, Captain Millbanks, please?' she greeted.

Turning, Millbanks looked first at the girl, a hint of recog-nition on his face, then he turned his gaze to Dusty for a moment, studied him with eyes which knew how to read a man's true potential.

'I'll be with you after I've settled a small matter here,' Millbanks replied.

'Come on, Cap'n Millbanks,' one of the nearby men put in. 'Let's see what kind of critter you've brung along.'

Nodding politely to the girl, Millbanks stepped along to one of the tubs in which the contestants for the fights could be displayed. Cautiously he opened and up-ended the box, shaking its contents out. A low mutter of surprise rose from the onlookers as they saw Millbanks' challenger. Lying coiled passively, the snake appeared to be no more than three feet long and slender, its head smallish and rounded, while bands of alternating black, yellow and red colour ran along its body.

'That sure is one fancy critter,' an onlooker remarked and eyed Millbanks. 'Can it fight?'

'There's one sure way to find out,' he replied. 'Drop it in the pit and see.'

'Air it pizeness?' inquired another of the crowd.

'Wouldn't want to put my hand in there and see,' admitted Millbanks. 'But I *will* put my money on this fancy old snake of mine.'

While the discussion of the fighting possibilities of the 'fancy' snake went on, Riegel and Fanning stood to one side and their eyes went to Belle.

'She went straight to Millbanks,' Fanning declared. 'Now we know she's Belle Boyd.'

'That's right. Now we know,' agreed Riegel.

'What do we do?'

'Arrange that accident – and here's how we do it.'

Unaware of the danger which threatened her, Belle stood smiling indulgently and watching Millbanks accept wagers on his snake. Despite his insistence that the snake be given odds, due to its never having fought before, she felt that he might not be making any mistake. Few of the crowd thought so, for all knew the deadly poisonous qualities of a diamond-back rattlesnake or a copperhead and had seen king snakes emerge victorious from combat with both. Belle did not mind the delay. Having seen the tensions under which a blockade-runner lived at sea, she could hardly begrudge Millbanks some relaxation, even of such a bizarre nature, while ashore.

At last the preliminaries had been taken care of, and some substantial wagers made on the result of the fight. With their money at stake, the gamblers in the crowd insisted on selecting an opponent and decided upon a king snake almost four feet long which had defeated more than one really big rattlesnake or copperhead.

Carefully Millbanks slid his contestant into the pit and at the other side one of the fight-promoters introduced the long king. Eagerly the crowd watched and waited for the action, but for almost two minutes nothing happened.

'Push 'em together!' a man called.

Taking up the long thin poles kept for that purpose, two of the promoters gently eased the snakes into the centre of the pit until they were only inches apart. Normally such an action would have been unnecessary, but even when up close the king showed no aggressive tendencies despite the fact that it ought to be hungry enough to want to make a meal of the first snake it saw.

'Make 'em come to taw!' suggested a spectator. 'Damn-it, neither of 'em wants to fight.'

As the promoter eased the king closer, the brightly coloured snake coiled, reared and struck, its fangs driving into the other's body just below the head. Fast though the king tore free and tried to throw its coils about the other, the gay-hued snake slipped away. Then the king began to thrash around wildly, knotting itself and beating its tail in frenzy as if fighting off some attack. Just what that attack might be, none of the crowd could imagine. Millbanks' snake had slithered to the far side of the pit and coiled up, ignoring the struggles of the king. At last the king stopped struggling and lay still.

Silence dropped on the crowd, their excited comments dying away. Not one of them could imagine what might have happened in the pit. Never had they seen a king snake laid low by a single bite; and from such a slender specimen of a critter too.

'Now's our chance!' Riegel hissed in Fanning's ear and caught the other roughly by the sleeve, turning him. 'You lousy cheat, there's something crooked going on here!'

Every eye swung towards the two men and suspicious, profane discussions began to develop. None of the crowd knew Millbanks' entry to be a harlequin coral snake the captain picked up in Mexico, or that *Elaps Fulvius'* poison

121

differed from that of the *Crotalids* over which the kings scored so many victories. While the pit-vipers – rattlesnakes, copperheads and water moccasins – used poison which attacked the blood of the victim, a coral snake's venom destroyed the nervous system; which accounted for the defeat of the king after only one bite. Not knowing the facts, the members of the crowd who had lost money on the result suspected that in some way they had been cheated.

'Let loose!' Fanning howled, following his part of the plan. Placing both his hands against Riegel's chest he began to push and yelled, 'Get your cotton-picking hands offen me!'

Releasing Fanning's arm, Riegel went reeling away as if out of all control. He hurled straight for where Dusty, Belle and Millbanks stood at the edge of the pit. Just too late Dusty saw their danger and tried to thrust Belle to one side. Riegel changed course slightly, cannoned into the girl and sent her sprawling over the edge of the pit. Shouts rose and some fights broke out as the over-excited crowd saw Fanning's action. Cursing, yelling warnings, 'the promoters rushed to protect and prevent being opened the boxes containing poisonous snakes needed for other fights.

Belle fell backwards, winded by the impact, and landed on the soft sand of the pit. Riding instincts helped her to break her fall, but what she saw jolted all cohesive thought from her mind.

Out in the centre of the pit, the coral snake had become aware of the open nature of the surrounding area; a condition it would never have endured in its natural state. The vibrations of Belle's arrival in the pit caused the coral to go into a defensive coil. Then it located the girl's body and, not recognizing Belle for a human being, saw only the cover and shade it craved. Swiftly the coral snake began to glide towards the girl.

Hearing the scream which broke unchecked from Belle's lips, Dusty forgot his intention of taking apart with his bare hands the man who caused the trouble. Without a moment's hesitation or thought of the danger to himself, Dusty leapt into the pit. His feet missed the snake's tail by less than half an inch and he did not fancy chancing trying to hit a moving, slender mark like the snake with a shot taken after a fast draw. Which left him only one thing to do.

Down shot his right hand, a hand capable of drawing a

gun with blinding speed – although his true potential in that line would not become fully perfected until in 1873 when the Colt factory produced its Model P, the gun which became the greatest fighting revolver ever made* – stabbed down and closed on the snake's tail. Dusty's original intention had been to jerk up the snake, crack it like a whip and snap its back in at least two places, immobilizing it quickly. However, something at the corner of his eye drew his attention to the side of the pit. What he saw caused him to change his plans for disposing of the snake.

Riegel stood on the edge of the pit, unseen by any of the crowd. Even Millbanks, busy explaining to objecting betters about his snake, failed to notice Riegel aiming a twin barrelled Remington Double Derringer down into the pit. If any of the arguing, excited crowd noticed the man, they must have thought him about to shoot the coral snake in an attempt to save the girl and Dusty.

Maybe Dusty would have thought the same had he not seen that the deadly little gun was aimed at Belle and not the snake. In that moment Dusty knew the incident was not accidental. The man deliberately pushed Belle into the pit and meant to kill her. Seeing his first plan fail, Riegel now meant to use his gun; either escaping in the confusion, or swearing that he tried to shoot the snake and how the girl moved into the line of fire as he squeezed the trigger.

With Dusty, to think had become nature to act. Even as his hand closed on the snake's tail, he had seen Riegel and formed his own conclusion. Whipping the snake up, Dusty flung it straight at Riegel's head. Even the most confirmed Union supporter, fanatically dedicated to destroying the South's top woman spy, would have flinched and forgotten his plans at the sight of that flying snake. Riegel served the Union for money and had no fanatical loyalty to support him. Desperately he threw up his gun-hand in an attempt to fend off the snake. He felt its sinewy length strike his arm, then coil around it. Like a flash, the enraged snake struck forward and up. Riegel screamed as he felt the burning sensation on the side of his neck. Horrified eyes turned towards him, staring at the gaily-coloured coral snake which swung by its jaws from his throat.

All quarrelling and fights became forgotten as the crowd

* Told in THE PEACEMAKERS by J. T. Edson. Wagon Wheel Western W315.

saw Riegel spin around then crash to the ground. The snake fell away and started to wriggle. Jumping forward, Millbanks stamped down with his boot, its heel crushing the snake's head to a pulp.

'Get the man who pushed him!' Dusty yelled, springing to Belle's side.

However, before anybody could think straight enough to obey, Fanning had fled without a trace. Nor would they learn anything from Riegel. The coral snake had not used much poison to kill the king and its venom sacs contained more than enough to write a speedy *finis* to Riegel; especially when bitten in the neck and so close to the controlling mechanism of the nervous system, the brain.

Millbanks sprang forward to help Belle out of the pit and Dusty looked around him, seeing no sign of Riegel's companion.

'What the hell happened?' asked Millbanks.

'I'll tell you later,' Dusty replied. 'Now let's get the hell out of here.'

## CHAPTER THIRTEEN

## MISS BOYD · MEETS AN INFORMER

LYING fully dressed on her bed in the best room of the Plaza Dixie Hotel, Belle Boyd looked up at the roof and smiled wryly. It seemed ironic that she who had given so much and taken so many chances for the South should be regarded as *persona non grata* in a Confederate Army officers' mess. Of course she realized that if she had announced her true identity, the mess door would be flung open and a welcome accorded to her; but she could not let it be known that she was Belle Boyd.

So Belle found herself alone. The local garrison issued invitations for 'General' Amesley and his staff to be guests at dinner and, rather than go into lengthy explanations or arouse suspicions, the three officers accepted. At which point a snag cropped up. While the local officers' ladies would have felt honoured to make the acquaintance of *the* Captain Dusty Fog of the Texas Light Cavalry, they strenuously and vocally objected to meeting a non-combatant general's *amie* on social grounds. Showing remarkable tact, the garrison commander avoided the issue by making the affair a strictly male function.

After some argument, Dusty and the other two left Belle in the hotel. Dusty warned her not to go out, remembering that one of the men who nearly caused her death at the snake-fight pit escaped and might want to try again. Smiling a little at the small Texan's concern for her welfare, Belle agreed to remain in the hotel and spend as much time as possible in the safety of her room.

After the incident at the snake-pit, things moved fast. First the local law was summoned and, sizing up the officer correctly, Dusty took him aside to tell him almost the full story. Being a stout Southron as well as a peace officer, the town marshal only needed to learn Belle's identity to make him willing to cover up the killing of Riegel as an accident.

With the legal side cleared, Belle spoke to Millbanks and found him willing to take them to Matamoros. He could not sail until the following afternoon, but Belle suggested that the bulk of the luggage, including most of the money, went aboard immediately. Accepting the girl's judgment, the men made all necessary arrangements and transferred the baggage to the safety of the *Snow Queen*. Doing so left them free to accept the garrison officers' invitation, but doomed Belle to a lonely, boring night at the hotel.

She wore one of her specially designed skirts and a plain white blouse, not bothering to dress formally when going to dinner in the hotel. Relaxed in her room after the meal, she turned over the events of the day in her mind. Given time, she could have tried to trace the man who made the attempt on her life. As she would be sailing the following day, the best she could do was hand the matter to the local branch of the Confederate States Secret Service. They knew of the existence of the ring and might possibly be able to trace it through the dead man.

A knock on the door interrupted her thoughts on how she would handle the investigation. Rising, she crossed the room to find the fat, pompous desk clerk outside.

'There is a person downstairs asking to see you, ma'am,' he announced in a voice which showed that he did not approve of the 'person' as being suitable to visit a guest at the hotel. 'He sent up this note.'

Taking the grubby envelope offered to her, Belle first noticed that its flap had been sealed down. Obviously the sender did not intend to have the message read by a snooping hotel employee during its delivery to Belle. Tearing open the flap, she extracted a sheet of equally grubby paper and looked down at the one line of writing upon it.

*'I have something to sell to you, Miss Belle Boyd.'*

Slowly Belle's eyes lifted to the man's face, but she had such control over her emotions that he never noticed any change in her expression. 'Who brought this for me, please?'

'A pedlar called Jacobs,' the clerk replied. 'He has a hat box with him.'

'Then you can bring him up.'

'Up *here*?' yelped the man.

'It's quite proper for a lady to interview a tradesman in privacy,' she smiled. 'He's probably bringing me a new hat I ordered.'

After the man left, Belle closed the door, went to her bed and drew out the small bag which contained her overnight items. Reaching into the bag, she took out an object which she concealed under the bed's covers. Shortly after, the clerk ushered in a tall, thin, bearded and dirty-looking man of Hebraic appearance. Pausing for a moment as if waiting for an invitation to stay and act as chaperon, the clerk gave an indignant sniff when it did not come, turned and left the room. Belle's visitor swung on his heel and thrust the door into a closed position and faced the girl – to look into the barrel of the Dance she produced from beneath the bed covers.

'I don't know you, Mr. Jacobs,' she stated.

'I'm only a poor Jewish pedlar, Miss Boyd,' he replied, standing very still. 'A famous lady like you wouldn't know the likes of me.'

'Then you want something?'

'Only to make a few cents trading.'

'What have you to trade?' Belle asked, looking down at the large hat box in Jacobs' hands.

'Something a bit more valuable than a hat.'

'Put the box down and tell me more.'

Setting the box on the floor, Jacobs looked up at the girl. 'Is that business, telling what I know before we talk money.'

'It's how I do business,' Belle warned. 'We'll start with you telling me how you know my name.'

'Come now, Miss Boyd,' Jacobs purred. 'A business man never tells his sec—'

His words trailed away as he stared at Belle. Still keeping the gun in her right hand lined at the man, Belle reached towards her middle with the left. The skirt she wore had been designed with the needs of her profession in mind and a pull on the buckle freed the waist band, allowing the skirt to drop free to the floor. Underneath Belle did not wear petticoats and the removal of the skirt left her lower regions exposed; which proved to be quite an eye-bugging sight. Her drawers were considerably shorter than a young lady of good-breeding usually employed as buttock covering. Suspender straps made black slashes down the white thighs and connected with black silk stockings. The contrast of colours served to show Belle's magnificent legs to their best advantage. High-heeled, calf-length shoes graced her feet and added to the general sensuous effect.

While never having heard the word, Belle was aware of the psychological impact the removal of her skirt and appearance it left would have upon Jacobs. He stood with his mouth trailing open and eyes bugging out like organ-stops, feasting his licentious gaze upon her lower limbs.

'I learned *savate* in a New Orleans academy,' she remarked. 'It's very painful, as you will find out if I don't get my answers.'

'Suppose I walk out? he asked, his voice a trifle hoarse.

Without taking her Dance out of line, Belle threw up her left leg in a standing high kick that rose with' sufficient power and height to rip off half his nose if it connected. Although Belle stood some distance away, Jacobs retreated hurriedly until his back struck the wall.

'Is there any need for all this foolishness?' he asked in what should have been a growl but came out as a whine. 'I came here in all good faith to see you—'

'How did you learn my name?' Belle interrupted and delivered a horizontal stamping side kick which dented the brass knob on the bed post, still without taking her gun out of line. 'Don't try to open the door; I'll shoot you and swear that you attacked me, if you try it.'

Jacobs hurriedly jerked his hand away from the door handle. Not for a moment did he doubt that the girl meant every word she said. Anybody playing the dangerous game of spying could only be a success and stay alive by possessing a ruthless nature and no false sense of the value of human life.

'I was on the dock this morning when the *Rosebud* came in,' he yelped. 'Feller next to me pointed to you and said, "That's Belle Boyd. I saw her in Atlanta". Well, I told this feller to keep quiet as we didn't know who might be listening and he shut his mouth. Only I'd heard him. Seeing's how I'd something that the South needs, I thought you'd be the best market.'

'You're *selling* information that could help the South?' she hissed.

'I'm only a poor man, Miss Boyd. Trade's become bad these days. A man has to make a living.'

'What have you to sell?' she snapped.

'It's worth a hundred dollars,' Jacobs answered. 'In gold.'

'Land-sakes!' Belle gasped. 'Do you have the entire war plans of the Yankee Army?

128

'No!' growled the man.

'I can't think of anything else that would be worth a whole hundred dollars in gold.'

'How about a buried telegraph wire running from Morgan City to the mouth of Atchafalaya Bay, the other end being visited by men from the Yankee blockade ships every night to take word of ships leaving the dock?'

'You're either joking, or lying,' Belle remarked, hiding the interest she felt. 'Which is it?'

'Can I open the hat box?'

'Do it real slow and watch what you bring out. Make sure I can see what you are doing all the time.'

Moving slowly, Jacobs raised the lid of the box and placed his hand inside. He used only the tips of his thumb and forefingers to bring an object into sight and toss it on to the bed.

'Go and lean forward with both hands against the wall and your feet spread well apart,' Belle ordered, not touching or looking at the object.

'Don't you trust me?' Jacobs whined.

'In a word, no,' the girl answered. 'Go do what I said.'

Not until Jacobs had assumed a posture which did not allow swift movement did Belle relax and study the object he tossed to her. Only by exercising all her will-power did she prevent an exclamation of surprise leaving her. The thing on the bed was a new model sending and receiving key which bore the markings of the U.S. Military Telegraph Department on it.

'Does this prove anything?' she sniffed. 'You can stand up and turn around.'

Obeying the order, Jacobs waved a hand towards the machine. 'It proves there is a telegraph station around here.'

'Or that you picked up the key from some soldier who collected it on the battlefield.'

'When I see the money, I'll tell you where the station is.'

Reaching into her vanity bag, Belle took out and flipped two double eagles to the man. He caught them and tested each with his teeth, but made no attempt to examine the dates.

'I said a hun—' he began.

'*If* we find the station you can collect the other sixty,' Belle replied.

Jacobs thrust the money into his pocket and gave a shrug. 'This's the last time I ever do anybody a good service.'

'You'll make me weep in a minute,' Belle answered. 'Where is it?'

'Down back of the cat-house – that's a—'

'I know what it is; and where.'

'Down back of the cat-house there's an old fisherman's cabin. Empty now, or was. The station's in there, keys hid under the floorboards.'

'Sounds awful chancy to me,' Belle said. 'Anybody might go in there and find the station.'

'Not many folks go down that way. The folks at the cat-house don't take to having prowlers around back. A lot of their sports wouldn't want it known they go down there.'

'I suppose not,' Belle smiled, then became serious again. 'Suppose they, the Yankees, miss that key?'

'It's a spare, I left the box it was in. Maybe they won't notice for days.'

'All right. Come around tomorrow and I'll give you the other sixty – if I find you've told the truth.'

'Are you going there yourself?'

'Me? Certainly not. I'll send along a troop of soldiers. Get going – and if you tell anybody my name, I'll see you regret it.'

'I'm an honest pedl—' Jacobs protested.

'I'm sure you are,' Belle purred. 'But watch what you peddle. A man could meet with a bad end, trading in some kind of goods.'

A few years later Belle's warning may have come back to Jacobs as he was shot down by a member of a criminal gang that he had tried to sell to the Texas Rangers.*

After Jacobs left Belle's room, the girl closed and locked the door. Swiftly she turned his information over in her head. Knowing the manner in which professional informers could gather items of interest, she wondered how much of Jacobs' story might be true. She doubted if he learned her name in the manner he claimed, although it could just possibly be true; she had been a blonde while working against the Yankee spy-ring in Atlanta and still used the same wig. Then her eyes went to the telegraph key. It was a model only recently introduced, not one of the old *Beardslee Patent Magneto-Electric Field Telegraph* machines with which the Yankees went into the War and that failed to stand up to

* Told in THE COW THIEVES by J. T. Edson. Wagon Wheel Western W329.

130

the rugged usage of active service. Of course the key could be a souvenir picked up on some battlefield, but it seemed to be in too good condition for that.

For a moment Belle thought of sending word to Dusty or the members of the local Secret Service field office and asking for assistance. Then a thought held her. Despite the fact that they had proved their worth many times over, Belle Boyd, Rose Greenhow and other female members of their organization still found a certain reluctance on the part of the Confederate States armed forces' top brass to recognize their use. Many of the senior officers clung to the belief that a woman's place was in the home and objected to Southern ladies being allowed to do such work as spying. If word got out that Belle had fallen for an ancient informer's trick and wasted good money on a false alarm, further fuel would be added to the flames of objection which blazed whenever the subject of women spies rose in high places.

So Belle decided to make the preliminary investigation herself. Nothing dramatic, of course, like trying to take the station single-handed, but enough to ensure that she would not waste time or lose prestige by sending the men from the field office on a wild-goose chase.

The overnight bag held her dark blue shirt, riding breeches and gunbelt and it was work of a moment to change out of the clothes she wore to dinner. After strapping on the belt and holstering her Dance, she drew back the covers and, using the bag, her wig and items from the room, made what would pass for a sleeping shape in the bed. If anybody should happen to look into her room, she did not want an alarm raised through her absence. Leaving the hotel offered no difficulty, even if she could not use the stairs and front door for obvious reasons. In case of fire, each room had a coil of rope secured to the wall near its window. Belle raised the window sash, tossed out the rope and slid down it hand over hand to the street at the rear of the hotel. Being used only for tradesmen delivering to the businesses lining the main street, nobody walked the area into which Belle slid. She paused for a moment to get her bearings, then walked along the back street. By keeping to the shadows, she hoped to reach her destination without attracting any attention.

After leaving Belle's room, Jacobs hurried downstairs and passed through the hotel lobby. The desk clerk scowled, but said nothing, figuring that the pedlar must have made a sale as he did not carry the hat box. On the street outside the hotel, Jacobs threw a cautious look in either direction before walking hurriedly away. He went fast, with many a backward glance. Making sure that he was not followed, Jacobs passed through the entertainment section of the town and reached the small, unobtrusive building which housed the Yankee spy-ring. Apparently he was known there, for the bouncer admitted him and led him to the office used by the madam.

Flora lounged on the couch when the door opened, but she came to her feet as she recognized her visitor.

'Well?' she said, as the door closed behind Jacobs.

'I saw her and did like you told me. She fell for it.'

'And she agreed to come look the cabin over?'

'Sure she—'

'You're a liar!' Flora snapped out. 'What did she really say?'

'Th – That she'd send soldiers.'

'That's more like the Boyd I know,' Flora purred. 'Now get the hell out of here and keep going. My men'll be watching to make sure you don't go near anybody else to peddle your wares.'

'I – I'm loyal to the North!' Jacobs wailed.

'Then the best I can wish is that you'd go over to the other side,' Flora replied. 'Get going.'

At the door, Jacobs turned and looked back at Flora. 'It looks like your idea didn't work.'

'Yes,' she agreed. 'It looks that way.'

However, after Jacobs left the room Flora gave a cold, calculating smile. While she expected Belle to tell the man that soldiers would make the investigation, Flora knew the Southern spy would only do this as a precaution, and was certain to look into the matter herself.

That was why Flora acted as she did. Why she sent the telegraph key and told of the message-passing station which had been set up at such hardship and effort. One of the spies exposed by Belle Boyd in Atlanta had been more than just a friend, he was Flora's brother and met his end standing back to a wall while facing a line of Confederate Army rifles. Since that time Flora had prayed for an opportunity to lay her hands on Belle Boyd. Now chance threw the rebel spy Flora's way and she did not intend to miss her opportunity – even if she had to use the most valuable secret her ring possessed as bait to draw Belle into her power.

Going to the room's second floor, Flora looked out and called, 'Beth, May!'

Two tall, buxom girls, a brunette and a blonde, entered the room. Wearing cheaply garish frocks and jewellery, they gave an impression of hard flesh under the tawdry finery.

'She going to be there?' asked May, the brunette.

'It's all arranged,' Flora agreed.

'We'll teach her that no lousy madam's going to open another place up close to our house,' Beth spat out.

While Flora reckoned her girls could be relied upon not to support either side in the War, she thought it might be better if the two selected to side her believed they dealt with a rival madam who planned to convert the old fisherman's cabin into a house which would steal some of their trade, rather than mention that the woman they were to attack was the South's most legendary Belle Boyd.

'Sure we will,' Flora agreed, glancing at the girls' hands. 'Take those rings off before we go.'

Both girls opened their mouths to object, knowing the value of the heavy, embossed rings offered for offence and defence. However, Flora insisted. The girls thought that all they would do was work their victim over, leaving her a battered but wiser woman. Flora aimed to make sure that Belle Boyd never spied again. Knowing that the disappearance of so important a person would cause a stir, Flora aimed to take no chances. The town marshal was no fool and knew an indecent amount of things one did not expect of a small town lawman – he had been a captain on the New Orleans Police Department before the arrival of the Yankees; keen, conscientious, the kind who kept up with the latest developments in criminal investigation. Flora intended to dump her enemy's body in the bay where the alligators would dispose of it, but knew that something might go wrong. Faced with a badly battered body, the marshal knew enough to understand the significance of any ring-cuts on the face. He would know that somewhere were rings that bore traces of human skin and blood. While the rings might inflict more damage on Belle Boyd, Flora did not want them using if doing so helped the law to locate her.

With the rings removed, the girls followed their employer from the house and went to the cabin where they made their preparations for the arrival of their prey.

## CHAPTER FOURTEEN

# A DEMONSTRATION OF LA SAVATE

APPROACHING the fisherman's shack, Belle Boyd studied it with distaste. Set close to the edge of Atchafalaya Bay, the building did not exude a welcoming air. Small, one-roomed, dark and deserted, yet still in reasonable condition, was how the cabin appeared to the girl. All around her the mangrove swamp and canebrakes closed in, making the winding path along which she walked gloomy, eerie almost, when one listened to the mysterious noises of the swamp-land at night.

If she had seen a light, or anything to hint that the telegraph station's crew were present, Belle would have returned to town and gathered assistance. No coward, Belle also did not rank folly among her achievements. While she could handle a revolver with some skill, matching shots against a bunch of desperate Yankee spies would prove too much for her. She knew her capabilities and recognized her limitations. If forced to by circumstances, she would have tackled the gang, but given a chance or choice in the matter, she intended to fetch help to make more certain the capture and destruction of the Yankee's message-distribution organization. Finding the building in darkness, she decided to check and confirm Jacobs' information.

Drawing her Dance, she approached the front door of the building. She doubted if the Yankees maintained a guard on the cabin when not using it; to do so might invite unwanted curiosity. In all probability the telegraph key would only be connected when in actual use and might even not be present at other times. However, the wires could not be rolled up and hidden between messages. Finding them would be all the proof she needed.

Gently she gripped the door handle, twisting and shoving at it. The door opened silently, a significant point that Belle grasped. If the cabin had been unused for some time, its hinges ought to screech a protest when working. Trying to peer through the stygian blackness of the building's interior, Belle moved forward. Eyes and ears worked hard to pick up any hint of danger; but her nose made the first detection. The significance of the faint aroma of perfume did not, however, strike her quite quickly enough. Even as she realized that such a scent had no place in a Yankee spy-ring's telegraph station, a hand caught her shoulder, jerked hard and heaved her towards the darkness in the centre of the cabin.

Taken by surprise, Belle had no chance to resist. The hand gripped her and pulled hard; as she shot forward, Belle heard the door slam to. The light flooded the room from a lantern hanging in the centre. Belle saw a big brunette stood with hands still gripping the lantern's covers, but that one did not constitute the immediate danger. Unable to halt her forward rush, Belle advanced straight into the round-arm swing the waiting Flora launched at her. Woman-like, Flora used the flat of her hand instead of her knuckles. Even so, the force of the slap sent Belle spinning across the room and caused her to drop her gun. Pain knifed through her and her head spun from the blow. Only just in time did she manage to twist herself around so that she struck the wall shoulders first instead of colliding face-on.

'Get her!' Flora screeched.

Only one thing saved Belle. The two girls aiding Flora expected to be confronted by a rival cat-house madam dressed in the conventional manner. Unable to see more than a blurred shape in the doorway, Beth carried out her part in the plan to perfection by grabbing Belle and thrusting her forward. Nor did May show any less ability in lighting the lantern at just the right moment. In doing so, she illuminated not a cat-house madam in a dress, but a beautiful girl wearing men's clothing and carrying a gun. The shock of the unexpected sight held Beth and May off for just that vital second Belle needed to regain control of her slap-scattered wits.

One thing Belle knew immediately and without needing any heavy thought, she must fight if she hoped to escape with her life. Although her Dance lay in the centre of the room, leaping for it would be suicide while all three of her attackers remained on their feet.

After screaming her order, Flora hurled herself straight at Belle. Fury and hate over-rode caution and made the red-head act without thinking of the consequences. Or it may have been that she believed a high-born Southern lady like Belle Boyd would prove easy meat. If that had been Flora's thought, she would swiftly find disillusionment.

Moving clear of the wall, and seeing the other girls recover from their surprise, Belle prepared to handle Flora's hair-reaching rush with something a damned sight more effective than curl-yanking. Up rose Belle's right leg until its calf was parallel to the floor and the sole of her high-heeled shoe aimed at Flora. Straightening her left leg, Belle leaned backwards slightly and thrust forward the right in a stamping high kick. Full into Fora's sizeable bust crashed the foot. Sick agony tore into the Union supporter; her eyes bulged and her mouth opened in a hideous shriek of pain. She stumbled backwards, momentarily out of the fight.

From her assault on Flora, Belle brought down her leg, pivoted and lashed up the kind of high kick which so impressed Jacobs at the hotel. Only this time she stood close enough to land home. The toe of her left boot caught Beth's top lip, although it must be admitted that Belle aimed to smash it under the other's chin, crushing the flesh up and splitting it before continuing to squash the nose. Squealing in agony, blood gushing from lip and nose, blinded by tears, Beth spun around and reeled away.

Fingers dug into Belle's hair from behind as her third attacker came within reaching distance. May lay on a one-handed hold, her other fist driving into Belle's back just above the kidney region. Even the back kick which Belle launched automatically, catching May just over the right knee, failed to release the tearing grip on the Southern girl's hair. It did, however, serve to hold the big brunette at arms' length instead of closing in to continue her assault. Fiery pain burst into Belle's head and almost drove thoughts of effective defence from it. Luckily she retained sufficient control to know that she must free herself before the other two attackers recovered and came to lend their friend a hand.

Tilting backwards as if dragged off balance, Belle brought up both hands to clamp over the fingers which still dug into her hair and pressed them firmly against her skull. Using her left leg as a pivot, Belle twisted around while still retaining her hold on the trapped hand and halted when she faced towards the other girl. May squealed as the leverage on her hand bent her wrist at an unnatural angle. On being released, her automatic reaction was to stagger back.

136

Up drove Belle's left foot, aiming at May's lower body. However, May had been in brawls before and, hurt or not, knew a thing or two. Her hands shot forward to catch Belle's kicking ankle.

'Come on, you pa—!' May began, feeling that her companions left too much for her to handle alone.

The words were chopped off, for Belle knew more than a few tricks and was prepared against the possibility of someone trapping her in that manner during a kick. Twisting her body, she brought her free leg up from the floor, turning so it passed over the trapped limb. Drawing the left leg back, Belle stabbed it out in a stamp to the centre of May's face. Again May felt the sickening impact of the kick and it cut off her demand for assistance. She lost her hold and stumbled away, hand clawing to her bleeding nose.

A hand caught Belle by the shoulder as she landed. Another came around, drove into her stomach and as she doubled over a knee caught her in the face. Belle crashed into the wall, half-blinded by tears of pain. Digging fingers into Belle's hair, Flora heaved and threw the girl across the room. Only Belle s superb co-ordination kept her on her feet. Again she managed to turn and hit the wall with her back, bouncing off it in the direction of Beth as the blonde rushed forward. Belle reacted almost without thought, yet she brought off the ideal answer to Beth's rush. Bounding into the air, Belle drew up her legs and thrust them forward with all her strength. Too late Beth saw her danger. Her own forward impetus added force to the kick as Belle's boots drove full into her bust. Screaming in mortal agony, Beth shot backwards, twisted around and crashed brutally into the wall.

Rebounding from the leaping high kick, Belle landed on her feet and found fresh trouble. Leaping forward, Flora smashed a blow which caught Belle at the side of the face. Behind the red-head, May came forward again. Desperately Belle drove out a roundhouse right which exploded on the side of Flora's jaw and sent her staggering to one side. May skidded to a hurried halt on seeing that she must again face alone the devastating fighting techniques of the other girl. Deciding to make use of her superior reach, May flung a punch at the black-haired girl's head. Throwing up her right fist, Belle caught the outer side of May's striking arm, deflected the blow and turned the brunette's body from her. A

137

swift side-step put Belle in position to deliver a stamping kick to the back of May's left knee. Even as the bigger girl lost her balance, Belle's left foot reached the floor and her right swung up to crash hard at the base of the brunette's skull. Already off balance, the kick flung May forward and, dazed and helpless, she smashed headlong into the wall. From there she collapsed in a limp heap upon the floor.

Before Belle could fully recover from handling May, she found fresh trouble. Flora flung herself forward, coming in at Belle's side. Two arms locked around Belle's waist and the impact knocked her sprawling to the floor with Flora clinging to her. On landing, Belle forgot all her knowledge of *savate* and her fingers dug into the mass of red hair. An instant later she felt as if the top of her head had burst into flames, for Flora retaliated in the same manner.

With both of Flora's girls out of action, the fight became equal. Over and over thrashed and turned the struggling gasping, squealing girls, first one then the other gaining the upper position and holding it until thrown over by the one on the bottom. In the earlier stages of the fight Belle's clothing gave her a greater freedom of movement than that afforded by the dresses of her attackers. Now the advantage meant little in the wild, close-up tangle the fight had become. Tearing hair, slashing wild slaps and blows, flailing with their legs, fingers digging and twisting into flesh, Belle and Flora churned about the room in a wild female fracas where skill had no place.

Slowly the Southern girl's superior physical condition began to show its effect. Flora did not lead a life conducive to perfect health and began to tire under the continued exertion. Slowly, but just as surely as when the king snake crushed out the diamondback's life at the snake-pit, Belle began to gain the upper hand. Blood ran from her nostrils; the shoulder and one sleeve of her shirt had been ripped away, but she ignored both as she fought for mastery over the half-naked, just as badly marked red-head.

A surging heave rolled Flora from the upper position. She landed on her back, too exhausted to make more than a token resistance as Belle threw a leg across her body and sat on her. Blind instinct sent Belle's fingers to the other's throat, for at that moment the Southern girl became the most primeval and deadly of all creatures, a furiously angry, hurt woman. All her upbringing and refinement was forgotten as her fingers tightened upon Flora's throat. Fear gave Flora strength. She arched her back in an attempt to throw Belle from her, but failed. Croaking, unable to breathe, her hands beat at the other girl's face, tried to claw at her shoulders, then went down, gripping the top of Belle's exposed underwear in an attempt to get at the flesh below.

At that moment sanity began to creep into Belle's mind again, or it may have been that some primeval instinct gave warning of her danger. Whatever the reason, Belle twisted her head around to see what the other two women were doing. May lay where she had fallen, but Beth dragged herself across the floor in Belle's direction. One hand supported and tried to give relief to the throbbing agony in the ultra-sensitive area which caught the impact of Belle's leaping high kick; but the other held a four-inch bladed push-knife such as gamblers and women of Beth's profession often carried concealed about their persons. While Beth had obeyed orders and discarded her rings, she retained the knife in its garter sheath. Seeing a chance to get at the woman who inflicted such punishment and suffering upon her, Beth drew the knife and started to crawl across the floor.

As if sensing what her companion planned, Flora clung even tighter to Belle's clothing. Struggling savagely, Belle tried to either rip the cloth or drag herself out of Flora's grasp, for she knew she must escape the hold – or die. Even as Beth gathered her pain-wracked body for a dive which would carry her on to Belle and drive home the knife, the Southern girl smashed a fist with all her strength into Flora's right breast. Shocking agony ripped through Flora, numbing her body and causing her hands to release their hold. Feeling herself free of the clutching fingers, Belle rolled from Flora. She did not move a moment too soon. Down hurled Beth, her pain-drugged brain failing to react to the changed situation. Instead of realizing that her enemy had gone, Beth carried through the plan formulated as she crawled across the floor – only she landed on Flora, not Belle. Down drove the push-knife, its point sinking just under the red-head's left breast and Beth's weight sent the blade in hilt-deep.

Landing on her back, Belle coiled up her legs and, as Beth reared up from the jerking, twitching body of the red-head, drove out both feet. The shoes smashed with sickening force into the side of Beth's head. Giving a low moan, she pitched off Flora and crashed to the floor.

For almost a minute Belle stayed on her back. Across the room, May moaned and tried to rise. The sight gave Belle an incentive to move. Dragging her aching body erect, she stood swaying and looking around at a room which seemed to roll and pitch like the deck of a ship. Seeing her gun lying on the floor, she staggered forward and picked it up.

The cabin's door burst open and Fanning entered. For a moment he stood staring in amazement at the sight which met his eyes. He did not recognize Belle as the woman he tried to kill at the snake-pit, but she identified him.

'What the hell?' he demanded, reaching towards his sagging jacket pocket.

Sick with exhaustion and pain though she might be, Belle could still react to such a threat. Up came the Dance she held, almost of its own volition it seemed – in later years Belle could never remember lifting the gun or pressing the trigger – and roared. In the confines of the cabin, the crack of the light gun sounded as loud as the boom of a Dragoon Colt. Through the pain-mists and powder smoke Belle saw the man jerk, stagger, hit the wall and slide down. Without waiting to see how badly hurt he might be, Belle ran staggering from the room and along the dark trail towards Morgan City.

Reaction to the events of the evening began to set in as Belle made her way towards the town. Her body seemed to give out a continuous throbbing ache, her head whirled with dizziness and nausea threatened to engulf her at any moment. Gun in hand she stumbled along the path, darting frantic glances about her.

Suddenly a man's shape appeared on the track ahead of Belle. She had just turned a corner which hid the shack from view and before she could halt saw the dark bulk blocking her way. Even as she tried to raise her gun, the man sprang forward and struck at her wrist. Feeling his fingers close around her arm, Belle acted almost instinctively. Up drove her knee, catching the man in a place guaranteed to make him release his hold. The man gave a strangled gasp of pain for, although Belle might be on the verge of collapse, the impact packed enough power to drive agony through him. Feeling the hand leave her wrist, she thrust the man aside, but three more shapes swarmed around her and other fingers closed on her.

'It's a gal!' announced a disbelieving voice.

Bending down, one of the others raised Belle's Dance, held its muzzle to his nose and sniffed at it. 'Hold down the talk!' he snapped in an authoritative tone. 'This's been fired. Then it was a shot we heard from down there.'

Relief flooded through Belle as she recognized the voice of Morgan City's efficient town marshal – who also ran the local field office of the Confederate States Secret Service; a detail he had not confided to Dusty.

'Sout – Southrons hear your country call you,' Belle gasped.

'What the—!' began the marshal on hearing the familiar password. 'Show a light here, but keep it down.'

'N – No light!' Belle objected. 'Down at the fisherman's cabin—'

'Get down there, two of you,' the marshal ordered. 'Keep alert at it. How'd you feel, Tom?'

' — terrible,' came the profane reply from Belle's assailant. 'That danged gal near on ruined me. Who is she?'

'B – Belle – Boyd—' gasped Belle, then collapsed.

'After covering up for you and asking no questions down at the snake-pit,' the marshal said grimly, 'I figure we rated some co-operation from you.'

Seated in the marshal's office, feeling stiff, sore and more than a little sorry for herself, although having received medical attention for her numerous bruises and minor abrasions, Belle nodded gravely.

'I didn't aim to go over your head, or try to show my superiority over you. But the information I *bought* might have been false and I didn't want anybody to know about that if it should be. And I'd no intention of moving in if there'd been a light showing or any sign of life.'

'How'd you get mixed in this game anyhow?' the marshal inquired. 'We've known about that outfit for some time, but couldn't get any proof. I began to get suspicious when I heard that soldiers and seamen were being filled with free liquor down there. That's not the cat-house way, unless somebody wanted the men drunk and talking. Anyhow, I sent a cousin of mine in, he's on furlough down here. He went dressed as a seaman and found that after he'd been liquored up, Flora started asking him questions about when his ship would be sailing and what she'd carry. So I figured it was time we moved in and took a look around.'

'Did you find the telegraph station?'

'Sure. That feller you shot, Fanning, he talked up a storm and showed us all we wanted. We raided the cat-house – don't know what the mayor'll have to say about it though.'

'Why should he have anything to say?' Belle asked.

'He was with one of the girls when we arrived – and him supposed to be at a meeting of the municipal council.'

'If he's married, he won't say a word,' Belle stated, and her guess proved to be correct. 'Did you destroy the station?'

'Nope. I aimed to, but when I found Flora's code books, I figured that it might be useful to be able to let the Yankees know what we want them to know.'

'It will at that,' Belle agreed. 'Can you get word out that there won't be any ships leaving, but that one is expected from the north tomorrow night?'

'Sure we can. The Yankees land to take any messages at midnight every night. I'll tend to it for you.'

'And how about that pedlar, Jacobs?' the girl went on. 'He was the one who told me about the telegraph station.'

'If I know old Jake Jacobs, he'll be long gone by now,' the marshal replied. 'Reckon that Flora sent him with the information for you?'

'She may have done. Did the two girls tell you anything yet?'

'Nope. May's in no shape to talk and all Beth knows is that you were supposed to be some cat-house madam who intended to open a place down there.'

'They weren't in the spy ring?'

'I doubt it. The bouncer, Flora and a couple more were the only ones involved in the ring. I'll pick up the odd ends tonight. Got the boys started on it right now. We've bust the Yankee spy-ring. Say, one way and another, the Yankees have been giving you a bad time.'

'I must have riled them for some reason,' Belle smiled. 'And now I'd best be getting back to the hotel. Lord knows what Dusty and the others will say when they see my face in the morning.'

A grin creased the marshal's features as he studied Belle's blackened right eye, scratched cheek, swollen lip and nose. 'You might try telling them you walked into a door and it fought back.'

## CHAPTER FIFTEEN

# A DIFFERENCE OF TABLE MANNERS

ALTHOUGH Belle's appearance attracted some comment among her friends, all found themselves too busy preparing for their departure the next day to go too deeply into the matter.

From the smooth manner in which the trip went, it seemed that the gods of war had relented and decided to smooth the path for their small band of devotees.

Slipping from her berth, the *Snow Queen* ran down the Atchafalaya Bay under sail power on the evening tide. The false message had done its work and the Yankee blockade gun-boats lay to the north awaiting the arrival of the non-existent ship. By running the *Snow Queen* through a channel skirting the mangrove swamps which lined the shore, Millbanks avoided detection and at dawn lay well beyond the enemy's range of vision. Once clear, the crew profanely informed the Texans, no damned Yankee scow ever built could lay alongside the ole *Queen* in a stern chase.

In good weather and bad, the *Snow Queen* ran down to the southwest at a steady thirteen knots. Showing masterly skill, Millbanks avoided the Yankee ships blockading Galveston, skimmed along the shore of Matagorda Island, beat out to sea to avoid the enemy off Corpus Christi and passed along the fringes of the shoals surrounding the elongated Padre Island. On approaching the mouth of the Rio Grande, the ship again put out to sea and slipped by in the night, unseen by a Yankee ironclad which lay a good three miles out from the entrance to the border river.

Thinking back on the trip, Dusty decided that Millbanks must have augmented his winter earnings by doing in-shore trading – a polite name for smuggling – as he knew all the tricks of avoiding detection by an enemy and every channel of deep waters along which a vessel could slip close to the shore. The thought gained support on seeing the way the

Mexican population of a small fishing village some twenty miles south of Matamoros greeted the *Snow Queen*'s arrival.

Using keg pontoons, Millbanks' men ferried ashore the carriage and horses brought aboard in Morgan City. Then the captain supplied a guide; a villainous-looking Mexican whom none of the Texans would have cared to trust without such good references. Certainly they had no cause to complain about his services. After arranging for Millbanks to wait in the area for a week so as to be able to carry the arms, Dusty's party took to a form of transport they understood. Their guide led them along narrow, winding tracks through the swamp-lands of the coast and across the range to the Los Indios trail. There he left them and, following their original plan, the party entered Matamoros as if they had crossed the Rio Grande up Mercedes way and come along the river trail.

Despite Ole Devil's predictions, the party had little trouble with the bad elements of Matamoros society. On their arrival Amesley presented his credentials to the garrison commander, a bulky French general very much of *du peuple* and, like many of his kind, determined to appear gentile. One meeting told Amesley all he needed to know of the French general's nature and at the earliest opportunity he broached the subject of the exchange of deserters. Amesley's judgment paid off. While the garrison commander wanted to lay his hands on French deserters, using their fate as a deterrent to other would-be absconders, he refused to accept responsibility for such an important matter. Nor would he flatly refuse the offer. As Amesley expected, the French general insisted that the Texans stay on in Matamoros as his guests until he could send a report to Mexico City and receive instructions from higher authority.

Given a good excuse to stay in Matamoros, Amesley settled down to enjoy himself. There were parties to attend, dinner invitations to accept. For three days the Texans and Belle relaxed, although each day saw Dusty and the girl at the dockside watching for the first sign of Smee's boat.

To avoid attracting too much attention, Dusty and Red had discarded their gunbelts and now wore the regulation type of equipment, one revolver butt forward in a closed-topped holster at the right side, and a sabre in the slings at the left. Neither their skirtless tunics nor the fact that

Dusty's Colt bore a white bone handle were out of character, as the Confederate Army allowed its officers considerable freedom in choice of arms and dress. Being introduced as Captain Edward Marsden, and the fact that he did not look how people imagined a man like Dusty Fog would be, prevented anyone suspecting his true identity. However, the open-topped holsters could have aroused suspicion, so Dusty left them off. He did not expect to need his weapons. True, there were some Yankee personnel in Matamoros, but they ignored the Southrons as became enemies meeting on neutral ground.

General Plessy laid great stress on his determination not to have trouble between Southrons and Yankees in his town. At the first meeting, he demanded that Amesley explain the rules of neutrality to the junior officers and warned that any trouble would result in all concerned, on both sides, being placed under arrest until the end of hostilities. With that in mind, Dusty and Red walked warily in the presence of such Yankees as they met and avoided conflict.

On the fourth afternoon a new ship had arrived and lay in the stream. Named the *Lancastrian,* she was an ugly vessel. A three-masted ship converted to steam propulsion, she retained her raised poop deck and standing rigging. The construction of the *Lancastrian* interested Dusty and Belle far less than the flag she wore.

'That's Smee's ship, Dusty,' Belle said.

'She's not coming right in,' he replied.

'I never thought she would. We'll go out by rowing-boat and visit with her captain.'

'*We* will,' Dusty agreed. 'But not the money until after I'm satisfied that the arms are worth it.'

'You've got a suspicious mind, Captain Fog,' smiled the girl.

'Why sure,' Dusty grinned back. 'But I only got it *after* I tied in with you.'

An hour later, after returning to the hotel which housed them and making all the necessary arrangements, Belle and Dusty sat in a shore-boat handled by a burly Mexican and skimmed towards the *Lancastrian*. The ship now rocked gently at anchor and a gangway hung down the side. With considerable skill, the Mexican boatman laid alongside the gangway and Dusty took out money to pay him.

Belle climbed the gangway ahead of Dusty and stepped

on to the deck, halting to look around her. Some half a dozen or so seamen dressed in the usual fashion stood about, eyeing her with interest, but she ignored the glances, directing her attention to the two men who approached. Captain Smee looked much the same as on their previous meeting; tall, gaunt, miserable of feature. However, she could not recall having seen the tall, powerful man who followed on his heels. Clearly this one was a ship's officer, for he wore the same style peaked hat as Smee, a frock coat and trousers tucked into seaboots.

'Good afternoon, Captain Smee,' Belle greeted, sensing that the man did not recognize her.

Then recognition came to Smee's face. 'It's Miss Tracey, isn't it?' he said. 'But you had—'

'We ladies do change the colour of our hair occasionally,' Belle smiled. 'May I present Captain Edward Marsden of the Confederate States army. Captain Marsden, this is Captain Smee, of whom I have told you, and—'

'My – mate,' Smee introduced, reading the question in Belle's unfinished sentence and inquiring glance at the other officer. 'Mr. Stone.'

Apparently Stone belonged to the strong, silent class, for he acknowledged the introduction with nothing more than a grunt and did not offer his hand. Ignoring the other's silence, Dusty looked around him and then turned to Smee.

'You don't have many men about, Captain.'

'They're all—' Smee hesitated and threw a quick glance at Stone, then went on. 'They're all ashore except for an anchor watch. I didn't want too many knowing about the arms.'

That figured; Smee could find himself in serious trouble if it became known that he sold arms to the Confederate States while in a neutral port.

'Speaking of the arms,' Belle put in. 'May we see them?'

'They're in the forward hold,' Smee answered. 'Do you have the money?'

'It's on shore, and will stay there until I'm satisfied with the consignment, Captain,' Dusty stated.

'Come this way then,' Smee growled.

With Stone following on his heels, Smee led Belle and Dusty to the hatch which gave access to the forward hold. Climbing down, he turned the wick of a lantern hanging from a beam and illuminated the cargo. He waved a hand towards a long row of variously shaped boxes.

'There they are. The same weapons Miss Tracey saw in England.'

'My apologies, sir,' Dusty answered. 'But I've my duty to do; and my orders are to check the arms before accepting them. You don't object?'

After throwing a quick glance in Stone's direction, Smee gave a shrug. 'Why should I object. There's a crowbar, open any box you want.'

Picking up the bar Smee indicated, Dusty walked along the row of boxes. He noticed that a couple had been opened recently and gave them his first attention. Forcing up the lid, he lifted out one of the rifles. Although smothered in grease, as one might expect, the weapon proved to be in excellent condition, and after a thorough cleaning would be ready for use. After selecting from three other rifle boxes, Dusty sampled among the boxes of ammunition, again finding everything to be satisfactory.

'They'll do,' he said, returning to the others. 'When we get outside I'll signal to my men to fetch the money along.'

'I explained to Captain Smee and Mr. Stone that we didn't consider it safe to have that much money standing on the dock for any length of time, Edward,' Belle remarked. 'The captain has invited us to take a meal with him while we're waiting. If it's all right with you, I've accepted.'

'You're handling the play, Miss Tracey,' Dusty agreed.

On the deck again, Dusty removed his campaign hat and waved it twice in an anti-clockwise direction over his head. Standing on the dock, Red saw his cousin's signal and signified to that effect by repeating it. Turning, the young lieutenant swung astride his waiting horse and rode back towards the better part of town.

With the formalities handled, Smee led his guests to a door set in the poop deck. Beyond it lay his quarters, two fair-sized cabins which gave him far greater space and comfort than that allocated to his officers or men. In the first cabin a table lay set ready and Smee waved his guests into their seats. The taciturn Stone followed the party in and drew up a chair without saying a word.

Dusty looked around the cabin, glancing at a couple of good pictures on the walls, then towards an open case holding a pair of fine *epee de combat*. While not mentioning the swords, he wondered about them. Smee did not strike Dusty as being the kind of man who would own such weapons.

Following Dusty's gaze, Smee seemed to think that an explanation was needed. 'I picked them up cheap,' he remarked, nodding to the case. 'There's always a good sale for a fine sword in Mexico.'

At that moment the door opened and a steward entered. Yet he was a most unusual type of man to be handling such a sedentary occupation, being six feet tall, burly and weather-beaten. Carrying a large tray, he approached the table and began to serve out the soup course.

Conversation did not prove to be a success during the meal. Although Belle tried to draw Stone into speech, he restricted his answer to non-committal grunts or terse comments of 'Yes' or 'no'. Nor did Smee improve matters, for he appeared to have little small talk. In fact he acted as nervous as a hound-scared cat, throwing many worried glances towards the cabin's main door.

While watching Smee, Dusty happened to glance in Stone's direction and noticed that the man held his knife in the left hand. So did Belle and Dusty if it came to that – but Smee used his right for the same purpose. Nothing Dusty had seen about Stone, apart from the mate's scarcity of conversation, hinted at a lack of knowledge of etiquette. Yet he sat holding his knife in the wrong hand – for a European.

A tingling sensation ran down Dusty's spine. At the same moment the steward leaned over to pass a plate to Smee and his white jacket trailed open. Underneath, strapped to his belt, hung a long-bladed sheath knife. Or was it just a sheath knife? A second look showed that the blade was curved and its handle had the shape of an old-time pistol's butt. Such a weapon had significant overtones to a man who studied weapons as Dusty had.

Casting a glance at Belle, Dusty tried to read from her face if she felt as concerned and uneasy as he did. Not by as much as a flicker of an eyelid could he decide and so sat back to await developments.

'Shore-boat coming off,' announced a seaman, poking his head around the door after knocking.

The door closed again and the steward moved around the table, approaching it from behind Dusty's back and reaching out big hands towards the small Texan. Suddenly, and without giving any indication of his intentions, Dusty

148

caught up the plate from before him and hurled it over his shoulder full into the steward's face. Taken by surprise, the man gave a startled yell as the plate shattered on striking him. He went back a couple of steps and before he caught his balance had Dusty's thrown-over chair wrapped around his legs.

In almost the same move that he hurled back the plate and thrust his chair from under him, Dusty's hands caught the edge of the table. With a heave, he tipped the table over into Stone's lap. The mate, starting to rise and reaching towards his waistband, let out a yell as plates, cups and other contents of the table cascaded into his lap. Pure instinct caused him to rise and back off hurriedly. His legs became entangled with his chair and it tipped over, bringing him crashing to the floor.

Smee began to rise, his face working and mouth opening to say, or shout, something. Under the circumstances Dusty did not dare waste time learning which. Coming erect as he hurled over the table, the small Texan pivoted and delivered a karate forward stamping kick which caught Smee in the centre of his chest, chopped off his speech unsaid and pitched him and his chair over.

'Get the hell out of here, Belle!' Dusty barked. 'It's a trap.'

Even as Dusty made his first move, Belle had been thrusting back her chair. Stone's continued silence had first aroused her suspicions, taken with the fact that she had not seen the man and been introduced to an entirely different first mate while in England. Nor had his breach of European table manners gone unnoticed by the girl. Belle had also seen the steward's knife, recognizing it for what it was. Everything added up to a highly disturbing fact. Somehow or other, she and Dusty had walked into trouble. Stone's silence meant that if he spoke, his accent would give him away as not being British. One did not need to be a mental genius to figure things out after reaching *that* conclusion.

Rising, Belle darted to the door of the cabin and pulled it open. The big seaman who brought word of the shore-boat's arrival stood outside. Seeing the girl, he sprang forward, hands lifting towards her. Belle rocked back a pace and slammed the door with all her strength; its sturdy timbers struck the man and staggered him back. Before he could recover and rush forward once more, Belle had slid home the bolts and spun around.

'Go through the night cabin and up on to the poop deck!' she shouted.

No seaman, Dusty did not know what the hell the girl meant by poop-deck; but he could only see one way out of the cabin now the main entrance was barred. Giving forth a string of good Yankee curses, the steward whipped out the naval dirk which had so interested Dusty – at that time the curved bladed variety still remained the more usual type issued to members of both U.S. and Confederate Navies and the pistol-grip handle was much favoured by Yankee seamen.

Steel rasped as the Haiman Bros. sabre slid from its sheath. Dusty cut across as the steward tried to block his way to the night cabin's door. A cry of pain burst from the man's lips as the blade of Dusty's sabre slashed into his right fore-arm. The knife clattered from a hand the steward would never use again and he reeled blindly aside, clutching at his wound as he went to his knees.

Belle made the door of the night cabin in one bound, jerking it open and running across to the companionway which led to the poop-deck entrance. Throwing a glance at Stone as the man rose and leapt towards the cased *epee de combat*, Dusty decided to put off a fight until after he warned his friends of their danger. Darting through the night cabin's door, he slammed it to and sprang across to the companionway, passing Belle without formality. One shove threw open the hatch cover and Dusty swung out on to the raised poop-deck. Already two of the seamen made their way towards the deck, cutlasses which had been kept hidden, but ready for use, gripped in their hands.

'Red!' Dusty roared, leaping to meet the men as they swarmed up the companionway. 'It's a trap. Yeeah, Texas Light!'

In the shore-boat, which held all their property ready for a hurried departure on going aboard the *Lancastrian*, Red and the others heard Dusty's yell mingle with startled, pure Yankee curses from the watching seaman at the head of the gangway. Even as the significance of the seamen's speech struck Red, he saw them produce cutlasses.

'Yeeah!' he yelled in answer to Dusty's war shout. 'Cold steel, Billy Jack. Watch the boatman, Major, Dick. Let's go. Up and at 'em, Texas Light!'

Remembering the warnings given by the French about

breaches of neutrality, Red thought fast and gave a necessary order. While a sword fight might pass unnoticed from the shore, one could be certain that the sound of shooting would attract attention. Apparently the Yankees appreciated that fact as well as did the Texans, for they met Red and Billy Jack's rush with cold steel instead of lead.

Belle drew herself on to the poop-deck as Dusty met the first rush from below and looked to see how she might best help out. A sound from below took her attention and she looked back in the direction from which she fled. *Epee* in hand, Stone burst from the day cabin and rushed up the companionway. While he saw Belle, he made the mistake of dismissing her as a factor. Going on his knowledge of Southern girls, gained in the days before the War, Stone expected Belle to do no more than scream a warning to the Texan who would most likely have plenty on his hands without that distraction.

Resting his sword hand on the edge of the hatch, Stone forced himself upwards. Like a flash, Belle raised her right leg and stamped it down hard. The high heel of her boot spiked into the back of Stone's hand, bringing a startled yelp and causing him to release his hold of the *epee*. Even as the sword clattered to the deck, Belle brought off a stamping kick to Stone's face and tumbled him back down the companionway. A glance across the deck warned her that she must help Dusty – and quickly before it was too late.

At first, Dusty held the two men from gaining a foothold on the poop-deck. Then he saw a third sailor in the act of swinging up from the main deck so as to climb the rail and attack from the flank. A swift bound to the rear carried Dusty into position, but he knew there would not be time to turn and use his sabre. Instead his left arm lashed around, the back of his fist driving full into the climbing man's face and pitching him off his perch. While he had removed one danger, Dusty saw that the other two seamen had reached the deck and came rushing at him, one slightly ahead of the other.

Around and out lashed the leading man's cutlass. Dusty shot back his left leg and went into a near-perfect turning *passata sotto*. As the cutlass hissed over his head, Dusty thrust upward. The point of his sabre bit in under his attacker's breast bone and drove up to split his heart.

Unable to reach Dusty with his blade, due to his companion blocking his way, the second man launched out a kick. The tip of his heavy seaboot smashed into Dusty's right shoulder and flung the young Texan over. Dusty's arm went numb and the sabre fell from his hand as he went rolling to the edge of the deck. At which point Belle took a very effective hand. A jerk at her waistband freed the skirt and she bounded clear to rush across the deck. For a vital instant the shock of her actions froze the seaman into immobility. While Belle had taken the precaution of wearing her riding breeches under the skirt, she still presented an eye-catching picture – more so to a man who had been at sea and away from female company for several months.

Sheer instinct made him beat at the flickering blade of Belle's *epee* and he realized that the girl meant her attack. Already two more men, one with his nose running blood, were climbing to the poop-deck and Belle knew she needed help.

'Red!' she shrieked, lunging and driving her *epee* into the first man's forearm. 'Get up here quickly!'

While willing to obey, Red found carrying out the request difficult. He and Billy Jack might be better hands with a sword than the two men blocking their path, but fighting upwards put them at a disadvantage. It was all the two Texans could do to hold off the slashes launched at them and neither found chance to make an offensive. Watching from the shore-boat, Amesley thrust himself to his feet and mounted the ladder. Behind him, Dusty's striker remained watching the Mexican boatman and protecting the party's baggage. Advancing until he stood behind the two Texans, Amesley drew his *epee*. For a moment he waited, then saw his chance. Out flickered the blade, passing between Red and Billy Jack to sink into the thigh of one of their attackers. Jumping forward, Red smashed the hilt of his sabre against the side of the wounded man's head before he recovered from the shock of the sudden attack. The seaman hit the side of the gangway and plunged into the water. A moment later his companion went reeling back from a cut to the body launched by the gangling sergeant-major.

'Get to Dusty quick!' Amesley ordered.

Springing to the head of the gangway, Red and Billy Jack raced towards the stern and hoped they might arrive in time. Bursting from the entrance where he had been guarding the

*Lancastrian*'s crew, a seaman charged along the deck. Amesley halted and met the attack. While handicapped by his injured leg, he still retained the marvellous control of his sword which made him famous as a *maitre d'armes*. Clumsy slashing had never been a match for the skilled use of a point; and so it proved. Two quick parries, then a lunge and Amesley's *epee* tore into the sailor's body, dropping him bleeding to the deck.

On the poop Belle displayed her skill with a sword by holding back the attackers who tried to get by her. Fighting desperately, she gave Dusty time to rise. With his right arm still numb and useless, Dusty bent and caught up the sabre in his left hand. He came alongside Belle, caught a slash launched at him, deflected it and laid open its deliverer's belly by a quick *riposte*. Then he saw Stone appear once more at the hatch top. Before he could disengage from the seaman, Dusty watched Stone make the deck. Turning, the small Texan left Belle to handle the seaman and sprang to meet the advancing Stone.

Never had the ambidextrous ability Dusty developed as a boy – a kind of defence to draw people's attention from his lack of height – been of such use. With his right arm too numb and sore to be of use, he could still handle the sabre almost as well with his left. In fact the left-hand style of fighting, which Dusty adopted completely, gave Stone, used to handling opponents who fought from the right, some trouble. Taken with the fact that Stone had become accustomed to wielding a naval sword designed, like the sabre, for cut-and-slash tactics, Dusty's left-hand style kept him alive. Even so he knew it would be a close thing in his present condition. The two men came up close, sword hilts locking together. At one side Belle gave a quick glance at the men as they strained against each other and she knew the fight must be concluded speedily before somebody on shore noticed it and informed the authorities.

'Dusty!' she called, parrying her man's slashing attack which came too fast for her to get home a thrust in reply. 'Re – member – family – motto—'

Up went her left hand, tearing off her hat and wig and flinging them into the seaman's face. Blinded and amazed at seeing the girl apparently tear off all her hair in one pull, the man staggered back. Like a flash Belle lunged and the *epee* took the man in the forearm causing him to drop his cutlass. He reeled back, struck the edge of the rail and fell to the deck.

Dusty's right foot rose and stamped down hard on to Stone's instep in a manner taught to him by Tommy Okasi. Pain knifed into Stone, causing him to yell and relax the pressure he put against Dusty's sabre. With a heave, Dusty thrust the man from him and Belle, turning from spitting the seaman, thrust her *epee* home. Steel bit through flesh, gliding between the ribs and into Stone's body. He stiffened, the weapon clattering from his hand as his knees buckled under him and he crumpled to the floor.

'Thanks, Belle!' Dusty said and sprang to the side of the deck.

Down below a battle raged between Red, Billy Jack and the remaining three Yankee sailors. Even as Dusty looked, Billy Jack received a slash across his shoulder, but Red ran one man through. Dusty's arm whipped back and he hurled his sabre downwards like a man throws a dart. Swinging up his cutlass to deliver a *coup-de-grace* to Billy Jack, the man who wounded the sergeant-major arched his back and fell, Dusty's thrown sabre sunk into his spine.

Seeing what had happened and that the small Texan left himself weaponless, Belle scooped up Stone's *epee* by hooking the point of her blade into its hilt.

'Dusty!' she called and flipped the weapon forward.

Catching the flying *epee*, Dusty started down the stairs to the deck and Belle followed him. Finding themselves outnumbered, the last two sailors threw down their cutlasses and surrendered.

'Now maybe somebody'll tell *me* what the hell this's all about,' Red growled.

'Secure the prisoners, Red,' Dusty answered, by way of explanation. 'Then start getting the baggage aboard. How is it, Billy Jack?'

'Hurts like hell, but I'll live,' the gangling non-com replied.

'Happen you don't,' Dusty said sympathetically, 'stay alive until after you help with the prisoners.'

With that, Dusty turned and looked around the poop-deck. Seeing Belle disappearing into the cabin, Dusty ordered the wounded men to go down to the main deck and then bounded after her.

## CHAPTER SIXTEEN

## CAPTAIN SMEE DELIVERS
## HIS CARGO

'You dirty, double-dealing, foul hound!' Belle hissed, her *epee* resting its needle-tip on Smee's adam's apple and holding him against the day cabin's wall. 'I ought to kill you.'

'It – it wasn't of my own free will!' Smee gurgled, eyes bulging in terror. 'That Yankee ironclad ran alongside me out beyond sight of land. Had me under its guns. I daren't disobey—'

'So you sold me out!' the girl purred, sounding as menacing as a she-cougar protecting her young.

'No!' Smee howled. 'They knew about my cargo. Put a boarding party here and told me if I caused them any trouble, they'd sink me out there without letting anybody get away to tell tales. I had to do what they said.'

'So?'

'Stone, he's the captain of the ironclad, and his men came aboard. They locked all my crew who weren't needed to work ship up forward, then stowed the rest away after we dropped anchor. I never told them who you might be. They knew it all along. Stone and his men dressed as civilians. That was why I left the case with the swords out, he couldn't wear his own, didn't dare use a revolver, and wanted a weapon handy without causing suspicion. I had to do what they said, I tell you. I just had to.'

'Can you get this ship out of here right away, Captain?' Dusty asked from the door.

'Near enough,' Smee agreed.

'Then free your crew and do it.'

'But—' Smee began.

'Mister,' Dusty growled. 'You make me one bit more trouble and I'll kill you where you stand. Then if I can't have the arms for the Confederacy, I'll see that nobody else gets them.'

'All I wanted to say was that the ironclad's still laying off shore,' Smee quavered. 'If she sees us coming out, she'll want to know why.'

'Likely,' Dusty agreed. 'In which case, we'll have to think up some mighty smart answers.'

The officer of the watch aboard the U.S. *Sinclair* lifted his speaking trumpet as he watched the *Lancastrian* approach through the gathering darkness.

'*Lancastrian* ahoy!' he bellowed. 'Captain Stone, sir!'

Sweat trickled down Smee's face as he prepared to reply. The barrel of Dusty's right-hand Colt bored encouragingly into Smee's ribs.

'Captain Stone took the rebels,' Smee called back. 'He and his men have gone ashore with their prisoners at Brownsville. He said for you to go in and take him aboard.'

Dusty stood at Smee's side and waited for what seemed like a very long time. Aboard the *Sinclair*, the first lieutenant gave a satisfied grunt. Maybe something had happened to change Stone's original plan for returning in the *Lancastrian*. Possibly his captain wanted a show of force on hand to impress the French garrison. Lifting his speaking trumpet, he pointed it towards the other ship.

'All right. Now get the hell out of here; and the next time we see you in our waters, we'll ram you – by accident.'

Slowly the two ships parted, the *Sinclair* heading towards Brownsville and the *Lancastrian* making due west – until out of sight of the other. Then she swung to the south and the waiting *Snow Queen*.

'We brought it off, Dusty,' Belle breathed as she came from the captain's night cabin and looked astern to the tiny lights which marked the departing ironclad.

'So far,' Dusty agreed. 'All we have to do now is find the *Snow Queen*, transfer the arms to her, put Stone and his men ashore, and run the Yankee blockade to land the arms.'

Belle smiled and looked at the small – no, she would never think of Dusty Fog as being small – man whose courage, reasoning power and guts had done so much to make her mission a success.

'I've a feeling we'll do it too.'

Belle's feeling proved to be correct. After an uneventful

voyage, and a narrow escape, the *Snow Queen* slipped through the waters of Atchafalaya Bay one night and delivered a cargo of arms, bought by Yankee gold, to Morgan City.

THE END

# The Rebel Spy

For Roy Toon, The Demon P.H.G.

# Chapter 1

## A Uniform of Cadet-Grey

While Captain Wormold, 5th Illinois Cavalry, did not profess to be a nervous man, he decided that he would feel a whole heap happier on completion of his present assignment. Not only did he have to take three wagons and a Rocker ambulance loaded with supplies across Arkansas to the Indian Nation outposts, but the real high brass saddled him with that damned runty civilian and gave all kinds of orders regarding his safety.

Any Union Army officer looked on supply-escort duty with misgivings. The rebels might be meeting with defeats back East and the tide of the War apparently turning in favour of the Union, but in Arkansas the Southerners gave no sign of following the general trend. From the time General Ole Devil Hardin assumed command over the Confederate States' Army of Arkansas, he not only halted the Yankee advance across the Bear State but inflicted defeats and held the Union Army on the verge of retreat. Given more men, arms, equipment, Ole Devil might even have pushed the enemy back, but the South could supply no further aid. So he held his position on the western banks of the Ouachita River and forced the Yankees to expend efforts that could be better used in breaking down resistance in the main Southern States.

The Northern States used their industrial superiority to produce new weapons and means of waging war. Already their blockade of the South threatened the Confederate's existence. New Orleans and much of the lower Mississippi lay in Yankee hands. While European countries might be willing to trade supplies for Southern cotton, the U.S. Navy held down the shipments to a minimum.

Despite all his difficulties, Ole Devil Hardin held on in Arkansas. Just a shade bitterly, Wormold realised that the North helped make Ole Devil's success possible. Wanting to strike down the heart of the South, the Federal Government concentrated its main efforts on the eastern battle-fronts. Little could be spared to allow the Union soldiers in Arkansas regain their ascendancy over the rebels. Supplies came, but a tendency developed to withdraw seasoned troops to go East and replace them with raw,

7

inexperienced men. Matched against the battle-tried veterans of the Confederate Army, who fought in conditions ideally suited to their ways, the superior numbers of the North achieved nothing.

More than that, it seemed the rebels relied on the Union Army to supply them with the specialised needs of an army in the field. Being Texas-born, the majority of Ole Devil's command were past-masters in the Napoleonic art of making war support war. Trained almost from birth by war against Indians, they turned the redskins' tactics to their advantage and, using the methods of their enemies, drew their needs from the unwilling hands of the Yankees.

A supply convoy like the one under Wormold's protection carried many items which the rebels would only be too pleased to acquire. Which accounted for why a full troop rode as its escort. While Wormold's troop fell some thirty short of the desired one hundred men complement, they carried Sharps carbines—the best general-issue arm at that time available—and, he believed, could put up a respectable defence against the normal run of rebel raiding force.

Of course other men had felt the same way; only to return in shame with a tale of soldiers killed and badly-needed supplies swept off to further the Southern cause.

Wormold felt again the bitterness at a fate which put him on the Arkansas battlefront when most of his West Point class-mates served in the East, with its attendant chances of distinction and acclaim. There would be little credit given at the successful conclusion of the escort duty, unless he should also bring off a victorious defence against raiding rebels. Even then the news would rate only a couple of columns on the inside pages of the important Eastern newspapers; and not even that should more important news be available.

Should he fail to bring off the assignment due to enemy action, it would be remembered against him beyond all proportion to recognition for success. So Wormold determined to take no chances. All day he kept his best men—a relative term when so few veterans were available to stiffen the ranks of green recruits —out on the flanks, ahead and to the rear, and receive no reports of sighting the enemy. By pushing the wagons hard, he hoped to have passed beyond the area in which the rebel cavalry concentrated their main efforts.

When night came, he set up camp on the shores of a small lake. While he might have hoped for more open land around him, he realised that such would not be available even should he

8

push on after watering the horses. A career soldier, Wormold knew his business and went about it in the dying light of day. Holding half his command as a grand guard by the wagons, he split the remainder into four picket sections and sent each group out some five hundred yards on the major points of the compass. Nor did they form the sole defence. Each picket placed out an arc of three vedettes, mounted sentries, between three and four hundred yards beyond them. Finally two mounted men rode a beat between each picket and the grand guard. Wormold would have a tired command the following morning, but felt the means justified the end as another day's hard travel ought to see them in safe territory.

Setting up the pickets and establishing the vedettes took time, and called for the efforts of Wormold, the first and second lieutenants, first sergeant, five sergeants and three corporals. Standing by the fire built for him, Wormold glanced at his watch and found the time to be almost ten o'clock. Cooking pots bubbled on section fires and steam rose, wafting the tempting aroma of coffee, from the muckets, as the troopers called the small 3-pint capacity kettles issued to them. Although the carbines had been piled by the men, they stood close enough to hand should an alarm be raised by one of the circle of watching sentries.

Satisfied that he had taken every precaution to safeguard the convoy, Wormold decided to join his two subordinate officers as they sat chatting to the small, dapper civilian who perched, as always, on the wooden box which formed his most prominent item of luggage. Wondering what might be in the carefully locked and watched-over box, Wormold became aware of a man walking from the darkness towards him. While he realised that something was wrong, his mind refused to accept the obvious answer given by his eyes.

Man might not be the correct term for the newcomer, for he looked to be in his late 'teens. Although not more than five foot six in height, his shoulders had a width that hinted at strength and he tapered down to a slim waist. His uniform differed in a number of respects from that worn by the 5th Illinois Cavalry. Not his boots, or tight-legged riding breeches, at first glance, for they conformed to regulations, even to the cavalry-yellow stripe down the pants legs. First major difference was his weapon belt. It hung a shade lower than usually seen, two matched white-handled Colt 1860 Army revolvers butt forward in holsters that not only lacked a top but left half the cylinder and all the trigger-guard exposed while being built to the contours of the guns. That started the differences. The tunic carried them even further.

9

Ending at his waist, it lacked the skirt 'hanging half-way between hip and knee', had a double row of buttons and stand-up collar which bore on either side triple three-inch long, half-inch wide gold braid bars; these served instead of decorated epaulettes as a means of knowing the wearer's rank. Instead of a cravat, the newcomer had a tight-rolled scarlet silk scarf which trailed its ends down over his tunic. Shoved back on his head, a white Davis campaign hat showed curly, dusty blond hair and a tanned, handsome young face with lines of strength and determination etched on it. The hat carried a different insignia to the United States shield inside a half wreath and bearing a bugle with the letter 'M' in its handle ring, being, like the Texas coat of arms, a five-pointed star in a circle.

Despite a growing tendency to standardise uniforms and equipment within the Union Army, some regiments still retained their individual style of dress. A few continued to wear sleeve decorations, but not that double braid 'chicken-guts' adorning the small newcomer's arms. And no *Federal* outfit wore uniforms coloured cadet-grey.

Still Wormold could not credit his eyes with seeing correctly, even though everything he saw told him the other did not belong to any *Yankee* regiment.

"Howdy, Captain," greeted the small newcomer, his voice a pleasant Texas drawl. "That coffee sure smells good."

"Coff—!" began Wormold, all coherent thought struck from him by the sight of a captain in the Texas Light Cavalry calmly strolling into a Union Camp.

From their lack of reaction to the sight, his men failed to realise their danger. Wormold let out a low hiss and reached towards his holstered revolver. The small Texan's left hand made a sight-defying flip across to and drew the right side Army Colt, thumbing back the hammer and sliding the forefinger on to the trigger as, not before, the barrel cleared leather and slanted towards Wormold. In a bare three-quarters of a second Wormold found himself looking into the levelled muzzle of a cocked revolver. The Yankee captain's hand had not even reached the flap of his holster.

"Your camp's surrounded, Captain," warned the Texan. "I don't want to kill your men, so tell them to surrender."

Already the occupants of the camp realised that something *far* out of the ordinary was taking place. Realisation did not bring reaction fast enough. By the time the Yankees shook themselves out of the shock caused by the small Texan's appearance, they learned he did not come alone. Suddenly, rising out of the ground it seemed, grey-clad soldiers appeared holding lined guns. Wormold needed only one swift glance to know the futility of resistance. Long before his men could reach their piled carbines, or draw revolvers, Texas lead would tear into them. Nor did the casually competent manner in which the Texans handled their weapons lead him to believe that they lacked ability in the shooting line. There might be a chance if—

"We'd've been here sooner," drawled the small Texan and killed Wormold's hope stone dead. "But it took us time to nail down all your pickets and vedettes." Then his voice took on a harder tone as his eyes, darting from point to point, saw something of importance. "Tell that green shavetail to sit fast before he dies a hero and gets a lot of men killed for no good reason."

The warning came just in time. Already Wormold's second lieutenant, showing more courage than good sense or judgement of the situation, tensed and sent his hand creeping towards his holster. If the shavetail drew, he would die and in doing so provoke an incident that might easily see Wormold's entire troop wiped out.

No coward, Wormold was also not a fool. He must balance the lives of the majority of his men against the very slender chance of saving the convoy. There could be only one answer. Surrender, let the wagons be taken, but save his men to fight another day.

"Sit still, Mr. Benson!" he barked. "Get your hand away from that gun."

"Now that's a whole heap more comfy," the small Texan remarked as Benson obeyed. "I'd be obliged, Captain, if you'd order your men to lie face down on the ground and with hands spread out."

Sucking in a bitter breath, Wormold gave the required command and watched his men obey it. Maybe his troops lacked veterans, but the men recognised the danger well enough not to resist the small Texan's wishes.

"Pluck their stings, Cousin Red," the Texan told his tall, well-built, freckle-faced and pugnaciously handsome first lieutenant, a youngster no older than the rebel captain and with a thatch of fiery red hair showing under his campaign hat.

Clearly every detail had been arranged. Without waste of time, half-a-dozen men moved forward under the lieutenant's command to collect the piled carbines and remove revolvers from Yankee holsters.

"Sharps linen cartridge breech-loaders, Cousin Dusty," enthused the lieutenant. "These boys're loaded for bear."

11

While the linen-cartridge firing Sharps lacked the Henry or Spencer repeaters' rate of fire, ammunition for them could be made in the South. So the Sharps found greater favour than the more advanced guns, which needed metal-case bullets, items only obtainable through the enemy and in short supply even there.

"We'll requisition them then," smiled the small Texan. "See them guarded, Red. Billy Jack, check what's in the wagons."

"Yo!" answered the tall, gangling, miserable-looking rebel sergeant major. "It's about time the Yankees shipped out some decent guns for us."

"I reckon I'd best have the officers' guns while I'm at it," remarked the lieutenant.

"It'd likely be best," agreed the Texas captain.

While handing over his weapon belt, Wormold raked his captor from head to toe with disbelieving eyes. Having heard the small Texan's first name, a thought sprang immediately to mind; yet Wormold wondered if it could be possible.

Could that small, almost insignificant appearing youngster—he would be no more than eighteen, and a young eighteen at that—be the man rated by many as among Dixie's top three fighting cavalry commanders? Was it possible that he might be the rebel who, in Arkansas, stood even higher than Turner Ashby or John Singleton Mosby? The man who voluntarily went behind the Union lines to give evidence at the court-martial of a Yankee officer falsely accused of cowardice and while there killed a much-disliked Federal general in a duel.* Or he whose raids over the Ouachita left havoc in their wake, while causing many a Yankee officer of great age and seniority to curse in impotent rage and wish he fought a more orthodox enemy.

Looking at the smart, disciplined efficiency of the Texans, Wormold concluded that he guessed right. By the worse kind of lousy luck, he had fallen foul of Dusty Fog. The smoothness with which the whole affair had been carried out showed a dash and flair few men could produce. Efficiency of that kind came only through excellent leadership. Not an imaginative man, Wormold could still almost picture the silent stalking which captured his vedettes and pickets before any of them might sound the alarm. That alone called for a degree of planning and organisation far beyond the normal run of officers.

"May I join you at supper after we've finished, Captain?" asked the small Texan. "My name is Fogg, Captain Dustine Edward Marsden Fog, at your service—up to a point."

"I called it right!" Wormold screamed mentally. "He *is* Dusty

*Told in *"The Fastest Gun in Texas"*.

Fog!" Then he stiffened into a brace. Hell's fire; he would be eternally damned if he allowed that rebel kid to out-do him in courtesy, or allowed the other to see just how he felt about being captured. So he drew himself to a brace and saluted. "It'll be my pleasure, Captain Fog. Wormold, Captain Rupert Ainsley Wormold."

Moving forward, Dusty's bugler gathered up Wormold's discarded weapon belt and looked into its holster. "It's a Starr, Cap'n Dusty," he said in a disgusted tone, showing the revolver.

"Unload it and put it back," Dusty answered and holstered his Colt.

One of Red Blaze's section stood alongside Lieutenant Benson, holding the officer's highly-prized Spencer carbine in his hands. Still seated, Benson glared fury up at the soldier as the latter spoke to Dusty.

"This here's a mighty fancy gun, Cap'n Dusty."

"Damn you!" Benson spat, face twisted in anger and mortification. "My mo—."

At a signal from Dusty, the soldier tossed the carbine over. As he claimed, it proved to be a fine piece, with a better finish and furnishings than the usual run of issue carbines.

"A private arm, mister?" Dusty asked.

"Yes—sir," Benson replied, the second word popping out before he could stop it.

"His mother presented it to him, Captain Fog," Wormold explained in a low voice.

Opening the magazine trap, Dusty caught the spring, slid it clear and tipped seven bullets from the tube into his palm. Pocketing the bullets, he worked the lever which formed the triggerguard and ejected the round from the breech. Then he offered the carbine butt first to Benson.

"With my compliments, mister," Dusty said and nodded to the special pouch containing ten loaded magazine tubes. "I'll have to take your ammunition, though."

"Thank you, sir," Benson answered and this time there was no hesitation in using the formal honorific.

"What's in the wagons, Billy Jack?" Dusty called, leaving Benson.

"Powder, lead, made bullets, linen cartridges for a starter, Cap'n Dusty," answered the sergeant major, sounding as mournful as if they were the prisoners and about to lose the convoy. "General stores in the others."

"Take them when we pull out," ordered Dusty. "Go through

13

the Rocker ambulance and turn out the medical supplies. Take one third of them."

"A third?" Wormold could not stop himself saying.

"We're short on medical supplies too, Captain," Dusty replied. "But I figure you have more casualties needing tending than we do."

Which, unpalatable as the thought might be, was perfectly true. Wormold felt a growing admiration for the small, young Texan and began to appreciate how Dusty won fame at an age when he should have just been starting in a military academy. The feeling did little to numb Wormold's sense of failure, however. Dusty Fog could act with his usual chivalry; return a mother's gift; prevent looting of personal property and abuse of captives; take only such medical supplies as his people needed; but he would leave Wormold's command without weapons, horses or equipment when he pulled out.

Already the disarmed Yankees had been allowed to sit up in lines, watched over by alert sentries. At the horse lines a sergeant and three men examined the Union mounts and exchanged laconic terms of Texas disgust when finding signs of inexperience-caused neglect. Born in a land where a horse was a way of life rather than a mere means of transport, they felt little but disgust for the Yankees from the industrial East, many of whom rode seriously for the first time on enlistment.

Having faith in his men, Dusty left them to their duties with the minimum of supervision. While looking around the camp, his eyes came to rest on the small civilian who still sat on the wooden box and had apparently been overlooked by the Texans. Telling Wormold to join the other Yankee officers, Dusty turned and walked towards the small man.

"I'm a civilian, not a soldier," the man yelped as Dusty drew near. "Henry S. Oliver, clerk to the Baptist Mission For Indian Betterment."

"Some of them sure need bettering," Dusty replied. "What's in the box, Mr. Oliver?"

"Religious tracts. The Good Book translated into the heathen Cherokee tongue so that the savages too may be shown the light."

"Mind if I take a look?"

"Do officers of the Confederate States Army rob civilians and men of the church?" demanded Oliver hotly, coming to his feet and walking forward.

"If tracts are all inside, they'll not be touched," Dusty promised. "Open it up, sir."

"Woe is the day when the work of the Lord shall be put down

14

by the un-godly and His servants beset by evil-doers!" moaned Oliver. "Can't you take my word as to the contents, brother?"

"As a man, yes," Dusty replied. "But as an officer with a duty to do, I'll have to see inside the box."

"Very well then," sighed Oliver resignedly and produced a key from his jacket pocket. "But I will not condone the Devil's work by opening it."

"See to it, Billy Jack," ordered Dusty and a faint smile flickered on his lips. "I reckon you're sinful enough for this not to make any difference."

"Happen it does," drawled the sergeant major, "I'll certain sure let you know about it."

With that, Billy Jack took the key and walked towards the box.

## Chapter 2

# A Box Full of Confederate Money

"Hold it, Billy Jack!"

The words cracked from Dusty's lips and brought the sergeant major to an immediate halt. Turning, he looked at his commander and waited to be told what caused the change of plans.

Almost three years of war and danger gave Dusty an instinct, or second sense which warned him of peril. Suddenly he became aware of the familiar sensations; something was wrong and he wondered what. Swiftly his mind ran through the sequence of events. He felt sure that the box contained articles more significant than mere religious tracts. If anything, Oliver spoke too glibly; and dressed wrongly for a member of an obscure church mission organisation.

When handing over the key to Billy Jack, Oliver for a moment lost his air of martyrdom. Only for a moment did it go, but during that time the man showed hate, disappointment and a little satisfaction. For some reason Oliver wanted them to undertake the actual opening of the box. In fact he had fallen back as Billy Jack approached it and stood so as to place Dusty between him and the sergeant major. All that had registered subconciously to Dusty, triggering off his warning instincts and causing him to stop Billy Jack. Unless Dusty was sadly wrong, Billy Jack might regret opening the box should he do so.

"What's up, Cap'n Dusty?" Billy Jack asked.

"Leave it," Dusty replied. "We'll take it back unopened."

"Let me do it for you," Oliver offered, stepping by Dusty and speaking in a voice which sounded just a mite shakey.

"Stop right there!" Dusty ordered. "I'm taking it back—."

"All right," answered Oliver and shrugged his shoulders.

In doing so, he pressed his left elbow against his side in what appeared to be a casual manner. Almost immediately his cuff jerked in a peculiar manner and a Henry Deringer Pocket Pistol slid from the sleeve into his hand. Smoothly done, the move showed long practice in controlling the pistol and its holster, which was built on the same lines as a card hold-out device used by crooked gamblers. Most people would have been taken by surprise by the sudden appearance of the pistol.

Dusty Fog proved to be an exception. Back home in the Rio Hondo country, he learned gun-handling from men well-versed in all its aspects. Part of his training covered concealment of weapons and the various methods by which a hidden pistol might be produced unexpectedly yet suddenly. Fortunately he had been watching the man, or he might have missed the elbow pressure required to set the hold-out's springs working.

Seeing the danger, a lesser person might easily have panicked, drawn, cut Oliver down and possibly have created a chain-reaction of shooting among the guards over the prisoners. Despite the urgency, Dusty realised the delicate nature of the situation and refrained from using his Colt as a means of recti-fying it. All too well he could see the Yankee enlisted men's reactions to the sight of a rebel officer shooting down a man of the church; as they imagined Oliver to be.

Realising that, Dusty acted accordingly. Even as he went into action, he became aware of Oliver's peculiar behaviour.

At the sight of the pistol, Billy Jack discarded his pose of lack-adaisical misery and showed himself to be a bone-tough Texas fighting man. Flinging himself to one side and down, he drew his right hand Colt while dropping to the ground. It appeared that he moved so fast, he caught Oliver unprepared. Certainly the small civilian made no attempt to correct his aim and con-tinued to line the Deringer at the box. So Billy Jack held his fire. Being all too familiar with Dusty's deadly speed, Billy Jack knew the small Texan could easily have drawn and shot Oliver. As he did not, Cap'n Dusty clearly required the man alive and Billy Jack respected his commanding officer's wants.

From where he stood, Dusty could follow the way in which Oliver lined the gun. The hesitation in following Billy Jack's diving body did not go with the smooth manner by which Oliver produced the hide-out pistol. Nor did there appear to be any point in the man shooting Billy Jack *after* the sergeant major turned away from the box. To Dusty's way of thinking, Oliver intended to hit the box—and a particular part of it at that.

Having reached that conclusion in a flickering blur of thought, Dusty set about dealing with the matter. He acted with the kind of speed that would in the future gain him the name as the fastest gun in Texas.

Out shot his hands, but he did not waste valuable time in trying to knock the gun from Oliver's grasp. Catching the man's right wrist between his hands, with the thumbs uppermost and fingers around the joint bones, Dusty pivoted to the left until standing almost with his back to and behind Oliver. Then he

17

drew the trapped arm until it was held before him and slid his left hand along to close over the pistol-filled fist. The action caused Oliver to lose his balance and stumble. Swiftly Dusty reversed the direction of the man by stepping back a pace and twisting on the wrist. Oliver went down on to his back, but the pain caused by his wrist and the momentum of his fall caused him to turn right over and land face down. Stepping around the man's head, Dusty turned the pistol and drew it from the clutching fingers.

As Oliver went over, he let out a screech far in excess of the pain he received. At the sound Benson began to rise, hot anger showing on his young face. Seeing an apparently unprovoked attack on the little civilian, he forgot all his previous thoughts on Dusty's chivalry. An uneasy ripple of movement passed through the seated ranks of Yankee prisoners and the watching Texans hefted their weapons to a more convenient position ready for use.

"Sit still!" ordered Red Blaze, twisting his right hand palm out and drawing the off-side Colt cavalry-style, to line it on Benson.

"Do it, damn you!" snapped Wormold, alert to the danger his shavetail's behaviour threatened to create. "First sergeant, make the men stay still." Then he glared at Red. "Does the Texas Light Cavalry make a habit of assaulting civilians, Mr. Blaze?"

"Likely Dusty had good reason," Red replied loyally. "Let's wait and see, shall we?"

"We'll do that," Wormold agreed, conscious that he could do no other.

"Lemme up!" Oliver whined. "I'm through."

Releasing the man's wrists, Dusty stepped clear. Already Billy Jack had regained his feet and stood looking at Dusty, wondering what the hell was going on. Moving slowly, as if hurt by his fall, Oliver raised himself on to hands and knees. Suddenly he flung himself forward, in the direction of the box. Out shot Billy Jack's right arm, catching Oliver by the scruff of the neck as he passed and heaving him backwards. Even so, the small man lashed a kick at the box and his boot narrowly missed colliding with its lock. Then he went staggering backwards in Dusty's direction.

At the second attempt by Oliver to destroy the box—for Dusty felt sure that lay behind the civilian's actions—the small Texan called off being gentle. As Oliver reeled towards him, Dusty struck in a certain way taught to him by his uncle, Ole Devil Hardin's personal servant. Although many people thought Tommy Okasi was Chinese, he claimed to hail from the Japanese islands. Wherever he came from originally, Tommy pos-

18

sessed some mighty effective fighting tricks and taught them to the smallest member of the Hardin, Fog and Blaze clan. Using the *ju-jitsu* or *karate* techniques passed to him by Tommy Okasi, Dusty could handle bigger and stronger men with comparative ease. Nor did his knowledge hinder him in dealing with Oliver.

Around lashed Dusty's right arm, the hand held open with fingers together and thumb bent across the palm. Its heel chopped hard against the base of Oliver's skull in the *tegatana*, handsword, of *karate*. While such a method looked awkward and might be judged unlikely to be effective by a man trained in Occidental fist-fighting. Dusty had no cause to complain. On receiving the blow, Oliver dropped like a head-shot rabbit and lay still.

"Hawg-tie him, Billy Jack," Dusty ordered.

"Yo!" answered the sergeant major and looked around. "Hey, Tracey Prince, bring over some rope from that centre wagon."

One of the troopers obeyed and Billy Jack swiftly secured Oliver. Dusty looked around the camp, seeing sullen resentment on Yankee faces and interest among his own men. However the Texans still had the situation well under control and Dusty aimed to keep it that way.

"What in hell made him act that ways, Cap'n Dusty?" asked Billy Jack after completing his task.

"Damned if I know," Dusty replied. "Give me the key and I reckon I'll find out about it."

Walking to the box, Dusty circled and studied it. By all outer appearances, Oliver took a lot of trouble and considerable risk for nothing. The box was maybe three foot long, by two high and deep, made of white pine, with a built-in lock to its hinged lid. Although Dusty held the key in his hand, he did not offer to use it. Unless he missed his guess, Oliver tried first to drive a bullet into the lock and then kick it. Not to jam its mechanism, for that would delay the opening only the few minutes required to smash through the lid.

So why did Oliver chance being killed by trying to shoot at the lock?

Slowly Dusty turned the box on end and examined its sides, but he saw nothing in their design of workmanship to interest him. Then he looked at the bottom. It had a stout framework screwed firmly around its edges to hold the base on to the sides.

"Never saw a box with its bottom screwed on afore, Cap'n Dusty," commented Billy Jack, standing behind the small Texan.

"Likely there's a good reason for it," Dusty answered. "Guidon!" The company's guidon-carrier came over from where he had stood awaiting orders. "Fetch me a screw-driver from one of the wagons."

"Yo!" answered the young man who carried the Company's identifying pennant on the march, while attending to the commanding officer's mount as required.

While waiting for the screw-driver, Dusty collected Oliver's Deringer from where it lay on the ground and walked over to the Union officers' fire.

"Why d'you reckon a man of the church carried a Deringer, Captain Wormold?" he asked, showing the small pistol to them.

"You mean he tried to shoot you?" asked Wormold.

"Something like that."

"He thought you meant to rob him," suggested the first lieutenant.

"That'd be a mighty Christian way to act, mister," Dusty drawled. "Shooting a man down to save some religious tracts. Especially when I'd told him that we'd not take them were that all he carried."

"Did he know you'd keep your word?" asked the first lieutenant.

"That depends on the kind of officers he's come across on your side, mister," Dusty answered. "And remember one thing, *mister*; when he made his move, he might easy have stirred up a mess that cost damned near all your men their lives."

"But Mr. Oliver's a man of peace," Benson put in. "He'd not know the danger, Captain Fog."

"I've got the screw-driver, Cap'n," called the guidon-carrier.

"Excuse me, gentlemen," Dusty said and turned to walk back to the box.

The short talk had been a waste of time in one respect, although it enabled Dusty to clarify his position over the incident. Despite having watched carefully, he failed to detect the slightest hint that the Yankee officers knew their passenger to be other than a member of the Baptist Mission For Indian Betterment.

Taking the screw-driver, Dusty knelt by the box and went carefully to work. After removing the screws, he moved the framework and slid away the bottom board. Before his eyes lay proof that Oliver had good reason for not wanting the box open.

"Whooee!" the guidon-carrier yelped, staring down with eyes bugged out like organ stops. "I never before saw that much money in all my life."

His comment was very apt. All the interior space of the box was filled with packs of new Confederate money. While the guidon-carrier looked down and saw no more than the bare sight of the money, Dusty stared and thought. The small Texan wondered why a Yankee civilian travelling on a Union Army supply convoy would be carrying a large sum of the enemy's money.

One answer sprang straight to mind. The U.S. Secret Service maintained spy-rings throughout Texas, Arkansas and the Indian Nations and its members needed rebel money for operating expenses. Most likely Oliver acted as pay-master for them. His actions earlier proved that he knew of the box's contents and sought to destroy them before they fell into the rebels' hands.

In which case Oliver became a catch of major importance. Most likely the Confederate Secret Service would be only to pleased to have in their hands a man so high among their opposite numbers that he carried payments for Yankee spies. With any amount of luck, Company 'C' ought to return to the Regiment's headquarters in time to hand over Oliver to a person who would know the best way to deal with him.

While studying the money, Dusty became aware of the apparent thickness of the box's walls. He took out three of the pads of money from level with the lock and looked into the space. It seemed that the inside of the box had been coated with a familiar-looking material. Unless Dusty missed his guess as he ran a finger over the box's lining, the material was wet-stretched pig's intestines coated with chemicals to make them inflammable and shellacked for a water-resistant finish. Self-consuming cartridges made of the same material sometimes came his way and he could not mistake the sight or touch of the lining. Nor did he feel the solid hardness of wood beneath the pig's skin, instead it gave slightly as if some softer substance separated it from the pine.

Dusty went no further with his experiments, preferring to leave the solving of the box's mystery to hands trained in such work. He put the three pads he had taken into his pocket, then telling the guidon-carrier to secure the box's base, Dusty called Red and Billy Jack to him. They saw enough of the contents to arouse their interest.

"Could be the lil feller didn't know what was inside," Billy Jack commented.

"Happen he thought it was the church funds," Red went on with a grin.

"You're a big help," Dusty answered. "This's why he tried to put a bullet into the lock."

"That wouldn't stop us opening the box for long," Red said. "We could easy bust in the lid."

21

"Didn't need to," Billy Jack put in. "He'd already give me the key—"

"And didn't make his move until after I'd told you to leave opening it up," Dusty pointed out. "I reckon we'll let an armourer take a look at that box."

"If you're thinking what I know you're thinking," Billy Jack said fervently. "Thanks for stopping me."

"It's my pleasure," Dusty assured him. "I'd rather have the devil I know than start getting a new sergeant major used to my ways. Get ready to pull out."

"You want the usual doing, Dusty?" asked Red.

Only for a moment did Dusty hesitate. No matter how often he did it, he could never quite reconcile himself to taking horses from his enemies.

"Do the usual," he said. "Take them all."

True to the code of the Texas range country, Dusty did not lightly set a man a-foot. An old Texas saying ran, 'A man without a horse is no man at all.' To the majority of people in the Lone Star State being set a-foot ranked as the worst possible fate and not infrequently led to the horse-less one's death.

However Dusty accepted that he must take all the horses; not only because his Company expected it, but as part of his duty as an officer in the Confederate States Army. He knew that the loss of the supplies would have a great demoralising effect on the Yankees—as also would his act of leaving them two-thirds of the medical supplies—and so he put aside his distaste in the interests of his duty.

Thinking of the medical supplies brought up another point and Dusty acted on it.

"Red," he said as his cousin turned to supervise the loading of the box on to a wagon. "Pick out two horses—no, mules if they have them—and leave them as a team for the ambulance."

"It'll be mules then," Red replied.

Strolling over to the officers' fire, Dusty said, "We'll be pulling out now, Captain Wormold."

"You didn't have your cup of coffee," Wormold answered, determined to prove he could accept defeat gracefully.

"I'll have it now then," Dusty smiled, glancing around him.

Already the wagons had been prepared to move, their teams hitched up by men assigned to the duty. Another party arrived with Company 'C's' horses and Billy Jack, without waiting for instructions, ordered half of the men guarding the Yankees to mount up. Everything ran with a smooth, orderly precision which allowed no opportunity for the Yankees to make a move at changing the situation. At no time were they left without armed men ready to quell any attempt at escaping or overpowering the rebels.

"You'll find your vedettes, pickets and riding patrols hawg-tied and gagged at the picket sites," Dusty remarked, sipping at the coffee.

"Are any of them injured?" Wormold demanded.

"Sore heads and rope-burned necks is all."

That gave Wormold the picture of how and why his circle of guards failed to raise the alarm. It also did nothing to lessen his admiration for the skill showed by the Texans. Stalking a lone vedette might be fairly simple, but silencing a full picket offered greater difficulty and that did not include the collection of the communicating patrols which passed constantly between the grand guard and pickets. Yet those Texans brought it off and performed most of the delicate work without any supervision from their officers. Wormold shuddered as he thought of the noiseless approach, the silent swish as ropes flew out to settle about Yankee necks, or gun butts descended to silence any Union out-cry. If the rebels were the sadistic, blood-thirsty fiends the liberal newspapers made them appear, Wormold would be burying at least half of his command the following morning instead of freeing hands and attending to minor injuries.

Sipping appreciatively at his coffee—the Union blockade of Texas' coastline putting it among the commodities in short supply—Dusty watched the final preparations to leave. Billy Jack sent the guidon-carrier and another man to collect Oliver and carry the bound man to the wagons.

"What's this, Captain Fog?" Wormold asked.

"I'm taking Mr. Oliver along," Dusty replied.

"As a hostage?" growled the first lieutenant.

"Wake up, mister!" Dusty barked. "Oliver's carrying a box full of Confederate money. He knew what he was carrying and it's likely for distribution to Yankee spies. So he's coming with me, mister. If our brass decide he's innocent, I'll be disciplined and he'll be returned with apologies."

Clearly the lieutenant understood the subtle differences between a harmless enemy civilian and an agent employed as pay-master and go-between for spies. If he did not, Wormold and Benson knew for they made no objections. In fact Wormold began to transfer his indignation and rage from Dusty to Oliver. No professional soldier cared for spies, although admitting they had their uses, and Wormold liked Oliver a whole lot less when

23

considering that the man had been willing to throw away many lives to safeguard his secret.

"We understand, Captain Fog," he stated.

"Then I'll thank you for the coffee and be on my way," Dusty replied. "I'm leaving you a couple of mules to haul the ambulance."

"Thanks," Wormold answered, understanding the reason for selecting that particular kind of team. Mules could not travel at the speed of horses and one trained for harness-work showed a strenuous reluctance to being saddled for riding. While Dusty left the Yankees with the means of hauling their medical supplies, he prevented them from using the animals as a way of sending for reinforcements. "You seem to have thought of everything."

"I try, Captain," Dusty smiled. "I surely try."

Looking around his denuded, disarmed, horseless camp after the sound of the rebel hooves faded into the distance, Captain Wormold decided that Dusty did far better than merely try—he made a damned good job of it.

## Chapter 3

## A Talented Yankee Gentleman

Captain Buck Blaze looked like a slightly older, not so pugnacious version of his brother Red. However he lacked Red's genius for becoming involved in fights, which might be thought of as a blessing. Annoyance of the kind which might have sent Red off on the hunt for a brawl filled Buck as he watched the way Miss Belle Boyd stood laughing and chatting with that preacher who came on a visit from back East to the Regiment.

Not that Buck had anything against preachers, even one as well-dressed and handsome as the Reverend Julius Ludlow. Nor, if the truth be told, could Buck lay any claim to Belle's affections. What riled him was that he had escorted Belle to the ball and, until one of their host's servants brought her a note which she read, she had behaved in a perfectly correct manner. Then, for no reason at all, she had excused herself and went over to lay the full weight of her charm on Ludlow—and, mister, that was a whole load of charm to be wasted on a visiting preacher.

Without a doubt Belle Boyd could claim to be the most beautiful and best dressed woman attending the ball. Of course, as the other ladies present repeatedly told themselves, the horrid Yankee blockade prevented people who didn't have influential friends from obtaining the latest fashion dresses. Perfectly true, too; and it seemed that Belle possessed the necessary qualifications for beating the blockade. The dress she wore was white silk, with a light blue sash about its waist, cut on the latest Eastern lines guaranteed to attract the attention of every male and envy of each woman present.

While the other women might make catty comments about her clothes, none could fault her in the matter of looks. A tall, willowy girl—but not skinny by any means—her neatly coiffeured brunette hair framed a beautiful face with lines of intelligence and breeding on it. Small wonder that she attracted attention among the guests at the ball.

Certainly Ludlow gave no sign of wishing to leave Belle's company. After coming from the floor at the end of a spirited Virginia reel, he listened to something the girl said, nodded and escorted her towards the open doors of the big room. Several of the women exchanged glances and disapproving clucks at the sight. Buck felt his annoyance grow. Normally he did not profess to sit in judgement on other people's morals; but he felt that Belle should remember who she was and, if she wished to use a mild flirtation as a means of relaxation, should select somebody more suitable than a preacher.

Then Buck found himself wondering if there might be some deeper motive behind the girl's actions. He could hardly believe that she found the need to relax in such a manner, even after her last trip. Maybe Belle possessed some deeper reason for her interest in Ludlow. If so, she might require help. Buck could not forget the slight, but significant change which came over Belle as she read the note. Although she had a mobile face, he knew it usually showed only such emotions as she wished to have seen. On reading the note, a blank, expressionless mask momentarily replaced her friendly attitude. Then she slipped the note into her vanity bag, excused herself in the formal way which gave no real reason, and left the party of young people with whom she had been talking. Going over, she began to exert all her charm on Ludlow and, preacher or not, he showed no reluctance to be so charmed.

"Come on, Buck, don't you-all stand day-dreaming," said his identical twin brother, Pete. "The Swinton gals want for you and me to take them home after the ball."

"Huh?" grunted Buck, coming out of his reverie. "Sure, Pete."

"It's lucky for you that I didn't say give me that new hoss of yours," Pete grinned. "You're not starting to think about Belle as your gal, now are you?"

"Nope. I'm just a touch curious."

"Over why she'd go for a preacher when there's a handsome, gallant, dashing young Cavalry captain all ready to lay his fame and fortune at her dainty feet?"

"Something like that," smiled Buck. "What's she see in that feller, Pete?"

"How's that?" Pete asked.

"Take away his fancy preacher's clothes, curly brown hair, good looks and soft white hands," drawled Buck, "and what've you got?"

"You," Pete replied. "Let's go talk to the Swinton gals. If Belle's wanting a change of company, she's old enough to pick it."

"But if she knows something about that preacher—," Buck began.

26

"She's full capable of handling it herself," Pete finished. "All you, or I, could do is spoil things for her and that'd get her riled."

"Which same I wouldn't want to happen," drawled Buck. "Come on, Brother Pete, you're keeping me and the Swinton gals waiting."

"It's hell being born into a family of ready liars," Pete sighed and the brothers walked across the floor.

Standing on the porch, Belle sucked in a deep breath and vigorously plied her fan.

"Lordy lord!" she said, looking at Ludlow. "Isn't it hot?"

"I'm afraid our host's house isn't large enough for his ambitions," he replied. "Inviting the General's staff and officers from the near-by Regiment as well as the local gentry does crowd everyone together."

"Could we possibly take a stroll, do you think?" Belle asked, peeking coyly over the top of her fan. "Lordy, isn't that forward of me. But I feel that if I go back inside just yet, I'll just melt right away."

"I wouldn't want that to happen," Ludlow answered and took her arm.

As they walked Belle prattled on in an empty-headed manner, sounding like the kind of rich, pampered, spoiled Southern belle portrayed on stage in the highly patriotic Yankee plays of the moment. Ludlow listened, making only such 'no' or 'yes' comments as the situation demanded. While doing so, he directed their feet towards the stables. Its doors stood open and lanterns hung inside to illuminate the interior. Edging Belle towards the doors, Ludlow peered inside to ensure that the building was unoccupied.

"And I said to Susie-Mae Swinton—," Belle continued with the pointless story she had begun when he suddenly thrust her through the doors and into the stables. Shock came to her face as she stared at the man. "Why—Why Julius Ludlow. And you-all a man of the cloth—for shame!"

"It won't work, Miss Parrish—if that's your name," Ludlow growled, moving towards her and taking what appeared to be a large, heavy key from his pocket. "I reckon you'd best drop that vanity bag."

Still maintaining her expression of fright and shock, Belle stared down at Ludlow's right hand. In it he held the key with three fingers through the ring handle, the fore-finger curled around a stud on the bar. Belle noticed that the bar of the key

27

appeared to be hollow. While aware of what the other held, she tried a bluff.

"Just what do you think you're playing at?" she asked. "You didn't need to push me in here just to show me your old church key."

"Drop it, Miss Parrish!" Ludlow growled. "That wig fooled me at first, but you're the girl I saw fencing with Buck Blaze at the camp. And even if I hadn't seen you there, I'd know. Up until the time you came over to me, you made real intelligent conversation. What was in the note?"

"Note?"

"I saw the coon bring it to you. And I won't ask you to drop that bag again. Do it right now."

"Why I don't know what you mean," Belle insisted and slipped the bag from her fingers. "I do really think you're deranged in your head, Ju—."

"No you don't," Ludlow answered. "And you're acting wrong again. If you really thought this was only an old church key, you'd be screaming your head off for help right now."

"I always heard one should humour crazy people," Belle said, her hands plucking nervously at the dress sash.

"Keep them where I can see them!" Ludlow ordered. "This key-gun's only .36 but this close it'll kill—."

Silk rustled as the sash and skirt of Belle's dress parted company from the bodice to slide down to the ground. What it revealed, along with the unexpected nature of her action, halted Ludlow open-mouthed and staring in his tracks. Belle wore neither under-skirt nor petticoats; understandable on such a warm evening, even if the Yankee blockade did not place such items in very short supply among the Southern ladies. However instead of the usual knee-long drawers one might expect a well-bred young lady to wear, Belle stood exposed in a pair of the most daring, short-legged black under-garments Ludlow had seen on, or off, a stage. Although of slim build, Belle had shapely legs muscled like a dancer's. A dancer's, or a—

Just a shade to late Ludlow thought of another type of person who acquired such muscular development in the legs; although it must be admitted at that time very few women came into that particular class.

The instant her action distracted Ludlow, Belle moved fast. First she flicked her fan at the man's face and instinctively he brought up his right hand to protect his features. In doing so he took the key-gun out of line of the girl. Up rose her right leg,

28

the white of the thigh flashing against the black suspender straps and black silk stockings, to drive the toe of her high-heeled calf-high boot with some force straight into Ludlow's groin.

Agony ripped into Ludlow with such severity that it caused him to double over and the gun dropped from his fingers. Nor did he find time to recover from the nauseating torment which filled him and prevented cohesive thought from warning him of danger. Bringing down her right foot from delivering the kick, Belle glided forward. No longer did her face look frightened, but held an expression of grim determination. Throwing her weight on to the right foot, Belle thrust her left leg up. Bending the left knee and pointing the toe down, she propelled it with all her strength to crash into Ludlow's offered face. The force of the attack caused Belle's knee to burst through the material of the stocking and lifted Ludlow erect. He did not stay that way for long. Drawing back her right fist, she whipped it across to collide with Ludlow's jaw. A solid click sounded and the man spun around, crashed into the side of a stall, then slid down into its straw.

None of Belle's attack gave any sign of being made by a thoroughly scared, scatter-brained girl of the kind she acted earlier. The punch whipped around with the skill and precision many a man might have envied; while the way she kicked would have done credit to any of the French-Creole *savate* fighters Ludlow had seen in New Orleans.

Blowing on her stinging knuckles, Belle worked the fingers and looked in Ludlow's direction. Unless she missed her guess, he would not be troubling her for at least a couple of minutes. So she decided to make herself more presentable. If any of the guests should happen to come to the stables, her state of undress would call for more explanation than she cared to give.

Taking up her sash and skirt, she gave them a shake to remove any traces of their contact with the ground. After donning the skirt, she took up her vanity bag and the key-pistol. Slowly she turned the latter over in her hands, making sure that she kept the barrel pointing away from her. Although Belle knew of such things, the pistol she held was the first of its kind to come into her hands.

From what Belle could see, the pistol had been well made. Its outer surfaces showed the dull, rust-pitted appearance one expected from the main key of an old church. The inside of the barrel had the clean, shining glint of new metal. Most likely it incorporated some kind of easily removable barrel-cap when not in use to prevent its true purpose being detected. She would know when they searched Ludlow.

Originally such pistols had been designed for use by jailers, serving to open the cell doors and provide an instantly available weapon should a prisoner try an attack. Belle knew the one she held must be of more modern construction and wondered how it worked. It might make use of the metallic cartridges becoming so popular among the Yankees; or take a charge of loose powder, ignited by a percussion cap, to fire its bullet. Although curious to learn, Belle knew better than to experiment. The time might come when she could use such a device, but she preferred to allow a trained gunsmith to learn how it operated.

Hearing footsteps approaching the stables, Belle dropped the pistol into her bag. She glanced again at Ludlow, seeing no sign of recovery, and moved towards the door. From the poor quality of his clothing, the man who approached her did not attend the ball as a guest. He was big, well-built, yet looked neither slow nor awkward. Studying the man, Belle concluded it might be unwise to try *savate* on him should he be an enemy. Given the element of surprise, she might be able to render him helpless. If she failed, he looked strong enough to half kill her.

So Belle slipped her right hand casually into the mouth of her bag. Ignoring the key-pistol, as she was unsure how to work it, the girl eased her fingers through the bracelet which rested in a pouch stitched to the side of the bag. She moved carefully, for the bracelet had a razor-sharp edge for use in emergencies.

"Southrons, hear your country call you," the man said quietly.

On hearing the first line of the militantly patriotic words General Albert Pike put to Daniel B. Emmet's song 'Dixie', Belle relaxed. The Confederate Secret Service used it as a password by which agents could identify themselves to each other. Satisfied that there would be no danger, Belle still retained her hold of the bracelet. In its way, that bracelet was every bit as much a weapon as the key-pistol and no more likely to be suspected.

"Up lest worse than death befall you," she replied, giving the counter-sign.

"Absom sent me, the name's Tolling," the man said, entering the barn and looking her over with approval. "So you're Miss Boyd. It's a honour to meet up with you, ma'am."

"I hope I'm not too much of a disappointment," Belle smiled.

Despite her light answer, Belle felt pleased with the man's obvious pleasure. It had been a hard struggle in the early days to gain male approval and acceptance by the Confederate States

30

Secret Service, but now she was firmly established and shared honours with Rose Greenhow as the leading female lights of that organisation. Between them, the two young women extracted much information and caused the Yankees untold trouble.

In an age when young women of good birth were expected to be fragile, sheltered creatures, Belle received almost a unique up-bringing. Born into a wealthy Southern family, she grew up with every advantage and luxury. However her father tended to be eccentric in some ways and made up for the disappointment of not having a son by teaching the girl to ride, handle a gun and other male accomplishments. A talented girl, Belle learned from her father without losing any of her femininity or forgetting to gain skill in female matters.

When the Civil War first began to rear its head in the distance, Belle's father stood out for the right of any sovereign state to secede from the Union if its interests clashed with the Federal Government; one of the main causes of the War, although the Yankees made much use of the slavery issue as being more likely to induce the masses to fight. Some weeks before the commencement of actual hostilities, a bunch of Union supporters attacked Belle's home. They killed her mother and father, wounding the girl and might have done worse if the family's 'downtrodden and abused' slaves had not arrived and driven off their 'saviours'. By the time she recovered, the War had begun. Belle put her increased hatred of the Yankees to good use. Joining her cousin, Rose Greenhow, she became an agent for the Confederate Secret Service, often delivering the information gathered personally. Stonewall Jackson himself referred to Belle as his best courier, after she brought news to him which helped make possible the victory at the first battle of Bull Run.

Since then Belle carried on the good work. While the Yankees knew her name, skilled use of disguises prevented her from being recognised. Pinkerton, soon to form his own detective agency, had his best operatives after Belle but without success.

Using information she gathered, Belle had recently completed an assignment. With Dusty Fog's aid, she captured a Yankee Army payroll and used the money to buy arms for the South.* Resting until orders arrived directing her to another assignment, she posed as one of General Ole Devil Hardin's kin on a visit from Texas. As such she naturally received an invitation to the ball. On receiving Tolling's message that Ludlow was not all he seemed, Belle forgot relaxation and went into action with all the deadly efficiency that gained her the name 'the Rebel Spy'.

*Told in "The Colt and the Sabre".

"Absom said you had black hair," Tolling remarked as they walked across to and looked down at the groaning, stirring man.

"This is a wig," Belle replied, touching her 'hair'. "Your note didn't say much about him. Who is he?"

"His real name's Byron and he's a real talented Yankee gentleman."

"One of their spies?"

"Paid by them for it, anyways."

"And his game?"

"Afore the War he used to work the riverboats," Tolling explained. "Making up to rich women, cheating at cards. Got him a way of becoming real friendly."

"And now?"

"There you've got me. He's one of a bunch who the Yankees sent out of New Orleans. Lucienne got on to them and sent me after him. Only he travelled faster'n me and I've only just caught up with him."

"We'll have to see if we can make him talk," the girl remarked. "Only we can't do it here or now. Can you keep him hidden until I find help to take him away?"

"I reckon so," Tolling drawled. "Only he'll likely make a fuss when he comes too. If he does, I'll whomp him over the head."

"You might do it too hard," the girl smiled. "They do say Yankees have soft skulls. I've a better way, if you fetch me some water."

Crossing the stable to a pump fitted on to a stone sink in one corner, Tolling took up the metal dipper which hung on its side. He worked the pump's handle, filled the dipper with water and returned to the girl. In his absence she had taken a ring with a large, heavy stone set into it from her bag. Holding the ring over the dipper, she touched its side and the stone flicked upwards at one side from the setting. A brown powder trickled out of the cavity exposed beneath the raised stone, dribbling into the water where it dissolved without a visible trace.

"That's neat," Tolling said as the girl pressed the stone back into place.

"Rose Greenhow suggested it and had one made for each of us," Belle replied. "Although I think she stole the idea from reading about the Borgia family in Italy. If he drinks that he'll give you no trouble."

"He'll drink it," Tolling assured her.

Although they both were prepared to deal with some reluctance on Ludlow's part, it failed to materialise. Most likely he would have objected to accepting a drink if he retained his normal quick wits. However Belle's treatment robbed him of them temporarily and pain gave him a thirst. So he drank greedily when Tolling held the dipper to his lips.

"He's taking it like a deacon at a whisky still," grinned Tolling.

Hearing the voice, Ludlow focussed his eyes first on the speaker, then past Tolling to where Belle stood. With a low curse, Ludlow tried to force himself up from the floor.

"Don't worry," Belle told Tolling as he reached down to restrain Ludlow.

Before Ludlow could do more than haul himself into a sitting position, the powder took effect. His body went limp and he slipped down to the floor again. Bending down, Tolling made a quick investigation and straightened up with a satisfied nod of his head.

"He's sleeping like a babe, Miss Boyd. That's real potent stuff. What is it?"

"I never learned its name," the girl replied. "Rose got a supply of it from the clerk of a river-boat. He claimed that a small dose would put the biggest man to sleep and keep him that way for a couple of hours; and it does."

At that moment they heard the drumming of rapidly approaching hooves. Telling her companion to hide Ludlow under the straw, Belle darted to the stable door and looked out. A sigh of relief came from her as she recognised the rider who came towards her. If anything, she would find the problem of secretly removing Ludlow made easier with the newcomer's arrival.

## Chapter 4

## A Fortune in Counterfeit Money

"Why Cousin Dusty," Belle greeted, walking towards the small Texan as he halted his horse. "I surely didn't expect to see you back here so soon."

For a moment the brunette wig fooled Dusty, then recognition came and he wondered what Belle might be doing at the stables.

"I only just got in," he replied, swinging from the saddle. "Was told back to the Regiment that Uncle Devil's here and so I came right over. Is he up to the house, Belle?"

"He surely is," Belle agreed, speaking as she had all the time in the world for she saw a young officer approaching them. "I just knew something would happen to spoil his evening. 'Beulah Parrish!' I said when I saw you coming, 'Cousin Dusty's bringing trouble for Uncle Devil for certain sure.'"

"You could be right at that, Cousin Beulah," Dusty drawled, grinning inwardly at the neat way in which Belle passed on her current identity. "Only it's nothing to spoil his night."

Catching Dusty's head shake, the officer steered his companion by without doing more than call a greeting. One look at Dusty's appearance told Belle that he had ridden long and hard. So she put aside her thoughts of asking him to help with removing Ludlow. Only a matter of some importance would bring Dusty to interrupt Ole Devil at the ball. With that in mind she reverted to her original idea of going to Buck Blaze for help.

"Why not let Tolling tend to stabling your horse?" she suggested.

"Who?"

"He works here," smiled the girl. "It will save time, Dusty."

Normally Dusty would not have thought to allow a stranger to take care of his horse, so he realised the girl must have good reason for making the suggestion. Looking to where Tolling came from the stable, Dusty noticed the man walked with a pronounced limp. All too well Tolling knew of the deserter problem which plagued both sides throughout the War. Figuring that a healthy man employed in such a menial capacity might otherwise arouse

34

comment, Tolling adopted a means of showing why he apparently did not serve his country.

"Let me have your reins, Cap'n," Tolling offered. "I'll see to it for you."

Before leaving the horse, Dusty took three pads of money from its saddle-pouches and slipped them into the front of his tunic. Tolling led the horse away and Dusty turned to Belle.

"I'd as soon not go into the ballroom dressed like this," he said. "Reckon you can fix it for Uncle Devil to meet me outside?"

"I'll see to it," she promised. "Go around the right side of the house and wait by the first door. I'll ask the General to meet you there."

On entering the main room, Belle passed with leisurely-seeming speed to where Ole Devil sat talking to their host. Catching the girl's slight signal, the General rose to his feet and joined her. Tall, lean, immaculate in his full-dress uniform, Ole Devil had a sharp, tanned, hawk-like face set in disciplined lines that rarely showed the true, generous nature underneath the hard exterior. When he heard of Dusty's arrival, he nodded and returned to the host. As Belle expected, Joe Hemming, their host, put his study at Ole Devil's disposal and she told the General that Dusty would be waiting at its outside door. So casually had both she and Ole Devil acted that none of the guests suspected anything might be wrong. After Ole Devil strolled off in the direction of the study, Buck Blaze drifted to Belle's side.

"You didn't have to slap that preacher's face, now did you, Cousin Beulah?" he asked with a grin.

"How'd you guess?" she replied. "I need your help, Buck."

"It's yours. What's up?"

"I'll tell you on the way to the stables," Belle promised. "Only let's make it look natural, so nobody guesses something's wrong."

Letting Dusty into Hemming's study, Ole Devil walked across to the desk, waved the youngster into a chair and sat down facing him.

"Well, Dustine," the General said. "What brings you here?"

"I'm not sure, sir," Dusty answered, taking the money from his tunic and placing it upon the desk before his uncle. "I just thought you'd be interested in this money."

"Why?" asked Ole Devil, picking up one of the bundles.

"We captured a Yankee convoy and found a box full of Confederate money in the possession of a civilian."

While Dusty spoke, Ole Devil thumbed through the notes. Then the General gave them a closer examination. When he raised his face to look at Dusty, the small Texan read interest and concern where most people could have seen no change of expression.

"A box full like this?" the General said.

"Yes, sir. I thought that the man might be taking it to the Indian Nations so he could have it passed to Yankee spies in Texas. Figured you'd be interested and as soon as we crossed the Ouachita I had the box loaded on a pack horse and came ahead of the company. They told me where to find you at Headquarters."

"The patrol went well?"

"Easy enough, sir. We hit the Yankee guard on Elk Crossing at sundown, ran them off without loss to us. There was only a half company of Stedloe's Zouaves and the Arkansas Rifles on our side gave us covering fire."

"Go fetch Miss Boyd," Ole Devil ordered when Dusty finished speaking.

Something in the General's brusque manner told Dusty that he made the correct decision in coming ahead of his Company and interrupting Ole Devil's relaxation. After the youngster left the room, Ole Devil remained seated at the desk and took up the other packets of money. Although his tanned face showed little or nothing, Ole Devil had never been more concerned than at that moment.

While walking towards the barn, Dusty wondered what caused Ole Devil's anxiety. Few people would have read the General's moods, but Dusty knew his uncle felt deep concern at the find. More than the mere capture of a Yankee spies' pay-master warranted on the surface. Ahead of Dusty, the man Belle had called Tolling emerged from the stables.

Hearing Dusty's approaching footsteps, Tolling quickly reverted to his painful-appearing limp; but suddenly realised that he had made a mistake. Not that it would matter under the circumstances; and he would never have made such a blunder in enemy territory. Anyway, Tolling mused, that small young captain—Belle had not thought to mention Dusty's identity—was unlikely to notice—

Even as the thought began to form, Tolling saw Dusty's right hand make a move. Then the man stared into the muzzle of the Army Colt which a mere three-quarters of a second before reposed harmlessly in the small Texan's left holster.

"Where'd you get the wound, *hombre*?" Dusty asked.

"At Antietam with the Hampton Legion, cap'n," Tolling answered, staring at the Colt like a snake-mesmerised cottontail rabbit.

36

Belle came from the stables, wondering to whom Tolling spoke. Halting, she looked from Dusty to Tolling.

"What's going on?" she said.

"Did you see the way this gent limps?" asked Dusty.

"Yes," smiled the girl. "It looked very bad."

"*Real* bad," drawled Dusty dryly. "Only it doesn't stay in the one leg."

"It's all right, Dusty," Belle chuckled. "I can vouch for Tolling."

"He's one of your crowd, is he?"

"Yes."

"Sorry, mister," Dusty said, holstering the Colt. "I figured you to be a deserter and reckoned the time to ask about it was after I made sure you couldn't argue about answering."

"You made sure of that," admitted Tolling. "I've never seen a gun come out so fast."

"I thought so too, the first time I saw it," smiled Belle and looked at Dusty. "Your business with Ole Devil didn't take long."

"He wants to see you as soon as convenient, Belle," Dusty answered.

"Which means right now, even though it's not convenient," the girl said. "Can you and Buck tend to things here, Tolling?"

"I reckon so," the man replied.

"Then I'll come straight away, Dusty," the girl stated.

Leaving the removal of Ludlow to Buck and Tolling, Belle accompanied Dusty to where Ole Devil waited for them. After seating the girl with his usual courtesy, Ole Devil told Dusty to go through the full story of the convoy's capture again. Belle realised that something of importance lay behind the order and listened intently. Certainly Ole Devil would not call her in merely to hear the story of a successful raid.

"What do you think, Miss Boyd?" asked the General when Dusty finished.

"The box would have had an infernal contrivance fitted to destroy its contents if they were important," the girl replied. "Which a shipment of money to pay their spies would be."

"And the money itself?"

"May I see some of it, General?"

"Help yourself," authorised Ole Devil, waving a hand to the three pads of notes on the desk top.

Taking one pad up, the girl studied the top note and then turned her eyes in Dusty's direction. "They were all new notes, Dusty?"

"All I saw, although I didn't take them all out to check."

Around Belle's neck hung a pendant with a large locket attached. Reaching up, the girl unclipped the pendant and removed it. Watched by the two men, she then eased off the glass cover of the locket. Drawing the top bill from one of the pads, she held the glass over it. From where he stood, Dusty could see that the glass was in reality a powerful lens and the girl used its power of magnification to examine the bill carefully.

"Well, Miss Boyd?" asked Ole Devil.

"How big was the box you took, Dusty?" the girl inquired, ignoring the question.

"About so big," replied Dusty, demonstrating with his hands. "There'd be a fortune in it."

"And unless I'm mistaken," Belle said quietly, "it's a fortune in counterfeit money.'

"Counterfeit?" Dusty repeated.

"You thought so too, General," Belle commented.

"I thought so," Ole Devil admitted.

"Likely printing their own's the only way the Yankees can lay hands on enough of our money to supply their spies, sir," Dusty remarked.

"It cuts deeper than that, Dusty," Belle put in. "Much deeper."

"Howd' you mean, Belle?"

"The Yankees could have found a mighty smart way to win the War."

"Miss Boyd's right, Dustine," Ole Devil went on. "If enough of this counterfeit money is put into circulation, it will ruin the South's economy."

"One box full, sir?" asked Dusty.

"The Yankees won't stop at just the one," Ole Devil replied and went on to explain how paper money only retained its value when its issuer possessed sufficient assets to cover its nominal value. "So if the Yankees can flood the South with this stuff they're printing, we won't be able to do so. Our economy will be smashed and that will end the War just as surely as if they whipped us on every battlefield."

"Which same they'll have to be stopped, sir," Dusty stated. "Only I'll be damned if I can see how to do it."

"The only way to do it would be to smash their printing plates and press," Belle said. "And to do that we'd have to learn where it is."

"Oliver might know," Dusty told her.

"He may," agreed Belle. "In fact he probably does. But a man fanatical enough to try to destroy that box at the cost of his own life won't talk easily."

"Even if he does, the chances are that the press'll be somewhere that we can't reach," Ole Devil pointed out.

"When will he be getting here, Dusty?" asked Belle.

"Noon tomorrow at the earliest."

"I'll see him when he comes—and don't tell me that it's not a chore for a woman, please."

"It's not," snorted Ole Devil. "But then, neither is spying—but you're still the best spy we have."

"Don't let Rose Greenhow hear you say that, General," warned Belle with a smile. Then she became serious again. "Dusty, did Oliver mention what he was doing travelling on a Yankee convoy?"

"Going into the Indian Nations to preach to the Indians," Dusty replied.

"And so was Ludlow," Ole Devil put in.

"So Mrs. Hemming told me," the girl breathed. "Is there any chance of our leaving soon, General?"

"Certainly."

"If I can, I'd like to be around when Ludlow recovers," the girl said. "He may know something and if he does, I might be able to make him talk."

"Do you think he's involved in this business?"

"I don't know, General. But he was one of a party who left New Orleans and scattered through the South. A man like him, smooth, with a way of charming people, could go anywhere and pass the money without arousing suspicion."

"You're right at that. He came with what seemed perfectly legitimate letters of introduction."

"Give Pinkerton and the U.S. Secret Service their due, General," Belle said. "They're thorough. They'd see that he came ready to get co-operation from you and the civil authorities too."

"What do you want to do then?" Ole Devil inquired.

"Question Ludlow first. According to Tolling, he's working for the Yankees for money and that kind break easier than somebody who's doing it out of loyalty or for his beliefs. As I said, I'd like to be on hand when he recovers."

"We can pull out in ten-fifteen minutes without arousing too much comment," the General told her. "Will that do?"

"Yes. It will give me time to change and make my arrangements after we reach the camp," Belle replied.

"Shall I ride out now, sir?" Dusty asked. "If folks see me here in these clothes, they'll start wondering what brought me back and tie it in with your leaving the ball."

"Go ahead, Dustine," Ole Devil confirmed. "Where's that box of money?"

"Locked in your office, with a guard at the door and window."

"Good. Have the armourer on hand ready for when I return."

"Could you leave the box intact, General?" Belle put in. "At least until after I've seen Ludlow."

"Certainly," the General promised. "Get moving, Dustine. I'll be along with Miss Boyd and my staff as soon as I can arrange it."

Saluting, Dusty left the room. He went along to the stables and collected his horse. There was no sign of Tolling, so Dusty concluded he and Buck Blaze had already left with their prisoner. After saddling his horse, Dusty rode away from the Hemming house in the direction of the Texas Light Cavalry's camp. On the way he caught up to his cousin and Tolling as they rode in the same direction, with Ludlow hanging limply across the saddle of a third horse. Pausing long enough to learn where they intended to place the man on their arrival, Dusty pushed on again at a faster pace than the others for he had things to do at the camp.

By the time Ole Devil arrived, Dusty and the armourer were waiting in his office. On the desk stood the wooden box, untouched since being brought into the room for safe keeping. Crossing the room, Ole Devil looked down at the box and took its key which lay on the lid.

"I wouldn't do that, General," the armourer warned quietly.

"And I didn't aim to," Ole Devil replied. "What kind of infernal contrivance're they using?"

The term 'booby-trap' had not yet come into use, but such things were made and employed by the Secret Services of both sides. As a soldier, Ole Devil did not fully approve of infernal devices; although he granted that they did on occasion have their uses.

"Haven't looked too close, sir," the armourer drawled, walking to the desk. "But from what Cap'n Fog tells me, I'd say the lock's a fake. Instead of works, there'll be a couple of percussion caps inside. So when somebody puts the key in and turns it, they pop a cap and fire off a charge. Only I can't say for sure until after I've had a chance to look real close."

"If you'll wait in the next room, you'll maybe have your chance to find out for sure," Ole Devil told him. "I'll send when I need you."

"Yo!" answered the armourer, saluting and marching from the room.

"Miss Boyd will be along soon, Dustine," the General said as

40

the door closed. "This's a serious business and I'd best see about notifying our Government so they can take precautions."

"Yes, sir," Dusty replied.

Taking up pen and paper, Ole Devil lapsed into silence and Dusty settled down to watch his uncle composing a concise report that could be passed in code over the telegraph wires to the Confederate Government. In addition the General would send a letter by courier to be passed East and give a fuller account of the affair. For a time the only sound in the room was the scratching of Ole Devil's pen. Then a knock came at the door. Rising, Dusty crossed the room. On opening the door, he found Belle outside and did not hesitate to let her enter.

No longer did Belle look the elegant Southern lady who attended the ball. In fact her appearance, as usual when clad in such a manner, drew a disapproving glance from Ole Devil. While the General reconciled himself to the girl making a success of the distasteful business of spying, he did not approve of her wearing her present kind of clothing.

With the wig removed, Belle proved to have deep black hair cut very short all round her skull. Instead of the ball gown, she wore a man's black shirt, riding breeches and boots; the shirt and breeches being tight enough to show off her slender figure to its best advantage and dispel any doubts as to her sex. Around her waist hung a gunbelt with an ivory-handled Dance Bros. .36 revolver—a Confederate copy of the 1851 Navy Colt—riding butt forward in the holster at her left side. Although it looked slightly incongruous taken with her clothes and appearance, she carried a lady's parasol in her left hand.

"We'll soon be ready, General," she remarked. "I've seen Tolling and he's prepared everything for me."

"Can we do anything for you, Miss Boyd?" Ole Devil asked, eyeing the girl's clothing in a frosty manner.

"I'd like Dusty's help during the questioning."

"Is that necessary? I don't want my officers getting a name for torturing prisoners."

"It will help me to have him along," Belle answered.

"I'm game to go along, sir," Dusty put in.

"Very well," Ole Devil growled. "Go. But this affair is not official in any way, you understand."

"Yes, sir," Dusty replied.

"There's one thing, Dusty," Belle said quietly. "If you come, you'll be under my orders. Do whatever I tell you without question and don't interfere with anything I do."

Watching the set, grim lines on the girl's face, Dusty found himself feeling almost sorry for Ludlow. He knew that Belle regarded the situation as being of vital importance and would brook no interference with her handling of the Yankee spy. Yet he also guessed that the girl would not employ crude torture methods until all other means failed. Dusty felt that watching Belle in action might be both interesting and instructive. So he nodded his agreement and then listened to what she wanted him to do.

## Chapter 5

# The Art of Gentle Persuasion

Sitting up on the bed, Ludlow blinked as the light from the lantern hung overhead dazzled him. He groaned as he swung his feet to the floor and clutched at his throbbing, aching head while fighting down the nausea filling his body. Slowly the throbbing and nausea died away and his dizziness ended, allowing him to take an interest in his surroundings.

He found himself in a small, stoutly-made one-room log cabin that had a small barred window in one wall faced at the other side by a door with a covered peep-hole cut into it. Significantly to Ludlow's mind, the door did not have a keyhole or latch in it. For furnishings the cabin held a bed, foot-locker, table and chair, all securely bolted to the floor. At first he could not imagine where he might be, then he realised that the cabin must be one used to hold captured Yankee officers before passing them on to a permanent prisoner-of-war camp. Securing the furnishings prevented them being used as weapons or a means of breaking down the door.

Even as Ludlow thought of that, pain bit into him and caused his hands to reach for the place where Belle kicked him. Recollection flooded back to him. Shock and fear creased his handsome face as his hands darted up to feel at his jaw. Staring wildly around the room, his eyes came to rest on a mirror hanging upon one wall. Rising from the bed, he lurched hurriedly across the room and studied his reflection in the shining steel surface.

"Thank God!" he croaked as he found that the swelling would have no permanent effect and leave no trace to disfigure his handsome features.

Before the thought that he might never again need his good looks as a means of making a living struck him, he heard the door's lock click and turned to see who entered. At first he barely recognised Belle without the wig and wearing male clothes. For all that, something told him that she, the burly civilian and small cavalry captain did not come merely to inquire about the state of his health.

"Go and sit at the table!" Belle ordered, standing with the parasol held lightly in both hands.

Seeing the futility of resistance, Ludlow crossed to the table and slid into the chair.

"What's the game?" he asked, sounding more than a shade uneasy.

"Lay your hands palm down on the table top in front of you," the girl said as if she did not hear a word he spoke.

Once again Ludlow obeyed, noticing that each of the male newcomers held lengths of rope in his hands. Giving Ludlow no chance to raise objections, Dusty and Tolling converged on him and grabbed a wrist. Fastening one of the pieces of rope around the wrist he held, Dusty drew its other end down to be secured to the top of the table leg farthest away from the prisoner. Moving no less deftly, Tolling tied Ludlow's other wrist in the same manner. Then, while Dusty secured Ludlow's arms further by fastening a rope from elbow to elbow, Tolling roped the man's legs to the chair. By the time they had finished, Ludlow sat held immobile and stared at them with growing concern.

"Now we're all set to have a little talk," Belle said.

"I don't know what you're playing at—," Ludlow began and looked at Dusty. "When General—."

"Don't look at Captain Fog!" Belle shouted. "I'm talking to you!"

"Maybe he don't reckon that a woman should be questioning him, Miss Boyd," Tolling put in.

"B-Boyd!" gasped Ludlow and stared at the girl. "So you're the Rebel Spy!"

"That's right, you stinking traitor," Belle replied, twisting at the handle of her parasol. "I'm the Rebel Spy and you're going to answer questions for me."

With that she drew the handle from the body of the parasol. Putting the lower section aside, she turned once more to face Ludlow. Instead of a piece of feminine frippery, she now held a deadly and sinister weapon. Dusty had noticed earlier that the parasol's handle appeared to be thicker than usual, but gave the matter no thought. Like Ludlow, he studied the thing Belle held and understood the need for the unfeminine thickness. Gripping the steel ball exposed by removing the parasol's upper section, Belle gave it a tug. Out slid a length of steel-coil spring and telescoped inside it was a foot of tubular steel connected to the ball.

Up and down flicked Belle's right hand and the coil-spring sent the steel rod whipping towards the table top with a force out of all proportion to her movement. A savage crack sounded as the metal ball struck the table and buried itself to half its depth

44

in the wood less than an inch from Ludlow's right hand. Giving a startled, frightened yelp, he tried to jerk his hand away but the rope prevented him from doing so.

"How did this filth use to earn his living, Mr. Tolling?" asked the girl.

"Cheating at cards—," Tolling began.

"A man needs supple hands for that," Belle purred. "Look at them, Tolling. Those hands have been cared for, kept soft and fancy. If they were broken—."

Again the wicked spring-powered billy snapped out, crashing into the wood even closer to Ludlow's hand. Sweat broke on to his forehead and fear twisted at his face. That a beautiful and sensual woman handled the billy made its effect so much worse. When Ludlow saw her remove the parasol handle, he expected to see it contain a knife-blade. Instead it held a far more terrifying device, for Ludlow did not doubt that the girl intended to use it against him. The steel ball would rip and smash his hands so that no doctor could repair the damage.

"You're a soldier!" he screeched, staring with terrified eyes at Dusty. "You can't let her torture me."

Again the billy whipped up and drove its ball into the table top. Dusty ran his tongue tip across dry lips as he saw the grim determination on Belle's face.

"Belle—."

"Keep quiet, Captain Fog!" Belle snapped. "I hold rank of colonel and I'm giving you a direct order. You came here at my request. So leave me to handle things my way."

While Dusty knew the girl spoke the truth about her honorary rank—given to put her in a position of authority when dealing with members of the Confederate armed forces—she had never made use of it in his presence before. Yet he knew she would not hesitate to invoke the full powers her rank gave if he interfered. So he stiffened into a brace and kept silent. Ludlow slumped in his chair as he realised that he could expect no further help from that source.

"Start talking, Byron!" Belle snapped after a brief pause to allow the full sense of his helplessness to fill the prisoner.

"I've not—," Ludlow began, then realised what name she used. "Who told you my name?"

"A man called Oliver," Belle answered, but saw no hint that Ludlow knew the name.

"And Gilpin sold you out to save his own neck back in New Orleans," Tolling went on when he saw Ludlow's negative response.

45

For a moment recognition flickered on Ludlow's face, showing that the name Tolling gave meant something to him. However he kept his mouth shut, wanting time to think how he might profit from his position and knowledge.

"You said the filth used to charm women, then bleed them by blackmail," Belle said gently. "He's handsome enough to do it, too."

With that she swung the billy sideways and its ball lashed at Ludlow's head. For a moment Dusty thought that the girl had struck the man's face. He heard Ludlow cry out and expected to see blood gushing from a wound. None flowed. Apparently the blow missed, but not by much.

Ludlow had felt the wind of the billy's passing and in his over-wrought state imagined that the metal ball grazed his skin. Far worse than the threat of mangled hands, to his way of thinking, would be the disfigurement of his face. Not only did his handsome features bring in money, but he prided himself on his looks. All too well he could imagine the horror in which the billy would leave him. An intelligent man, he possessed sufficient imagination to picture the work of the steel ball as it tore his features to a bloody, barely human ruin. Nor did he doubt that Belle meant to carry out her threat. The Rebel Spy had plenty of good reasons to hate Yankee spies and her abhorrence of Southern-born traitors would hardly be less.

"Talk, man. Why be ruined," Tolling said. "Gilpin sold you down the river quick enough to save his own hide."

Although Tolling lied on the matter, Ludlow did not doubt his story. Being an unprincipled rogue himself, Ludlow could not imagine other men acting differently than he would under a set of circumstances. So he accepted the lie that Gilpin, who died without talking, betrayed him. For all that, he hesitated to talk and hoped for time to think how he might put his informaion to the best use.

"I don't know much!" he stated hurriedly as Belle's lips tightened. "They told me to come out here, make my way across to the Indian Nations and meet one of their people in the Choctaw Indians' main village."

"And that's all you know?" Belle asked.

"That's all I know," agreed Ludlow.

"Bring in that box, gentlemen," the girl ordered.

"Sure, Miss Boyd," Tolling answered and left the room followed by Dusty.

"Captain Fogg captured a Yankee agent on his way to the

Choctaw village," Belle explained to Ludlow. "Maybe his property will tell us something of your mission."

Watching the man, Belle noticed him give a shocked start as he saw the box Dusty and Tolling carried in. She drew the key from her pocket as the men set the box down before Ludlow, placing it between his hands on the table. Fear flickered across Ludlow's face as she walked forward. Then his features set into hard lines. Realising that he stood a good chance of dying, Ludlow found some comfort in the fact that the girl who humiliated and captured him would also be killed. Anger at Belle for out-smarting him over-rode his knowledge of what would happen when she inserted and turned the key.

"Hold it, Miss Boyd!" Tolling said urgently, just before the key entered the lock. "There may be an infernal contrivance in the keyhole."

"That's true enough," the girl admitted and stepped back. "Could you break the lock with a bullet from outside the room, Dusty?"

"Easy enough," Dusty replied.

"Then we'll go outside and watch you do it."

Although Belle, Tolling and Dusty retired from the cabin, they left Ludlow inside. Desperately he strained at his bonds, but the ropes held firm. Out in the open, at the far edge of the door's light, Belle and Tolling stood watching as Dusty took out his right side revolver then aimed in the direction of the box. If any member of Company 'C' had been watching, they might have felt surprise that Dusty took so long in his aiming at a target.

Sweat began to trickle down Ludlow's face as he realised that he, and he alone, would be caught in the raging inferno when the bullet struck the box's lock. While reconciled to dying as long as Belle went with him, he did not relish meeting his end in such a manner when she stood in safety.

"Don't shoot!" he screeched. "Don't shoot. I've something to tell you."

"Hold your fire, Dusty," Belle said and walked back into the cabin. Halting, she looked down at the man. "All right, Ludlow, what is it?"

"That box'll expode if you put a bullet into it."

"We'd an idea it might."

"I can tell you how to get into it without getting killed."

"So can the armourer here in camp," sniffed the girl. "Anyway, there's nothing of importance in it, I'll bet."

"You'd be wrong!" Ludlow growled. "It's full of counterfeit Confederate money."

"How do you know that?" Belle asked.

"What's in it if I talk?"

"What do you want?"

"My life," Ludlow said simply. "I know what'll happen to me if you send me for trial. It'll be a rope, or firing squad, and I'm not wanting to die."

Belle watched the man and knew that she had won. After placing Ludlow in the cabin, Tolling and Buck Blaze had removed some of the chinking—mud packed between the logs and allowed to harden there so as to keep out draughts—and made a hole large enough for them to keep him under observation from outside. Using the vantage point, Belle had studied the man on his recovery. She noted his concern for his face and based her subsequent actions on what she saw. First she played on his fears of hand-damage and disfigurement to weaken his resistance and then brought in the box on the odd chance that he might recognise it and be aware of its contents. Without the first shock treatment, he might have hidden his knowledge; but in his disturbed state failed to do so. Unless the girl missed her guess, Ludlow meant to tell all he knew. She hoped the time spent would prove worth the effort.

"Go ahead," she ordered.

Instead of answering the girl, Ludlow looked at Dusty. "I want your word as a Confederate officer that I'll not stand trial if I talk."

"Isn't *my* word good enough?" smiled Belle.

"I don't trust any of you Secret Service bunch on either side," Ludlow told the girl and turned to Dusty. "How about it, Captain?"

"I'll do all I can for you, *if* Miss Boyd says your information's worth it."

"That's not good enough. I want your assurance that I won't have to stand trial if I talk."

"These're three bars on my collar, mister, not three stars in a laurel wreath.* I don't have authority to make that kind of agreement."

"But I do," put in Ole Devil's voice and he entered. "Sorry to butt in, Miss Boyd, but I've been watching through that hole you had made in the wall. I always wanted to see some of you Secret Service crowd using 'gentle persuasion'."

*Three stars in laurel wreath: Confederate General's collar insignia.

48

"I suppose that General Hardin's word is good enough for you?" asked Belle.

Only for a moment did Ludlow hesitate. All too well he knew the iron code by which the true Southern gentlemen lived. If Ole Devil gave his word, he would stick by it. No matter that the people present would say nothing should he fail to do so, the General could be relied on not to go back upon his given word. As the Commanding General of the highly-successful Army of Arkansas, Ole Devil wielded considerable influence. Not even the leaders of the powerful Confederate States' Secret Service could countermand his orders. Nor would the South's Government attempt to interfere with any decision he made.

"Your word's good enough, General," Ludlow stated.

"You have it then. If, in Miss Boyd's opinion, your information has sufficient value, I give you my word that you won't stand trial for your actions."

While that placed a whole lot in Belle's hands, Ludlow realised he was in no position to argue.

"All right then," he said. "The box's full of counterfeit money—."

"You'll need to give us a whole heap more than that," Belle warned him.

"The Yankees plan to ruin the South with it!"

"With one box full?" snorted the girl. "Don't waste our time, man."

"They've more than one box full. This's only the start, Miss Boyd. They're printing more and plan to flood the South with so much counterfeit money that it'll ruin everybody and end the War."

"Do you know where they're printing it?" demanded Ole Devil.

"You might save your neck if you do," the girl went on.

"It's being printed down in New Orleans!" Ludlow blurted out.

"That's a mighty big area, but one well-covered by our spies," Belle pointed out. "How is it that they've learned nothing about the plot?"

"It's been kept a real close secret."

"Then how did you learn about it?" the girl snapped.

"Pickings've been mighty slim in New Orleans since the Yankees took it. So I grabbed when Gilpin came up with an offer to make some money. They didn't tell me much, but I learned what the game was and all about it."

"Go on," the girl prompted, knowing a man like Ludlow would

have methods of gaining information that exceeded those of her own people; especially as he found himself with such a good starting point.

"Like I said," he continued, "I kept my eyes open and followed Gilpin without his knowing. I learned all the game, including where they're printing and holding the money."

"And where is it?" Belle asked.

"Is this important enough to save me?" inquired Ludlow.

"If you're telling the truth."

"I'm telling it, so help me!" Ludlow insisted, with such sincerity that the girl felt sure he told the truth. "A feller called Gaton's doing the printing and the stuff's held at his place on St. Charles Avenue."

"That's in the old city," Belle pointed out.

"Sure. A big old house standing in a garden with a high wall around it," agreed Ludlow. "Gaton's working for the Yankees, has been ever since they took over. That's the truth, Miss Boyd."

"I hope for your sake that it is," the girl said quietly.

"How about him, Miss Boyd?" Ole Devil asked.

"I'd say keep him alive, but a prisoner, until we've found a way to verify his story," the girl replied. "If it's true, turn him loose. If not—."

"If not you won't need to deal with him," Ole Devil growled. "I've men under me who learned torture from the Indians. We'll see if they can make him tell the truth. I'll do what you say. Release him, Dustine."

"Yo!" Dusty answered and obeyed.

After releasing Ludlow, Dusty left the cabin, fastening its door with the padlock which took the place of the usual fitting. Then he walked after the others in the direction of the house used as Ole Devil's headquarters.

"He talked easy enough," Dusty commented as he caught up to Belle.

"Easier than I expected," Tolling admitted.

"Of course he was only doing it for money," Belle put in. "That kind break easier than a fanatic. I'd have bet, when we watched him, that we wouldn't need to do more than threaten to use violence."

"Would you have carried out your threats, Belle?" Dusty inquired.

"If necessary," the girl replied quietly. "This isn't a game I play, Dusty, it's a vicious, dirty business without any rules. The thing now is to destroy the counterfeiting plant, its plates, inks and paper. If we can do that, it'll put back the Yankees' plot for long enough to allow us to counter it."

"Can your people handle it, Miss Boyd?" Ole Devil asked.

"I mean to try, General," she replied.

"You?"

"Of course. I know New Orleans fairly well, but I may need help."

"You want for me to go with you, Miss Boyd?" Tolling wanted to know.

"No. I'd like you to go into the Indian Nations and see if you can find out who Oliver was to contact. I don't think you're going to be any too happy about me, General Hardin."

"Why?" said the General.

"Because I'm going to make a formal request that you assign Dusty to help me wreck that plant."

"You realise what you're asking, Miss Boyd?" Ole Devil snapped, halting and facing the girl. "I know Dustine helped you collect those arms, but he travelled and worked in uniform. That won't be possible this time."

Which meant, as Dusty knew without needing telling, that if he fell into the Yankees' hands, he could not claim the rights and privileges accorded to a captured officer. If he went in civilian clothing, he classed as a spy and would be shot. For all that, Dusty felt a touch of pride when considering Belle Boyd, the fabled Rebel Spy, requested his assistance on a desperate and dangerous mission.

Ole Devil did not appear so eager. "Do you consider Dustine's presence necessary, Miss Boyd?"

"Essential, General," the girl assured him. "I need a man of courage and on whom I can rely implicitly. Dusty fills that need."

A frown creased Ole Devil's face. Apart from personal considerations, he had his command to consider. Losing Dusty for a further indefinite period would lessen his fighting strength and the balance of power hung delicately in Arkansas. However he realised that should the Yankee counterfeiting plant not be destroyed, the War must be lost. He also appreciated the risks and difficulties facing Belle. Having a good man—which, despite his youth, Dusty was—at her back might make the difference between success and failure. So he made his decision.

"Very well, Dustine," he said. "You will accompany Miss Boyd and give her every possible aid. Good luck to you both."

"Thank you, General," smiled the girl. "I've a feeling we'll likely need it."

## Chapter 6

# A Different Way of Travelling

Due to the urgency of the situation neither Dusty nor Belle found time to sleep much on the night of Ludlow's interrogation. They had their preparations to make for the journey. First they would ride to the nearest town on the Red River and there go by steamboat down to Alexandria, after which some way must be found by which they could reach New Orleans.

During the first stages of the journey, Dusty would travel in uniform. To avoid attracting too much attention, he elected to wear a jacket which followed the dictates of the Confederate States Army's *Manual of Dress Regulations*, including the issue-type sword and pistol belt. His dress for New Orleans would be civilian clothing of a fairly nondescript kind; town suit, boots and hat. Nor could he take along his gunbelt and matched Army Colts as they would attract too much unwanted attention. That left him with the problem of selecting a suitable weapon for his needs. Texas born and raised, Dusty believed in a gun of .44 calibre as the only type on which a man might place complete reliability. Yet none of them were small enough for easy concealment. Finally he elected to take along one Army Colt. It would be carried in his waistband, hidden under his jacket and be readily accessible when needed. Of course he would be unable to draw with his usual speed, but reckoned to be fast enough when dealing with men unused to range-style gun-handling.

Belle too made her preparations for the assignment. It seemed highly unlikely that she would need her specially designed ball gown, so she decided to leave it behind until her return. Instead she would travel to Alexandria in an outfit suited to the part she intended to play; that of a well-to-do Southern lady on a journey. In addition she meant to take her male clothing, gunbelt and another of her special dresses, this time of a cheaper appearance and cut on the style a lady's maid would wear. Using a capacious carpetbag as her one item of luggage, the girl packed in her spare clothing on top of the gunbelt and Dance. Already inside lay a jewellery case holding the 'Borgia' ring, her lens locket and various trinkets. The parasol, taken down into its two parts went in the bag, as did a purse heavy with Yankee gold and a spare wig. She left the materials for destruction of the counterfeiting plant to be supplied by the South's agents in New Orleans.

So quickly did they work that on the night following the capture of Ludlow, Dusty and Belle boarded a riverboat and started upon the first and easiest leg of their journey.

While the boat carried him down the Red River, Dusty spent much of his waking time wondering what means they would use to reach New Orleans. In July the previous year, the Yankees finally took Vicksburg and gained control of the lower Mississippi River. On their last assignment Dusty and Belle avoided the problem that this posed by going along the Atchafalaya River to Morgan City, so by-passing the Big Muddy completely. Unfortunately they could hardly do so to reach New Orleans. Confederate armoured river-boats raided along the Mississippi, even slipping by the shore-batteries at Vicksburg and Baton Rouge to attack Yankee shipping on the lower reaches, but did not meet Dusty and Belle's needs. Running the gauntlet of the Yankee heavy artillery, or the U.S. Navy's efficient Mississippi Squadron would be too risky in a big river-boat when they had so much at stake. Of course they might take horses and pass along the fringe of the Yankee-held territory, then try to slip through to New Orleans over-land, but doing so was certain to take far too long to be of any use.

As the last major Confederate town on the Red before it joined the Mississippi, Alexandria lived in a constant state of readiness for war. On the down-stream side batteries of heavy-calibre cannon covered the water ready to repel any Yankee attack. Armoured vessels occupied most of the berths which before the War housed steamboats loaded with cotton and flatboats carrying produce of lesser importance down to the major cities along the country's greatest waterway.

On her arrival, Belle presented her credentials to the relevant authorities. She left Dusty to be taken on a tour of the city's defences while she saw various officials to arrange for their passage to New Orleans. Knowing something of Alexandria's defences, the girl made a request and backed it with Ole Devil's written orders that she be given every assistance. The General's name packed enough weight to ensure compliance and he arranged for a different way of travelling to any that Dusty might have guessed.

Shortly after dark Belle and Dusty entered a closed carriage and drove through the town. The girl wore male clothing and Dusty dressed as a civilian. With a range-dweller's sense of direction, Dusty guessed that they did not head for the main riverfront area. In fact they left Alexandria behind and went down-river. At last the carriage halted and they climbed down. Before them a narrow path wound off through a thickly wooded area. Standing in the centre of the path, a tall, slim, bearded young Confederate Navy lieutenant armed with sword and Navy Colt faced them.

"This's Lieutenant Cord Pinckney, Dusty," introduced Belle. "Cord, allow me to present Captain Dusty Fog."

"Captain Fog," greeted Pinckney. "Excuse the lack of formalities, but we'd best be moving."

Without saying more, Pinckney led the way along the winding path. Water glinted through the trees, a large lagoon off the main flow of the Red. At the lagoon's edge rested a kind of vessel Dusty had heard about but never before seen.

"A submersible," he said. "So that's how we'll do it!"

"That's just how we're going to do it," agreed the girl. "This is the Confederate Navy Ship *Jack the Giant-Killer*. Lieutenant Pinckney designed her himself specially for river work."

Basically the *Jack* looked little different to the other *David*-class torpedo boat-rams which operated off Charleston and gave the blockading Yankees as much trouble as did Dusty's Company in Arkansas. Fifty-four foot in length, she looked like a cigar with an oblong cockpit, funnel and torpedo-elevating spar rising from her deck. The torpedo itself, a copper container holding 100 pounds of gunpowder, rode submerged at the end of a fourteen foot hollow iron tube fitted to the bows, but could be raised to an operative position when needed. However the *Jack* rode higher in the water than the usual *David* which was ballasted down so hardly more than the cockpit showed above the surface.

Although smaller than any steamboat, the *Jack* still would show up on the river surface. Or so Dusty imagined as he looked at the little vessel. He was given no time to think of the matter. Already the *Jack's* three-man crew stood by ready to leave. Smoke rose from the stack and the stoker tossed fuel on to the furnace, but its mouth had been masked so that none of the glow showed outside the hull.

"It'll not be as comfortable as travelling in a riverboat," Pinckney commented as his coxswain took the passengers' bags and stowed them at the rear of the cockpit. "And I hadn't counted on one of you being a lady."

"Neither did my father when I was born," Belle smiled. "He learned to live with it. I'm used to travelling rough, Mr. Pinckney."

54

"It'll be that," Pinckney replied. "We'll travel all night and as far as we dare during the day. It'll be uncomfortable, dangerous and uncertain. I've my orders to deliver you to New Orleans and aim to make a try. But I feel it's my duty to warn you of the dangers involved."

"And we accept them," Belle assured him. "Where do you want us to ride?"

Not that there would be much of a choice, the *Jack's* sole accomodation being the tiny cockpit.

"Sit at the stern, the back end," ordered Pinckney, translating for the benefit of folks he did not expect to understand nautical terms. "Once we're under way, you can move about—as much as possible—unless we sight the enemy."

"And if we do?" asked Dusty, wondering what the tiny vessel could hope to accomplish against even one of the small 'tin-clad' river gun-boats, so-called because of their very light armour plating.

"You'll return to the stern, sit down and keep quiet," Pinckney replied. "I hope it doesn't come to that, though."

With his passengers aboard, Pinckney ordered his men to cast off. Despite using a rear-screw, as opposed to the twin side-wheels of the riverboats, the *Jack* handled well and showed a surprising manoeuvrability. After being poled away from the shore, the little submersible gathered way and headed across the lagoon. Ahead lay a narrow gap barely wide enough for the boat, but Pinckney guided it through with little change of speed and once on the river headed downstream.

Clearly the *Jack's* crew knew their work and went about it without needing orders. In addition to their cutlasses and Navy Colts, the men had two shotguns and a pair of Sharps carbines for armament.

"Which same stops us coming alongside and trading broad-sides with any Yankee we meet," Pinckney drawled as he saw Dusty studying his ship's weapons. "Mind you though, apart from those Yankee steam-launches, there's not a craft on the Big Muddy can catch the *Jack* running with the current and we'd give a launch a good run for its money."

Even as Pinckney spoke, one of the crew men hauled on a cable which raised the torpedo spar from the water. Then the sailor swung over the cockpit and advanced along the deck to stand by the elevating spar. He looked down at the water intently, giving an occasional direction over his shoulder to the coxswain. On shore the shapes of the guardian batteries showed, gun crews on the alert but not challenging the little ship.

"We're passing through the frame-torpedoes," Belle breathed. "That's why they raised the spar."

Dusty did not need to ask why. Frame-torpedoes—the name 'mine' had not yet come into use—were copper or cast-iron shells filled with explosives, mounted on wooden frames firmly anchored to the river's bottom. Fixed to come just below the surface, the shells carried percussion caps to be ignited when struck by an enemy vessel coming up-river. However it did not pay to knock or jolt the torpedoes from any angle and Pinckney took no chances.

Even the *Jack*'s crew members looked relieved when they had passed through the frame-torpedo maze. On went the little boat, its screw propeller making only a small sound instead of the thrashing thump a side-wheeler's paddles gave out. With the current behind them and the engine turning the propellors steadily, they made a steady fifteen miles an hour.

Suddenly Dusty heard a gurgling sound and became aware that the *Jack* appeared to be settling deeper in the water. None of the crew showed the slightest concern, although the cox'n turned the wheel over to Pinckney and watched the river's surface creeping higher. At last, with the water lapping at the very bottom of the cockpit, the gurgling stopped. Pinckney swung the wheel and the *Jack* moved across the river, turned back and resumed its course downstream. Nodding in satisfaction, Pinckney gave an order and the smallest member of his crew ducked out of sight under the deck. Turning over the wheel to his cox'n, Pinckney smiled at his passengers. It seemed that he noticed their agitation for the first time.

"I've just been ballasting her down," he explained. "Run water into two tanks so that we lay lower and aren't so easy to see. Most of the time we'll be at normal level, but we'll have to go down when we're passing Yankee ships or batteries. When we're by, we pump out the water and go on as before."

"That's smart thinking," Dusty drawled, trying not to reveal that he had been worried.

"The *Hunley* was a better one," Pinckney answered. "She'd got right under water. The crew stayed down for just over two and a half hours once."

"If we could have found some way to power her, it would have made all the difference," Belle remarked.

"It'll come one of these days," prophesised Pinckney.

Even in Arkansas word of the submarine *Hunley*'s exploits had been heard. Lacking engines, for steam could not be generated under water, the crew operated handles on a crank shaft to propel it through the water. After experimentation and some loss of life, the *Hunley* went down in a successful attempt to destroy the U.S.S. *Housatonic*.

While unable to submerge completely, the little *David*-class boats achieved greater success than the true submarine.

Despite the fact that the Red River remained in Confederate hands, one member of the tiny crew stayed on the look-out all the time. The U.S. Navy's Mississippi Squadron sometimes sent raiding vessels off the main river and even a steam-launch's crew submerged to cockpit level, crept by the Confederate batteries guarding the mouth of the Red and swung out on to the wide Mississippi.

"I never knew it was this big!" Dusty breathed as daylight gave him his first view of the main river.

"It's even wider lower down," the girl replied, then looked at Pinckney. "What do we do now?"

"Go on as far as we can, then find a place to lie up until night-fall," he replied. "We have to pass the towns at night, the Yankees have garrisons in some of them."

Dusty and Belle exchanged glances. All too well they realised the extreme urgency of their mission; and understood what such an extensive delay might cost the South. Yet there did not seem to be any way of slipping unseen by the Yankee garrisons along the river's banks.

While thinking about the problem, Dusty glanced upstream and saw something bobbing in the current some way behind them. Even as he opened his mouth to give a warning, he realised the thing was a large tree either cut or torn down up-river and, having fallen in, came floating down on the current. From the lack of interest in the sight shown by the *Jack*'s crew, Dusty concluded it must be a reasonably regular occurence. Pinckney confirmed the view when Dusty put a question to him.

"Trees? Sure, you see plenty of them; bushes too. I've seen what looked like whole islands floating down-river at times."

"Reckon the Yankees'd be used to seeing them, then," Dusty drawled.

"I'd say so," agreed Pinckney.

Looking at the wooded banks of the river, Dusty sucked in a breath. He did not wish to appear foolish and hesitated before offering what might be an impractical suggestion.

"I've got a fool notion that you might like to try, Mr. Pinckney," he said, and after explaining it finished, "Mind, I don't know sic 'em about boats or if it'll be possible to do."

"It'd be possible all right, but riskier than all hell," Pinckney answered. "Just how important is this mission you're on, Miss Boyd?"

"So important that its failure could cost us the war," Belle told him. "And any delay increases the danger."

"Then it's important for us to take the chance," Pinckney decided. "We'll give your 'fool notion' a whirl, Captain Fog. Take her ashore, cox'n."

Deftly swinging the *Jack* nearer to the bank, the cox'n watched for a place where there would be sufficient water close in for them to stop without running aground. Not until two miles fell behind them did he find the kind of place he wanted and during that time Pinckney explained Dusty's scheme to his attentive crew. If the grins of the three men proved anything, they felt no concern at chancing their lives to the small Texan's 'fool notion'.

With the *Jack* bobbing in a bay just deep enough to keep her afloat, but offering some slight shelter should any Yankee warship happen to pass, the party went to work. Taking the field glasses used by the look-out, Belle went to a place from which she could keep watch on the river and left the men to handle the work. Putting aside all thought of rank, Dusty and Pinckney helped the three enlisted men to cut branches and bushes, then take the material to the boat. With a sense of urgency driving them, the men secured their gatherings until all the upper deck and its fittings lay hidden under a ragged, yet natural-appearing, mass of vegetation. While the sailors added the finishing touches, Pinckney and Dusty discussed the dangers which lay ahead.

"We'll have to go with the current when anybody's watching," the lieutenant warned. "And stay as far away as possible from whoever is watching. It'd be best if we ran by Baton Rouge in the dark, too. The Yankees only have small garrisons in most places, but they hold the major cities with strong forces."

"How about fuel?" asked Dusty.

"We'll need to pick some up. I know of a couple of secret supplies left by the cutting parties from the different woodings."

Having made a long trip on a riverboat, Dusty knew about woodings. Professional wood-cutters made their living by hewing timber and collecting it at established points along the river for sale to passing boats. Pinckney explained that the Yankees destroyed some of the woodings, but maintained others to supply fuel for their vessels. Under the guise of co-operating, some of the wooding owners laid on secret wood-piles for use by such Confederate ships as might need it while on raiding missions along the river.

With everything ready, the party ate a meal made up from

58

supplies brought aboard in Alexandria. Then they boarded the foliage-draped *Jack* and started moving once more. After a few adjustments had been made, the cox'n announced that he could see well enough and discovered that the boat answered to the wheel in a satisfactory manner.

For three hours they travelled downstream without seeing anything to disturb them. Before the War there would have been other boats on the move, people working on the banks, but most activity had been suspended due to the danger of becoming involved in a clash between the two opposing forces. Suddenly the look-out turned from where he peered through a gap made in the foliage.

"Boat dead ahead, sir," he said, offering Pinckney the field glasses.

"Stop engines!" the lieutenant ordered after studying the approaching vessel briefly. "Run us as close as you can to the starboard bank, cox'n. Not a sound or movement from any of you after that."

With the engine stopped, the *Jack* drifted on the current. Gradually and in as near a natural manner as he could manage, the cox'n steered them across the river and then held the boat so that it continued to move but did not swing in the direction of the approaching enemy craft.

"It's a steam-launch," breathed the sailor at Dusty's side as they peered through the foliage.

Dusty studied the other craft as it drew nearer, holding out in the centre of the wide river and making good speed even against the current. In appearance it resembled a large rowing boat, but with a powerful steam-engine installed. A twelve-pounder boat-howitzer rode on a slide-carriage at the bows, while the launch's spar torpedo hung on slings alongside instead of extending before the vessel as it would when ready for use. Although only thirty foot in length, the steam-launch carried a crew of seven men and possessed sufficient armament to blow the *Jack* out of the water even without using the spar-torpedo.

Nothing Dusty had ever done in action or during his patrols ever filled him with a nervous strain to equal that of watching the Yankee steam-launch go by. Born on the great open plains of Southern Texas, the largest river he had seen until joining the Army was the Rio Hondo and that looked like no more than a stream compared with the width of the Big Muddy. His eyes flickered to the Sharps carbines and his right hand touched the grip of the Army Colt at his waistband. Neither weapon offered much comfort when he considered the strength of the enemy's armament.

Belle could sense Dusty's tension and smiled a little, which helped relieve her own. However, having seen the small Texan's cold courage at other times, she knew he would do nothing that might endanger their mission.

On came the launch, drawing closer, coming level and then passing them. Not one of the Yankee sailors did more than glance at the floating foliage. Soon the two vessels lay so far apart that Pinckney decided they might chance using their own engines. With the added thrust of the Jack's propellors, they quickly ran the Yankee launch out of sight.

"How'd you like it, Captain Fog?" grinned Pinckney.

"Well, I'll tell you," drawled Dusty sincerely. "Give me leading a cavalry charge any old time at all."

## Chapter 7

# A Matter of Simple Priorities

The *Jack* continued to make good time, without meeting any other shipping or needing to do more than cut off their engines while passing some river-edge town or village. At around three in the afternoon, Pinckney told his passengers that they would soon be stopping to take on fuel at a secret dump left by Confederate supporters working out of Mendel's Wooding.

"We'll have to run in there behind that island," he went on, pointing ahead. "Unless it's silted up or something, there's more than enough room and water for the *Jack* and we'll be hidden from anybody who might happen to be coming along the river in either direction."

"It may be as well to take a look before we pull in," Dusty suggested. "If you put me ashore, I'll go."

"Two pairs of eyes are better than one," Belle remarked. "I'll go with you."

"Follow the bank then," Pinckney told them. "You'll see a flowering dogwood tree about a hundred yards along it and the wood-pile's hidden under a dead-fall near to it."

"Mind if I take one of the carbines?" Dusty asked. "A dead-fall's a good place to find a bear, if you have bear down here."

"We've some," admitted Pinckney. "But there's a Yankee garrison at Mendel's Wooding and if they hear a shot, they'll come running."

"Looks like a carbine won't help us then, Dusty," Belle said and opened her bag to take out the parasol handle. "It doesn't make any noise—."

"And won't stop a bear, either," grinned Dusty. "We'll just have to hope there's not one there."

"I'll come with you," Pinckney decided. "I know just where the wood is and can tell whether it'll be any use to us."

Parting the foliage, Dusty, Belle and Pinckney slipped through, into the water and waded ashore. Back on his native element, Dusty moved with easy confidence, gliding ahead of the other two and searching around him with careful, all-seeing eyes. Coming to a halt, he waited for the other two and pointed ahead.

" 'Gator," he said. "Just look at the size of it, too."

Belle and Pinckney were more used to seeing alligators, but admitted to themselves that the specimen ahead could be termed a real big one. Full sixteen feet long, with a bulk which told of good feeding and long years, the alligator lay with its broad, rounded and flat-looking snout pointing to the water of the channel. Hearing Dusty's voice, it lifted its powerful body on legs which appeared too slender to support it. Letting out a long hiss, it plunged into the channel's water to create a considerable disturbance before disappearing under the surface.

As the water parted under the impact of the alligator's arrival, something black, rounded and inanimate showed briefly above the surface. Briefly or not, Belle and Pinckney saw enough.

"A torpedo of some kind!" the girl exclaimed.

"Looks that way," agreed Pinckney.

"Then the Yankees have found the wood-pile," Dusty growled.

"Not necessarily," Pinckney replied. "They'd figure this channel'd be a place where one of our raiders might hide and left a torpedo here instead of having to guard it."

"We'll have to move it before we can fetch the Jack in," Belle stated.

"That's just what we'll have to do," agreed Pinckney quietly.

"Can you do it?" the girl asked.

"I've had to do it a couple of times."

"It might be as well for us to make sure there's enough wood on hand for it to be worth while," Dusty commented.

"There's that," Pinckney agreed.

Going first to the flowering dogwood tree and then making a circle of the dead-fall, Dusty found no sign of new or old tracks which would tell that the hidden wood had been discovered. While he did not put himself in Kiowa's class as a reader of signs, Dusty reckoned he knew enough to locate any left by in-experienced men. Finding nothing, he went to the dead-fall—a tree fetched down in a storm and supported on a clump of rock in such a manner that a hollow remained underneath. Under the dead-fall, hidden by what looked like part of the tree's branches, lay piles of cut timber. Calling up the others, Dusty told them of his negative findings. Then he stepped aside and allowed Pinckney to take his place.

"What'd you expect to find?" Dusty asked, after the lieuten-ant rose from examining the wood.

"An old riverboat trick was to hollow out a log, fill it with gun-powder then plug up the end so it looked natural," Pinckney explained. "Then when the stokers tossed it on to the boiler fire—."

"I don't reckon it did the boilers any good," grinned Dusty. "Is this lot all right?"

"As far as I can see," Pinckney replied. "Let's see about that torpedo."

"What kind is it?" asked Belle.

"I didn't see much," Pinckney answered. "But I reckon it's a Brooke, or a copy of it. The Yankees've fetched a few in unexploded, I'd say."

"They might know about Turtle torpedoes too," warned the girl.

"Hell's fire, yes," Pinckney barked. "I'd forgotten all about them."

"What're they?" Dusty asked.

Belle explained how the Brooke torpedo consisted of a copper case holding the explosive charge and bearing either percussion or chemical detonators positioned to be struck when a passing boat made contact. As an added aid to the built-in buoyancy chamber, the Brooke rode on a wooden-spar that extended down to its anchor; which made the fast-developing art of mine-sweeping more difficult. As an added precaution against removal, the Turtle torpedo had been developed. Looking roughly like a turtle's shell, the torpedo lay on the bottom with a length of wire connecting its detonating primer to the Brooke. Should anyone attempt to drag away the Brooke torpedo, its weight activated the Turtle's primer and one hundred pounds of explosive went off beneath the surface.

"So we'll have to send a man down to check," the girl concluded. "And if there is a Turtle, he'll have to cut it free."

"Which's dangerous," Pinckney continued. "The Brooke might've moved and pulled on the Turtle's primer so that a touch sends it off. If that happens while I'm cutting the wire—."

"In that case," Dusty interrupted. "You'd best let me do it."

"You?" asked Pinckney.

"It's a matter of simple priorities," Dusty replied. "You can't be spared, Cord, or there'll be nobody to run your boat. Nor can any of your crew. And Belle has to reach New Orleans. I can't handle her work. So that makes me the most expendable of us."

True enough, as a matter of pure, cold-blooded logic, but not the kind of decision most men would have cared to make.

"How well can you swim, Dusty?" Pinckney asked, dropping the formal mode of address for the first time.

"Well enough, under and on top of the water. Tell me what to look for and how to handle it, then I'll have a try."

"I've got some wire cutters in the *Jack*—."

"Let me fetch them," Belle suggested. "You tell Dusty what to do."

"Go to it," Pinckney confirmed and after the girl left went on, "find the Brooke, but don't touch it. Then if you dive you can follow its spar to the anchor. I don't reckon the water'll be more than ten, twelve foot deep if that. Feel real carefully around the anchor until you touch the Turtle's connecting wire. Then come up and let me know what you find."

Stripping off all but his underpants, Dusty entered the water. Pinckney watched and decided that the small Texan could swim well enough to handle the work ahead. On locating the Brooke, which—being designed to handle shallow-draught riverboats— did not lie too deep, Dusty sucked in a breath and dived. He found little difficulty in locating the anchor, merely following the wooden spar down to the bed of the channel. Before his air ran out, he traced the edge of the anchor block and felt the thin wire. With cold apprehension he realised that the connection between the anchor and the torpedo was taut.

Long practice had taught Dusty to keep his eyes open under water and he could see a little way in the dark canal. Forcing himself to stay down, he kept one finger touching the wire as he followed it from the Brooke. Not three feet away lay the rounded shape of the Turtle. Before Dusty could do anything more, lack of air sent him to the surface. By that time Belle had returned, but she swung her back to Dusty as he broke water and gasped in a long breath.

"It's a torpedo," Dusty declared. "With a Turtle on the bottom. The wire's taut, too."

"That's bad!" Pinckney growled.

"Maybe," Dusty said. "I'm going to try to lift the Turtle and move it closer to the Brooke, then cut the wire."

"That'll be risky!" Belle gasped, throwing aside the proprieties and turning to face Dusty.

"No more risky than cutting the wire while it's tight," Dusty pointed out and dived again.

Going down seemed longer, but Dusty forced himself to concentrate on his object. He found the Turtle and lowered his hands, fingers probing around its edges and finding them partly buried in the gravel bottom of the channel. At last he managed to get a grip on the underneath. By that time his lungs felt on the point of bursting, but he forced himself to carry on. Going up

64

for air and diving again would not be easy and he preferred to get the business over in one go if he possibly could. So he tightened his grip and lifted. For an instant the Turtle remained stuck, but then it moved. Dusty forced himself to think, not acting blindly. Whatever he did, he must move the Turtle towards the Brooke. If he drew it away, the pressure might pull hard enough to operate the primer and fire the charge.

Slowly the Turtle rose and moved in the direction of the Brooke's anchor. Setting down his burden, Dusty gently felt for the wire. Relief flooded through him as he found it to be hanging loose. The main danger had passed. All that remained to do was clip the wire and remove the Brooke torpedo. Gratefully Dusty rose once more to the surface. One look at his face told the watching pair of his success without needing words.

"Pass me the wire clippers, Belle," Dusty requested. "I reckon it's safe to cut them apart now."

"Everything's all right then?" she asked, handing him the powerful instruments collected from the *Jack*.

"I'll tell you better the next time I come up," Dusty grinned. "If I come up slow enough that is."

"You be careful!" Belle ordered. "If anything happens to you, it's me who will have to go back and explain to Company 'C'."

"Now there's concern for you, Dusty," Pinckney chuckled.

Once again Dusty dived down through the water, following the Brooke's spar until he could see the Turtle resting in its new position. However the task proved more difficult than he imagined. After three attempts Dusty managed to clamp the jaws of the clippers around the wire. Fighting against the time when lack of air would drive him back to the surface, he applied pressure on the handles. It must be a straight cut. Any jiggling or twisting at the wire in an attempt to weaken it might drag out the primer and explode the Turtle. Then the wire parted, its separated ends falling away.

Even as Dusty realised he had completed his task, a feeling that all was not well bit into him. As his danger-instinct screamed out its grim warning, he became aware of a shape moving through the water in his direction and travelling with an ease that no human being ever attained under such conditions.

Since reaching a greater length than most others of its kind, the bull alligator ruled that stretch of the Mississippi and claimed the channel as its especial den area. While it might dive into the water at the approach of man, the alligator feared nothing when in its native element. Sensing the presence of another large creature under the channel's surface, it came back to defend its territory. Gliding forward with the effortless-seeming way of its kind, the alligator located Dusty and moved in to attack. With a thrust of its powerful tail, it surged in the small Texan's direction.

Never had Dusty's lightning-fast reactions stood up to such a test. From seeing the alligator rushing at him to doing something about it took only a split second. Nor would there have been time for any greater deliberation on the problem. Digging his feet into the channel's bed, Dusty propelled himself backwards. Yet so close was his escape that the alligator brushed against him in passing. Desperately Dusty threw one arm around the alligator's thick neck, while his legs locked around the rough scaled body. With his grip established, Dusty hung safe from the brute's jaws and tail; but felt like the man who caught a tiger by the tail. If he released his hold, the alligator would turn on him again.

"I think he's going to make it!" breathed Belle as the seconds ticked by.

Suddenly the even surface of the water bulged and churned. Once more the Brooke torpedo's head showed briefly, but neither Belle nor Pinckney had eyes for it. Both stared at the sight of Dusty clinging to the alligator as they swirled into sight and disappeared once more beneath the surface.

"Lord!" Belle gasped, reaching for her Dance. "We forgot that bull 'gator!"

Although both she and Pinckney drew their weapons, neither offered to fire. Not only could they see no sign of Dusty, but both realised that the sound of shooting would attract any nearby Yankees as effectively as if the torpedoes went off. If it came to a point, Belle doubted her ability to hit the alligator in its brief appearances, with Dusty clinging so close to it.

"Bring me a cutlass, cox'n!" Pinckney yelled, reaching the same conclusion as Belle and aware that the weapon's arrival might come too late.

Equally aware, Belle made her decision. Swiftly she twirled the Dance back into its holster, then unbuckled and allowed the belt to slide to her feet. Darting forward, she gripped the metal ball of the parasol handle, tugging to draw out the full wicked length of the billy. Even as Pinckney realised what the girl meant to do and opened his mouth to order her back, Belle plunged into the water.

Rising again Dusty and the alligator rolled into sight, the small Texan being raised clear of the surface. Although Belle struck out hard, she knew she would reach the spot too late for that appearance. Then something happened which lent an added urgency to the need for rescuing Dusty. Lashing around, the alligator's tail struck the water scant inches from the Brooke torpedo's head. If the tail struck, or the brute's body collided with the swaying torpedo, an explosion must surely result. Once more man and reptile disappeared beneath the boiling surface of the channel. Belle swam closer, conscious of her own danger. While Dusty held the neck and body, he could not grip and keep closed the murderous jaws. Seeing the girl's arms or legs as she swam, it might grab hold of her.

The danger did not take form and Belle saw the struggling pair rising to the surface. Treading water, she watched and waited. Up they rolled, with the small Texan retaining his hold with grim and deadly determination. Stripped to his underpants, his powerful muscular development showed. Biceps bulged, their veins standing out from the skin, under the effort of holding on. Dusty's face showed strain and approaching exhaustion as he opened his mouth to drag air into his tortured lungs. Yet he still retained his hold and did not seem aware of Belle's nearness.

Sucking in her breath, the girl took aim and struck with all her might. The force of her effort caused her body to rise in the water. Around, up and down lashed the murderous billy. Its coil-spring bowed and snapped straight, propelling the pliant but powerful steel shaft with increasing force. All too well Belle knew the danger. If the metal ball of the billy caught Dusty's arm, it would splinter bone and cause him to lose his hold.

Never had the billy seemed to move so slowly. Then it descended, the ball smashing on to the top and centre of the alligator's skull. Although unaware of the girl's arrival, Dusty heard the wicked crack of impact and felt a convulsive shudder run through the alligator's giant frame.

"Let go, Dusty!" Belle screeched. "Turn him loose and head for the bank."

The words meant nothing to Dusty in his dazed, half-drowned condition. Yet he sensed a difference in the alligator's behaviour as it began to sink again. Instead of forging its way down, the reptile sank slowly and in a limp manner.

Flinging her billy ashore, Belle dived after and caught Dusty under the armpits in an effort to drag him back to the surface. She failed to do so, but help came fast. Disregarding the cutlass his cox'n waved while dashing along the bank, Pinckney also discarded his belt—he had removed his sword on entering the *Jack* so as to conserve the boat's limited space—and plunged into

67

the water. Striking out fast, Pinckney reached Belle and dived under to help. Between them, Belle and Pinckney managed to haul Dusty back to the surface. In his half-drowned condition, the small Texan could not maintain his hold on the alligator. As he felt the body slip away from him, Dusty's head broke the surface and he sucked in air. On being released, the alligator's body continued to sink until it came to rest on the bed of the channel.

Belle and Pinckney hauled Dusty towards the bank, while the cox'n plunged forward, wading in to lend them a hand. A few seconds later Dusty lay on solid land and looked weakly up at the anxious faces around him.

"Wh—Where's the 'gator?" he gasped.

"Belle got it," Pinckney replied. "Although I'm damned if I know how she did it."

"I just whomped that ole 'gator over the head with my billy," the girl smiled. "It's not the first time I've done it. When I was around eleven back on the plantation I and a boy cousin made a regular game of killing 'gators by sneaking up and cracking them over the skull with a piece of timber. Lordy me! I'll never forget mama's face when she learned how Willy and I carried on while we were out walking."

"Thanks, Belle," Dusty said. "And you, Cord. Lord, I'll be old afore my time working with you pair."

For the first time Belle realised the exact scanty nature of Dusty's attire and came hurriedly to her feet. Nor did her soaking shirt and pants lead to modesty, so she decided to make adjustments and save embarrassment all round.

"I think I'd better find something dry to wear and go get changed into it," she said casually.

"Go to it," Pinckney replied. "We'll see to moving the Brooke, bring the *Jack* in and take on the fuel. You take a rest, Dusty, you've earned it."

Shortly before sundown the *Jack*, loaded with fuel and under the mass of foliage, crept out of the channel. Before leaving, Pinckney stripped the detonators from the torpedo and replaced its harmless shell back in position. If the Yankees had left the Brooke, they would find it in place should they check. Expecting the torpedo to be connected to the Turtle, it hardly seemed likely any inspecting crew would attempt to raise the Brooke in order to make a close examination. So they might continue to assume all was well and never suspect the guardian of the channel rode impotent and useless on its spar.

"Not that I'm ungrateful," Dusty drawled as the journey

resumed. "But you could've got killed coming in to help me. The idea was for me to take all the risks and chance getting blown up."

"Like I said," Belle replied. "It would be me who had to face Company 'C' if anything happened to you."

"You think you've got problems," grinned Pinckney. "I'd not only've had Dusty's company after me, I'd be running from your bosses too, Belle, if that 'gator managed to kill both of you."

"Damned if I guessed it," Dusty said in a resigned voice. "But I had the least to worry about of us all."

## Chapter 8

# A Snag to Miss Boyd's Plans

Before the War came, New Orleans ranked as the United States' second greatest port; and at the height of the cotton-gathering season its volume of trade exceeded even New York's. The city's waterfront area spread along the river for four miles and at times ocean-going or river-boats filled almost every inch of the front-age, in some cases lining out three or four deep. Then there had been a constant coming and going, boats arriving or departing with cargoes and helping the New Orleans banks to hold a greater combined capital than those of any city in the land, with the possible exception of gold-rich San Francisco.

The War changed all of that. When Farragut brought his fleet of iron-clad ships into the Mississippi, all hope of peaceful trading ended. Such riverboats as could fled up the river, others were sunk by the Yankee ironclads' guns. When defeat became inevitable, the waterfront glowed red as stocks of cotton, sugar, molasses and other produce were set on fire to prevent them falling into enemy hands.

Altogether the Federal garrison at New Orleans topped the fifteen thousand mark, while the Mississippi Squadron numbered forty-three major vessels and many smaller craft. However their ships took up only a portion of the riverfront and much more lay empty, deserted, with blackened, gutted ruins bleakly facing the mighty river.

Shortly before midnight, three days after leaving Alexandria, the *Jack* crept through the darkness towards a derelict stretch of wharf. Ballasted down to the limit of safety, the little boat had wended its way past Yankee artillery batteries and by U.S. Navy guard ships. The covering of foliage which served them so well during the majority of the journey had been discarded that day at sundown and within sight of the city, for it would attract too much attention and might be investigated.

After disarming the Brooke torpedo and tangling with the alligator, the remainder of the trip proved uneventful. Once they lay up for two hours against a mud bank while a Yankee trans-port took on fuel at a wooding. During the second night they drifted silently by one of the big *Conestoga*-class gunboats, with

Pinckney breathing curses at the turn of fate which made him pass up such a tempting and open target. The Yankee vessel went on its way, crewmen acting like they rode on a pleasure-cruise and blissfully unaware of the danger so narrowly averted.

As they approached the dock, a gurgling sound told Dusty that the *Jack* pumped out its ballast. Slowly the boat rose higher in the water, but instead of stopping edged between the piles of the wharf. An air of alert tension filled the *Jack's* crew and the cox'n went forward with a hooded bull's-eye lantern in his hand. Standing on the wet deck forward, he darted an occasional glimmer of light by which Pinckney at the wheel steered. It was an eerie sensation, passing between the piles supporting the wharf. Then the light showed a small jetty and Pinckney brought his boat to a halt alongside it.

"This's as far as we go," he told his passengers in a low voice. "Look around, cox'n and make sure all's secure."

"Aye aye, sir," the cox'n replied and stepped on to the jetty to fade away into the blackness.

"This's some place you have here, Cord," Dusty remarked when the cox'n returned with the news that all was safe.

"A bunch of us *David*-class captains rigged it up when we saw that New Orleans must fall," Pinckney replied. "We only use it in emergencies, but the Yankees haven't found it."

"How long can you lay here, Cord?" Belle asked.

"We're short on food, but I can stay until tomorrow night. Likely have to, there won't be time to run clear of the defences before morning. Will that be any good to you?"

"Hardly. It'll take all tomorrow at least to get what I need. If I can get food for you, are you game to wait two more nights?"

"I can get my own food," Pinckney assured her. "All right, I'll stay on for three days, but I'll have to pull out by just after sundown on the third night."

"Thank you, Cord," Belle said sincerely. "If we aren't back by then, go. In that case Dusty and I will take our chance of slipping through the Yankee lines and make our way north through our own territory."

"When do we start, Belle?" asked Dusty.

"Not before morning," the girl answered. "I don't know if the Yankees still impose a curfew, but even if they don't we'd attract attention walking through the streets at his hour."

"You sure would," agreed Pinckney. "I say grab some sleep and leave here at around eight or so in the morning. That way there'll be enough folks on the streets for you to have a chance."

71

"That's what we'll do," confirmed Belle. "And the sleep will be welcome."

Although the hidden dock offered none of the comforts of home, the *Jack's* party slept well. Next morning Belle went behind some of the pilings and changed into one of her dresses. She then worked on a wig, altering its hair-style to fit the part she must play. When finished, the girl looked like a lady's maid in the employment of a rich family. With her other property packed in the bag, she and Dusty accompanied the cox'n through a trapdoor cut in the floor of a gutted warehouse and came out on a deserted side-alley.

"Go down that ways and you'll come out on Thrift Street," the cox'n said. "Do you know it, ma'am?"

"Well enough to go to where I'm going," Belle answered.

"Good luck then," the man said, admiration on his face.

Dusty had often marvelled at the manner in which Belle could slough off her natural air of charm and good-breeding. On changing clothes she walked and talked like the wearer of such dress would.

Any doubts Belle might have felt about Dusty faded away. Without his uniform he became small, insignificant in appearance, an attribute he would turn to his advantage on more than one occasion during later years.*

"Where're we going?" he asked as they mingled with the early morning crowd on Thrift Street.

"To see one of our best agents," the girl replied, then raised her voice as a pair of Yankee soldiers approached them. "Don't you-all drop the bag, Jeremiah, or the mistress'll tan your fool hide for sure."

Neither of the soldiers, members of an infantry regiment on garrison duty in the city, as much as glanced at the passing pair. Dusty grinned at Belle and started to look back at the soldiers.

"Whooee!" he began. "I never thought to pass—."

"Don't look back!" Belle hissed. "Act like you're used to seeing Yankees around."

"Why sure," Dusty said. "I'm sorry, Belle."

"Don't be," the girl told him. "I'd make mistakes handling your work."

"Talking of that," Dusty drawled. "Do something nice for both of us in future, Belle gal."

"What?"

"Don't ask for me on another chore like this. It's plumb rough on the nerves."

*One occasion is told in "The Floating Outfit".

A faint smile flickered across Belle's face at the words. Most spies felt concern when they passed through enemy-controlled streets. Certainly Dusty handled himself well, considering that it was his first mission.

Although the girl had to pause and think a couple of times and once ask a passing man for directions, she and Dusty made good time through the streets. They passed other Yankee soldiers and sailors, with Dusty studiously ignoring his enemies. To help take his mind off the tricky nature of their business, Belle told him something of the person they went to contact.

"Her name is Madam Lucienne and she runs what used to be one of the most popular—and expensive—dress shops in New Orleans."

"A dress shop?" Dusty asked, for the nature of the business did not seem to go with the dangerous work of spying.

"Don't sell her short," Belle smiled. "Madam Lucienne had a 'past', or so Mama always used to tell me. Of course she never told me what the 'past' was; but you know what it means."

"It sure covers plenty of ground," Dusty replied.

Having a 'past' might mean no more than coming from the wrong section of society, or gaining a divorce after an unfortunate marriage. Being connected with the theatre might also give a woman a 'past', or any of a number of other things. Whatever aspect put Madam Lucienne in the category of having a 'past', she appeared to have overcome it if she ran a successful business in the old city of New Orleans.

" 'Past' or not," Belle said. "She's the best agent in New Orleans, with contacts all over the city."

"Reckon she can help us?"

"She probably knows about the counterfeiting plot all ready, if not of the plant's location. Even if she doesn't, she'll know where we can find the men we need for the work."

"I'd been wondering how you planned to handle things," Dusty remarked. "It looked like a chore for more than the two of us."

"It'll need more than us, for sure," Belle agreed. "We'll need somebody who knows how to break open the safe, for a starter."

"And Madam Lucienne knows somebody like that?"

"Knows the right man, or how to find him. We're nearly there, Dusty. It's around this corner and along the street."

Naturally the rich Creoles did not wish anything so sordid as a business section close to their homes; nor would they want to wander too far when shopping. The street on to which Belle and Dusty turned catered to the whims of the elegant and wealthy

73

citizens. Before the War every shop along it would have been open and doing good business. Only a few remained in operation, but all seemed to find trade, if from a different class of customer.

Across the street from the shop bearing the discreet sign announcing that Madam Lucienne owned it, a smart carriage drawn by two good horses stood at the sidewalk. A colonel, wearing a uniform that carried the scarlet facings and trouser stripe of the artillery, escorted his wife into a milliner's shop, having just left the carriage. Apart from the colonel and his driver, a smartly-dressed artillery private, who already mounted the carriage seat again, there was no sign of Yankee troops. As the woman was in her late middle age, plump, homely and well-dressed, Dusty assumed her to be the officer's wife. The small Texan could also see how some of the street's occupants still found business.

It was Dusty's first visit to a big city shop and he found a big difference from the places to which he had become accustomed. Even in Arkansas, a comparatively civilized area, shops tended to be on the general store lines, with their wares exposed attractively on display. Not so in Madam Lucienne's exclusive establishment. Dusty could see no sign of the clothing she sold, only comfortable tables, chairs dotted about the tastefully-decorated front room, and fitting cubicles erected along the walls.

Behind the small, elegant counter which faced the front entrance stood a tall young man who failed to blend into the surroundings and looked out of place in the room. He wore a good suit, had a sallow, lean face with an expression of supercilious condescension, with lank long hair and a general impression of needing a good wash. Looking up from the thick, leather-bound ledger he was reading, the man studied Dusty and Belle.

"Is Madam Lucienne here, sir?" Belle asked mildly, ducking a curtsy to the man and her very attitude warned Dusty that all was not well.

"No," the young man answered, his voice holding a Northern accent. "I'm her—assistant."

Dusty darted a glance at Belle, finding her to be expressionless yet tense. While completely inexperienced in such matters, Dusty felt Madam Lucienne would be highly unlikely to accept such a man as her assistant in a fashionable business.

"I came to collect Mrs. Beauclaire's new ball gown," Belle told the man. "Is it ready yet?"

"Not right now."

74

Even as the man replied, a voice sounded from the open door behind him and which led into the rear of the building.

"It's no use, Kaddam. There's no sign of the old bitch's rec—!" While speaking, another tall, lean young man appeared at the door. Apart from a drooping moustache, he looked much like the first. Halting, he chopped off his words and looked across the counter. "Who're they?"

"Couple of servants," Kaddam replied. "Come after Mrs. Beauclaire's new ball gown."

"Get them out of here."

"You heard Mr. Turnpike. Get out."

"Yes sir," Belle answered meekly, nudging Dusty in warning. "We'd best go, Jeremiah."

"Hold hard!" Turnpike barked as Belle started to turn.

"What's wrong, Melvin?" Kaddam asked.

"There's something about this I don't like," Turnpike answered and began to move forward, reaching into his jacket's right side pocket.

Moving with his usual speed, Dusty scooped up the heavy ledger—which Kaddam closed and laid aside on their entrance—and spun it sideways. Its hard edge caught Turnpike in the face, halting his advance and causing his right hand to emerge empty from the pocket.

In a continuation of the move Dusty's left hand slapped down on the counter top and he vaulted upwards. Kaddam began to take action a good five seconds too late. Out lashed Dusty's left leg, driving his boot full into Kaddam's advancing body. Caught in the chest by a solid boot heel, powered by a leg toughened from long hours of hard travelling, Kaddam croaked and reeled backwards. Going over the counter even as he kicked Kaddam, Dusty landed before Turnpike. Spluttering curses and spitting blood from his damaged lips, Turnpike threw a wild punch in Dusty's direction. Dusty ducked under the blow, slamming his right fist hard into Turnpike's solar plexus. With an agonised croak Turnpike went back and doubled over. On the heels of his first blow, Dusty whipped up his left hand to meet the down-swinging jaw. A click like two colossal billiard balls connecting sounded and Turnpike snapped erect once more. Glassy-eyed and limp, he shot back through the door and landed sprawled out on the floor.

Although Belle wished to avoid trouble, she realised that she must take a hand in Dusty's play. Leaping forward, she stamped her right foot on to the back of Kaddam's rear knee. Thrown off balance as his leg doubled under him, Kaddam went to his knees. Before the man could recover, Belle hitched up her skirt and kicked again. She sent her left foot crashing into the centre of Kaddam's shoulders and propelled him head first into the wall. When Kaddam hit the wall, he arrived with enough force to knock himself unconscious.

"Who are they?" Dusty asked as Kaddam collapsed limply to the floor.

"Some of Pinkerton's men," the girl answered. "They must have caught Madam."

"Looks that way. Or killed her. Reckon we ought to look around and see?"

"There's no time. They were looking for her records and more of them might be coming. She's not a prisoner here and we can't help her if she's dead. Empty the cash draw, take the money with you."

"Make it look like we robbed the place, huh?" Dusty said.

"That's it," Belle agreed. "I'll take the ledger, what they were looking for is in it."

"Won't they think things when they find it's gone?" asked Dusty.

"We'll have to chance it and hope they think we took it along for the leather binding," Belle replied. "This's going to make things difficult for us, Dusty."

"It sure is," Dusty answered, scooping the money from the cash drawer into his jacket pocket. "What'll we do now?"

"Find someplace safe where we can look through this ledger and see what we can learn."

"And if we don't learn anything?"

"I'm trying not to think of *that*," Belle admitted frankly. "But if we don't I've another contact. He'd help for money, not through loyalty to the South."

Despite her calm words, Belle knew just how much harder grew the situation. Yet, no matter what happened to her, Madam Lucienne would try to leave some message behind. On their previous meeting Lucienne had said if anything went wrong the ledger would tell Belle where to find help, but did not have a chance to explain how.

Picking up the book, Belle opened it and glanced at the first page. It held nothing but a list of customers' names, addresses and prices paid. Nor did the subsequent pages prove any more enlightening to the girl's rapid examination. Not that she really expected they would. Madam Lucienne would hardly make the prying loose of her secrets all that easy.

"I reckon we'd best get moving, Belle," Dusty said quietly.

"You're right," she replied, and tucked the book under her arm.

With Dusty carrying the girl's bag, they made for the door. Unnoticed behind them, Turnpike dragged himself to his feet. Almost maniacal rage mingled with the pain that twisted his face as he lurched to and leaned against the side of the door. From his pocket he drew one of the metal-cartridge firing .32 calibre Smith & Wesson revolvers popular among Northern supporters who hailed from the less firearm-conscious East, lined it at Dusty's back and fired a shot. Still feeling the effects of Dusty's handling, Turnpike did not have a steady hand. So his bullet passed between the pair without touching either of them, flying on to pass through a glass panel of the door.

At the sound of the shot, Dusty let Belle's bag drop and whirled around. His right hand fanned across, gripped the Colt's butt and slid the weapon from his waistband. Going into what would one day be known as the gun-fighter's crouch—Colt held waist high, in the centre of his body and aimed by instinctive alignment—he cut loose in the only manner possible under the circumstances: for a kill. Only one thing stood between Turnpike and death, the fact that Dusty carried his gun in a different manner than usual. Drawing from the waistband made just the slight alteration which turned what should have been a bullet between the eyes to a nasty graze across the side of the head. Even so, Turnpike jerked back, spun around, and fell out of sight through the door.

"Get the hell out of here, Belle!" Dusty barked, unsure of how seriously he hit Turnpike and conscious that the other did not drop his gun before disappearing.

Swiftly Belle scooped up her bag, knowing Dusty might need both hands free, and darted to the door. Keeping his Colt lined on the opening behind the counter, Dusty followed. Without looking back, Belle jerked open the door and stepped out. Clearly the bullet breaking the window attracted attention. Across the street, the carriage's driver stood up on his seat and looked in the girl's direction. Not that he worried Belle; her interest centred on another pair of soldiers further down the street. Although cavalrymen, they were on foot and worked for the Provost Marshal's Department (Military Police as such did not yet exist). Their main function was dealing with breaches of the peace and acting in place of the normal New Orleans police.

On hearing the window break, the two men halted and waited to see what caused it. When Belle appeared, they started towards her. At that moment Dusty joined the girl. Although he no longer held his revolver, the soldiers increased their pace and slipped free their clubs. Dusty realised that to start shooting would not be advisable and glanced across the street.

"Head for the carriage, Belle!" he ordered.

Even though the driver saw Belle and Dusty headed his way, he took no action. Driving his commanding officer's carriage did not call for carrying weapons, so he wore neither sword nor revolver. Instead of making some move, he just stood up in the carriage and stared. Against a man like Dusty Fog such hesitation could only bring disaster. Bounding up on to the seat, Dusty lowered his head and butted the driver in the body. Taken by surprise, winded by the force of Dusty's attack, the driver shot backwards off the seat and landed rump-first on the sidewalk.

Belle pitched her bag into the back of the carriage and followed it. Before she could do more than enter, Dusty grabbed the reins and slapped them against the rumps of the two horses. There was not even time for him to feel grateful to a fate which put a sedentary non-combatant soldier as driver instead of a veteran who would have been far more difficult to handle.

"Yee-ah!" Dusty whooped. "Giddap there!"

A spirited pair, the horses needed no further encouragement. Lunging forward, they threw their weight into the harness and almost jerked the buggy's wheels clear of the ground as they started it moving. Dusty thought back with gratitude to buggy-races between the Regiment's young officers. From them he learned how to handle a fast-moving vehicle and pair of team horses. That knowledge came in very useful as he guided the carriage away. Although the two cavalrymen gave chase, on foot they stood little chance of keeping up with the speeding carriage and neither thought to use their guns.

"Keep going, Dusty!" Belle said. "We've got to get away."

# Chapter 9

## A Dress for an Engineer's Wife

While the two cavalrymen fell behind, they still kept up the chase and in doing so attracted the attention of other soldiers. Holding the two horses to a fast gallop along the centre of a street, Dusty saw a man dart from the sidewalk in an attempt to catch hold of the reins. Taking up the carriage whip from its holder, Dusty sent the lash slicing forward. For a snap shot he aimed well and the leather curled about the man's head, causing an immediate withdrawal.

Seeing what happened to the soldier, a second man tried a different method of halting the carriage. Racing forward, he came in behind and grabbed hold of the rear of the passengers' seat. Only he failed to take one thing into account and his plan met with a check. Rising up before the surprised man, Belle lashed around her right fist in a punch which snapped his head to one side and caused him to lose his hold. Before the man landed on the street, Dusty started to swing the racing carriage around another corner.

Shouts rang out, whistles blew and hooves clattered as members of the Provost Marshal's mounted patrol headed for the disturbance area. Luck favoured Belle and Dusty for none of the riders came their way. However they realised that they must leave the carriage at the first favourable opportunity. It did not come for some time and the sound of pursuit kept at about the same distance behind them. Sensing trouble, the citizens disappeared into their homes, or entered business premises, with the intention of disassociating themselves and so as to be unable to help the Yankees should they be asked.

Swinging the horses on to a street which ran behind big buildings that in time of peace housed businessmen, or supplied town homes for plantation owners, Dusty saw his chance. Nobody appeared to be watching them and their pursuers had not yet come into sight. So Dusty hauled back on the reins and slowed the carriage.

"Get out, Belle!" he snapped.

Bag in hand, the girl obeyed. She thrust open the carriage door, paused to catch her balance and leapt down. Lashing the reins on to the whip, which he had thrust back into its holder, Dusty rose on the seat. He let out another yell, which caused the horses to lunge forward into the harness once more and start running, then sprang clear. As Dusty lit down on the sidewalk, the carriage tore away along the street.

"Down there, Dusty," Belle suggested, darting to the small Texan's side.

Flights of steps ran down into small areas that opened into the houses' basement kitchens and Belle led the way out of sight. No sooner had they gone than feet clattered, hooves drummed and some of their pursuers turned on to the street. Gun in hand, Dusty flattened himself by Belle against the area wall and listened to their hunters pass them.

"So far, so good," Dusty breathed. "Only we'd best find some better place than this to hide afore they find that buggy's empty."

"Let's see if we can get into the house. Most of them are empty, their owners went up river when the Yankees came," Belle replied, walking to the door and reaching for its handle. "This's probably a waste of time—Hey, it's not."

At Belle's turn of the handle and push, the door swung inwards. Followed by Dusty, the girl entered a kitchen, that, before the War, would have held several servants. Only a pair of elderly Negroes stood in the room, the man reaching for a butcher's knife on the table at which they stood.

"Put it down and keep quiet, friend," Dusty said quietly, holding his Colt but not threatening the man.

"What do you want, mister?" the man asked, still holding the knife.

Before Dusty could answer, an old white woman entered the kitchen. Despite her faded old clothes, she still retained an air of breeding. Tall, slim, the woman stood studying the newcomers and her face showed no fear.

"What is it, Sam?" she asked.

"Don't be frightened, ma'am," Dusty told her.

"I wasn't aware of being frightened, young man," she answered. "May I ask what brings you here. And put that gun away. This isn't Texas and you won't need it."

Clearly the old woman recognised a Texas drawl when she heard one. Her eyes darted from Dusty, as he returned the Colt to his waistband, to Belle. The girl spoke up:

"We're in trouble, ma'am."

"*That* strikes me as being obvious. Come here, girl, and show me your hands."

Flashing a smile at Dusty, Belle crossed the room towards the old woman. The small Texan remained at the door, holding it open a little so as to watch and listen to the noises in the street. With her hands held out like when, as a child, she stood inspection before going in to meet the guests at a tea party, Belle allowed the woman to scrutinise her carefully. Then the old woman glanced at the bag and ledger Belle set down on the table before showing her hands.

"You're dressed as a maid," the woman remarked. "But you've a lady's hands and voice. A lady and a Texan who's obviously a soldier and doesn't look like the kind to be a deserter. I may say that you two interest me. Just what are the Yankees after you for?"

"Robbing a shop and shooting a man in it," Belle replied.

"Killing him?"

"Possibly."

"Was he the owner?" demanded the old woman, a different note coming into her voice and a glint flickering in her eyes.

"No," Belle answered. "I believe he was one of Pinkerton's men."

"A member of the Yankee Secret Service?"

"He certainly didn't work for Madam Luciene."

"Is that why you took the ledger?"

Belle nodded agreement. Realising that she stood in the presence of a very shrewd, discerning woman, she decided to tell the truth. Unless Belle missed her guess, she could rely on the woman's loyalty to the South and need not be afraid to disclose her identity.

"My name is Boyd—," she began.

"One of the Baton Royale Boyds?" asked the woman.

"My father was Vincent Boyd of Baton Royale," Belle admitted.

"Who had only one daughter, Belle by name. Belle Boyd, who is also known as the Rebel Spy."

"That's what they call me. Although I doubt if the Yankees know it's me they are hunting."

"Then they won't search so thoroughly," guessed the old woman, directing an inquiring glance in Dusty's direction.

"May I introduce Captain Dusty Fog?" Belle said. "He is assisting me on my present assignment."

"My pleasure, ma'am," Dusty drawled, closing the door and crossing the room.

Even in occupied New Orleans Dusty's fame had spread amongst the Southerners and the old woman beamed delightedly.

However she did not allow her pleasure at meeting Dusty to interfere with the business on hand.

"It may be as well if you go and hide in case a search is made," she stated.

"How about your servants, ma'am?" asked Dusty.

"You can trust Sam and Jessie as you trust me," she answered. "Come along."

Leading Belle and Dusty into what had once been a comfortable study, but which showed signs of having various furnishings removed, the woman—she introduced herself as Mrs. Annie Rowley—supplied them with a very good place of concealment. At times members of many New Orleans families found the need to keep out of sight for a few days: maybe to avoid somebody wishing to issue a challenge; or, when duelling became illegal, to hide after a duel until a suitable arrangement could be made with the court to overlook the matter. Clearly the Rowleys belonged to that class, for the old woman operated a disguised switch and a section of wall pannelling slid back to reveal a small, comfortable and ventilated room.

"Go in. I'll have food brought for you," she said.

Dusty and Belle exchanged glances as the same thought ran through their heads. Life in the occupied city could not be easy for Mrs. Rowley. Too old to work, her normal sources of revenue taken by the War, she clearly had to sell items of her property to support herself. So feeding two extra people would create a serious drain in her resources. Yet she might take offence at any offer of payment. Receiving a nod of agreement from Belle, Dusty took a chance.

"May we offer to help pay for the meal, ma'am?" he asked.

"I would like a lemon if one can be bought," Belle went on.

"There was a time when your offer would have offended me," Mrs. Rowley admitted. "But I'm afraid the War caused many things to change in my life—."

"This's stolen money," Dusty warned with a grin as he started to empty his pockets.

"I thought 'booty' was the term when it's taken from the enemy in time of war," smiled the woman. "It'll spend well enough at the market no matter what we chose to call it."

"Can your servants raise a lemon?" Belle asked.

"Land-sakes, girl," Mrs. Rowley answered. "That's a strange fancy. There are lemons for sale, I'll have Jessie bring some."

"Only one," Belle corrected.

"I'll tell Jessie," promised Mrs. Rowley. "Now you two had best hide."

Like most of its kind, the secret room offered reasonable comfort in the shape of a bed, table and chair. Entering, Dusty and Belle watched the door start to swing shut behind them. Then Dusty rasped a match on his pants' seat and lit the lamp on the table. With a sigh Belle stretched on the bed, the ledger and bag at its side. She glanced at the closed door, then to Dusty.

"Well," she said. "Have we made a mistake?"

"We're caught in a box canyon if we have," he answered, thinking how much the Yankees would pay for the capture of the Rebel Spy and himself. Taking a small box from his pocket, he opened it to expose twelve combustible cartridges and a similar number of percussion caps. "I'll fill that empty chamber just in case. Then we'll grab some rest."

Neither really thought the old woman would betray them and were fatalistic enough to realise they could do nothing but wait to find out. So, after Dusty replaced the discharged round and put out the lamp, they settled down to rest. Neither had any idea how long they lay in the darkness, Dusty seated on the chair with his boots on the table and Belle on the bed. At last they heard a creaking and the door began to inch slowly open.

Gun in hand, Dusty came to his feet and Belle rolled from the bed gripping her Dance ready for use. Then both knew they did not need to fear treachery. Slowly the door continued to open, allowing light to creep gradually into the room in a manner which permitted their eyes to grow accustomed to no longer being in complete darkness. If there had been a betrayal, the enemy would just jerk open the door and move in while the sudden advent of light dazzled the pair inside.

"It's all clear now," Mrs. Rowley said, smiling in at them.

"Did the Yankees come?" asked Belle, returning her Dance to the bag.

"Came and searched the house, then went away satisfied," replied the old woman. "From what their sergeant said, it's assumed that you're just ordinary thieves and slipped back to the waterfront area. He didn't hold out much hope of finding you."

"The two men at the shop couldn't have talked yet then," Dusty commented. "Likely the one I shot can't and it'll be a spell afore the other's able to, the way you slammed him into the wall, Belle."

"I've a meal ready for you, and your lemon," the woman told them. "And Sam's watching the street in case the Yankees come back."

After eating a good meal, Belle took her bag and ledger to the table and started to work. From the bag she lifted her jewel case and extracted the brooch which held the lens. With it she examined each unused page of the book. To do so she stood by a window and allowed the light of the afternoon sun to fall on the paper. The lemon had not been bought for eating purposes and its use soon became apparent.

"I can't find any traces of pen-scratches," she said at last. "But I'll try the usual tests."

"You figure Madam Lucienne used invisible ink?" asked an interested Dusty.

"She left information in the ledger some way," the girl replied. "We use two kinds of invisible ink. One appears when you apply lemon juice to the paper and heat produces the other."

Although both tests were tried on various pages, no writing appeared and at last Belle reluctantly admitted that however Madam Lucienne left her message, invisible ink had not been used.

"Could be inside the ledger's bindings," Dusty suggested.

"It could be," admitted Belle. "Could we have a knife, please Mrs. Rowley."

"Of course," answered the old woman, having been an interested spectator.

Carefully Belle slit open the leather binding of the ledger, checking its inner side and the stiffeners without result.

"Nothing," she said. "Yet Madam Lucienne told me the information was in it."

"She might have written a message in among the other writing in it," Dusty offered.

"It's possible," the girl said. "Let's try and see."

Turning to the first page, Belle started to read. She tried taking the first letter of each order, but they made no sense. Then something caught her eye. Somebody in Baton Royale had bought a ball gown, a person she had never heared of and at a plantation which Belle could not recall. Yet the name did not help her any nor the address and she cursed the bad luck which prevented Madam Lucienne from being able to give her more information when they met; the meeting had been terminated by the arrival of a Yankee naval captain and his wife at the shop.

After the failure with the address, Belle read on to learn how a Mrs. J. Bludso of the Busted Boiler Inn in New Orleans bought a silk ball gown. Finishing the page, Belle turned over no wiser than when she began. Nor did enlightenment come until three more pages went by. Suddenly the girl stopped, sat staring thoughtfully at the ledger for a moment and then turned back to the first page.

"Something, Belle?" Dusty asked.

"Listen to this and tell me what you think," she answered. "One silk ball gown for Mrs J. Bludso, the Busted Boiler Inn, price twenty-five dollars."

"So?"

"On the next page the order is repeated and on the third."

"You said Madam Lucienne was mighty popular," Dusty pointed out. "Likely a woman'd keep going to her if she got good service."

"Three times in less than two months?" Belle replied.

"I would for bargains like that," Mrs. Rowley put in. "You show me any place that can supply a silk ball gown for twenty-five dollars."

"If I find one, I'll keep quiet about it, buy some and make a fortune," smiled Belle. "The Busted Boiler's in the waterfront district; it's, or used to be, the gathering place for the riverboat engineers."

"And young Jim Bludso was engineer of the Prairie Belle," Mrs. Rowley recalled. "Only she went down trying to ram one of Farragut's gunboats before the surrender. I know engineers made good money, but not enough for one to shop regularly at Madam Lucienne's."

"This's what we want, Dusty," Belle stated. "It must be."

"She'd be taking a big chance putting it down that way," Dusty objected.

"Not so big," Belle replied. "I doubt if a man would see any significance in the entries. I might not have but for that false address in Baton Royale above the first mention of Mrs. J. Bludso."

"What're we going to do then?" Dusty asked.

"Go to the Busted Boiler and see Jim Bludso," the girl replied.

"Do you know it?" asked Mrs. Rowley.

"We can find it," Belle answered.

"Wait until after dark and I'll send Sam to guide you," the woman suggested. "It's little enough I can do for the South, so don't argue."

Accompanied by the old Negro, Belle and Dusty passed through the evening-darkened streets. Clearly the Yankees attached little importance to their visit to Madam Lucienne's shop, for only normal patrols moved through the streets. Even if the two men should be dead, the military authorities most likely took the attitude that the killers had disappeared into the city and organising a search capable of producing results would take more men than they had available. Whatever the reason, none of the patrols met during the journey gave Belle, Dusty and the Negro more than a casual glance in passing.

At last Sam halted. They had long since left the elegant area behind and walked through streets which grew narrower, dirtier, more crowded. Much of the atmosphere of the waterfront departed with the city's surrender. In times of peace the area boomed with unceasing life and gaiety, as wild and hectic as in any gold camp or—in later years—town at the end of the long cattle drives from Texas to Kansas. Many of the saloons, dance or gambling halls and other places of business were closed, but some remained open in the hope of grabbing trade from the U.S. forces.

The Busted Boiler was a small hotel set back off a street facing the river and comprised of businesses concerned with the riverboat trade. At one time it served as a gathering point for most of the riverboats' engineers; and there had been sufficient of them to ensure the owner a steady custom. After directing his companions to the place, Sam disappeared into the darkness and they walked towards its doors. In passing they glanced through the windows at the right of the door and did not like what they saw. Yankee sailors and marines sat around the dining room, or leaned at the bar. Only a few civilians were present, mingling with the uniformed men and apparently on good terms with them. At a table in the centre of the room, a big, wide-shouldered man whose curly black hair showed from under a pushed-back peaked civilian seaman's hat sat dining with a trio of U.S. Navy petty officers and clearly all enjoyed their meal.

"What about it?" Dusty asked.

"I don't know," Belle replied. "Stay out here and cover me while I go ask for Bludso."

"Are you taking your bag?"

"No—but I'll take the parasol."

After assembling the parasol into its harmless form, Belle left her bag in Dusty's keeping and entered the hotel. The arrival of a woman attracted no especial attention, although Belle saw men studying her with interest. Then a bulky Negress waitress came to a halt before the girl.

"You wanting something?"

"Is Jim Bludso here?" Belle inquired.

"He sure am, gal," grinned the Negress. "Does you-all want him?"

86

"I'm his sister," Belle replied.

"Ain't dey all, gal?" asked the Negress and ambled away.

Crossing the room, the Negress halted by the big civilian with the three petty officers. A puzzled expression flickered across his face as the woman spoke and indicated Belle. One of the petty officers made a comment and his companions laughed, then the civilian rose and walked in Belle's direction.

Studying the man, Belle formed an impression of strength, toughness and capability. He wore a short coat, open-necked shirt, trousers tucked into sea-boots and a long-bladed knife hung sheathed at his left side. Good-looking in a rugged, tanned way, he grinned as he drew near.

"Why howdy," he greeted. "Are you-all a sister on my mammy or pappy's side?"

"Why Jim," Belle replied. "Pappy's for sure. He told me to come here and speak to you about your extravagant ways. Three silk ball gowns for your wife, for shame."

If the words carried any special meaning to the big man, he gave no sign of it. The smile never left his lips and he took the girl's right arm in his big left hand. Gently but firmly he turned her towards the door.

"Let's us go someplace quiet where we can talk about it," he suggested.

"Why I just adore big strong men," Belle purred. "But I don't need force—"

"You keep on walking like we the best of friends, gal," Jim Bludso ordered. "If you don't, I'll bust your arm."

Belle carried the parasol in her left hand, but did not offer to take it apart as a means of defending herself. To do so in the hotel invited capture. Once outside, she and Dusty between them ought to be able to handle Jim Bludso. Unresisting, she allowed herself to be steered towards the front door.

## Chapter 10

## Another Talented Lady

With Bludso retaining a grip on her arm, Belle left the hotel. She darted a glance in either direction as she walked through the door, but could see no sign of Dusty. Wondering where the small Texan might be, she allowed Bludso to steer her along the sidewalk and into the alley at the left side of the building.

"Just what's the game?" she demanded, realising that she ought to be saying or doing something.

"What do you know about those ball gowns?" Bludso countered, not relaxing his grip.

"Only what Madam Lucienne wanted me to know."

"Who're you?"

"Would you believe me if I said I was her dress designer?"

"No——," Bludso began.

At that moment he heard a soft footfall behind him. So did Belle, but with a difference—she could guess at who approached quietly from behind them. Even as Bludso sent his left hand towards the hilt of the knife he wore, Belle made her play. With Dusty so close at hand, she decided not to release her skirt. Although retaining the garment lessened the methods by which she could defend herself, she felt adequate to the present situation.

Raising her left leg, Belle stamped backwards to drive the heel of her shoe hard against Bludso's left shin. A croak of pain broke from his lips and he involuntarily loosened his hold on the girl's arm. With a heave Belle freed herself and shot her elbow back to collide with Bludso's solar plexus. Taken unawares by the attack, Bludso rocked back and struck the wall. A tough, hard man—riverboat life did not breed weaklings—he threw off the effects of Belle's stamp and blow fast; the recovery might not have been so speedy if the girl used her full power. Before Bludso could make a move, Dusty stood before him with a lined Army Colt.

"Hold it right there, mister," the small Texan ordered and the cocking click of the gun added its backing to the command.

Bludso was no fool. Maybe he lacked a comprehensive knowledge of gunfighters' ways, but he knew enough to recognise top class work when he saw it. Small the man before him might be,

88

but he handled the Colt with a casual, assured ease that told of long practice. From his voice, he hailed out of Texas and the Lone Star State had already begun to build its reputation for producing skilled revolver-handling men. Significantly the small Texan stood just close enough to ensure a hit, but too far away to allow a successful grab by Bludso at his weapon.

In addition Bludso could not overlook the manner in which the girl defended herself. Not in panic, but with deadly, skilled purpose and just at the right moment when his attention was divided between her and the approaching man.

"Southrons hear your country call you," Belle said quietly.

"Up lest worse than death befall you," Bludso replied, feeling just a touch relieved at the familiar password. "Why didn't you say you were one of us?"

"You never gave me a chance," Belle pointed out. "I think they've got Madam Lucienne. There were two of Pinkerton's spies at the shop when we arrived."

"So it was you pair who downed Turnpike and Kaddam," Bludso said. "Come with me, this's not the place for us to stand talking."

With that Bludso turned and walked through the alley towards the rear. He showed such complete trust that Dusty and Belle did not hesitate to follow. At the back of the hotel a flight of stairs ran up to a first floor room and Bludso began to climb them. Not until then did Belle request advice.

"Where're we going?" she asked.

"This's where I live and I can't think of a better place for us to talk," Bludso answered. "It's better we go this way than through the front door. Those Yankee brass-pounders're used to me meeting gals, but not when the gal has a feller along with her."

"It's your play," Dusty stated.

At the top of the stairs Bludso opened his room's door and walked straight in. Deciding that the man probably did not need to use correct manners with his normal run of lady-friends, Belle followed and Dusty brought up the rear. As soon as they entered the room, its door slammed behind them and a lantern's light burst out from under cover. Dusty cursed, bringing up his gun, but was so dazzled by the sudden light that he could not see anything more than a milky-white blur. Nor did Belle fare any better. Dusty carried her bag in his left hand, which allowed her to jerk the head from her parasol and free its deadly billy. Armed in that way, she still could barely see enough to use the billy. Clearly Bludso expected the light. On entering, he must have kept his eyes closed and avoided the main impact of the glare. Out came his knife and he dropped easily into a knife-fighter's crouch. Facing Dusty and Belle, he darted a glance at the woman who stood holding a bucket with which she had covered the lighted lantern until it was required.

"You sure fell for that one, Belle gal," the woman said with a broad grin.

"Don't shoot, Dusty!" warned Belle, recognising the voice.

When Dusty's eyes cleared, he saw a plump, jovial-looking woman with hair that retained its red tint through liberal use of henna dye. Even clad in a cheap dress such as a woman of the dock-area might wear, she gave off an air of theatrical leanings and looked as if she played a part rather than belonged to the district.

"You know them, Lucy?" asked Bludso.

"Not the feller, but the girl is Belle Boyd."

"So you're safe after all, Lucienne," Belle said, reassembling her parasol.

"Sure," Madam Lucienne replied. "I see you worked out where to come from my ledger. I didn't have time to take it with me when I lit out."

"Sorry, Miss Boyd," Bludso said, sheathing his knife. "I didn't know who you might be and wasn't in a position to raise the question. So I figured that it'd be best to get you up here where Lucy and me could tend to your needings. Let's get sat down, in case I have callers."

Sitting around the table, the quartet got down to business. After Dusty had been introduced, Madam Lucienne told how she escaped from the two Yankee agents.

"I don't know how they found out about me," she said, "but I recognised one of them and pulled out the back when they came in at the front. I came down here, changed and have been with Jim from this morning. We aimed to see if we could get into the shop and collect the ledger tonight."

"We've saved you that chore," Belle told her. "Is there anything else of importance in the shop?"

"Nothing that they can find, or would help them if they did," Lucienne replied. "I never kept written records if I could help it and all my other gear's safe. What brings you and Captain Fog into New Orleans, Belle?"

"Something really important," the girl replied, darting a glance at Bludso. "How do you fit into this?"

"Jim and I work together," Lucienne explained. "He passes on the information our folks gather when he goes up river."

"The Yankees need good engineers," Bludso went on. "I'm one of the best and they can trust me. I've helped keep some of their boats working—."

"After he and his men damaged them in the first place," grinned Lucienne. "So you can trust Jim all the way."

"Of course," smiled Belle.

"I don't trust folks on face value either," Bludso said with a grin. "Which you may have noticed."

Which put the meeting on a friendly basis again. Bludso, being a cautious man, did not object to Belle showing the same traits. Both worked in a business where the penalty for failure was death, and had learned early not to take any unnecessary chances.

Quickly Belle told of the discovery made in Arkansas and explained the serious threat posed by the counterfeiting for Bludso's benefit. Soon the engineer's face set in grim lines and he nodded his head.

"We'll have to stop it," he stated. "Thing now being, how to do it."

"We'll have to raid Gaton's place," Dusty said. "Only before we do it, I'd admire to know what force he has guarding it. We may need help."

"That I can supply," Bludso replied. "And I can fix it to learn all we need to know about Gaton's guards. Got the combustibles we'll need stashed away, too."

"Do you have a man who knows how to break open a safe?" asked Belle.

"I don't reckon so," admitted Bludso.

"That's where I can help," Lucienne put in. "I can take you to a man who'll supply a safe-breaker for a price."

"I've five hundred dollars in gold in my bag," Belle told her. "Will that be enough?"

"If not, we've our own supply to back you," Lucienne replied. "While Jim learns all he can about Gaton's place, you, Dusty and me will go visit this feller."

"Who is he?" Belle asked.

"Harwold Cornwall."

From the way Lucienne merely said the name, she concluded it to be enough and ought to tell the others all that was necessary. The name meant nothing to Dusty, although the time would come when he took an interest in the affairs of Harwold Cornwall.* Certainly he was the only one present who did not know the man named.

*Told in "The Man from Texas".

"Hell, Lucy!" Bludso burst out. "You can't take a lady like Miss Boyd into Cornwall's place."

"Can we trust him?" Belle asked, ignoring the man's comment.

"About as far as you could throw a bull by the tail," Lucienne replied. "But if the price's right he will do what he can for us."

"You have to excuse a half-smart lil country boy like me," Dusty drawled. "But just who is this Cornwall *hombre*?"

"A thief," growled Bludso.

"And just about the biggest in New Orleans," Lucienne went on. "He's smarter than most and the law's never proved a thing against him. But he's behind most of the law-breaking in the city."

"Most of his kind got out before the Yankees arrived," Bludso continued. "I reckon they thought there wouldn't be any pickings."

"Not Cornwall though," Lucienne finished. "He runs a place called the Green Peacock not far from here. It's real popular with the Yankees."

"And you figure *he'll* help us?" asked Dusty.

"If the price's right he will," Lucienne agreed. "Not that we'll let him know why we want the safe-breaker. If he learns later, he won't dare open his mouth about it. Anyway, I know enough about Cornwall to keep him quiet."

"Let's go then," Belle suggested. "We've only three days to handle this business."

"Why the rush?" Bludso inquired.

"A submersible is coming to pick us up three nights from now. So we'll have to move real fast."

"We'd best start right away then," Lucienne stated. "You see to your end of it, Jim. I'll take Belle and Dusty to see Cornwall."

"Will it be safe for you to walk through the streets, Lucienne?" asked Dusty. "With the Yankees looking for you and all."

"A change of clothing and hair-style's all I need," the woman assured him. "And I've had both of them here. Don't forget that it was mostly the wives of the Yankee officers who knew me—and there'll be none of *them* where we're going."

"How about the pair we had a run-in with at your place?" Dusty went on.

"From what I heard, neither of them are in any shape to be walking the streets tonight," Lucienne answered.

"We have to take that chance anyway, Dusty," Belle warned. "Lucienne can deal with Cornwall better than either of us."

"That's for sure," agreed Lucienne. "I talk his language,

Dusty. Come on, Belle. We'll go to my room and fix ourselves up."

"Something more suitable in clothing is definitely called for," the girl admitted, running a hand down her dress.

Watching the girl leave, Dusty wondered what she intended to change into. Certainly the travelling suit would not fit into the scene at a fancy New Orleans saloon any more than the maid's outfit.

While waiting for the women to return, Dusty and Bludso talked. Although the big man could shed no light on Lucienne's past, or guess how she might know a man like Harwold Cornwall, he seemed certain that she could gain the criminal's co-operation. In the course of their conversation, Bludso admitted that he knew of the secret submersible dock, but did not blame Belle for her reticence on the matter. He also seemed just as sure that he could learn all they would need to know about the lay-out and personnel at Gaton's house.

"My striker off the old Prairie Belle'll do it," Bludso stated confidently. "Ole Willie's real slick at learning things."

"How about the combustibles?" Dusty asked.

"We've all we need in a safe place."

"Best not make plans until we know exactly what we'll need, though, Jim."

"Nope. But I can raise all the men we might want at short notice."

After that the conversation turned to more general matters; the progress of the War in the East and Arkansas was discussed, then Bludso spoke of conditions in occupied New Orleans.

At last the door opened and the women entered. Used as he had become to the way in which Belle could change her appearance, Dusty still stared hard at what he saw. To the best of his knowledge, the girl brought along only two dresses and the male clothing. Yet she walked into Bludso's room clad in a manner more suited to a saloongirl than a travelling lady or a maid.

A blonde wig replaced the other and her beautiful face carried stage make-up like any saloongirl's. Although she wore a black skirt still, it clung tighter to her and glinted flashily instead of being drab. Above the skirt, a sleeveless white satin blouse hugged her torso, left her shoulders bare and its decollete was cut low enough to allow the valley between her breasts to show. Despite its excellent quality, the jewellery she wore looked cheap and flashy when taken with her general appearance. Nor did the deadly parasol look out of place.

"Well?" she asked.

"That'd really make Uncle Devil bristle," Dusty grinned. "How'd you do it?"

"Turned the skirt inside out and tightened it," the girl explained. "Took the sleeves and part of the top off my blouse and turned it inside out too. Will it do, Dusty?"

"Do? I wouldn't know you if I'd seen you passing in the street," Dusty enthused. "Do all women's clothes have such fancy fittings?"

"No," Belle replied, then nodded in Madam Lucienne's direction. "But I have a very smart seamstress."

"I'll be the last to deny that," grinned the woman.

Turning his attention to Lucienne, Dusty realised that he stood in the presence of yet another talented lady. In addition to being able to design clothes ideally suited to a female spy's specialised needs, Lucienne proved to be almost Belle's equal at changing her appearance. She too now looked like the kind of woman who frequented saloons, with her hair and dress changed so that they met the required state. In fact both she and Belle looked so different that Dusty could understand their confidence at not being recognised.

At the corner of the Busted Boiler, Bludso left Belle, Lucienne and Dusty and went to organise his part of the business. The trio walked along behind the buildings for a time and then came out on to the street. With Lucienne guiding them, they passed quickly through what had been the centre of better-class waterfront entertainment before the War. Even with the Yankees in occupation several saloons remained open and drew trade.

The Green Peacock proved to be the biggest, best and most popular place on the street. In fact it drew such a volume of business that Dusty wondered if some special entertainment brought in the crowd. Music blared from a tolerably good band, mingling with laughter, droning conversation and the clatter of glasses. Naturally the majority of the customers wore Federal uniforms, although some civilians were present. Clearly the saloon rated highly, for Yankee Army, Navy and Marine personnel of various ranks gathered in it.

In the centre of the room stood a raised wooden platform, square in shape and with an upright post at each corner supporting two tight ropes which stretched all the way around. Dusty recognised the construction as a 'ring' of the kind used to stage fist fights. While the Texas Light Cavalry preferred more basic methods of settling their differences, or laid their sporting emphasis on events involving the use of horse or gun, a near-by

Confederate infantry regiment went in for pugilism and often held prize fights to relieve their boredom between spells of active service.

Knowing that prize fights often were staged by saloon-keepers, Dusty wondered if the crowd gathered that night to witness one of exceptional merit.

At first nobody took any notice of the trio's entrance. Then a passing waiter threw a glance their way and came to a halt.

"You bunch wanting something?"

"We've come to see Harwold Cornwall," Lucienne replied.

"Looking for work?" asked the man.

"Could be," she answered. "Tell him that it's Auntie Buck-halter wants a word in private."

"I'll tell him," sniffed the waiter. "Only he's entertaining a couple of Yankee Navy captains and likely won't see you."

"You've a big surprise coming," smiled Lucienne as the man walked away to deliver the order he carried before passing on her message.

"I tell you it's the same girl!" declared a voice from a table close to where the trio stood. "It's Jim Bludso's 'sister'."

Turning her head slightly, Belle saw Bludso's three companions from the Busted Boiler. They sat entertaining a trio of the saloon's girls and the tallest of them pointed straight at her.

"That one was a lady's maid and not a blonde," a second man objected.

"I tell you that's her," the first insisted.

His voice carried to more than Belle's ears. Swinging around in her seat at the next table, a stocky brunette glared first at the speaker, then in Belle's direction. At the brunette's side, a sharp-faced little man spoke quietly but urgently in her ear. Ignoring the man, the brunette thrust back her chair, rose and stalked grimly towards the slim girl. Halting on spread-apart feet and with arms akimbo on her hips, the brunette looked Belle up and down with cold eyes.

"Have you been hanging around Jim Bludso?" the brunette demanded.

Almost as tall as Belle, the woman weighed heavier, was reasonably good-looking and showed hard muscles on her bent arms. In view of the question, and recalling the comment of the Negress at the Busted Boiler when she asked for Bludso, Belle could have groaned. The last thing she wanted was to have trouble with another of Jim Bludso's 'sisters' and it seemed the brunette belonged to that class. Fortunately at that moment a

95

troop of acrobats appeared on the stage and drew the attention of most of the room's occupants in that direction.

Most, but not all. The trio of petty officers watched the two women and exchanged knowing grins.

"I don't know what you mean," Belle said meekly.

"Was she the one, sailor?" the brunette asked, glancing at the tallest of the trio.

Even then trouble might have been averted, but the petty officer had no wish for it to be. Flickering another knowing leer at his companions, he nodded his head.

"It sure was," he stated. "A man wouldn't forget one of old Jim's 'sisters' who's that pretty."

Turning a cold, angry face to Belle once more, the brunette hissed, "I've warned you lobby-lizzies* to steer clear of Jim Bludso. When I've done with you, there won't be so many of you wanting to bother him."

With that the brunette laid her right hand on Belle's bust and shoved her. Even as Belle struck the wall, she saw the woman draw back and drive out a clenched left fist. Noting the skilled manner in which the brunette acted, Belle knew she could take no chances. Especially against a woman as strong and capable as the other showed herself.

Just before the fist reached her face, Belle ducked and swayed aside. She timed the move right, allowing no opportunity for the brunette to halt the blow. Hissing harmlessly by the girl's head, the brunette's hand smashed with sickening force into the wall. A squeal of pain broke from the woman's lips and Belle held back the punch she automatically prepared to launch. Gripping her injured hand, the woman tottered backwards.

"Ruby!" yelped the little man, having watched every move. Concern showed on his face as he sprang forward. "Let me see that hand."

"Leave it, Belle!" Lucienne snapped, catching the girl's arm.

"I want to see if she's badly hurt," Belle objected.

"The waiter's coming back," Lucienne replied. "Forget her, she asked for it."

*Lobby-Lizzy: A prostitute.

96

## Chapter 11

## The Price for Cornwall's Aid

Comparatively few of the crowd witnessed the incident. Seeing the brunette sink to her knees, moaning and cradling the damaged hand, those who saw decided that the scene possessed no further dramatic possibilities, so turned their attention to the acrobats on the stage.

"The boss'll see you in his office," announced the waiter as he came up, showing more respect than on their arrival. Then he darted a glance at the injured brunette and a startled expression crossed his face. "What happened to Ruby?"

"She ran into the wall," Lucienne replied calmly. "Let's go see Cornwall, shall we?"

Looking to where the waiter came from, Dusty saw a tall, well-dressed man rise from a table he shared with two Yankee Navy captains and walk in the direction of a door marked 'Private'. A big, heavily-built hard-case moved across the room in the man's direction, swerved off as if at a signal and lounged casually shoulder on the wall and back towards the door.

Standing behind his desk in the office, Harwold Cornwall looked at the trio as they entered. He gave most of his attention to Lucienne, staring hard at her face. At last a hint of recognition came to his hard, heavily moustached features.

"I heard you'd died, Annie," he said. "Who're the other two?"

"Friends of mine. I need your help, Harwold."

Before any more could be said, a knock sounded at the door and the waiter entered. Dusty stepped by Lucienne and halted alongside Cornwall's side of the desk as the door opened, but made no move. Scowling at the waiter, Cornwall growled that he left word not to be disturbed.

"Wilf wants to see you real important, boss," the waiter replied and the brunette's companion came into the office, crossing to the desk.

"What's up, Wilf?" Cornwall demanded.

Leaning across the desk, the man spoke in a low voice. A soft curse broke from Cornwall's lips and he threw a furious glare in Belle's direction. Then he listened again to the small man and made a reply too low for Dusty, Belle or Lucienne to catch.

Straightening up, the man turned and walked towards the door. Dusty saw Cornwall nod meaningly to the waiter, who followed the man out.

"You've put me in a hell of a fix, Annie," Cornwall remarked in a friendly tone and drew open his desk's drawer. "And I reckon you should—."

Fooled by Dusty's insignificant appearance, Cornwall failed to regard him as a factor in the affair. Too late the saloonkeeper learned his mistake. Like a flash Dusty's right hand disappeared under the left side of his jacket and came out holding the Army Colt. Although he could not produce his full, blinding speed when working from the waistband, the Colt still made it's appearance in a manner amazingly fast to eyes unused to range-country gun-handling. Certainly Cornwall had never seen anything so fast and his first intimation of danger came when the cold muzzle of the Colt touched his ear. The shock caused him to jerk his hand away from the open drawer. He sat as if turned to stone, ignoring the Adams Navy revolver scant inches beneath his fingers.

Down swooped Dusty's left hand, taking out the Adams. He tossed it to Belle without taking his Colt away from Cornwall's ear. Deftly catching the Adams by its butt, Belle swung to face the door and covered the burly hard-case as he entered. The man came to a halt, staring from Belle to Cornwall as if in search of instructions. Receiving none, the hard-case wisely stood still.

"What's gnawing at you, Harwold?" Lucienne asked.

"Do you know who your gal crippled out there?" he countered.

"No," Lucienne answered. "Put up the guns, you two."

"It was Ruby Toot," Cornwall explained, signalling for his man to leave.

"And who's she?" Lucienne inquired, her companions leaving her to speak for them. With the man gone, Dusty slid away his Colt and Belle returned the Adams.

"Just the gal who was going to fight English Flo tonight," Cornwall growled.

"Fight her?" Lucienne repeated.

"In the ring, Annie. The customers got tired of seeing male pugilists, so I put English Flo and another gal in one night. When I saw how they went for it, I started training up more gals. So did Ross down the street. Ruby Toot's his best gal and we fixed the match for her against English Flo. There'll be all hell pop if I have to tell that crowd the fight's off."

"I'm sorry about it, Harwold," Lucienne stated. "But the big gal laid into Becky here first."

"You didn't know anything about this then?"

"No."

"There's been a lot of money bet against Flo. I thought maybe—."

"No. I didn't bring Becky here to get that gal hurt so the bets will be called off," Lucienne said. "I came here to ask you to find me a safe-breaker in a real hurry."

"Can I ask why?"

"I know where I can pick up some Yankee gold, Harwold. The War ruined my business and I've been lying low watching for this chance. Now I know where I can make enough for a fresh start."

"Here in New Orleans?" asked Cornwall, his tone indicating that the prospect would not please him.

"No. Out in California. Can you get the man I want tonight?"

"Maybe—for a price."

"How much?"

"Not much. I want a replacement for Ruby Toot."

Although she knew what Cornwall was driving at, Lucienne asked, "How do you mean, Harwold?"

"Wilf told me how your girl handled herself against Ruby. If you taught her, she can take care of herself. Put her against Flo and I'll find the man you want."

"Like he—!" began Dusty.

"How much money, Harwold?" interrupted Lucienne.

"No money. The gal fights, or no help."

"All right," Belle put in quietly. "I'll do it."

A grin creased the saloonkeeper's face as he studied the girl. Most likely she could put up a reasonable show, and her good looks would distract the crowd, while English Flo should beat her easily.

"It's on then, Harwold," Lucienne declared, throwing a warning glance at Dusty. "Becky'll be ready to fight *when* you get the feller here. I want to be sure he's worth her trouble."

"Hell!" Cornwall snorted. "I'm not sure how long it'll take to find a good safe man."

"Then start looking!" Lucienne snapped. "When I've seen the feller and made my deal, Becky'll go out there and fight."

"I'll see what I can do," Cornwall growled. "And I'll see about fixing your girl up with some clothes. She can't go into the ring in that dress."

"If you don't find a safe man. don't bother," Lucienne said calmly. "And no tricks, Harwold. I know things about you the Yankees'd be pleased to hear."

"Such as?"

Leaning across the desk, Lucienne whispered in the man's ear. Whatever she told him, the effect proved satisfactory. An expression of shocked anger crossed the man's face and he opened his mouth to ask a question, but thought better of it, and rose to his feet.

"I'll see what I can do," he said and walked from the office.

"Reckon we can trust him?" Dusty asked.

"No," smiled Lucienne. "But he daren't doublecross us after what I told him. Especially as I let him know how I left letters behind to be passed out if anything happens to us."

Ten minutes later Cornwall returned to the office. He brought in a middle-sized man of indeterminate age and who dressed like a respectable craftsman.

"This's Saul Paupin—," Cornwall began, then found his introduction unnecessary.

"Annie!" Paupin gasped, advancing with his right hand held out. "Annie Buckhalter. I heard that you were dead."

"So did a lot of folks," smiled Lucienne and turned to Cornwall. "You've done good, real good, Harwold."

"Then how about doing your part?" Cornwall asked. "They're getting restless out there."

Clearly Lucienne regarded the man as entirely satisfactory for she asked only if he would help her by opening a safe and he agreed eagerly. Telling Dusty to stay with Paupin, Lucienne followed Belle and Cornwall from the room. Paupin asked no questions about the proposed robbery during the few minutes before Cornwall returned and asked if they wanted to see the fight.

"I'll put you at a table by the office here," he offered. "If you want anything to drink—."

"A glass of beer'll do me," Dusty replied and Paupin requested the same.

Maybe Cornwall hoped to pump Dusty about the robbery, but the chance did not present itself. Even as he seated Dusty and Paupin, a waiter came up with word that the main guests of the evening requested their host's company.

Suddenly a hush fell on the room, then a low rumble of excitement rippled through the crowd. Three women crossed from a side room and climbed up to enter the ring. Clad in dresses, two of the trio carried a bucket, bottle of water, towel and the other gear prize-fight seconds used.

Not that Dusty paid much attention to the pair, being more interested in the third woman. She would be two inches shorter than Belle, although out-weighing the Rebel Spy by several pounds. Medium long blonde hair, gathered in a bunch on either side of the head, framed a sullen yet good-looking face. Standing in her corner, the blonde looked even more blocky than Ruby Toot, yet had hard flesh not flabby fat. Clad in a sleeveless bodice, which showed plainly she wore nothing beneath it, and black tights, the woman gave an impression of strength and power.

"I hope your gal knows what she's doing," Paupin remarked. "English Flo's near on as good as any man I've ever seen."

So was Belle, Dusty mused, but in a different style of fighting. Dusty knew little about prize-fighting, but doubted whether her knowledge of *savate*, or the *karate* and *ju-jitsu* moves he taught her during the sea voyage to and from Matamoros, would be of use, as they might contravene the rules.

In the ring, the referee announced to a suddenly silent crowd that Ruby Toot had met with an injury. Disappointed and angry murmurs rose and he hurriedly assured his audience that a substitute had been found. Although some of the crowd began to complain, they fell silent when Belle made her appearance. Accompanied by Lucienne and one of Ruby Toot's seconds, Belle walked to the ring and climbed in.

True to his word, Cornwall rigged the girl with a ring costume. Dressed in the same manner as English Flo, with the garments fitting just as snugly, Belle's appearance more than compensated the women-hungry male crowd for Ruby's absence.

Possibly the worst part of the ordeal for Belle was facing the crowd in such scanty attire. Not even her male clothing was so revealing as the borrowed outfit and she rarely wore the shirt and breeches when in general company. However the thought of her mission's importance drove down her objections and she forced herself to ignore the comments of the crowd. To take her mind off the audience, she studied English Flo. Although the blonde had the advantage of weight and possibly strength, Belle doubted whether she would be fast-moving. Speed then would be the weapon Belle must use, relying on her superb physical condition to out-last her more experienced opponent.

The preliminaries went by fast, with the referee warning the girls that biting, gouging, scratching and jumping on an opponent who was down would not be tolerated. Going back to her corner, Belle turned and waited for what seemed a long time until the bout commenced.

"Time!" ordered the timekeeper, seated outside the ring.

Rounds as such did not exist, each lasting as long as both girls kept their feet. When one went down, the round ended and she must toe the line ready to fight on after sixty seconds or lose the bout. The timekeeper's function was the check on the period between a knock-down and toeing the line.

Flo studied Belle with interest as they approached each other and figured the slim girl knew enough about fist-fighting to be dangerous. For her part, Belle watched Flo adopt the typical style of the male pugilist. While bare-fist pugilists of the day tended to stand up and slug, the lightly-built Creoles of New Orleans already used foot-work which, along with dodging and weaving, would oust the old style fighters eventually. Having learned her lessons well, Belle used the *savate* stance. She kept her elbows into her sides and pointing downwards, right arm in front and its fist just below eye level, left just above the height of the solar plexus. Although *savate's* main emphasis centred on kicking, the fists were also used; so the stance she adopted offered good offensive and defensive possibilities.

Before the blonde came within punching distance, Belle made use of her longer reach. Three times in rapid succession Belle's raised right fist stabbed out to smack into Flo's face. Even at the end of their flight, the punches stung enough to halt the blonde's advance. Rocking back a step, Flo shook her head and thrust forward determinedly. In doing so, she left herself open for a body kick and Belle prepared to launch it. Then Belle hesitated. While no mention of kicking had been made by the referee, she felt sure it would be against the rules.

While hesitating, Belle learned that Flo could move with deceptive speed. Taking her chance, the blonde lunged forward and crashed a solid right into Belle's ribs. Belle gasped, for the blow had not been light, and danced back just too late to avoid Flo's follow-up punch to the side of her jaw. As Belle staggered, Flo bored in and flung punches with both fists at the slender body. Pain and anger cause Belle to hit back and the girls exchanged punches in the centre of the ring.

That proved the wrong way for Belle, being out-weighted by the stocky blonde, although it took almost thirty seconds for the idea to sink home. Dancing clear, Belle avoided a hook aimed at her bust and ripped a hard right to Flo's cheek before going out of range.

Following her decision, Belle danced around the blonde and tossed long-range punches over the other's guard. Although the blows reached her opponent, Belle could not land them at full power. However they stung the blonde and Belle hoped to goad the other into some rash move. The hope did not materialise. Despite using the same tactics as male pugilists of the day, Flo clearly used her brains and did not rely on brute force. She quickly realised Belle's intention and countered it by doggedly ignoring the stinging fists while trying to crowd the other girl into a ring corner.

For almost three minutes Belle managed to avoid being trapped or taking more than the occasional punch. She landed a few hard blows in return and her stinging knuckles homed often enough to leave a reddened patch under Flo's left eye and to start the blonde's nose trickling blood. Each time Belle found herself at close range it came about through her preparing to kick and calling off the move at the last moment.

After sinking a hard left into Flo's chest, Belle again began to wind up for a kick and held it back. She felt Flo's left fist rip into her stomach, croaked and began to double over. Across whipped the blonde's right, colliding with the side of Belle's head before she had time to recover from the left. Down went Belle, sprawling on to the canvas-covered wooden floor. Dazed, winded and hurt, Belle tried to rise. She felt hands take hold of her arms and lift her erect. Supported by Lucienne and the borrowed second, she was returned to her corner and seated on a stool while receiving treatment.

"That kid's good," Paupin remarked to Dusty.

The small Texan did not reply, but his concern grew as he watched Belle rise for the start of the second round. Knowing her, he doubted if she would follow the safe course of avoiding as much punishment as possible while giving the crowd a reasonable show, then fail to toe the line after the end of a round. Unless he missed his guess, she intended to carry the affair through to its conclusion.

So it seemed as Belle began to fight the second round. Some of the crowd had not seen girls fighting in a ring before and came along expecting nothing more than a good laugh. The derision they might have felt rapidly died away as Flo and Belle put on a bout every bit as tough as could any two men.

Belle lost the second round, going down after a dogged pursuit found her trapped against the ropes. In addition to being able to hit hard, Flo could take punishment; and she needed to, for not all Belle's punches landed at the end of their flight. Yet when she did get within range, Flo handed back as much, if not more than she received.

More than that, Flo knew the game far better than Belle. In the third round, having taken a punch in the right eye which partially blinded her, Flo was wide open and Belle went in to make the most of the chance. Sinking a wicked left into Flo's bust, the girl drew a moan of agony and sent the blonde stumbling away. Before Belle could do more, Flo slipped to one knee and ended the round. Nor did Flo give Belle a chance to capitalize on the advantage. At the first hint of trouble in the fourth round, the blonde cut her losses and sank down again.

By the time the fifth round started Flo had thrown off the effects. She took Belle by surprise, moving straight in and making a two-handed attack. With punches raining on her body, or jabbing into her face, Belle could not use her footwork or speed. So she hit back, throwing both hands as fast and hard as she could. Cheers and yells of encouragement rose from the crowd as the girls slugged it out toe to toe, drowning Lucienne's yelled advice. So Belle did not hear her friend telling her to go down and end the round. Instead she took a beating.

So did Flo. Closing, she locked her arms around Belle's body and began to squeeze. Belle croaked, feeling as if her rib cage would be crushed at any moment. Yet the referee made no attempt to separate them. Placing her head under Belle's chin, Flo forced upwards, holding herself so close that the other girl could not use her fists. On other occasions when Flo used that devastating bear-hug, her opponent forgot fist-fighting and grabbed that conveniently fastened hair; to waste valuable energy on something which hurt but did little damage.

Only this time she fought a girl skilled in more than one form of self-defence. Remembering a trick Dusty taught her, Belle pressed her thumbs into the sensitive mastoid area under the ears and at the hinge of the jawbones. Although the pain did not incapacitate Flo, it caused her to loosen her hold. With a thrust of her hard body, Flo bellied Belle backwards. Winded, exhausted and body throbbing in pain, Belle doubled over and fell against the ropes. To her amazement, she saw Flo's foot driving up to catch her in the body. Gagging with nausea, Belle collapsed to the floor.

Half a minute's seconding was needed before Belle recovered enough to be able to understand what Lucienne said to her. Lying back on the stool, her body a mass of pain, nose bloody, left eye swollen and discoloured, Belle looked up at her friend and the words began to take effect.

"Give it up, Belle," Lucienne said. "You've done enough."

"Sh—She kicked me!" Belle gasped, indignation preventing her from taking the advice.

"She's allowed to, and use any standing wrestling holds," the second put in. "Hell, didn't you know that?"

"No!" Belle admitted. "But I do now."

Flo did not expect Belle to come out and toe the line. Even seeing the slim girl approach the ring centre, she doubted if there would be any trouble in ending the fight that round. So she advanced confidently, yet watchful and alert.

So far Belle had only used her fists, giving no sign of either kicking or using any of the standing wrestling holds permitted by the rules. She aimed to change all that. With only the tights covering her feet, she realised kicking with the toe would hurt her more than Flo, but she had other methods at her disposal. Rotating half a turn to the left before Flo reached punching range, Belle tilted her body over from the waist. She drew her right leg up and shot it outwards. Rising up, the bottom of her heel drove into the point of Flo's jaw with considerable force. Back snapped the blonde head as Flo halted in her tracks, dazed and momentarily helpless. Nor did Belle give her time to recover. Bringing down her leg from the horizontal high kick, Belle used it as a pivot to turn and snap a wicked stamping kick full into the pit of the blonde's stomach. Although the blonde had taken hard punches down there without any undue distress, the force of the kick doubled her over like a closing jack-knife.

Jumping in close, Belle sent her left knee crashing full into the centre of the blonde's face. Its force pulped the nose to bloody ruin and lifted Flo erect. Just as when she dealt with the fake preacher in Arkansas, Belle finished the attack with a vicious right cross that exploded her fist against Flo's jaw and sent the woman sprawling head first into one of the ring posts.

A minute dragged by, with Flo's seconds doing all they could to revive her. Although they worked hard, she still lay limp and helpless in her corner when time was called.

"I—I've won!" Belle gasped to Lucienne.

"You won," she agreed. "Now let's get out of here as quick as we can."

## Chapter 12

# A Mighty Persuasive Young Man

Although the officers at Cornwall's table expressed a desire to entertain Belle in honour of her victory, Lucienne insisted that the girl's injuries must be treated first. Avoiding all other attempts to delay them, the woman hustled Belle across the room. Dusty and Paupin rose, following the women into Cornwall's office where Lucienne sent the second to collect some of the gear deliberately forgotten on helping Belle from the ring.

"How'd you feel, Belle?" Dusty asked as the girl sank exhaustedly into a chair at the desk and Lucienne closed the door behind the second.

"Not good," Belle admitted and winced as she touched her ribs. "I don't think anything's broken, though."

"Get your blouse and skirt on, Belle!" ordered Lucienne, bolting the door. Then she gathered the remainder of the girl's property from where it lay on the desk and went on, "I want to get out of here."

"Belle needs time to get over that fight," Dusty objected.

"Only we don't have time to let her," Lucienne pointed out. "Look, Dusty, Cornwall can't just pull out and leave those officers. I want to get clear before he can."

"How do we get out, Annie?" Paupin asked.

"Through that door there," Lucienne answered, indicating the room's second exit. "It leads into the side-alley. Reckon you can unlock it?"

"I've yet to see the lock I can't open," Paupin stated calmly.

Watching the man cross the room and bend to examine the lock, Lucienne grinned and said, "I bet Cornwall didn't know Saul and I're good friends. He'd've tried to get somebody else if he had known."

Working slowly, for each move cost her plenty in pain to her aching, bruised body, Belle drew on her blouse, shirt and shoes over the borrowed bodice and tights. By the time she had dressed, Paupin straightened from the lock and pulled the door open. Dressed, Belle looked passable. The second had managed to stop her nose and mouth bleeding during the rests between the final two rounds, so only the girl's enlarged upper lip and swollen eye gave visible signs of the fight. That would not be noticeable once on the streets, although Belle could not move at any speed.

With Belle's parasol in one hand and underclothing tucked under her arm, Lucienne stepped cautiously into the alley separating the Green Peacock from the neighbouring building. Dusty and Paupin took the girl's arms and helped her along as Lucienne led them to the rear of the building.

"Where'd you keep your tools, Saul?" she asked. "We'll collect them and you can spend the night with us."

"It'd be best," he admitted. "Watch we're not followed, Annie. I've a room not far from here."

Taking Paupin's advice, Lucienne kept a careful watch as the safe-breaker led them to his home. She saw nothing to disturb her and felt certain that leaving so soon after the fight took Cornwall by surprise. At last Paupin halted and indicated a small rooming house as his home. Telling the others to wait, he entered the building.

"Reckon you can trust him, Lucienne?" asked Dusty.

"Like I trust Jim Bludso, or you two," she answered. "Enough to take him back to the Busted Boiler with us and tell him the truth."

"Is that wise?" Belle inquired, leaning against Dusty's arm.

"Saul lost his brother and son fighting the Yankees. He's no love for them."

The subject lapsed, for both Belle and Dusty knew they could rely on Lucienne's judgement. Soon after, Paupin came from the house and joined them with a leather bag in his hand.

"Have you everything you'll need, Saul?" Lucienne said.

"Sure," he replied. "Let's go." Then as he turned, a change came over him. "Keep walking and talking," he ordered.

With the bag in his hand Paupin could not help Belle, and Lucienne took his place. At first he strolled along with them, but dropped back as soon as they turned a corner. Flattening himself against the wall, he peeped cautiously around in the direction from which they came. Satisfied that his early view had been correct, Paupin followed and caught up to the others.

"Cornwall's smarter than you figured, Annie," he declared. "When I came out of the house, I caught a glimpse of Slippery Sid watching me from up the street."

"I should've figured on it," the woman answered. "Cornwall would know we'd come here to collect your tools. We'll have to stop Slippery following us."

"Happen we can find the right sort of place," Dusty drawled. "I'll see if I can persuade him to leave us be."

"You'd best not start shooting, Dusty," Lucienne warned.

"Don't figure to," Dusty replied.

"Slippery's not the biggest, nor toughest jasper Cornwall hires," Paupin put in, "but he's good with a razor and he's got Latour to back him up. They're a rough handful."

"I'll mind it," promised Dusty. "Let's find the right kind of place.

Tell us what you want and we'll try to find it for you," Belle stated, having the advantage of knowing Dusty's ability in the art of bare-handed defence.

The two men following Dusty's party knew their work and kept well back in their attempts at avoiding being seen. Much to their annoyance, Slippery and Latour noticed their victims turn off into almost deserted streets which did not make for easy dogging. However the emptiness worked two ways in that they could hear the other party ahead of them even when out of sight. When the opportunity presented itself, the two men moved into visual range. They saw Lucienne and Paupin on either side of the girl, with Dusty walking ahead and carrying the safe-breaker's bag. After winding about for a time, the quartet turned a corner and disappeared from sight. Realising that the others had entered an alley and might be lost, Slippery increased his pace and Latour followed obediently. Turning the corner, both men saw the bulk of the party ahead of them.

Standing flattened against the wall just around the corner, Dusty watched his friends walk away and listened to the sound of approaching feet. With Belle so exhausted, there would be no chance of losing the following men any other way. So he prepared to make his move.

Sometimes the subject of spies had come up for discussion in the Regiment's mess, with many a comment on the easy life such people must lead being passed among the younger officers. Dusty now realised just how wrong they had been. None of his friends back at the Regiment even started to think of the numerous details a spy needed, at his, or her fingertips. Nor would any of them have guessed at the kind of things that could go wrong on a spy's assignment. Not the least being that the spies had aroused the avarice and interest of a dangerous criminal. It fell on Dusty to remove the menace from their tracks.

One thing Dusty knew for sure, he could not act in a sporting manner when dealing with the two men. Too much hung in the balance for him to give Slippery Sid and Latour an even break. So he waited, tense and ready, as the men turned the corner. Slippery Sid stood six foot, with a lean, gaunt frame, while

108

Latour was a couple of inches smaller and stocky. Which meant both of them possessed a considerable height-weight advantage over the small Texan. However Dusty had surprise on his side.

Lunging forward, Dusty heard a startled expression break from Latour, and struck at Slippery Sid. While most Occidental men of the period would have crashed a fist into Slippery's jaw, Dusty knew a far more effective way of handling him. The small Texan struck with a clenched fist, but not in the accepted manner. Instead he used the *hitosashiyubi-ipponken,* the forefinger-fist, with the forefinger's knuckle projecting beyond the others. Such a blow could be directed against the solar-plexus, or the *jinchu* collection of nerve centres in the centre of the top lip, with devastating effect; but Dusty aimed for neither. His hand struck home under Slippery's chin, smashing into his prominent adam's apple. In striking, Dusty tried to land his blow hard enough to create a temporary paralysis and unconsciousness, but not so as to seriously injure or kill the man. A croak of agony broke from Slippery and he stumbled backwards, feeling as if somebody had thrust an iron knob into his throat.

Already Latour began to turn and face Dusty, right hand fanning to his pocket. Having thought ahead, Dusty did not need to plan further action. From striking Slippery, he whipped straight into a *mae keri* forward kick that slammed his boot full into the pit of Latour's stomach. Letting out a winded screech, Latour doubled over. His hands clawed at his middle though he still retained enough control over himself to stagger forward in an attempt to avoid a knee to the face. Although Dusty had hoped to end the matter with his knee, he wasted no time in trying to move to a position where he could. Bending his right arm, he swung it up and down. His elbow struck home right where it would do most good, at the base of the skull, and Latour went down like a back-broken rabbit.

Only just in time Dusty heard the sound of Slippery's muffled gasping draw nearer. In his desire not to strike too hard, Dusty had erred the other way. While feeling half-strangled, the thin man was still on his feet and, if anything, even more dangerous than before. Around lashed the open cutthroat razor in Slippery's hand in a wicked downwards slash. The steel missed, but by a very slender margin, to be whipped back upwards again. Such a blow had succeeded on other occasions when the first slash missed and the victim tried to close with Slippery. It might have again, for Dusty had begun to move forward. Seeing his danger, Dusty thrust himself rearwards and once more avoided the murderous blade.

109

Up went the razor and Dusty moved as if to try to block it. Having witnessed the small Texan's speed, Slippery hurried his roundhouse cut just as Dusty hoped. Checking his forward motion, Dusty swayed his torso out of the radius of the razor's swing. Unable to stop himself, Slippery bent over and the razor pointed towards the ground away from Dusty. Even as the man prepared to cut up again, Dusty pivoted into a stamping kick which thudded home against the other's rib cage. Slippery cried out in pain as two ribs broke and the force of the kick propelled him into the wall of the nearer building. Leaping over the razor, which had fallen from its owner's hand when the kick landed, Dusty drove a *tegatana* chop with the edge of his hand against the back of the man's neck. Down went Slippery and Dusty heard a footstep behind him. Whipping around, he prepared to deal with whoever made it.

"Dusty!" gasped Lucienne's voice urgently. "It's me. Are you all right?"

"I reckon so," he replied. "This pair won't be following anybody for a spell though."

A match rasped and in its glow Lucienne studied the two sprawled out shapes on the ground.

"You're right about that," she breathed and awe as much as a need for secrecy kept her voice down. "I don't know how you do it, but you're a mighty persuasive young man. Come on, Belle insisted that one of us came back to see how you made out. Let's show her you're all right."

"Reckon there's any chance of Cornwall finding us now?" Dusty inquired as they walked along the alley.

"I doubt it. He'll maybe try, though."

"To help the Yankees?"

"To cut himself into a share of the loot. Only he'll have to find us first."

Whatever action Cornwall might decide to take, he would need to locate Dusty's party first. Clearly he regarded the two as ample to trail them to their hideout, for Lucienne and Paupin kept a careful watch without seeing any sign of more of the saloonkeeper's men. Paupin appeared surprised at being taken to the Busted Boiler and remarked that it would be the last place Cornwall thought of looking for them. Letting them in by a rear door, Lucienne led the way upstairs to the room which had been prepared as her hideout.

Not until seated in the room, behind drawn curtains and a locked door did Paupin learn the truth about the safe he would be asked to break open. He hesitated only for one minute, then nodded his agreement.

"I'm still on," he stated.

"There'll be five hundred dollars in Yankee gold for you after you've done it," Belle promised.

"I'd do it for nothing, young lady. It's for the South."

"How about when it's done?" asked Dusty. "What'll Cornwall do?"

"What can he do?" Belle countered. "He'll know what's happened, but he can hardly say anything."

"I'll make sure of *that*," Lucienne promised grimly. "To-morrow morning I'll send him a warning that if he tries another trick like with Slippery, I'll let the Yankees hear what I know. And after the job's over, I'll let him know that if he talks I'll fix it so the Yankees hear he planned the whole thing."

"Will he believe you?"

"He'll be too cautious not to, Dusty," Belle guessed. "Especially as he's managed to keep his place going and bringing in money. I'd say he'd not chance spoiling it."

As his companions appeared satisfied that Cornwall did not pose a serious threat, Dusty relaxed. Soon after, Jim Bludso returned. Seeing Belle's facial damage, he forgot to give the news that his part of the affair was well in hand.

"What the hell happened to you?" he growled.

"I met another of your 'sisters'," Belle answered coldly. "Sister Ruby."

"Ruby Toot?" Jim said. "I'd forgotten about her. I'm sorry about that, Miss Boyd. See, she was going with a Yankee Army engineer working on the new defences they set up. I got to know her and picked up details of the work they did. Trouble being the engineer left soon after and Ruby figured I should take his place."

"What if Cornwall sends somebody around here asking questions?" Dusty put in. "He'll likely learn what caused the fuss between Belle and that Toot gal."

"He won't learn a thing," Jim replied. "Early tomorrow I'll see those Yankee brass-pounders and let on that you stayed the night here with me, Miss Boyd."

"You'll ruin my good name," smiled the girl. "But Cornwall may move sooner than that."

"What do we do then?" the engineer asked.

"Play smarter than he does," Belle replied.

At about the same time that Belle laid her plans to circumvent Cornwall's efforts to find her, the man learned of the failure to follow her party to its hideout. He had made excuses to his guests on learning of Belle's departure and contented himself with the knowledge that Slippery Sid and Latour waited at Paupin's home ready to trail them. When the battered pair returned, interrupting an enjoyable evening, Cornwall started to ask questions. First he learned the cause of the trouble between Belle and Ruby Toot. Talking with the three petty officers, Cornwall could not decide whether the girl had been one of Jim Bludso's 'sisters' or merely a victim of mistaken identity. While the most sober of the petty officers insisted that the 'sister' visiting Bludso had been a brunette, as opposed to Annie Buckhalter's girl having blonde hair, Cornwall decided to check. Calling over one of his most reliable men, Cornwall gave orders.

"Yeah?" Jim Bludso called sleepily in answer to a knocking at his room's outside door. "What's up?"

"Got a message for you, Mr. Bludso," a male voice answered.

"Can't it wait until morning?"

"No, sir."

Outside Jim's door, the man saw a lamp lit and its glow drew closer. From all the signs, Jim had just left his bed. Naked to the waist and supporting his pants with one hand, bare-foot and with hair rumpled untidily, the big engineer scowled at his visitor in the light of the small lamp.

"Who-all is it, Jim honey?" asked a girl's voice from inside the room.

"Hush your mouth, gal!" Jim barked.

By moving around in a casual manner, the visitor found he could make out the bed. A shape moved uneasily in it and, although unable to see much, he judged it to be the female speaker. Further than that, a mass of brunette hair showed in contrast to the pillow.

As if noticing the man's interest, Jim reached out a hand to draw the door shut and hide his 'bed-mate' from view. Then he growled out a demand for information as to the reason for the visit.

"There's Yankee ironsides due in early tomorrow and they want you to gather a gang ready to help clean its engines," the man answered.

Although he received a blistering cursing for disturbing Jim with such unimportant news, the man went away contented. Returning to the Green Peacock, he told Cornwall that the brunette was still with Jim Bludso. Cornwall decided that the Yankee petty officer either made a mistake, or deliberately stirred up trouble with Ruby Toot in the hope of seeing a fight before the one arranged in the ring. While disinterested in Ruby's injury, Cornwall cursed bitterly, his invective being directed at the time wasted in checking the story. There would be little or no chance of finding where the safe was that 'Annie Buckhalter' planned to rob in time to grab off a portion of the loot, if she intended to strike that night. Maybe it would be for the best. He would not be too sorry to learn that the woman brought off her proposed robbery and slipped safely out of New Orleans; 'Annie Buckhalter' knew far too much about him for comfort.

Jim Bludso put out the lamp when the man reached the foot of the stairs, but did not return to his bed. Instead he stood by the window and watched his visitor depart, while drawing on his shirt.

"I reckon he fell for it, Miss Boyd. Shall I follow him?"

The bed creaked as Belle swung her bare feet out of it. Dressed in her male clothing, less the riding boots, she crossed the room and halted at Bludso's side.

"I'd say let him go and tell his boss," she replied. "He's certain that you have a girl in here and I'm sure Cornwall will think the Yankee brass-pounder made a mistake."

"I'm not sorry that jasper came," Bludso stated. "If he'd held off much longer, I'd've been asleep."

"I *was*," put in Dusty Fog's voice from the side of the room.

"And me," Paupin went on. "That's a smart scheme you thought up, Miss Boyd, but now let's grab some sleep shall we?"

"Go ahead," smiled the girl, crossing to the interior door and opening it. "I doubt if they'll try again, so I'm going to bed. Good night."

With that, the girl left Bludso's room and went to the one she would share with Lucienne. All in all Belle felt that the boredom of waiting in the dark for a visit from Cornwall's man had been worth while. She felt sure that the saloonkeeper would be fooled and thrown off their trail. That only left the main problem, the destruction of the counterfeiting plant, for them to worry about. Nothing could be done about that until they learned more about the Gaton house's defences. She wondered if the men she met at Lucienne's shop had recovered and made a guess at her mission or identity.

So far neither had. In a room at the military hospital Kaddam lay unconscious and with a fractured skull, while Turnpike waited for the drugs prescribed by the doctor to overcome the pain of his throbbing head and let him sleep. Before he could think of the events at Madam Lucienne's shop, sleep claimed him and he did not wake up until late the following morning.

Even then Turnpike did not rush to resume his interrupted work. Legarthy induced by the drugs kept him content to lie in bed until a recurring thought nagged its way through to him. Had there been more to the affair at the shop than a mere attempt at robbery? Before being sedated, he had learned all he could about the couple's actions and escape; but the doctor insisted that he must sleep before doing anything about it.

Sitting up, Turnpike called for his clothes. For all that, it was late in the afternoon before he entered Lucienne's shop. Making a thorough examination, he found the till empty and the ledger gone. His own people had searched the shop withouf finding anything to lead them to its owner, or tell of her activities. Yet he felt sure that his information as to her being a Confederate spy was true.

Could the theft of the ledger be more than coincidence? Did Lucienne send those two with orders to collect it and prevent whatever it contained falling into the wrong hands?

Certainly such skill with a gun as the small man showed could not be found in the normal sneak-thief. Turnpike would never forget the speed with which the man drew and fired at him.

Leaving the shop, Turnpike returned to his department's office and read through records, trying to find some report of the small man. Night came with him no nearer to an answer. He sat alone in the office, thinking about the small man. Then he turned his attention to the woman, remembering that she did all the talking and showed a fair turn of speed in handling Kaddam.

Going into the shop, knowing it to be in Yankee hands, called for a special brand of courage. One name leapt instantly to mind in connection with such an act. Belle Boyd, the Rebel Spy, had the audacity and nerve to do it. Yet she was reported to be in Arkansas. It seemed highly unlikely that Lucienne could have contacted Belle Boyd so quickly. Of course the Rebel Spy might have come to New Orleans on some other mission. Turnpike could think of only one thing in New Orleans big enough to attract Belle Boyd. Rising, he dashed from the office in search of a carriage.

## Chapter 13

## The Raid

"Six men?" Dusty Fog said in surprise, looking at the big, powerful Negro at Jim Bludso's side.

"That's all," replied Willie, Bludso's striker. "They turns out all the coloured folks afore dark."

"Maybe they move a guard in after dark," Dusty remarked.

"No, sir," Willie answered. "Once in a while they has visitors, but only one or two of 'em at a time. I asked around among the house staff and they know."

"It's possible that they think they don't need a big guard, Dusty," Belle pointed out. "They don't know that we stopped the consignment and hope to avoid attention by not having the house heavily guarded."

"They sure ain't like that Yankee colonel along the street from 'em," Willie commented. "He's done got thirty men on hand all the time guarding him."

"That's a mighty big guard for a colonel's residence, even in occupied territory," Dusty stated. "It's near on half a company."

"There's not been sufficient civic unrest to warrant that big a guard," Belle agreed. "How close to the Gaton house are they, Willie?"

"A quarter of a mile, ma'am," the Negro replied. "Only they'd not need to shout for help. There's a telegraph wire running down the back from Gaton's house to where the colonel lives."

It was mid-afternoon and Dusty's party gathered in Jim Bludso's room to hear Willie give his report. Clearly the big Negro possessed excellent methods of gathering information, for he gave a very clear picture of the house. In far less time than Dusty would have believed possible, Willie had gathered enough details to make planning the raid feasible.

No white man could have done it in so short a time. Posing as a freed, but unemployed slave, Willie visited the Gaton house's servants' entrance and asked for work. Being big, strong, jovial and attractive to women, he ingratiated himself rapidly among the household staff. While it turned out that they could not hope to gain permanent employment for him, the staff let him stay with them. In return for helping with their work, they gave him much information and permitted him to see around both building and grounds. He noticed that the gardens appeared in need of attention, but his offer to do some tidying up met with refusal. For some reason or other, Massa Gaton gave orders that none of the staff must stray from the paths and had discharged one man who started to go amongst the bushes. Although unable to make a search of the garden and learn the reason for the ban, Willie managed to see the telegraph wires.

"They runs across the garden from a downstairs window," he said. "And the one to the colonel's house ain't on its own."

"There're more of them?" asked Dusty.

"Sure are, Cap'n. I saw two more. Only they was fastened about eighteen inches above the ground and to the bushes. Couldn't see where they went and didn't find a chance to look closer."

"You know what they are, Dusty?" Belle put in, the words a statement rather than a question.

"Trip wires," he replied. "The Yankees used them and ground torpedoes up around Little Rock. One end of the wire's fastened to a pull-primer and when you hit it, the charge goes up."

"That's what I thought," the girl confirmed. "Maybe they'll have the torpedoes in place too."

"Give them their due, those Yankees are smart," Dusty said. "Just six men at the house, but a good-sized guard on hand. Not in the house to draw attention and start our folks wondering why they're there, but close enough to arrive in a hurry if they're needed."

"The telegraph manned day and night, most likely," Belle went on.

"You can count on that, ma'am," Willie remarked. "Least-wise there's one room downstairs that's allus got a man in it. Maid I asked allowed he'd got him some scientifical instrument in there, but she didn't know what it was. Way she described it, I'd say it was a telegraph key like I saw a few times on the river."

"Which room, Willie?"

"First on the right at the foot of the main stairs, Cap'n. Door was shut all the time I was there."

"Locked?"

"If it was, the gal didn't mention it."

"I never did like them too easy," Belle sighed. "If we set off whatever's at the end of one of those trip-wires the telegraph operator starts sending a warning, even if the soldiers don't see and hear the explosion."

116

"Or goes to tapping his key should anybody slip through the wires and get into the house," Dusty continued.

"Can we break in?" Bludso demanded.

"We're going to make a try," Dusty assured him. "We'll have to go tonight, too if we can."

"The longer we wait, the better chance for Cornwall to find us," Lucienne put in. "Or for the Yankees to hear something and get suspicious. I'd say tonight, if it can be done."

"Are you set, Jim?" Dusty wanted to know.

"Got all we need, Cap'n. We cut open some incendiary shells and poured the stuff into small barrels. A couple of them ought to do all we need. How many men do you want?"

"As few as we can manage with. You, Willy, Saul and—."

"And me," interrupted Belle. "No arguments, Dusty. This's my assignment and I mean to see it through."

"Belle and me then," Dusty finished and grinned at the man. "Giving in to her straight off saves time. She sure is a strong-willed gal."

"Will that be enough?" asked Lucienne. "You don't need more men?"

"It ought to be enough," Dusty answered. "We have to go quietly, so the smaller the party, the better."

"How about you, Lucy gal," Bludso grinned. "You want to come along?"

"Not me," the woman laughed. "The days when I went in for that kind of stuff are long over. I'll stay here ready to do anything that needs doing. How do you intend to play it, Dusty?"

"This's how I reckon," he replied and outlined his plans.

Night found the party Dusty named standing before the Gaton house. With Jim Bludso and Willie as their guides, they passed unnoticed through the town and that despite the kegs and other equipment they carried. For the most part they went by back streets and other deserted ways, but occasionally needed to pass other people. At such time the men gathered around Belle, who was definitely feminine despite her male attire, and gave an impression of being a group of revellers on their way home from some celebration.

Luck favoured them in that they found St. Charles Avenue deserted. The big gates of Gaton's house were closed and locked.

"We'll have to go over the wall," Belle breathed.

"Around the side then," Dusty replied and led the way.

Even in the alley separating Gaton's home from its neighbour, the surrounding wall rose ten feet high and carried pieces of broken glass fixed to its top. When Dusty heard of the added protection, he laid plans to circumvent it. Unfastening the thick roll of blankets he wore slung across his shoulders, Dusty looked to make sure Belle kept watch and then walked to the base of the wall. Already Jim Bludso and Willie had set down the small kegs they carried and stood waiting to do their parts. Placing his right foot into Bludso's cupped hands, Dusty thrust himself upwards with the left. At the same moment Bludso began to lift and Dusty rose up the wall. Willie's hands went under Dusty's left foot and the two big men hoisted the small Texan into the air until he was level with the top of the wall, then held him there.

Supported by the two men, Dusty spread a thick pad of blanket over the top of the wall. Although the broken edges of the glass made uncomfortable bumps, they could not cut through several thicknesses of the folded material. Sitting astride the padding, Dusty gave the grounds a quick scrutiny and saw no sign of guards. Already Paupin was being hoisted up by the two men and at Dusty's signal took a seat facing him. Leaving her post, Belle joined the men. She unslung the coil of rope from her shoulder and tossed one end to Dusty so he could haul up Paupin's tool bag. Next Belle came up and joined the two men on top of the wall.

"I'll go down first," she whispered.

Gripping the rope, Belle slid down it to the ground with Dusty holding the other end. The girl kept close to the wall, taking the bag which Paupin lowered and then the two kegs. On the other side of the wall, Willie handed Bludso up to the waiting men and then received their help to climb up and drop down, joining Belle.

"Keep close to the wall!" Dusty ordered.

When making his plans, Dusty gambled on there being no trip-wires or ground torpedoes close to the surrounding walls, or on the main path to the house. Unless he missed his guess, the Yankees would expect an attacking party to approach through the cover of the bushes and must have laid their defences accordingly. So he planned to reach the house by the front path; doing the unexpected often paid dividends.

"I'd like to unlock that gate before going to the house, Cap'n," Paupin breathed. "If we have to run for it, there won't be time."

"It's your game we're playing, Saul," Dusty answered. "Go to it."

By the time they reached the gates, Dusty knew the first part of his gamble had been successful. They had encountered no trip-wires or ground torpedoes so close to the wall. Nor had Paupin found any difficulty in opening the heavy lock securing the gates. Before going further, the party took precautions against being recognised. Each one carried a cloth hood, made up that evening, designed to cover the head and trail down to the shoulders. In addition the men wore clothes which could not lead to their being identified. Slipping on their hoods, taking care that they could see through the eye-holes, the party advanced silently along the edge of the path.

Lights glowed in the main hall and a few other rooms, showing that at least some of the six men were present and not yet in bed. The sight did not cause any thought among the party that Dusty's plans were going wrong. Working on the assumption that the Yankees would expect any such an attempt to come between midnight and dawn, Dusty arranged for them to reach the house just after nine o'clock. In that way, he hoped to take the defenders by surprise.

Not that Dusty intended to rush the front door. Close to the house, he left the path and walked along the side of the building. According to Willie, the servants could walk around the outside of the house provided they stuck close to the wall. So Dusty took a chance that there would be no protective devices in that area. He hoped that the Yankees did not go to the trouble of rigging trip-wires or ground torpedoes each night and removing them before the staff arrived in the morning. For all that Dusty walked along with extreme care, feeling at the ground ahead delicately before chancing his weight on it.

At last they reached the rear of the house and found it, as Dusty hoped, silent without signs of occupation. Moving by the small Texan, Paupin took the lead. He had already decided that tackling the kitchen door would be a waste of time as it was bolted in addition to the lock. So he examined one of the windows and nodded in satisfaction. Opening the tool bag, Paupin took out a can of molasses and a sheet of thick paper. After smearing some of the molasses on one side of the paper, he applied its adhesive surface to the pane of glass separating him from the window catch. Next he drew a glazier's glass-cutter from his bag and carefully ran its working edge around the sides of the pane. Dropping the cutter into his jacket pocket, he took hold of the edge of the paper with one hand and tapped its centre with the other. A faint click sounded and the pane moved inwards a trifle. With a firm but gentle pull, Paupin drew the pane, firmly held to the paper, towards him and passed it to Belle.

"I'll go in and unfasten the door," Paupin offered, slipping back the window catch and raising the sash.

Slipping silently through the open window, Paupin disappeared into the building. In a surprisingly short time the kitchen door opened and he grinned at the surprised faces of his companions.

"That was quick," Dusty said.

"The key was in the lock," Paupin admitted. "Everything's quiet enough."

On entering the kitchen Dusty and Belle crossed straight to its inner door. Bludso and Willie set down their kegs while Dusty eased open the door and looked along the dimly-lit passage which led to the front of the building. Followed by Belle, the small Texan crept along the passage. Ahead of them lay a corner and, around it, the main hall. Just as they approached the corner, Belle and Dusty heard footsteps coming towards them.

The man who came around the corner clearly had no suspicion of their presence. Seeing them before him, he came to a halt and stared. Given a chance, he might have made trouble for he had size and weight in addition to a Navy Colt stuck in his waistband. Only he did not receive the opportunity to make use of either his heftiness or the firearm. Up lashed Belle's right foot, driving hard into the pit of the man's groin. Coming so unexpectedly and hard, the kick stopped any outcry the man meant to raise and doubled him over. Dusty followed up Belle's kick with remarkably smooth timing and team-work. Around lashed his left arm in *a tegatana* chop to the back of the man's neck, dropping him silent and unconscious to the floor.

"One!" Belle breathed.

"Hawg-tie him, Jim!" Dusty ordered. "Let's see to some of the others, Belle."

Leaving Bludso and Willie to attend to securing the first prisoner, Dusty and Belle continued to move stealthily along the passage. When making his plans, Dusty decided that Paupin must stay in the background until after the occupants of the house had been secured. They could not replace the safe-breaker if he should be injured, so Dusty refused to take any chances. On reaching the end of the passage, Dusty and Belle looked into the main hall. A wide staircase ran down from the first floor to the centre of the hall. Doors gave access to various rooms off the hall, but only one of them interested Dusty. First item on his agenda was the capture of the telegraph key so that no warning might be passed to the waiting soldiers. From where he and Belle crouched at the side of the stairs, they could see through the open door of the first room on the right. It appeared to be empty; certainly no man sat at the table on which rested the telegraph key.

Voices sounded as a door at the left of the hall opened and footsteps thudded, coming in the direction of the stairs. There would be no time to back off into the passage, nor dare Dusty and Belle chance crouching by the stairs in the hope of not being seen.

Thrusting himself forward, Dusty landed before the men. He went straight into a gun-fighter's crouch and the Army Colt flowed from his waistband. Combined with their surprise at Dusty's sudden, unexpected appearance, his speed on the draw caused the men to freeze. There were four of them, all in their shirt-sleeves and none armed. That left only one to be accounted for, unless Willie had made a mistake in his reckoning.

"Don't make a sound, any of you!" Dusty growled, his gun making a casual arc that seemed to single out each man individually without losing the drop on the remainder. Slowly Dusty and Belle moved forward and he went on, "Back towards the wall real easy and quiet."

Obediently the quartet backed away, keeping spread out just far enough to prevent any one of them taking cover behind the rest. Dusty wanted to get the men in a position where he could make them lean with palms on the wall and bodies inclined so that sudden movement would be impossible. Then tying them up would be easy.

Unnoticed by either Dusty or Belle, a plump, well-dressed man appeared at the head of the stairs. He took in the scene and backed away silently into a room, to emerge a second or two later holding a Navy Colt. Although he lined the gun on Dusty, the man held his fire. At that range he doubted if he could make a hit, and so he began to tiptoe down the stairs. Although Dusty and Belle saw the glances darted behind them by the quartet, each suspected a trick. However the girl started to turn her head, meaning to look and make sure no danger threatened them.

Having finished tying up the first captive, Jim Bludso came into sight, his knife in his hand. He saw the man on the stairs. Even without recognising the man as Gaton, the Confederate printer who sold his skill to the Yankees, Bludso could not have acted in any other way. Even as one of the quartet prepared to yell a warning, Bludso threw his knife so that it passed between the stair case rail in its flight at Gaton. Steel flickered through the air, sinking into Gaton's plump throat. He gurgled, jerked and fired the Colt, but its bullet did no more than shatter a vase

121

by the door. Then, gagging and choking on his own blood, the traitor crumpled forward and crashed down the stairs.

Instinctively Belle and Dusty swung their heads in the direction of the shot. Leaping forward, the biggest man struck down Dusty's gun arm, gripping it in both his hands to try to shake the revolver free. A second leaped to lock his arms around Belle, holding her as he yelled an order.

"Get to the telegraph!"

After throwing his knife, Bludso charged across the hall, tackling the third man and Willie dashed towards the telegraph room. Swinging around at its door the Negro faced the approaching fourth member of Gaton's guard and they disappeared into the room.

Deciding that wearing her gunbelt might attract unwanted attention, Belle had left it at the Busted Boiler. However she had the special bracelet on her left wrist. The man gripped her around the upper arms and from the side, in a position where she could not kick him hard enough to effect a release. That did not stop her getting her hands together. Quickly she eased the bracelet off with her right hand, then raked its razor-sharp edge across the man's upper wrist. With a yell of pain he loosened his hold. Even as Belle drove her left elbow crashing into the man's ribs to send him stumbling away, she saw Dusty's assailant sail over the small Texan's shoulder.

Willie came sprawling through the door of the telegraph room, his hood twisted around so that its eye-holes faced the rear. Before he could save himself, he crashed to the floor. Snarling in rage, the fourth man appeared at the door. Then he realised what he must do and put aside thoughts of attacking the Negro. Turning the man started to make for the table again.

Racing across the hall, Belle hurdled over Willie and as she landed bounded into the room again. Her feet smashed into the white man's shoulders, hurling him across the room. On landing from the leaping high kick, Belle flung herself at the table in an attempt to unscrew the wires from the key. While she tried to free the first wire, a hand fell on her shoulder. Swinging around faster than the man pulled, Belle lashed up her right hand to rake the bracelet across his face. Blood spurted and the man fell back a pace in agony. Placing her foot against his stomach, Belle shoved hard. In the hall Willie was just turning his hood so he could see again when the man came backwards through the telegraph-room's door. Still on his knees, the Negro linked hands and smashed them into the back of the man's knees to bring him crashing down.

Crouching ready to attack again, Belle saw Willie leap on to the man and gave her attention to the urgent matter of disabling the telegraph key. Swiftly she disconnected the wires, hurled the key-box against the wall and then darted into the hall ready to help her friends. She found her services would not be needed and the situation under control. Although Bludso knelt holding his side and muttering curses and Dusty had lost his hood but gained a bloody nose, they need not worry for the four guards sprawled all around them.

"Are you all right, Belle?" Dusty asked.

"I'll live," she replied. "How about you?"

"I'm the same as you. Make a start with Saul while we tend to this bunch."

Leaving the men to tie up their groaning, helpless enemies, Belle went to the foot of the stairs. Her face showed distaste as she knelt by Gaton's body and searched its pockets in the hope of finding the safe keys. Failing to do so, she and Paupin went up-stairs and made a quick but thorough examination of the man's room. Again they failed to produce the keys.

"It's as I expected," Belle admitted. "He probably hands them to the soldiers after the house staff leave at night. Let's take a look at the safe."

Returning to the hall, Belle and Paupin entered the study as being the most likely place to house the safe. The guess proved correct and Paupin looked over the steel box with faint contempt.

"They're sure easy," he commented. "I could open it with a bobby-pin."

"Do you want one?" Belle smiled.

"Naw! I've brought my tools, so I may as well use them. Go tell the fellers to start getting ready to leave. This won't take long."

## Chapter 14

## Miss Boyd Renews an Acquaintance

Although Paupin probably could not have opened the safe with a bobby-pin, he found little difficulty in doing so using his tools. While the safe-breaker handled his part of the affair, all the others worked hard. Half an hour later Belle Boyd stood watching the counterfeiting plates, faces scratched and marred, bubbling in a container of acid to complete their destruction. In the cellar Dusty Fog waited to start the fire which would consume all the money already printed and the paper to make more. The printing-press had been ruined, inks, dyes and chemicals poured out of their containers.

"Ready, Belle?" he asked as the girl entered.

"When you are," she replied and passed a thick notebook to him. "Put this in your pocket. It's details of the entire business, what shipments they've sent off, where to, stuff like that."

"It'll be handy," Dusty admitted. "Willie and Jim've gone up to clear those jaspers out of the house."

"I saw them," the girl smiled. "Willie's taking along a bottle of whisky he found, says it will cure his rheumatism—if he ever gets it."

"There's nothing like being prepared," Dusty grinned. "I'll start the fire, Belle. Get going."

By the door of the cellar Dusty rasped a match on his pants' seat and tossed it into the centre of the room. At first only a tiny finger of flame rose, but it grew by the second. A composition of benzole, coal tar, turpentine, residum and crude petroleum could be relied upon to burn well, as the makers of the incendiary shells from which it came knew. Watching the fire spread and grow, Dusty doubted if the Yankees would recover any part of their counterfeiting plant. To slow down any fire-fighting force which might arrive, Dusty spilled the last of the composition on the floor and up the cellar's wooden steps. Almost before he reached the top, he saw the first fingers of flame creeping after him.

All the lights were out in the hall by the time Dusty reached it. Already Bludso and Willie had dragged the bound and gagged Yankees from the house and far enough along the path to be safe should the whole house take fire. On Dusty joining them, the party hurried along to the main gates. So far no sign of the fire showed and muttered congratulations passed among the raiders.

Pulling open the gate, Jim Bludso allowed Belle to lead the way. Followed by Paupin, then Willie, the girl stepped on to St Charles Avenue. Just too late she heard the grass-muffled feet of approaching men and saw several soldiers running towards her. By keeping to the wide, tree-dotted grass border of the street, the soldiers had escaped detection until almost too late.

Clearly the men came ready for trouble. Without challenging, the leader of the approaching party brought up his revolver and fired. Then a rifle cracked and its bullet struck the gate just in front of Dusty, causing him to take an involuntary pace to the rear. In doing so, he prevented Bludso from leaving.

"Run for it!" Belle shouted.

More shots rang out as the girl darted off along the street, closely followed by Willie and Paupin. Gun in hand, Dusty tried to go through the gate. Once again lead drove him back and a glance told him that there could be no leaving through the front entrance.

"We'll have to try the back, Jim!" he snapped, throwing a couple of shots at the rapidly approaching soldiers.

While Dusty did not hit any of them, he caused the soldiers to slow down. Turning, Dusty raced with Bludso along the path. Half of the soldiers approached the gates cautiously and the remainder charged by in hot pursuit of Belle's party. Already a small glow of fire showed in the house, but Dusty and Bludso ignored it. Hurdling the bound men, they ran along in front of the house, swung down the side and reached the rear. By sticking close to the wall again they avoided the chance of running into trip-wires and reached the rear gate. Although Dusty was prepared to shoot open the lock, the need did not arise.

"They'd got slack!" Bludso said. "The key's in the lock."

Swifly the engineer turned the key and Dusty drew open the bolts. Opening the gate, they stepped out. Nobody challenged them, the narrow street at the rear of the houses being deserted. Dusty transferred the key to the outside of the gate and turned it in the lock as Bludso closed the exit. With that done they moved off silently and could hear the first of their pursuers running towards the gate.

"It's locked!" yelled a voice. "They must still be in the grounds."

"Guard the gate, two of you," barked another. "The rest come with me to see if we can put out that fire."

"But those two—."

"Leave them. If they're roaming around the garden, we'll soon know it."

"Where now, Jim?" Dusty whispered.

"Back to the Busted Boiler as quick as we can. If I know Willie, he'll be taking Miss Belle and Saul there. Likely we'll meet up on the way."

Lead sang its eerie 'splat!' sound around Belle's head as she ran along St. Charles Avenue, but none of it touched her. By keeping to the edge of the street, she and her companions offered a far harder target for the Yankee soldiers. The quarter moon did not give much light and the trees which lined the Avenue threw shadows not conducive to accurate shooting. Realising this, the soldiers stopped using their rifles and concentrated on running their quarry down.

The strenuous activities of the previous day and night, following upon a long journey in the cramped conditions aboard the *Jack* did not leave Belle in the best of physical condition. While Lucienne had shown her skill as a masseuse to remove most of the stiffness from Belle's bruised body that morning, she could not entirely eradicate the effects of the prize-fight. So the girl felt herself weakening. Discovering that they drew ahead of her, the two men slowed down.

"K—Keep going!" she gasped and tried to run faster.

Then her foot slipped on the projecting root of a tree and she stumbled. At another time she might have saved herself, but she moved too slowly. Bright lights seemed to be bursting in her head as she crashed into the tree's trunk and she slid down in a dazed, helpless heap to the ground.

Hearing Belle's cry of pain, Paupin and Willie skidded to a halt. Yells rose from the pursuing soldiers and one's rifle cracked. The bullet flung splinters from the tree, causing Paupin to stop as he went to help the girl. Bayonets glinted dully on the soldiers' rifles, a more deadly threat than bullets in the poor light. It would be certain capture, or death, to stay and fight; but to run away meant that Belle Boyd, the Rebel Spy, must fall into enemies' hands. Paupin realised that the result would be the same for Belle no matter which way he acted. However if he and Willie escaped to take the news to Dusty—always assuming the Yankees had not caught the small Texan—something might be done to rescue the girl. It was a slight chance, but better than no chance at all.

"Run, Willie!" he snapped, knowing what fate a Negro helping in such an affair could expect. "We've got to find Cap'n Fog."

Only for a moment did Willie hesitate. His thoughts on the matter ran parallel in all respects to Paupin's. So both men turned and ran on again, striding out at their best speed. Behind them, Belle tried to rise and to order them to save their own lives. Exhaustion welled through her and she became conscious of men around her and voices which seemed to come from a long way off reached her ears.

"One of 'em's down!" yelled the leading soldier, swinging his bayoneted Sharps rifle into an attack position.

Next moment another of the party jerked the cover from a bull's eye lantern he carried and illuminated Belle with its light.

"Hold that cat-stabber back," bawled a sergeant. "That's a woman."

Immediately the man with the ready bayonet held his thrust and the rest of the party came to a halt as they stared at Belle. Although the sergeant urged most of his men on after Paupin and Willie, the pause allowed the two men to increase their lead still more.

Slowly the dizziness left Belle and her eyes focused on the scene. Four soldiers formed a loose half circle in front of her, standing tense and watchful in the light of a lantern. Looking beyond them, Belle saw a trio of civilians approaching. The white bandage around the centre civilian's head identified him even before Belle could see his face. It seemed that Dusty's bullet had done less damage than they guessed, for Turnpike came towards Belle with his companions. At Turnpike's right side stalked a big, burly, bearded young man. The third of the group was smaller, thin, with a weak face and narrow, shifty eyes.

"So you managed to get one of them," growled the burly man, sweeping by the soldiers and bending over Belle. "Hey! It's a woman."

"I'd never've guessed," grunted the senior soldier present. "Reckon he must've learned things like that in college."

Although the burly civilian threw a savage glare at the soldier, he chose to ignore the comment. Instead he turned back to Belle and reached towards her hood. Suddenly he changed his hand's direction, shooting it down to grab her left wrist. Not until he had drawn the bracelet off did the bearded man offer to remove Belle's hood.

"We've got one of their big ones here, boys," the bearded man stated. "Only their best get these bracelets."

"What's wrong with the bracelet, Ike?" asked the smallest of the trio.

"I saw one of our men with his throat slit near on from ear to ear with one after he went to arrest Rose Greenhow," the bearded man answered. "This slut—."

"I recognise her!" Turnpike yelped, thrusting by the other. "She's the one who came to the shop."

"Are you sure, Melvin?" asked the bearded man.

"I'm sur—."

"Fire! Fire!"

At the sound of the two words shouted from along the street, Turnpike and his companions jerked around. A faint red glow showed over the wall around Gaton's property, growing brighter by the second.

"They've done it!" snarled the bearded man. "They've done it!"

"It wasn't my fault, Lorch!" Turnpike yelled back. "Damn it, you and Bartok know I did all I could."

When Turnpike had dashed from his office, he had failed to find any transport. Not fancying such a long walk, he had waited in the hope of seeing a passing hire hack, but none came. At last Lorch and Bartok, two more agents, returned in a carriage from making some investigation of their own. When Turnpike explained matters, the two men agreed to accompany him. On their arrival at the colonel's house, Turnpike met the guard commander and caused a further delay. Instead of telling the officer of his fears, Turnpike asked for the telegraph service to be tested. When no answer came, he knew that he guessed correctly. The guard turned out and moved fast, but too late as the fiery glow at Gaton's house showed.

"Get down there and see if you can save anything!" Lorch growled. "The safe ought to come through a fire and it's locked."

"I'll send some of the soldiers in to carry it out," Turnpike answered. "The officer of the guard has the key."

With that he turned and raced back towards the house. After watching Turnpike depart, Lorch took a pair of handcuffs from his jacket pocket and secured Belle's wrists behind her back. Then he hauled her roughly to her feet and gripped her right arm in his big left hand.

"You come quiet," he warned. "Make fuss for me and I'll break your arm. I'm not one of your Southern gentlemen and I don't think it's wrong to hit a woman."

"You'd probably find it easier and less dangerous than hitting a man," she replied and the soldiers chuckled.

"Easy there, college boy!" growled the oldest soldier as Lorch gave Belle a hard jerk. "I'm not Southern neither, but I don't stand for no man-handling a gal."

Nor did his companions if their low growls of agreement meant anything. So Lorch held down his anger at the interruption and started to walk towards the burning house. Belle went along, but she knew that she had never been in a tighter spot than at that moment.

Turning a corner which momentarily hid him from the following soldiers, Willie tore off his hood and threw it aside. "Keep going, Massa Saul!" he ordered. "Draw 'em off. I's a-going back to see if I can help Miss Belle or learn where they-all taking her."

"Where'll I go when I lose 'em?"

"Head back towards the Busted Boiler. If you go the way we come, you ought to meet the others."

With that Willie swung behind a tree. Leaping up, he caught its lowest branch and hauled himself up. Hardly had the Negro swung his feet out of sight than the soldiers rushed around the corner. Paupin kept running at the fringe of the shadows and yelled as if encouraging his companion. Then the soldiers went by and Willie cautiously dropped to the ground. Taking the bottle of whisky from his pocket, he looked sadly at it.

"Lordy Lord!" he sighed, drawing the cork. "What a waste."

After splashing a liberal amount of the whisky on to his clothes, Willie filled his mouth and then spat it clear again. Moving carefully, he slipped across the street and stalked along in the shadows until close to the gates of the Gaton house. Assuming a drunken stagger, he walked across the street and when the two sentries at the gate saw him they concluded that he came from a house on the other side of the Avenue.

"W'a's going on, gents?" he inquired in a drunken voice, breathing whisky fumes into the nearest soldier's face.

"You'd best get going, Rastus," the soldier replied, drawing back a little. "It's none of your concern."

Willie saw Belle standing handcuffed inside the gate, but knew he could not hope to achieve anything in the way of a rescue. Playing for time, he pretended to be concerned about a cousin who worked at the house and watched Turnpike returning, followed by Bartok.

"They've bust open the safe!" Turnpike snarled. "Everything's gone. Killed Gaton, too."

"And he was the only one we've got who could make up the right inks," Bartok wailed. "It'll be months before we can get

129

things going again. They may have found the record book, it wasn't in the safe."

"All right," Lorch answered, taking hold of Belle's head with one hand. "So we've got a mighty important prisoner here. She'll know where we can find the rest. Once we get back to our headquarters, we'll soon make her talk."

"It's not that easy," Turnpike warned. "That damned soldier told his officer about the girl. The stupid, sentimental old fool insists she's his prisoner and insists we hand her over to him."

"Like hell!" Lorch barked.

"You aiming to argue it with him?" Turnpike inquired. "He says we're not to torture her and that if we try it, he'll stop us."

"He might, if he found us at it," Lorch answered. "We'll take her—."

"He knows where our headquarters is," Bartok interrupted.

"And that's where he'll go looking for her," Lorch replied. "Only she won't be there. We'll take her to—."

"Madam Lucienne's shop," Turnpike put in. "There'll be nobody around and I've got a key. While we're at it, we may as well learn if there's anything in the shop. She may know."

"The shop it is then," barked Lorch.

While talking, the men had been walking Belle along. Suddenly they became aware that somebody followed them. Turning, the men looked at Willie who wobbled uncertainly along in their wake. A white man would have been immediately suspect, but none of the trio connected a Negro with Belle.

"Where're you going?" Lorch demanded.

"I'se been to a marrying and's going home, sah," Willie answered, breathing a cloud of whisky fumes into the bearded face. "Down that ways, sah."

As Willie had taken an opportunity to wash his mouth out again, Lorch did not doubt his drunken appearance. Watching Willie stagger off, Lorch gave a snort.

"Do you reckon he's all right?" Bartok asked.

"He's drunk," Lorch answered. "Come on, let's get the carriage. The soldier reckons they've two of the rebs cornered in the garden and he's setting up sentries to keep them in until morning. We've time to be on our way before he misses us."

"He'll never think of looking for us at the shop," Turnpike purred, laying a hand on Belle's shoulder and sinking his fingers into her flesh. "I'm looking forward to this."

Belle did not reply. Not a flicker of expression had she allowed her recognition of Willie to show. Darting a glance over her shoulder while pretending to free herself from Turnpike's grasp,

Belle saw that the Negro had already disappeared into the alley between two houses. While she guessed that Willie was going as fast as he could to fetch help, Belle wondered where he might find it.

Cursing the officer of the guard for his insistence that they did not torture the girl, Turnpike, Lorch and Bartok hustled her back to the big house from which they came. On arrival they found that a well-meaning servant had unhitched, fed and watered the two horses from the carriage. Calling the man a number of things—but not a poor, down-trodden victim of the vicious rebels, their usual term for a Negro—Bartok and Turnpike went to re-harness the team. Although only Lorch remained with her, Belle knew better than try to escape. The bearded man watched her too carefully and was so powerful that she could not hope to defeat him with her hands secured behind her back.

With the horses hitched, Bartok took the driver's seat and his companions placed themselves on either side of Belle in the back. The quickest way to Madam Lucienne's shop would have taken them by the front of the Gaton house, but Lorch ordered Bartok to turn in the other direction. If the officer saw them leave that way, he would think they were going to their headquarters. Long before he learned his mistake, Lorch expected to have gained all the information possible from the girl. After that it would be up to Allen Pinkerton, as head of the Secret Service, to make excuses to the Army.

"What's your name?" Lorch growled as the carriage clattered through the darkened streets.

"Martha Lincoln," Belle replied. "You may know my husband, Abraham."

"Have your fun while you can, girlie," Turnpike snarled.

"She's a spunky little devil, that's for sure," Lorch went on and laid his hand on Belle's thigh. When she tried to pull away, he grinned at her. "Don't worry, peach-blossom, there's not enough room here."

With that, he nipped the tender flesh on the inside of her thigh. Only with an effort did Belle hold down a gasp of pain. She felt afraid, more so than ever in her life, as the man released his hold. All too well she knew what kind of men held her in their power. Young intellectuals, well-educated, but with all the bigotry and intolerance of their kind, hating all Southerners for daring to oppose their beliefs, the trio would not hesitate to torture her, or worse, if they could do so without risk to themselves.

Belle wondered what had happened to Dusty and Bludso. Although the Yankees believed the two rebels to be in the garden,

Belle doubted it. Knowing the dangers, Dusty and Bludso would not stay in the house's grounds unless they had no way out. She did not dare try to raise her hopes by imagining the two men would be able to effect a rescue.

No chance of escape presented itself during the drive to Lucienne's shop, despite the fact that it took twice as long as it should. Given a practical piece of work, Bartok proved sadly lacking in ability. When it became apparent that Bartok was lost, Lorch insisted they stopped and asked a passing patrol for directions. Even then the bearded man found it necessary to keep a check on Bartok to prevent him from taking a wrong turn.

At last the carriage rolled along the dark, deserted Le Havre Street and halted outside Lucienne's shop. Climbing down, Turnpike took a key from his pocket and went to the shop's door. While Lorch and Bartok made Belle leave the carriage, Turnpike entered the shop. He found and lit a lamp, standing it on the counter.

Bringing Belle in, Lorch shoved her on to a straight-backed chair. He bent her torso forward until he could haul her arms over the back of the chair and growled orders to his companions. Held in such a manner Belle could not struggle and Bartok brought a length of stout cord which Lorch used to fasten the handcuff's links to the rear legs of the chair.

"You're going to talk now, peach-blossom," he told her and gripped the neck of her shirt.

With a savage jerk Lorch ripped the shirt down the front. He continued pulling and tearing until Belle sat naked to the waist. Lust showed on all the trio's faces as they stared at the round swell of her bust.

"You've been in the wars, peach-blossom," Lorch purred, fingering the mottling of bruises on her ribs. "I thought you messed up your face when you fell against the tree. Who did it?"

"Maybe it was some nigger she used to mistreat as a slave," Turnpike sneered, eyes fixed as if by a magnet to her naked torso.

"Whoever it was, she proved a damned sight tougher than you," Belle hissed.

"Why you—!" Turnpike began, lunging forward with the intention of driving his fist into her face.

Belle kicked up, hoping to catch him where it would do the most good. Instead of striking his groin, her boot collided with his shin. Letting out a howl, he hopped on the other leg and clutched at his pain-filled limb. Then he flung himself back just in time to avoid a second kick. Almost foaming at the mouth in his rage, Turnpike drew his Smith & Wesson and lined it at the girl.

"Quit that!" Lorch bellowed, shoving Turnpike's gun-arm aside. "If you kill her, we'll learn nothing."

"Let me work on her face with the butt then!" Turnpike snarled.

"Not just yet," Lorch answered and moved around to where Belle could not kick him. Cupping his hand almost gently under her left breast, he flicked its nipple with his thumb. "Let's try another way first."

"Get your filthy Yankee hands off me!" Belle said and the contempt in her voice raked Lorch like a whip. "I'd as soon be mauled by a pig."

Drawing back a pace before the raw scorn showed by the girl, Lorch glared at her for a moment. Then he slashed his left hand around, driving the back of it viciously into Belle's bust. The girl's body stiffened and she could not stop a cry of agony bursting from her lips.

133

## Chapter 15

# A Man Who Deserved to Die

"There's somebody coming, Jim," Dusty Fog said as they stood in a dark alley some distance from the Gaton house. "Only one man, travelling fast."

"It's not a soldier either," Bludso guessed. "Maybe it's one of the others."

After slipping out of Gaton's back garden, Dusty and Bludso had not been followed by the Yankees. They heard the shooting on St. Charles Avenue and wondered how their friends fared. Knowing they could do nothing to help at that moment, Dusty and Bludso reluctantly made their way towards the first of the prearranged rendezvous points. There they waited in the hope that all of their friends might join them. Silence had fallen in the direction of Gaton's house, at least as far as shooting went. A red glow grew higher in the sky and the two men heard distant yelling as soldiers fought the fire.

While waiting Dusty reloaded his Colt's two empty chambers, working deftly with only an occasional need for Bludso to light a match and illuminate his work. By the time they heard the approaching footsteps, Dusty once more held a gun with six full and capped chambers.

Coming up to the waiting pair, Paupin wondered how they would take the news that he escaped while Belle fell into the Yankees' hands and Willie returned to try a rescue. Quickly he told Dusty and Bludso the full story, expecting to hear savage condemnation when he finished.

"You did the right thing, Saul," Dusty said quietly. "If they'd taken you all, it would have been a long time before we heard about it."

"And Willie stands a better chance than any of us to get close to Belle," Bludso went on. "What do you reckon, Dusty?"

"That we make a stab at saving Belle. What'll Willie do?"

"Learn what he can, do whatever he can. If he sees he can't save her, he'll try to find out where they're taking her."

"We'll need help, likely," Dusty said. "Let's give him ten minutes to come here, then head back to the Busted Boiler and make plans."

"It'd be best," agreed Bludso. "Anybody after you, Saul?"

"Nope. I led them around to draw them away from Willie, then lost them and cut back this way."

"We'll give him ten minutes then," Dusty decided.

Never had time dragged so slowly as during the minutes Dusty stood in the dark alley. The mission had been a success, with the counterfeiting plant destroyed, its operator dead and details of the whole scheme in the small Texan's pocket. It would be a long time before the Yankees could make a reorganisation of the size needed to start the counterfeiting chain from printer to distributors and before then the Confederate Government could take precautions. Many people would regard the affair a success should Dusty make good his escape with the news; but he could not go and leave Belle a prisoner. He must at least make some determined attempt to rescue the girl, even at the risk of his own life and freedom.

"We'd best go, Dusty," Bludso said gently.

"I suppose so," Dusty answered in a disappointed voice, knowing the time to be up. "Willie'll foll——."

At that moment they heard the padding of feet approaching and fell silent. Breathing hard, Willie loped up to the trio and halted to lean on the wall. After a few seconds, the Negro looked first at Saul Paupin then to the other two men.

"See you made it, Massa Saul."

"What'd you learn, Willie?" Dusty put in.

"Miss Belle's in bad trouble, Cap'n. Three fellers done took her off in a carriage."

"Soldiers?"

"Naw. They was some of Pinkerton's men. Leastwise one of 'em was. I'd know his whiskery face any ole time, Cap'n. He's a mean one, real bad. 'Nother of 'em looked like somebody done whomped his ole pumpkin head with a club, way it was all bandaged up."

"That'll be Turnpike, Dusty," Bludso growled. "I thought you'd shot him up real bad."

"There wasn't time to take careful aim," Dusty explained. "Happen I get another crack at him I won't make the same mistake."

"I'd say they'll be taking Belle to their headquarters for questioning," Paupin put in.

"They ain't," Willie answered. "Seems like the Yankee officer of the guard figured they aimed to abuse Miss Belle real bad and wouldn't have it. So they done snuck off someplace to work on her secret-like."

135

"Do you know where, Willie?"

Although the words left Dusty in a soft, almost gentle whisper, they brought a chill to all the listeners.

"They allowed to take her to Madam Lucienne's shop," Willie answered.

"Let's get going!" Bludso growled.

"Not you, Jim," Dusty replied. "One way or another there'll be a big hunt for us by tomorrow dawn at the earliest. If I rescue Belle, the sooner she's out of New Orleans the better. If not—well, it'd be best if the *Jack's* gone by morning."

"So?" Bludso asked.

"I want you to go to the Busted Boiler, get Belle's and my gear and take them to the *Jack*. Tell Cord Pinckney to be ready and pull out by three in the morning whether we're there or not."

"How about you?"

"Willie can get me to the shop, Jim. I reckon we can handle three like Turnpike. There's no time to argue it, anyway."

Bludso knew Dusty spoke the truth. Already a messenger would be rushing to the Garrison Commander and most likely New Orleans would be swarming with Federal soldiers searching for the party who had destroyed a valuable piece of Union property. So far no organised effort had been made by the Yankees, but each minute drew them closer to when it would be.

"How about me, Captain?" Paupin inquired.

"Stay with Jim. He'll hide you until we can have you moved out of town and to somewhere safe."

"I'll get you on to a foreign boat when one comes in with a skipper I can trust," Bludso promised.

"Damn it, I'm not bothered about that!" the safe-breaker barked. "I meant what can I do to help Miss Boyd?"

"Go with Jim, Saul," Dusty said gently. "If I can't get to Belle, he'll maybe need an expert at opening locks."

"That's for sure," Bludso admitted. "Let's go, Saul."

"I'll maybe not run across you again, Saul," Dusty said, offering his hand to the man. "But if there's ever anything I can do for you, just get word to me."

With his hand tingling from Dusty's grip, Paupin watched the small Texan fade off into the darkness at Willie's side.

"There goes the biggest man I know," the safe-breaker remarked.

"He's all of that," Bludso agreed. "Let's go. I've an idea of my own and you can help me on it."

Guided by Willie, Dusty passed through the streets of old

New Orleans but at the rear of its stately mansions. By following the routes used by coloured servants, they avoided the notice of soldiers heading towards the Gaton place. When reaching Le Havre Street, on which stood Madam Lucienne's shop, Dusty and Willie found it deserted. However a carriage stood before her establishment and a light showed through its front windows.

"They're here, 'cap'n," Willie breathed. "That's their carriage."

"Let's go then," Dusty replied, Colt sliding into his hand.

Silently they moved along the sidewalk and Dusty peeped around the edge of the window. Behind him, Willie heard a low growl of rage. Then Dusty went by the window and the Negro looked in to see Lorch drive a hand at Belle's naked bust. Even as the blow landed, Dusty hurled himself like a living projectile at the shop's door.

With Belle's scream ringing in his ears, Dusty burst into the room and his coming took the three Yankees by surprise. So completely had their attention been on Belle that none of them heard or saw Dusty pass the window. They did not even suspect his presence until the door flew open and then it was too late.

For once in his young life Dusty allowed anger to override thought in a dangerous situation. By his treatment of the helpless Belle, Lorch was a man who deserved to die; but he did not hold a gun and so presented less of a danger than the armed Turnpike. Normally Dusty would have dealt with Turnpike first, but the expression of pain on Belle's face caused him to forget that elementary precaution.

Even as shock and fear wiped the lust-filled sneer from Lorch's bearded features, Dusty shot him in the head. Although the bullet would have done a satisfactory job, Dusty thumbed off a second on its heels. Lorch pitched backwards, struck the counter and slid to the floor as dead as a man could be with a .44 bullet ranging upwards through each eye.

Terror knifed into Turnpike as he recognised the small Texan. Seeing the manner in which Lorch died did nothing to lessen Turnpike's fears. Having twice witnessed the Texan's superlative skill in handling a gun, Turnpike had no wish to try conclusions with Dusty again. A way out of the difficulty presented itself close to hand and Turnpike took it, fast. Lunging forward, he thrust the muzzle of his Smith & Wesson against the side of Belle's head.

"I'll kill the girl!" he yelled in a voice high with fear.

Dusty took in the situation rapidly. At Belle's right side stood a man so scared that he might pull his gun's trigger in blind panic. To her left, Bartok—no less scared-looking—reached for the Colt Baby Dragoon in his jacket pocket. With Belle's life and his own as the stake, Dusty knew he must handle the matter just right. Swiftly he studied the two men, assessing their natures and forming his conclusions. Even as Belle opened her mouth to advise him to go ahead and shoot, Dusty acted—although not in the manner she would have expected.

Giving a dejected, beaten shrug, the small Texan reached up with his left hand to take hold of the Colt by its cylinder. Still wearing the attitude of a man thoroughly whipped, he reversed the Colt with his left forefinger through the triggerguard. Supporting the gun lightly on his remaining fingers, he offered it butt pointing upwards towards Turnpike.

"I surrender. My name is Captain Dusty Fog, Texas Light Cavalry, and I demand the privileges of my rank as a prisoner-of-war."

A mixture of rage and hate twisted at Turnpike's face as he listened to the words. Before him stood one of the people responsible for wrecking a scheme designed to bring the South's economy crashing into such ruins that it would be unlikely ever to recover, even if such misguided fools as President Lincoln offered the chance, as seemed likely, after the War. The utter and complete destruction of the hated white Southerners had been the aim behind the plan when formulated by Turnpike and others of his kind, not merely the bringing about of a speedy and less bloody ending to the War.

Nor did Dusty's part in destroying the counterfeiting plant form Turnpike's only reason for hatred. The small Texan had proven himself more capable than the Yankee agent and had performed deeds that the other knew he could not hope even to approach. Like all his kind, Turnpike hated any man who did something he could not and Dusty's small, insignificant appearance made matters worse.

The sight of the Texan standing in an attitude of abject surrender drove some of Turnpike's fear away. Then a thought struck the Yankee. Already that night he had seen one example of military chivalry, in the officer of the guard's determination that no ill-treatment should come the female prisoner's way. A man with Captain Dusty Fog's reputation could expect good treatment from most Federal regular soldiers, who would have respect for a brave and honourable enemy. Nothing so lenient must be allowed to happen. Alive, Dusty Fog could testify to their treatment of the girl. Far worse, he would be living proof of Turnpike's inadequacy and failure.

With that thought in mind, Turnpike swung the Smith & Wesson's barrel away from Belle's head and played right into Dusty's hands. Gambling on Turnpike's knowledge of firearms being, by Texas standards, rudimentary, Dusty prepared to try a move often practiced but never used in earnest by him until that moment.

When reversing the gun in apparent surrender, Dusty left its hammer drawn back at full cock. The lack of objection to the state of his gun by Turnpike or Bartok increased the small Texan's confidence. With the Smith & Wesson turning away from Belle, all Dusty needed to do was get the Colt's butt into his hand and squeeze its trigger.

Professional duellists had discovered how twirling and spinning a pistol on its triggerguard strengthened the fingers and helped develop increased accuracy. The information passed West, where men frequently found the need for skilled use of a hand gun under less formal conditions than the *code duello*. During spells of gun-juggling, Dusty developed a trick later to become famous, or notorious, as 'the road-agent's spin'. It was a trick of desperation and one only likely to work, even before its latter-day publicity, against a man lacking in knowledge of practical gun-handling matters.

Waiting until the Smith & Wesson passed out of line with Belle's head, Dusty gave his left hand a slight jerk upwards. At the same moment he released his hold of the barrel with his other fingers. With his forefinger as its pivot, the Colt's butt rose upwards and curled over to slap into his waiting palm. Instantly Dusty's remaining three fingers folded around the curved bone grip and he squeezed the trigger with unhurried speed.

Too late Turnpike saw his danger. Being unable to use his gun left-handed, it never occurred to him that others might be able to do so. Nor did he possess the kind of lightning fast reactions which might have saved him. Flame ripped from the barrel of Dusty's Colt and a bullet tore into Turnpike's chest. Reeling under the impact, the Yankee retained his hold of the Smith & Wesson. Again Dusty fired, angling his shot upwards. The bullet ripped into Turnpike's throat, sending him backwards and the gun clattered from his hand as he fell.

Terror lent speed to Bartok's movements and he had spent more time than his companions at learning to handle a revolver. Jerking out his small Colt, he swung it up to line at Dusty. Belle saw there would be no time for Dusty to deal with both Turnpike and Bartok, so took a hand in the game. Using all her strength, she flung herself and the chair over to crash into Bartok's side. A yelp of surprise left the man and his Colt jerked aside just as it fired. Hearing the shot, Dusty swung from firing his second shot at Turnpike. One glance warned the small Texan that he faced a man with some gun-skill. Enough for there to be no taking chances with him.

Cocking the little Colt smoothly, Bartok prepared to shoot again. Dusty threw himself to one side, dropping to the ground. As he landed, the small Texan lined up his Colt and missed death by inches as the Baby Dragoon spat out another .31 ball. Once again Dusty found himself in a position where he must shoot to make an instant kill. So he took that extra split-second necessary to aim. Then the Colt bucked in his palm, its deep roar echoing in challenge to the lighter crack of the small calibre weapon in Bartok's hand. Driving up, the bullet Dusty fired tore into the soft flesh beneath Bartok's jaw, passing on upwards through the roof of his mouth and into the brain. Dusty did what he had to do, achieved an instant kill, and Bartok's body collapsed like an unstuffed rag doll across Belle's legs.

Partially winded by landing on the floor, her fastened arms prevented any chance of breaking the fall, Belle lay gasping in pain. Willie burst into the room as Dusty rose and together they approached the girl. Bending down, the two men lifted the girl and the chair upright.

"Are you all right, Belle?" Dusty asked.

"I've felt better," she admitted. "The bearded one has the key."

While Willie used a cut-throat razor to sever the cord holding Belle to the chair, Dusty searched Lorch's body and recovered the key of the handcuffs. On her wrists being freed, Belle gasped and raised her right hand to rub at the left shoulder. Then she remembered the state of her clothing and tried to cover up her naked torso. Dusty thrust the Colt into his waistband and removed his jacket to give to the girl. Slipping into it, Belle glanced at Willie as the Negro went to the shop's door and stood listening.

"We'd best get going, Cap'n," he said. "There's folks coming a-running and they's wearing heavy boots."

"Can you walk, Belle?" Dusty asked.

"I'm game to try," she replied. "Let's get going. Out of the back way, too."

Although the building had been thoroughly searched, Turnpike's men did not trouble to take away the back door's key. Belle followed Dusty's action in locking the door after them on leaving. Already they could hear running feet drawing closer to the shop, but not from its rear. Darting a quick glance around, Belle suggested that Willie took them by the least conspicuous route to the Busted Boiler.

"There's no need for that," Dusty told her. "Jim's collected our gear and he'll be taking it to the *Jack*. We've done what we came for, Belle. It's time we got out of New Orleans."

## Chapter 16

# A Way of Life

Dawn crept greyly into the eastern sky and Lieutenant Cord Pinckney watched the ever-growing light with care. Although they had crept by the main New Orleans' up-river defences, there was always the chance of meeting some U.S. Navy craft returning from a journey. Or if a chance-passing cavalry patrol happened to see them from the shore, it would only be a matter of hours at most before a fast launch or two came after them.

On arrival at the hidden dock, Dusty, Belle and Willie found everything ready. Each night, when the smoke would not be seen rising from among the ruins, Pinckney's men built enough fire to raise a head of steam capable of giving the *Jack* motive power. So they needed only to pole their vessel out from under its hiding place and set off up-river.

Already the alarm had been raised and the first part of a massive search campaign begun. While the main body of men concentrated on the area around Gaton's house, the U.S. Navy started to put out guard boats on the river so thickly that sneaking through them in the *Jack*, even ballasted down to the limits of safety, invited disaster.

Jim Bludso came up with the answer. In fact he had been preparing for it through his return to the Busted Boiler and carrying the gear to the dock. Once he had delivered the two bags and given Dusty's message to Pinckney, Bludso told the lieutenant of his own idea. Before the others arrived, Bludso left to put the plan into operation. With the aid of Paupin and three trusted men from the Busted Boiler, Bludso stole a steam launch used as picket boat by the Yankee fleet, making sure that the theft would be discovered quickly. Then he and his men headed downstream as if trying to escape through to the sea. Rockets flamed into the air and steam whistles whooped a warning, drawing guard boats and such larger craft as had enough steam up to follow down river and away from the *Jack*.

Timing their moves just right, Bludso's men abandoned the stolen launch and left it tearing along with a locked tiller to be sunk by shell fire from the pursuing vessels. After swimming ashore, Bludso and his party made good their escape. While the Yankees searched for survivors, and eventually concluded that the launch went down with all hands, the *Jack* passed up-river unnoticed.

The journey north took longer than coming down to New Orleans. There could be no travelling by day under a pile of bushes as that would only attract attention. So at dawn each day the *Jack* halted at the first suitable spot and hid in some way until darkness left them free to move on again. Clearly the Yankees did not suspect their method of escape, for no search of the up-river side of New Orleans was made.

At last they turned off the Mississippi and up the Red River. Despite being in comparatively safe waters, Pinckney waited until nightfall before trying to reach Alexandria. So far the Yankees did not know of the *Jack's* presence on the Upper Mississippi and he wanted to keep it that way. So he chanced dangers of passing through the spar-torpedo field in the darkness rather than make an appearance in the city's dock area during daylight and in view of possible Yankee spies.

Dusty and Belle landed at the same lagoon from which they embarked. Nor did they waste time in celebrating their successful mission. As soon as she could arrange, Belle and Dusty boarded a sidewheel riverboat and carried on with their trip to rejoin Ole Devil.

"You've done well, Miss Boyd, Dustine," said the General in a grim satisfaction as he listened to their report. "And how about your friends?"

"I don't know, sir," Belle admitted. "You've heard nothing?"

"Not a thing."

After the War Dusty learned that Madam Lucienne and Paupin made good their departure on a British ship after being kept hidden by Bludso until the Yankees gave up an extensive search for the wreckers of the counterfeiting plant. No suspicion fell on Bludso, although Pinkerton himself conducted an investigation into the deaths of Turnpike's party. For the rest of the War Bludso served the South well and with peace returned to being a riverboat engineer on a new Prairie Belle.

Not that Dusty and Belle knew anything of their friends as they sat in Ole Devil's office on their return.

"Any news for me, General?" asked the girl.

"You're to go as soon as possible to Atlanta," Ole Devil replied. "Dustine, that damned guerilla Hannah's come into our area again. Tomorrow you'll take your company, a sharpshooter and mountain howitzer and bring in the whole stinking bunch."

A mission had been completed at great risk, but that did not end the War. Short of men, Ole Devil could not afford the luxury of keeping his favourite nephew and a full company of men sitting idle.

"I'll be gone when you come back, Dustine," the girl said as she and the small Texan left the office. "Thanks for everything."

"What'll you be doing in Atlanta, Belle?" he inquired.

"I'll not know until I reach there."

"Why don't you give it up while you can, Belle?" Dusty said. "You nearly lost your life this time."

"I can't give it up. It's in my blood, Dusty. Lord knows what I'll do when the War's over. There'll be no more need for me or my talents then."

And Belle laughed. Neither she nor Dusty realised that the War would soon be over; or how there would still in peace be work for the Rebel Spy.

Author's note: *For details of Dusty's hunt after Hannah's Guerillas and his next meeting with the Rebel Spy, read* THE BAD BUNCH.

# To Arms! To Arms in Dixie!

For Richard and David of Replica Models (UK) Ltd., whose Winchesters, Colts, Thompson and Smith & Wessons, and not forgetting the Remington Double Derringers, have won many a gun battle for me.

# TO ARMS! TO ARMS, IN DIXIE!

Author's note: *In answer to numerous requests I have received, here are the words which General Albert Pike, C.S.A., put to Daniel D. Emmet's minstrel song 'Dixie'.*

Southrons, hear your country call you,
Up, lest worse than death befall you,
To arms! To arms! To arms, in Dixie!
See the beacon fires are lighted,
Let Southron hearts now be united,
To arms! To arms! To arms, in Dixie!

*Chorus:*

Advance the flag of Dixie! Hurrah! Hurrah!
For Dixie's land we take our stand and live or die for Dixie,
To arms! To arms! We'll fight the world for Dixie!
To arms! To arms! We'll fight or die for Dixie!

Hear the Northern thunders mutter,
Yankee flags in South winds flutter,
To arms! *etc.*
Send them back your fierce defiance,
Stamp on that accursed alliance,
To arms! *etc.*

*Chorus:*

Fear no danger, shun no labour,
Take up rifle, pistol, sabre,
To arms! *etc.*
Shoulder pressing close to shoulder,
Let the odds make each heart bolder,
To arms! *etc.*

*Chorus:*

How the Southland's heart rejoices,
To the sound of loyal voices,

7

To arms! *etc.*
For faith betrayed and pledges broken,
Wrongs inflicted, insults spoken,
To arms! *etc.*

*Chorus:*

Strong as lions, swift as eagles,
Back to their kennels chase those beagles,
To arms! *etc.*
Cut the unequal bonds assunder,
Let Yankees hence each other plunder,
To arms! *etc.*

*Chorus:*

Swear upon the Southland's altar,
Never to submit or falter,
To arms! *etc.*
Until the Lord's work is completed,
And the spoilers are defeated,
To arms! To arms! To arms, in Dixie!
*Chorus:*

## CHAPTER ONE

# THIS IS RECONSTRUCTION!

Raising his open, empty right hand with its palm turned forward, high above his white-turbanned head, Sabot the Mysterious paused in an impressively dramatic manner. From the orchestra's pit, a deep, continuous rolling of the drums gave a warning that something special—possibly even the high spot of the evening's entertainment—was about to happen.

Clearly the audience deduced the required message from Sabot's attitude and the sound of the drums. Although his assistant—a beautiful, voluptuous brunette who wore the type of flimsy, revealing garments expected of a girl who had been 'rescued from a life of sin in the Sultan of Tripoli's harem'— and a committee comprising of three men and an elderly woman shared the stage with him, the magician alone held the watchers' attention. Which was, of course, how it should be.

Stocky, of medium height, Sabot's sallow face sported spike-tipped moustachios and a sharp-pointed chin beard which combined to suggest foreign birth and upbringing. Nor did his Occidental black evening suit, frilly bosomed white silk shirt and flowing scarlet silk cravat lessen the impression of the mysterious Orient created by his features and jewel-emblazoned turban.

Pausing to permit his audience's anticipation to build even higher, Sabot found himself pondering upon the possible cause of the vague, uneasy sensation that was eating at him. Something was wrong and, try as he might, he could not decide what it was.

Of course, even such an experienced performer as the magician might have been excused if he should feel perturbed under the prevailing conditions. Yet Sabot felt sure that his lack of ease was stemming out of another, more subtly disturbing influence. Unless he missed his guess, the cause of his concern had evolved out of something he had seen—or failed to see properly—since coming on to the stage. It did not, he believed, come from the wings or down in the well-filled auditorium.

That meant the sensation had its source in the committee, if indeed it existed at all.

Instinctively, if covertly, Sabot was watching the committee to make sure that their attention stayed on him and did not wander to the wings, where they might see something that should remain unobserved until the correct moment. He failed to detect any hint of what might be disturbing him. The three men were of the type who could be expected to come out of any audience. Prosperous-looking town-dwellers, they were clearly enjoying their active participation in the show and the proximity of the scantily attired Princess Selima Baba Nothing about such a commonplace trio could be responsible for his uneasy sensation, of that he felt certain.

Which left the woman as a possible suspect; and she appeared to be an even less likely candidate than the men. Tall, or she had been before age had bent her shoulders, and slenderly built, she had a face that was heavily powdered in a not too successful attempt to conceal its lines and wrinkles. For all that, in its day it could have been very beautiful. Drawn back in a tight bun, her dry, lifeless-looking grey hair supported an ancient, curly brimmed, flower-decorated black hat. She wore a shapeless, stiff dark grey Balmoral skirt that had been designed for a more bulky figure. Its matching paletot coat had long sleeves and was buttoned from the neck downwards like a military tunic. Black lace mitts covered sufficient of her hands and fingers to prevent her marital status from being revealed. She gripped an ancient vanity bag in both hands, nursing it protectively on her lap. Earlier, in the course of a trick, Sabot had produced a watch belonging to one of the male members of the committee from her bag and had seen all its meagre contents. Since then, she had sat clutching it tightly as if she feared that other, more incriminating items, might be plucked from it.

Sabot allowed his gaze to linger briefly upon the woman. Going by her appearance, it seemed strange that she should have consented to come on to the stage. There was an air of faded gentility and respectability about her which hinted that she had known better, more affluent days, yet did not lend itself to exhibitionist tendencies. Her kind usually shied well away from actions which might be construed as making a public display of themselves. Yet she had been one of the first to rise, when Sabot had made his usual request for a committee to scrutinise his tricks at close quarters and try to explain away how each was performed.

Diverting his glance, Sabot darted a scowl at his assistant. Although shapely and visually attractive in her 'harem' costume, Selima left a lot to be desired in the way she performed her duties. A more astute member of the act would have evaded the woman's offer to join the committee, especially under the circumstances. Even in normal conditions, such a person would not have been a good choice. Knowing the woman's type, the audience might believe that she was a shill in his employ and not a genuine patron of the performance. However, he consoled himself, his present audience should have small cause for complaint even if she had been a shill.

The Grand Palace Theatre at Shreveport, Louisiana, was packed to capacity that night. Its patrons formed much the same general cross-section of the population as had attended the other performances during Sabot's ten-day engagement. Being a major stopping point on the Red River, drawing custom and profit from the north- and south-bound traffic, the town had thrown off most of the poverty left in the wake of the War Between The States. Sufficiently so for theatre-going to have returned, as a regular diversion, to a level where it was profitable for performers of Sabot's standing and importance to include the Grand Palace in their itineraries.

Not that tonight's show would be profitable in a monetary sense. Out of gratitude for the excellent attendances during his stay, Sabot had offered to donate one final appearance—before moving north to Mooringsport on the riverboat *Texarkana Belle* at midnight and commencing a tour of Texas's towns—without charge to all such members of the late Confederate States' Army and Navy as might care to attend.

In view of the local situation with regard to the United States' Army, especially that section of it based on the outskirts of town, the offer might have been considered—to say the least—tactless and ill-advised. However, the camp's commanding officer, Lieutenant Colonel Szigo—a bitter, disappointed man whose dislike of the South and Southrons showed in his clinging to the outmoded title of garrison—had had no cause for complaint over the magician's apparent discrimination. On the night after his arrival in Shreveport, Sabot had donated an equally profitless performance for the men under Szigo's command.

Such apparent favouritism might have cost Sabot dearly by alienating him from the civilian population of Shreveport, who had had little reason to hold friendly feelings for the soldiers. That it had not was a tribute to his smooth talking and knowledge of human nature. In a statement to the *Shreveport Herald-Times*, concerning his generosity to the 'Yankees', he had pointed out that the War ended back in 'Sixty-Five and how many a gallant ex-Rebel now wore the blue uniform of the United States' Army. That might have had little effect in a town where the senior Army officer insisted on speaking of his command as a 'garrison', with all its connotations of the recently ended Reconstruction period. However, Sabot had gone on to declare that he believed the citizens of Shreveport were sufficiently fair- and open-minded not to hold the soldiers' free performance against him. In a less enlightened and forward-looking community, he had continued, he would not have dared to make such a gesture, but felt certain that he could do so in Shreveport.

Faced with such a comment, the citizens' civic pride had compelled them to lay aside any objections they might have wished to express. Some of the more responsible members of the community had even hoped that, as a result of the free shows, a better and more friendly relationship with the Army might be forthcoming.

Certainly Colonel Szigo had shown an eagerness to improve matters which he had not previously displayed. Despite the general consensus of public opinion, he had raised no objections to the show for the ex-Rebels. In fact, he had even gone so far as to make what amounted to a gesture of good will. To ensure that there would be no incidents or open clashes between his soldiers and the local population—which had been an all too regular occurence in the past—he had placed the whole town off limits to all military personnel on the evening of the civilians' free performance.

How much of that sensible decision had been influenced by Sabot, only Colonel Szigo and the magician could have said. Throughout his show's stay in Shreveport Sabot had worked hard to win the confidence of the Army's officers and the town's leading, most respected citizens. Judging by Szigo's response—and the presence of those same citizens in the audience—he had met with some success in his endeavours.

The rolling of the drums ended without Sabot having reached any conclusion as to why he was experiencing the uneasy sensation. In the breathless hush that followed, Selima undulated her way to the garishly coloured and decorated prop box. From it, she lifted an inflated red balloon. Exhibiting the balloon prominently to the audience, she tossed it into the air.

Rotating his raised wrist, so that he displayed both sides of it, Sabot plucked a shining, nickel-plated Remington Double Derringer apparently out of thin air. All in the same motion, he aimed upwards and fired. Hit by the charge of minute birdshot, with which he had replaced the usual solid lead ball of the pistol's .41 rimfire cartridge, the balloon disintegrated in a violent puff of bright red smoke.

At which point, before the sense of anticlimax could start to creep home on the audience, the evening's previously harmless, enjoyable entertainment began to take on a very serious, even alarming, note.

Coinciding with the explosion of the balloon, four large portraits unrolled from where they had been suspended, concealed by the upper fringes of the stage's decorative curtaining. The sight of them, or rather a realisation of the subjects which they represented, brought a startled, concerted gasp from the people seated at the various tables in the auditorium.

The first portrait on the right depicted a background of burning houses and crops stretching off towards the horizon. In the foreground was an excellent likeness of the Federal Army's General William Tecumseh Sherman, wearing a dark blue dress uniform and holding a flaming torch. In a speech balloon, he was ordering his brutal and clearly delighted soldiers to, 'Loot and burn all you want, men. I'll see that you're not punished for it.'

Having as its background the sidewalk outside the First National Bank of New Orleans, the front of which was clearly named, the second painting showed the Union's General Benjamin F. Butler emerging from the broken-open main entrance. Grasping a large sack labelled 'Bank Deposits', he was exhorting villainously featured Yankee enlisted men—who were engaged in tearing the clothes from a well-dressed, terrified woman and two young girls—to, 'Go to it, men. Treat all their women like common whores!'

On the third poster, in front of scenes of Union soldiers torturing Confederate prisoners, General Smethurst gloatingly supervised the crew of a Gatling gun as they fired at a group of bound and gagged victims in one of the prisoner-of-war camps which he had commanded. He was complaining, 'I wish I had more of these Secessionist scum to test the gun on.'

The final portrait was more recent in its text. Topped by a large, printed message in glaring red ink which read, 'THIS IS RECONSTRUCTION!', it illustrated a mob of drunken Negroes wrecking and looting a general store. In the foreground, a burly, vicious-looking blue-clad sergeant was using the butt of his rifle to club down the white, civilian owner of the store and warning, 'You aren't allowed to stop them robbing you, Johnny Reb, they're black!'

If the subject matter of the four paintings had been intended as a joke, it fell remarkably flat. More than that; in view of the local situation with regards to the Army, they might be considered more than tactless reminders of the past and could be dangerous. However, the surprises of the evening had not ended.

Almost before the portraits had completely unrolled from their places of concealment, a figure grasping a twin-barrelled, ten-gauge sawed-off shotgun appeared at each of the four exits. They wore plain-coloured, almost nondescript suits devoid of any identifying features. The desire for anonymity was carried even further. Each of them wore a black mask, suspended from the brim of his hat to below the level of his chin, which effectively concealed his face.

From their positions on the stage, the committee were unable to see the fronts of the portraits. They could, however, tell by the reactions of the audience and the appearance of the masked men that something far out of the ordinary was happening. Then they had further cause for alarm, and much closer to hand.

Three more masked men walked from the left side wings. Only one, the bulkiest if not tallest, was openly armed. He too carried a sawed-off shotgun. By his clothing, which matched that of the watchers at the exits, he was of inferior social standing to his empty-handed companions. One of them was taller than the armed man, although slighter in build. The other was something over medium height, well-made and carried himself with a brash, straight-backed swagger seen mainly amongst arrogant, rank-conscious Army officers. Their attire was that of wealthy gentlemen attending an informal, yet important, social gathering with their equals.

Showing symptoms of alarm, the three male members of the committee rose hurriedly from their chairs. The woman also came to her feet, moving with considerable speed for one of her age. Darting a glance towards the intruders as they

14

approached, she made as if to move towards the front of the stage.

'No sudden moves, fellers!' warned the bulkiest of the trio, gesturing with his shotgun and employing a tone in keeping with his clothing. 'Just sit down a spell and nobody'll get hurt.'

From his perplexed expression, Sabot had been completely taken aback by the unexpected turn of events. His whole being left an impression that he had no idea what was going on. Then the burly man's growled-out words seemed to jolt him out of his state of shock and aroused an instinct to protest. Bracing back his shoulders, he stalked grimly towards the masked intruders.

'How dare you come in here,' the magician demanded, bristling with righteous indignation, 'interrupting my perform——'

Striding by his better-dressed companions, the burly man snapped around his shotgun with casual-seeming, yet trained precision. Its butt thudded against the side of Sabot's jaw and knocked him staggering to sprawl on to the floor at the rear of the stage. As the magician collapsed in a huddled heap upon his hands and knees, a rumble of protest rose from the audience. Immediately, the men at the exits elevated their weapons to a greater position of readiness. It seemed likely that the people in the auditorium would rush the intruders and avenge their benefactor.

'That's for you, you Yankee-loving son-of-a-bitch!' bellowed Sabot's assailant, in a voice that carried above the protests of the audience. 'Anybody's foot-licks to the blue-bellies like you do deserves anything he gets from a loyal Southron.'

Backed by the very real, deadly menace of the shotguns at the exits, the man's statement served to quieten down the expressions of disapproval. His words recalled certain feelings many of the audience had harboured concerning Sabot's friendship with the disliked blue-bellies. Remembering, they were less inclined to take active measures to avenge his injuries. Especially when doing so might result in death or injury for many of themselves. At least, they would not make the attempt without another, stronger and more personal reason for doing it.

Inadvertently, the female member of the committee suggested just such a reason.

'Wha-what do you want?' she shrilled, clutching even tighter at her vanity bag and displaying far greater alarm or concern than Princess Selima Baba was showing. 'If this is a robbery——!'

Again the menacing rumblings crept through the audience. Men who would have hesitated to take action on behalf of a 'Yankee-lover' were prepared to be defiant in defence of their property.

## CHAPTER TWO

# YOU WON'T STOP ME LEAVING

Clearly the taller of the unarmed intruders on the stage did not underestimate the potential danger to his party that had been caused by the elderly woman's suggestion. The mask he wore concealed whatever expression might be on his face, but his whole attitude was one of quiet reassurance as he swung in her direction.

'Calm yourself, ma'am,' the man requested politely. His voice was that of a well-educated Southron gentleman. 'I assure you that we have not come here to commit a robbery.' Turning from the woman, he faced the audience and raised his arms in a signal for silence. 'Please remain seated, ladies and gentlemen. There is no cause for alarm. You have my word that we mean no harm to any of you.'

Such was the apparent honesty in the man's tone that the audience started to relax once more. Even the most unthinking of them realised that outlaws would hardly go to so much trouble to commit a crime that would yield only small returns. The loot that they might hope to gather would hardly justify the risks.

To strengthen the point made by their spokesman, the watchers at the exits relaxed. The shotguns sank to point at the floor, implying that their wielders no longer felt a need to remain vigilant. Natural curiosity caused the men and women at the tables to settle down and await further developments.

'You there, shameless foreign woman!' barked the second of the weaponless newcomers, in a hard, commanding voice that had traces of a well-educated Southern accent. 'Go over and attend to your master.'

'Sure thing, mister,' Selima answered, with a remarkably American-sounding voice considering that she had been 'rescued from a life of sin in the Sultan of Tripoli's harem'. 'Anything you say.'

Crossing the stage with the same sensually jaunty, hip-rolling gait that had graced all her movements—drawing numerous lascivious glances from the men on the committee and causing the elderly woman to deliver almost as many disapproving glares—the girl halted and bent over her employer. She did this in a manner which prominently displayed the full curvaceous quality of her buttocks under their flimsy pantaloons. Nothing in her posture and behaviour implied that she harboured fears for her own safety, nor concern over her employer's possible injuries. Rather she comported herself with the air of one who was playing a well-rehearsed scene from a melodrama—but was playing it remarkably badly.

Watching the way in which Selima carried out his companion's order, the taller of the unarmed pair made a gesture that might have indicated annoyance. It almost appeared, to at least one observer, that he took exception to the brunette's too casual acceptance of what should have been an alarming and unprecedented sequence of events. However, he made no comment on the matter. Instead, he returned his attention to the restlessly moving audience.

'Ladies and gentlemen!' the tall man boomed out, his words reaching every corner of the auditorium. 'You are all probably wondering why my companions and I have seen fit to intrude upon your evening's entertainment in such a manner. This charming lady'—he indicated the elderly woman as she sat staring intently at him and bowed slightly in her direction—'suggested that we might be contemplating a robbery. That is not so. Instead of taking from you, we hope that we may be able to help you regain something that we have all lost. We want to give you back your—FREEDOM!'

An excited, yet also disturbed rustle of conversation arose amongst the audience, swelling louder in the dramatic pause which followed the speaker's final shouted word. Most of Sabot's guests were aware that, taken with the four dangling portraits, the speech they had heard carried serious, dangerous implications. The civil law enforcement authorities and, more particularly, the local Army commander might easily call it treason.

Despite their understanding, the men in the audience hesitated. As usual in times of stress, or when faced with a situation completely out of the ordinary, the majority were waiting for guidance on how to act. They were also hoping that somebody else in their number would accept the responsibility of becoming their leader.

Aware of how a crowd's mentality worked, the spokesman of the intruders scanned the auditorium. He saw a figure stand

18

up at the table reserved for the most important members of the audience.

'You have a question, sir?' the masked man inquired amiably, pointing in the other's direction.

'No, sir,' replied the man from the audience. 'I intend to leave.'

Instantly every eye focused upon the speaker. Tall, slim, in his early fifties, he dressed fashionably and in perfect taste. His whole appearance hinted at military training and self-confidence. Most of the audience recognised him as Colonel Alburgh Winslow, attorney-at-law, a member of the Louisiana State's Legislature and owner of the *Shreveport Herald-Times*. Well-liked, respected as a pillar of the community, the people in the auditorium figured that his lead in the affair would be worth following.

So the rest of the audience sat back and waited to see what the masked men's response would be. And, more important, to discover how Colonel Winslow would react if his intention of leaving should be opposed.

'You served in the Army of the Confederate States, sir?' asked the spokesman of the intruders, in flat, impersonal, but neither threatening nor angry tones.

'I had the honour to command the 6th Louisiana Rifles under General Braxton Bragg, sir,' Winslow answered, returning politeness with civility. 'But I have also taken the oath of allegiance to the Union——'

'That was your right, sir,' the spokesman conceded courteously. 'Most of us present took it in good faith and the belief that the Yankees would honour their side of it.'

'They sure as hell didn't do that!' bawled a male voice from the rear of the auditorium and a mumble of concurrence rose from his area.

'You are free to leave, sir, if you so wish it,' the masked spokesman stated, when the hubbub had died away. 'All I ask is that you will give me your word as a Southern gentleman that you will not speak of what is happening here before tomorrow morning at the earliest.'

'You won't stop me leaving if I do?' Winslow asked.

'Your word will be sufficient guarantee for us, sir,' replied the spokesman. 'We've no intention of stopping *anybody* leaving. All we need from those who go is an assurance that they will do nothing to prevent the rest of us from continuing with this meeting.'

There was a shuffling of feet, but still nobody showed any inclination of accepting the offer to depart. They were still awaiting Winslow's lead.

'I'll go further,' the shorter of the unarmed intruders went on, drawing the elderly woman's gaze to him until she seemed to be hanging on to his every word. Through the slits in his mask, his eyes raked the six prominent citizens who shared Winslow's table. 'We, *all* of us in this room, would prefer those who aren't loyal to the South to leave immediately.'

'Let the gentleman pass there,' the spokesman ordered the guard nearest to Winslow. 'Let anybody pass who wants to go.'

'Thank you, sir,' Winslow drawled, after a moment's thought. 'I'll stay and hear you out.'

Taken with the second man's comment on loyalty to the South, Winslow's refusal to accept the offer to depart brought to an end the muttering and inclinations amongst the other patrons who had intended to leave. They were mostly businessmen who had regained some measure of their prosperity after being impoverished by the War. Some drew an appreciable amount of their business from the Army, so had no desire to take a part in what Colonel Szigo would certainly regard as a treasonable assembly. On the other hand, they had no wish to label themselves as disloyal to the Southern States. That could be just as damaging, perhaps even more so, to their local business prospects. So they concluded that they would accept Winslow's guidance and remain. Later, if necessary, they could disclaim any association with the sentiments expressed by the intruders.

Assisted by Selima, Sabot the Mysterious dragged himself erect. Leaning on the girl's shoulder, with a trickle of blood running from the corner of his mouth, he scowled at his assailant. Jerking a thumb contemptuously in the magician's direction, the spokesman instructed his armed companion to remove the Yankee-loving trash and attend to his injury. Going over, the burly man herded Selima and Sabot into the wings and beyond the audience's range of vision. The couple went without protest. Any concern the guests might have felt was lessened by the reminder of Sabot's 'Yankee-loving' tendencies and the thought that his hurts would receive attention.

'Ma'am, gentlemen,' the masked spokesman said, drawing the elderly woman's gaze from the departing magician, girl and their escort. 'Perhaps you would oblige me by returning to your seats in the auditorium?'

'We sure will, mister,' confirmed one of the male members of the committee, rising with alacrity.

Sharing their companion's desire to be disassociated with the masked intruders, the other two men showed an equal haste to quit the stage. Although she flashed another quick look at where Sabot's party had disappeared into the wings, the elderly woman wasted no time in following the three citizens.

With the stage cleared of all but himself and his smaller companion, the tall, imposing, masked figure commenced a carefully thought out and excellently delivered speech. He started by reminding the audience that, from the earliest days of its conception, the United States had agreed upon one certain matter of policy. If any State should feel that its policies and domestic arrangements were not in keeping with the remainder, or that the Federal Government's decisions were against its best interests, it had the inalienable right to secede, withdraw, from the Union.

'This is the *right* that the people up North refused to grant us,' the man went on, his voice throbbing with emotion. 'They begrudged us our heritage, envied our way of life and culture. But they wanted to keep right on digging their grasping Yankee hands into our pockets. They didn't want the Southern States, but they *did* want the money which was wrung from us in taxes. And that, ladies and gentlemen, is why those noble Abolitionists up North fought to retain the Union.'

Going by the growl which sounded from the main body of the hall. there was considerable agreement with the man's words. At the table holding the important members of the community, more than one pair of eyes darted worried glances at Winslow. Giving a quick shake of his head in reply to the unasked questions, he flickered a look towards the elderly woman. She sat on a lower-priced table, subjecting both the masked men on the stage to a careful scrutiny and listening intently to the response to the speech.

Covering the South's original victories, the speaker touched briefly upon the behind-the-scenes reasons why the first thrust of successes had not been exploited to the full. He also intimated that, in the event of another clash with the Yankees, there would be no such loss of advantage. Then he praised the gallantry, courage and loyalty of the Confederate States' Army and Navy as they had battled against a numerically, industrially and economically superior enemy.

'They might have had better arms, food and supplies,' he stated proudly, 'But, by the Lord, they didn't have better *men*!'

'And this time we won't be fighting them alone,' the second man announced, after the thunder of applause which had greeted the other's declaration had ebbed away. 'Our friends in Europe are willing to send arms, equipment, supplies to help us fight the Northern oppressors.'

'Which friends in Europe?' Winslow challenged.

'We can't mention the country, for obvious reasons,' the spokesman answered. 'But I give you my word as a Southern gentleman that a powerful European country is prepared to back us in our fight for freedom.'

'For what price, sir?' Winslow demanded.

'That will be decided between our two Governments,' the spokesman replied, hiding any displeasure he might be feeling at the questions. He pointed to the first portrait on the right, continuing, 'You may ask why we should need the aid of a foreign country. There is the answer. That is how the Yankees make war. Not against soldiers, but against the harmless, defenceless civilian population.'

Without giving Winslow an opportunity to extend the questioning about the identity of the European country that was willing to ally itself to the Confederate cause, the spokesman enlarged upon the horrors of Sherman's 'march to the sea'.

Winslow realised that he was being frozen out, but did not try to force the issue. To do so might swing the crowd even further in the masked intruders' favour. Its more impressionable members would recollect that the spokesman was willing to take Winslow's word as a Southern gentleman on the matter of keeping silent after he had been allowed to depart. So the Colonel ought to return the compliment by accepting the spokesman's assurance—backed by his word—that the European ally existed.

Deftly the spokesman drew a lurid picture of how Sherman had implemented a policy of wholesale arson during 'the march'. Not content with the hardships that had been caused to the civilian population, he had given his verbal and written assurance that no man under his command would be placed on trial or punished in any way for looting.

'And so, my friends,' the spokesman continued. 'Whole families were stripped bare of their possessions and left destitute, while Yankee officers and enlisted men amassed fortunes under those damnable orders which gave them the right to loot and pillage with impunity. Yet, debased as they were, Sherman's marauders did not sink to the depths of Butler or Smethurst.'

There would be few in the audience to argue against *that* point.

Enlarging upon the former officer, the spokesman told of how he had 'acquired' and converted to his own use some eight hundred thousand dollars held in the Dutch Consul's office in New Orleans. Probably, the masked man went on, he had further increased his fortune by other, undisclosed thefts. Certainly he had permitted his soldiers to go even further in their excesses than Sherman had allowed and to do worse than burn or loot. Butler's most notorious order—which, although the man omitted to mention the fact, General U. S. Grant had rescinded as soon as it had come to his attention—had read, '*If any woman give insult or offence to an officer or soldier of the Union Army, she shall be regarded and held liable to be treated as a woman of the streets plying her avocation.*' According to the spokesman, Butler's troops had eagerly grasped the opportunities offered by such a vicious, ill-advised command decision.

Since the end of the War, Butler had allied himself with the most radical section of the Republican Party. He was notorious for his inflammatory speeches advocating strict controls and restrictions being retained on the Southern States; which did little to make ex-Rebels forget his iniquities in New Orleans. Butler's behaviour made an even more telling point than Sherman's, for the latter had proven a humane and moderate man in peace.

Although Smethurst's command of the Union's prisoner-of-war camps had been notorious with stories of deliberate starvation, wanton brutality, vicious torture and general mistreatment of the captives, Winslow felt that he was a weak link in the intruders' arguments. There had been rumours of prisoners being used to test experimental weapons—hotly denied in the North, but firmly believed below the Mason-Dixie line—but he had been killed in Texas after the War had ended.* So, while the memory of his misdeeds remained, the crowd would be less inclined to hate Yankees in general on his account.

* Why and how Smethurst was killed is told in *The Hooded Riders.*

The speaker pointed out that conditions had undoubtedly been bad in the South's Andersonville prisoner-of-war camp, but explained that there had been mitigating circumstances. Due to the United States' Navy's piracy and blockade on Confederate ports, food and medical supplies had been in short supply all through the South. While the camp's staff had done their best, obviously the prisoners had had to take second place to Southron needs. In the event of a further confrontation, the undisclosed European country would ensure that similar shortages did not occur.

Much as Winslow would have liked to make a further investigation into the identity of the European ally, he was denied the opportunity. Launching straight into the subject of the last poster, the spokesman was on firmer, more familiar ground.

Vividly the spokesman catalogued the abuses and injustices perpetrated by Union officials and carpet-bagger politicians who had been sent to administer the beaten Southern States. In this he was helped by the fact that the kind of situation illustrated on the portrait had been very close to the actions and sentiments of the North's occupying Armies during the early days of Reconstruction. Memories were still fresh of Negro 'committees' set up to govern communities; many of which had been comprised of a drunken rabble intent on defiling or destroying everything white, knowing that the Army's bayonets would back them up no matter how bad their actions.

In Winslow's opinion, the spokesman had just made his best argument. The behaviour of the soldiers under Szigo's command had served to keep alive the resentments of Reconstruction.

'And, my friends, that is what Yankee "fair dealing" and Reconstruction has meant—Nay! Still is meaning to the South!' the masked man thundered. 'For too long we have been held in bondage by the grasping Yankees. You have all witnessed and suffered from the arrogance of the garrison in your town. Do you wish to continue living under its heels?'

If the thunderous response from the cheaper tables at the rear was anything to go by, at least one section of the audience had no wish for the prevailing situation to continue. To give them their due, the occupants of the lower-priced tables were the citizens who had seen and suffered most from the worst aspects of the soldiers' behaviour. It was at their saloons or

24

entertainments that the antipathy had flared many times into open conflict. So there was little love lost between the blue-clad troops and the people who saw them at their worse. Especially as the commanding officer had never seen fit to give compensation to those who had suffered financial losses through his men's bad conduct, nor to control and punish the offenders.

'May I ask, sir,' Winslow boomed, springing to his feet in an attempt to prevent the intruder from stirring up even greater ill-feeling against the soldiers. 'Why you have come here tonight?'

'Because the day of reckoning is at hand for the Yankees,' the spokesman replied. 'The time for striking back is drawing near.'

'You mean for us once again to secede from the Union?'

'That, sir, is exactly what I mean!'

'Are we ready for such an extreme step?' Winslow inquired, hoping to sow the seeds of doubt amongst the audience. 'It would mean open war with the North.'

'We didn't flinch from *that* before,' the spokesman pointed out.

'But we were prepared——' Winslow began, meaning to point out that the South had been in a condition of readiness for war which no longer existed.

'And we're prepared to fight again!' the man interrupted. 'We were willing to continue the fight in 'Sixty-Five, but our leaders made peace. No, gentlemen, I don't blame General Lee for doing so. He acted, according to his belief, for the best and according to his orders from our Government. They were men of honour, deluded by the belief that they were dealing with honourable men. So they stopped the fighting, accepting honourable terms. But did the Yankees keep to their end of the bargain?'

'Like hell they did!' roared a voice from the rear, and rousing cheers echoed the sentiment.

'As our friends says, like hell they did!' the spokesman shouted. 'So, I say to you, we Southrons are no longer bound by the Yankees' dishonoured allegiance. The time is coming when the South will rise again. To arms! To arms, in Dixie!'

As if in answer to the clarion call of the man's final words, a large Stars and Bars flag of the Confederate States unfurled—apparently of its own volition—at the back of the stage. Raising his baton, the conductor of the attenuated orchestra—

Sabot's charity had not extended to paying the theatre's regular staff of musicians and he had been making do with only his own four men—gave a signal. The familiar strains of a tune rose from the orchestra pit. It was 'Dixie', long since adopted as the anthem of the Confederate States.

Snapping into smart military braces, the two masked men on the stage began to sing General Albert Pike C.S.A.'s fiercely patriotic words to what Daniel D. Emmet had originally composed as a cheerful, innocent minstrel song. Wood scraped on wood as man after man stood up. Slowly, yet with an ever-increasing volume, the singing spread through the hall.

> *'Southrons, hear your country call you!*
> *Up, lest worse than death befall you!*
> *To arms! To arms! To arms, in Dixie!*
> *See the beacon fires are lighted!*
> *Let Southron hearts now be united!*
> *To arms! To arms! To arms, in Dixie!*

Standing as straight and proud as any member of the audience, Winslow added his voice to that of the others. His eyes met those of the elderly woman who had been part of Sabot's committee and he could read the deep concern and worry on her face.

## CHAPTER THREE

# TELL THE FRENCHMAN ABOUT IT

'Well, Alburgh,' said the plump, perspiring president of the Shreveport Rivermen's Bank as their party left the theatre. 'What do we do now?'

'We gave our words in there that we wouldn't do anything before tomorrow morning,' Cullinan, owner of the town's biggest livery barn, grain and fodder store, pointed out.

'That we did,' agreed a third, equally prominent, member of the party. 'And, let us not forget, they've taken Sabot's girl along with them as a hostage against his good behaviour. If we should set the law on to them, they might think he'd done it and harm her.'

'Would they go that far?' the bank's president inquired. 'The two on the stage sounded like gentlemen.'

'And both know what they can expect from the Yankees if they're caught after tonight,' Cullinan answered. 'Are *we* prepared to take the chance that they *won't* harm her?'

'Well, *I* for one don't intend on going back on *my* word,' declared another of the party. 'I gave it of my own free will and I'll keep it. So I'm going straight home and staying there.'

'Szigo's going to be riled to hell when he hears about it and that we didn't go immediately to tell him what had happened,' warned the president of the bank. 'He might even claim that we were a party to it and will certainly say that we should have done something to prevent it happening.'

'That's for sure,' Cullinan agreed, sounding worried. A large proportion of his profits came from supplying the Army's needs. 'The fact that we gave our words not to report the incident until morning won't carry any weight with him.'

'Szigo's no longer in command,' Winslow remarked quietly.

'No longer in command?' Cullinan repeated. 'I hadn't heard any mention of him being replaced.'

'Nor had he,' Winslow replied. 'I want you to treat this as confidential, boys, although there'll be no great need after tomorrow. A friend of mine in Washington heard of Szigo's behaviour and passed it on to the War Department. They're putting a new man in command. I met him this afternoon, before he went out to the camp. Take it from me, Colonel Manderley's not like Szigo.'

'So what do we do, Alburgh?' Cullinan insisted.

'Here's Hector with my carriage now,' Winslow answered, pointing along the street. 'I'm going home. What I suggest is that you boys leave it with me.'

'There's no great point in breaking our words, anyway,' said the man who had insisted he would not. 'That fifteen minutes' grace they had us grant them will have given them time to make good their escape.'

'They're long gone already and will be well clear before the Army can start looking for them,' Cullinan decided, sounding relieved at the other's support to his conclusions. 'I'm all for doing as Alburgh says. There's nothing to be gained by going to the Army and making a fuss.'

'That will only keep the affair in the public's eye,' the president remarked. 'We'd do better to let it be forgotten. Who wants a ride home with me?'

'I'll come,' Cullinan offered. 'Let us know what this new colonel thinks about it, Alburgh.'

'I'll do that,' Winslow promised, and watched his party disintegrate as its members went to their waiting carriages.

'Could I trouble you for a ride, Colonel?' asked the elderly woman, crossing the sidewalk before Winslow could board his own vehicle. 'A poor old body like me's not used to such exciting goings on.'

'It'll be a pleasure, ma'am,' Winslow replied, doffing his hat gallantly. 'Allow me to help you to enter.'

If any of the excited, chattering crowd streaming from the theatre noticed the woman addressing Winslow, they attached no significance to the sight. Their heads were too full of what they had witnessed in the building for them to think about what was perfectly natural behaviour on Winslow's part. A Southron gentleman of the finest kind, he could be expected to render assistance if it was requested by a member of the opposite sex.

Slouching casually in the doorway of the cafe adjacent to the theatre, two big, burly men paid greater attention to Winslow's activities. Bare-headed, with close-cropped hair, they had hard, clean-shaven, tanned features. Their long black civilian cloak-coats effectively concealed all their other garments

28

except for highly polished, spur-decorated, Wellington-leg riding boots. Retaining their positions, they watched Winslow open the door of his carriage and help the woman to climb in.

'Well, that's done,' said the shorter of the pair, sounding pleased, as Winslow followed the woman.

'How'd you mean?' demanded his companion.

'We don't need to keep watching him. He didn't come out before the others. Now he's got that old gal with him, he'll not be going to the camp or the marshal's office.'

'The Colonel said for us to follow him——' began the larger man.

'And stop him if he looked like he was going to fetch the law——' the other interrupted.

'*And* trail him home if he went there.' the larger reminded the shorter coldly. 'Then we wait for the other boys to join us.'

'Aw, Matt——'

'Don't forget, Winslow's the main one we're after,' Matt growled, watching Winslow's carriage drive by. Its curtains had been drawn across the windows and he could not see inside. 'Let's go.'

Followed by his scowling companion, Matt went to where a buggy stood in an alley. Taking the reins as he climbed aboard, Matt started the horse and guided it after Winslow's carriage.

If the hard-faced pair had been able to see into their quarry's vehicle, they would have received a surprise. Letting out a long sigh of relief, the 'elderly' woman straightened and flexed her 'age-bent' shoulders.

'Whew! That's better,' she ejaculated, in a vibrant Southern drawl far different to the tones she had used in the theatre. 'Stooping that way's not the easiest thing to do for any length of time.'

'I don't suppose it is,' Winslow answered, showing no surprise at his passenger's remarkable change of voice. 'You did it very well.'

Reaching up, the woman removed not only her hat but her grey 'hair' at the same time. Doing so exposed black locks which had been cropped boyishly short to the contours of her skull. Producing a bandana from her vanity bag, she rubbed vigorously at her cheeks. The powder and 'age' lines departed, leaving behind a beautiful face that showed intelligence and strength of will.

'I was getting worried that the magician had realised I was disguised,' she remarked at the completion of her metamorphosis. 'He kept glancing at me in a nervous manner. This wig is good, but it's not the same as real hair.'

Unconsciously, the girl had struck upon the cause of Sabot's perturbation. He had noticed, in passing, a slight unreality in the 'elderly woman's' hair and the memory of it had remained in the back of his mind but was unable to break through.

'What did you make of it, Uncle Alburgh?' the girl inquired.

'I didn't like any part of it,' Winslow admitted.

'Most of the audience seemed to,' the girl pointed out. 'They cheered him loud and long when he finished speaking. And nobody offered to leave for the full fifteen minutes after he and his men had gone.'

After the singing of 'Dixie', the spokesman for the intruders had stated that the meeting had lasted as long as was safe for his party or the audience. Then he had taken precautions against the intruders' departure. First the magician had been returned to the stage. Sabot's face was no longer bleeding and he had declared that he was unharmed. However, his assistant was to be taken as a hostage by the masked men. If there had been no pursuit, they had undertaken to return her in time to catch the *Texarkana Belle*. Promising that he would behave, he had begged the audience not to do anything which might endanger Selima.

Next the spokesman had asked the audience—directing his words mainly to Winslow's party—that they should give their words not to inform the authorities until the following morning, by which time he and his men would be out of harm's way. Lastly, he had requested that the audience remain seated for fifteen minutes after his party had taken their departure. That would, he had assured them, give adequate opportunity for their escape.

'He was smart, without a doubt,' Winslow observed. 'Although he claimed they were only taking the girl to ensure Sabot's good behaviour, he knew that we would hesitate to do anything that might endanger her. And we, my party, were those most likely to report the meeting to the authorities. Blast it, Belle, I should have followed my inclination and walked straight out.'

'I'd say the men knew you,' answered the girl. 'Or read your

30

character pretty well.'

'I don't follow you.'

'Anybody who *knows* you would realise that, without forc-
ibly detaining you, they couldn't have made you stay against
your will. And you're too popular for them to want to use
force. So they offered to let you go, knowing they could trust
your word if you promised not to report them.'

'They could.'

'So they were gambling on you being curious enough to
stop, just so long as it was clear that nobody was trying to
make you,' the girl went on.

'Huh!' Winslow grunted, but made no further comment on
the girl's assessment of his character and motives. 'If I'd left, a
lot would have followed.'

'Not after the other man's speech about loyalty to the
South,' argued the girl. 'And I feel sure that they'd made
arrangements to deal with anybody who did try to leave. Tell
Hector to stop, please.'

'What's wrong?' Winslow asked, after he had complied with
the request.

'A whole lot of things,' the girl replied. 'What was your
impression of the man who did most of the talking?'

'He was well-educated, shrewd and as hard as nails. A
gentleman by birth and upbringing,' Winslow decided, after a
moment's thought.

'Did he, or his companion, strike you as being French?'
asked the girl.

When Winslow's carriage had come to a halt, Matt had been
compelled to keep his vehicle moving. They were on a deserted stretch of street and the buggy would have been too
conspicuous if he had stopped. Warning his companion, whom
he addressed as 'Hermy', not to display interest in the carriage
as they passed, he steered the horse to go by it. Continuing for
about fifty yards, he found an intersection. Turning out of
Hector's sight, he reined in the horse.

'Go keep watch from the corner,' Matt growled.

'You're a mite free with your orders,' Hermy protested
sullenly. 'Them three bars on your sleeve don't count for a
heap on this chore.'

'So tell the Frenchman about it,' Matt sniffed. 'Only make
your will *afore* you do it. You won't get a chance *after* you've
said your piece.'

'Ain't he the mean bastard,' Hermy remarked in a conciliatory manner, turning to lift a corner of the blanket which covered something behind their seat.

'Leave the hat there, blast it!' Matt snapped in exasperation, showing no sign of being mollified. 'If somebody sees you wearing it, they could come and start asking questions.'

Removing his hand, Hermy climbed from the buggy. He swaggered away as if keeping the carriage under observation had been his own idea. The cloak-coat trailed open as he walked, exposing his legs. The dark blue riding breeches which showed had a yellow stripe along the outside of each thigh.

'No,' Winslow declared, after considering the girl's question. 'I don't think either of them was French.'

'Did you recognise either of them? I mean, did they seem familiar?'

'Not that I could put a finger on it. And I know all the men of their class in Caddo and Bossier Counties. Do you know something about them?'

'Not much,' the girl answered. 'I've heard a little about their activities.'

'Do you mean that they've done this kind of thing before?'

'Nothing so blatant and open. But I was told that Shreveport would be different from the other meetings which have been held throughout the South.'

'How did you become involved, Belle?' Winslow inquired.

'I'm a member of the United States' Secret Service,' the girl explained, sounding just a mite defensive and challenging.

'Dad-blast it, Belle!' Winslow barked, showing no great surprise at her answer. 'I never took to the notion of you and Cousin Rose playing the spy in the War——'

'Not *playing*,' the girl protested indignantly. 'We both did useful work for the South.'

That was a point which Winslow could not deny. Rose Greenhow and the girl facing him, Belle Boyd, had carried out their originally self-appointed—but soon officially recognised —duties in a most satisfactory manner. Each had achieved considerable fame and success. Gathering information had been Rose's forte. Belle had specialised in delivering the results of her cousin's work through the enemies' lines. Later, she had graduated to handling assignments of a tricky and frequently dangerous nature.* The Yankees had named her

* Told in *The Colt and the Sabre*, *The Rebel Spy* and *The Bloody Border*.

the Rebel Spy and her efforts had caused them a great deal of trouble.

'I'm not gainsaying it,' Winslow stated. 'Vincent Boyd always wanted a son and at times I'll swear he had one.'

'Why thank you 'most to death, as a good friend in Texas says,' Belle replied, looking very feminine and not at all like anybody's *son*.

'Blast it, girl, he taught you to sit *astride* a horse and swore you could outride any man in Baton Royale County. He had you handling a sword and a gun when most girls of your age were playing with dolls——'

'Fencing and shooting were more fun,' Belle interrupted. 'And I always enjoyed *savate* lessons better than dancing. But mama saw to it that I didn't neglect the more ladylike accomplishments. If it hadn't been for Tollinger and Barmain, I'd probably have forgotten all about riding, shooting and *savate*, married and settled down to a life of dull respectability.'

'Tollinger and Barmain!' Winslow snorted, knowing them to have been the leaders of a drunken pro-Unionist rabble who had attacked the Boyd plantation before the start of the War. Belle's parents had been murdered and she was wounded. On her recovery, she had become a spy, seeking revenge against the pair. 'If I could have laid my hands on them——'

'I did,' Belle said quietly. 'Down in Mexico, just after the War. In a way, that was how I joined the Secret Service.'*

'I wondered why you insisted on going to the theatre in disguise,' Winslow commented, knowing that it was neither the time nor the place to seek further details of his niece's adventures.

'There wasn't time to explain. I only arrived this afternoon and knew that, as it was Sabot's last performance, whatever was due to happen must happen at it. I went in disguise because I wasn't sure if anybody would recognise me.'

'You are after them?'

'Yes,' Belle agreed, a touch defiantly. 'Despite their loyalty to the South, I'm after them.'

'*Loyalty!*' barked Winslow. 'I yield second to no man in *my* loyalty to the South. But, by cracky, I fail to see how starting another war with the Yankees will help Dixie.'

'Or me,' Belle said quietly. 'Uncle Alburgh, just how dangerous do you think the situation might be?'

* Told in *Back to the Bloody Border*.

'It could be very serious,' Winslow replied. 'Or it could fade into nothing. I'll have my paper treat it as no more than a stupid practical joke. After a night's cool and sober thought, I think that the rest of the audience will decide peace beats war any time. It'll all be forgotten in a week.'

'Unless something happens to keep it in the public's eye,' Belle warned.

'Such as?'

'I only wish I knew. They certainly didn't go to all that trouble just to make a speech and then sit back and hope for developments. It's my belief that they plan to make sure their words aren't forgotten.'

'How?' Winslow asked.

'I've no idea,' the girl admitted. 'But, if the Frenchman is involved, it won't be pleasant; whatever it might be.'

'The Frenchman?' Winslow repeated. 'Is France the country to which the man kept referring?'

'I've no proof of that. I only know that this person called "the Frenchman" is a leader in the plot. With the emphasis they placed on the Army's activities, it could be an incident involving the local soldiers. I hope that new commanding officer isn't delayed.'

'He's here.'

'And not before time, from the stories I've heard. But that doesn't tell us why they held their meeting tonight.'

'Perhaps they hoped to stir up trouble before Manderley took over?'

'It's possible,' Belle conceded and stood up. 'The answer might be at the theatre. If so, I intend to find it.'

Peeling off and dropping the mitts, Belle unfastened and removed her coat. She laid it on the seat and slipped out of the Balmoral skirt. That left her slender, willowly figure clad in an open-necked dark blue shirt, form-hugging black riding breeches and calf-high Hessian boots. Nor did her unconventionally masculine attire end there. About her waist, previously concealed by the stiff, over-large skirt, was strapped a wide black leather gunbelt of Western fashion. Butt forward in the contoured holster, which was secured to her right thigh by pigging thongs, rode an ivory-handled Dance Bros. Navy revolver. Although percussion-primed and firing a ·36-calibre combustible paper cartridge, it would still be an effective weapon in trained hands.

'I'll come with you,' Winslow offered, studying her preparations.

'No, thank you,' Belle refused.

'Blast it, girl. You can't go back there alone——!'

'I can, and mean to. If I was looking for trouble, I'd welcome you. But I'm only going to scout around. And I can do that far safer alone.'

'If all you're going to do is scout around,' Winslow growled, 'why don't you go back in your disguise?'

'If there's trouble, I don't want hindering by skirts,' Belle explained. 'And they wouldn't be any protection for me. The Frenchman wouldn't bother about me being a woman if he caught me.'

'In that case, I'm coming with you!' Winslow stated.

'No, Uncle Alburgh!' Belle replied, speaking in a grim and definite manner. 'I have to handle things my own way. This is my work. I wouldn't try to tell you how to run your newspaper, or how to defend a law case. Anyway, there's probably nothing to find at the theatre. But I'll feel easier if I've checked.'

'Suppose there *is* something at the theatre?' Winslow challenged.

'Then I'll do my level best to get away undetected,' Belle promised with a smile. Becoming more serious, she continued, 'You'll find an addressed envelope in my trunk. If I'm not back by morning, write a report of everything that has happened and mail it in the envelope.'

'If you think that's all I'll do——'

'Very well. If I'm not back by midnight, go and tell the new commanding officer what's happened.'

'Damn it! I'm going with you——!' Winslow commenced, then he shrugged. 'Oh, do things your own way! You Boyd females have a most unseemly habit of doing as you please. I should know. I've married one. What if this Frenchman is there?'

'If he is and I get the chance,' Belle answered, and her voice throbbed with cold, angry hatred, 'I'll kill him.'

Giving her uncle no opportunity to speak, Belle opened the door and dropped lightly to the sidewalk. She glanced in each direction, then strolled away. For all the emotion he displayed, the aged Negro on the driving box might have had an elderly woman enter and a slender, beautiful girl emerge from his carriage every day of the week.

'Shall us wait for Miss Belle, Colonel?' Hector asked.

'No,' Winslow replied, wondering why the note of deadly hatred had come into his niece's voice each time she had mentioned 'the Frenchman'. 'Go home, Hector. She'll come when she's finished her business.'

Jerking back his head as the girl quit the carriage, Hermy felt certain that he had escaped being observed by her. He peeped cautiously around the corner and saw her turning to walk off in the opposite direction. Frowning, he swung on his heel to return to the waiting buggy.

'I don't know where the hell she come from,' Hermy told Matt in wondering tones. 'But a gal wearing pants just got out of Winslow's carriage.'

'A gal, *wearing pants*!' the burly man repeated, eyeing his companion with cold suspicion. 'What're you try——?'

'Go see for yourself,' Hermy suggested.

'Which way did she go?' Matt demanded, making as if to leave his seat and follow the other's suggestion.

'Back the way she come. Here's Winslow's carriage.'

'We'll keep going after him,' Matt decided, sinking back on to the seat.

'How about the gal?' Hermy inquired, unaware of certain suspicions he was arousing. 'She might be headed back to the theatre.'

'All right,' Matt grunted. 'You go watch her. I'll tend to Winslow.'

'What do I do if she is headed for the theatre?' Hermy wanted to know.

'Make sure she doesn't come away alive,' Matt replied and set the buggy into motion.

## CHAPTER FOUR

# A NATIONAL DISASTER

*Belle Boyd's deep and bitter hatred for the person she knew only as 'the Frenchman' had had its beginning aboard the Mississippi riverboat* Elegant Lady, *as it lay alongside a dock at Memphis before continuing south to New Orleans.*

'There's a gennelman to see you-all, Miss Winslow,' announced the coloured stewardess, entering Belle's stateroom on the *Elegant Lady* and using the name under which the girl was travelling.

Telling the Negress to show the gentleman in, Belle wondered who he might be and, more important, what he wanted with her. That he was in the Secret Service seemed obvious from his knowing her assumed name.

Taking a well-earned vacation, after completing an assignment that had not been without danger, she was on her way to New Orleans. Of course, her superiors had been informed of her destination and the route by which she would be travelling. Every Secret Service organisation insisted upon keeping in touch with its members, even when they were taking a holiday. Given luck, the visitor would only be another agent, paying a friendly, courtesy call.

That hope ended abruptly with her first sight of the visitor.

Soberly and plainly dressed, the man was below middle height, lean and with a prissy, self-important air. He looked like the owner, or manager, of a successful business; arrogant, within the bounds of his power, to underlings and a stickler for protocol as it affected himself. Belle recognised him as Alden H. Stenhouse, senior co-ordinator of the Secret Service along the middle reaches of the Mississippi River.

One thing was for sure. Stenhouse was not the kind of man who would pay a purely social call to a mere agent; even to one of Belle's prominence.

'Good afternoon, Miss B—— Winslow,' Stenhouse greeted, looking uneasy.

'Good afternoon, Mr. Stenhouse,' the girl answered, knowing that he would not be travelling under an assumed name.

'Can I have the stewardess bring you a drink or anything?'

'No, thank you,' Stenhouse refused. 'I have come to see you on a confidential matter of some importance.'

'Feel free to do it,' Belle drawled as the stewardess left the stateroom and closed the door. 'The boat doesn't sail for three hours.'

'You won't be leaving with it,' Stenhouse warned brusquely, as if wanting to get things straight immediately.

'I won't?' asked Belle, a hint of challenge in her voice.

'No,' Stenhouse stated. Another, bigger man might have tempered the word with a more polite, apologetic refusal. Conscious of his authority, he made no attempt to do so. 'I have an assignment for you.'

'You realise, of course, that I'm on vacation?' Belle demanded, annoyed by his behaviour.

'General Handiman assured me that you would be willing to return to duty,' the man replied, wanting to impress upon her that his demand carried top-grade, official backing. 'This is a matter of considerable importance, Miss Boyd. I can't overestimate just *how* vital it is. In fact, it might even develop into a national disaster.'

'Sit down and tell me about it,' Belle suggested, curiosity overriding any resentment she felt at the intrusion, or over Stenhouse's attitude.

'I hardly know where to begin,' the man admitted, taking a seat.

'They do say that the beginning's the best place to start,' Belle commented. 'And the more I know, the better I can handle my part in it.'

'I suppose the beginning was in Topeka, Kansas,' Stenhouse said, producing a notebook from his jacket's inside pocket and flipping it open. 'But we aren't concerned with that——'

'Not even if it helps me to see the full picture?' Belle interrupted, more to annoy her visitor than for any special reason. 'I'd hate to keep asking for you to clear up some point I haven't heard about.'

'Very well,' Stenhouse sniffed. 'A group of Topeka businessmen, in early 'Sixty-Five, decided that they would raise a regiment of cavalry——'

'They left it late in the day,' Belle commented, for that had been the year which had seen the end of military hostilities.

'Probably they hadn't foreseen how close we were to victory,' Stenhouse replied tactlessly. Realising that the girl might not be pleased with the reference to the South's defeat, he did not offer to apologise. 'Anyway, they set about organising what would have been the 18th "Kansas" Dragoons.'

'*Dragoons?*'

'It would have been in name only. They were to be equipped with Burnside hats, standard uniforms and accoutrements, but armed with Henry rifles.'

'That would have cost money,' Belle remarked.

'Yes,' conceded Stenhouse. 'Most of it would have been raised by public subscriptions. However, what with one delay or another, the War ended before the Dragoons had acquired their full requirements. In fact, they had obtained only sufficient uniforms and arms for one hundred men. Although the businessmen cancelled the rest of their orders, they had to purchase those which had been filled. So they found themselves stuck with the rifles and equipment.'

'I feel for them,' Belle said dryly. 'Why didn't they sell them?'

'There was no market for surplus military equipment when they decided to do so. It's my belief that they hung on hoping to have their regiment retained on a permanent basis, but failed to do so. They left it too late to dispose of even the Henry rifles at so much as their cost price.'

'The new, improved Winchester Model of 1866 certainly reduced the value of the Henry,' Belle admitted. 'So what did the speculators do?'

'They held on, hoping for the opportunity to dispose of their purchases at, if not a profit, something close to the original cost.'

'Which they eventually managed?'

'Yes. Two men, calling themselves Duprez and le Beausainte, made an acceptable offer. They said that they were commissioned by the Legislature of Oregon to purchase arms and equipment for the State's militia. Their price was satisfactory and the spec—businessmen—didn't check on the story. However, one of their number had misgivings. What nationality do the names Duprez and le Beausainte suggest to you, Miss Boyd?'

'French, or Creole,' the girl replied without hesitation. 'But the speculator had reasons to doubt that they were either.'

'Yes,' Stenhouse confirmed. 'Their accents were unmistakably—*Irish*!'

'Huh huh!' Belle said non-committally, although she could

guess in which direction the conversation was heading.

'Fortunately the spec—businessman had the good sense to mention his misgivings to a U.S. marshal who was in Topeka at the time,' Stenhouse went on, studiously avoiding the term 'speculator' when mentioning the Kansas citizens. 'Marshal Cole——'

'Solly Cole?' Belle interrupted.

'Yes. Of course, you worked with him.'

'I did. He's a smart lawman.'*

'Smart enough to see the implications in the disparity between the two men's names and their accents,' Stenhouse agreed. 'You understand my meaning?'

'Yes,' Belle replied. 'I understand.'

In 1872, the international membership of the *Alabama* Arbitration Tribunal had completed its long investigations and deliberations. It had rendered a decision most favourable to the United States. For permitting the Confederate States' naval cruisers like the *Alabama, Florida* and *Shenandoah* to be built in and operate from their ports—as well as being involved in other activities which had aided the South—the Government of Great Britain had been ordered to pay compensation to the tune of £15,500,000.

Since that event, the U.S. Congress had trodden very warily where British interests were concerned. Given an opportunity, the British would be only too willing to invoke a similar international body and try to retrieve some of the money. In general, Congress realised that Ireland and British–Irish affairs might easily supply the required excuse.

Over the years, large numbers of Irish nationals had emigrated to the United States. While a few might have fled to escape persecution, or to avoid the consequences for acts of political violence, the majority had merely come in search of new homes and a higher standard of living. The love which many of them expressed for the 'ould country' had increased enormously with the distance they had put between themselves and it.

Although many of the emigrants had frequently discussed 'liberating' Ireland from British domination, only some of the wealthier and better educated—who may have been motivated by thoughts of great opportunities for social, business or political advancement as 'saviours' of their native land—had

* Details of Marshal Solly Coles' career are given in *Calamity Spells Trouble*.

turned their attention to actively achieving that end.

So far, however, the efforts of the Irish–American 'loyalists' had not reached noticeable proportions, Politicians of Irish descent had frequently attempted to invoke official action by the United States against British rule. For one reason or another, every session of Congress had refused to sanction such measures.

With the commencement of the '*Alabama*' Arbitration Tribunal, there had been a growing awareness of the danger to chances of a satisfactory decision if even unofficial intervention in Irish affairs should be launched from the United States. So General Philo Handiman, head of the Secret Service, had been ordered to stay alert for, and to prevent, such incidents.

'Marshal Cole telegraphed the story to General Handiman,' Stenhouse went on. 'He also instituted inquiries in Salem. The Oregon Legislature had not commissioned the two men. Nor, Cole learned, had the consignment been sent west. It was taken to Kansas City and sent down the Missouri to St. Louis. One of our agents was waiting for its arrival and travelled on the same boat to Memphis. Once here, the consignment was disembarked and placed into a warehouse owned by Phineas Molloy, who is Irish.'

'He certainly doesn't sound French,' Belle could not resist remarking.

'My agent——' Stenhouse continued stiffly.

'Does he have a name?' Belle interrupted.

'It's Horatio A. Darren. Do you know him?'

'We haven't met,' Belle replied, tactfully refraining from mentioning that she had heard of Horatio A. Darren and was aware of his relationship to Stenhouse. 'What has he been doing?'

'He kept watch on the warehouse for two days, but the boxes carrying the consignment weren't brought out again. So, last night after it was closed, he broke in and examined them.'

'What did he learn?'

'That they are still sealed and are marked, "To Await Collection".'

'Nothing else?'

'What else could he learn?' Stenhouse demanded. 'He didn't want them to know he'd been there and he could hardly have made a more detailed examination without leaving traces of his presence.'

'I should have seen that,' Belle drawled. 'But where do I

come in?'

'Hora—Agent Darren may need assistance,' Stenhouse explained, looking evasive but sounding as if he doubted that such a need could ever arise. 'So General Handiman suggested, as you were in the vicinity, that I should make use of your services.'

'Why, I just hope that I can live up to your trust, sir,' Belle said, with such humble sincerity that she might have been speaking the truth.

'Shall we go and make a start?' Stenhouse asked.

'There's one problem,' Belle objected. 'When I came aboard, my trunk was placed in the hold. I wasn't expecting to need it and getting it out again before New Orleans will be inconvenient for the captain.'

'Is it imperative that you have it?'

'Most of my equipment is in it, wigs, special clothing, things I need for disguises——'

'You won't need any of them,' Stenhouse assured her. 'All I need is for you to assist Hor—Agent Darren. In all probability you'll be able to continue your journey on the next boat. We, of course, will defray any expenses this puts you to—within reason.'

'Why thank you 'most to death,' Belle said sardonically. 'You can start by paying for a telegraph message I'm going to send.'

'To whom?'

'A friend in New Orleans. She can collect and hold my trunk when the *Elegant Lady* arrives. I'll arrange with the captain for it to be handed over.'

'Is your friend trustworthy?' Stenhouse wanted to know.

'If she isn't, somebody's made a bad mistake,' Belle replied. 'It's Madame Lucienne and she's with the Secret Service, just like us. Where do I meet Hora—Agent Darren, Mr. Stenhouse?'

## CHAPTER FIVE

# I'LL PROTECT YOU, MISS BOYD

Belle Boyd had not been impressed by Stenhouse and she found herself even less inspired by his nephew. Neatly dressed in a grey suit of the latest Eastern fashion, white shirt with one of the newfangled celluloid collars and a sober blue tie, Horatio A. Darren was tall, brown-haired, reasonably handsome—although dark lines under his eyes suggested that he had been losing sleep recently—and had an athletic build. A revolver raised a noticeable lump under the left side of his vest; being the more noticeable due to his habit of drawing attention to the protuberance by a variety of gestures. There was about him an air of smug, self-satisfied, complacent superiority that the girl found both amusing and irritating. Going by his response when his uncle had performed the introductions, Darren clearly considered that the affair was firmly under his control and it was obvious that he resented Belle's intrusion.

For all that, Darren had struggled to prevent his feelings from showing. He was torn between the desire to impress his attractive visitor and his annoyance that anybody could believe *he* would require assistance on any assignment. Helped along by Belle's appearance and attitude, the former emotion won.

All in all, Belle presented an attractive picture. She wore the normal travelling garb of a well-to-do, fashionable lady. The brown two-piece jacket and Balmoral skirt set off her slender, shapely figure, just as the small, neat hat and brown wig—the latter to prevent her short black hair from drawing attention—combined to accentuate the beautiful lines of her face. However, the garments concealed a dark blue shirt, black riding breeches and Hessian boots. These had all been available in her stateroom aboard the *Elegant Lady*. Having been made to her measure by a master cobbler, the boots were so comfortable that she preferred them to more conventional footwear and had had them on her feet when Stenhouse had arrived. Her gunbelt and the Dance Bros. Navy revolver had been in her trunk aboard the riverboat. So, if she should need a weapon, she would have to rely upon the Remington Double

Derringer in her vanity bag or the specially designed parasol which dangled negligently in her right hand.

The meeting was taking place in a room hired by Darren, at a small hotel which stood across the street from Molloy's warehouse.

After Belle had packed such of her belongings as were in the stateroom, and made arrangements for the disposal of the rest of her property, she had accompanied Stenhouse to the Travellers Hotel. An expensive, new establishment, the hotel had two advantages. One, it was close to the river and much used by travellers with money to meet its high tariff; two, neither Stenhouse nor his nephew resided there. Having settled in and, while an impatient Stenhouse waited in the foyer, changed into her male attire, Belle had been escorted by him to the rendezvous. With the introductions performed, Stenhouse had left the agents to their own devices.

'Come to the window, Miss Boyd,' Darren requested briskly, as the door closed on his departing uncle. The words came out as an order, for he wanted to establish who was running things. 'You can see the consignment from it. I don't need to tell *you* to make sure that you're not seen looking, do I?'

'Why I'm *so* pleased to have you remind me of that,' the girl purred, dripping honey spiked with strychnine in every word. 'I might have spoiled all your good word if you hadn't.'

Eyeing Belle speculatively, Darren could read only what he took for an expression of respectful admiration. Being a young man with more than his fair share of ego, he preferred to accept that it *was* her true feeling about him. He felt certain that he was making a satisfactory impression on her, both as an expert in their mutual trade and as a masterful member of the stronger, dominant sex.

Ignoring Darren, except to follow his unnecessary advice regarding concealment, Belle stood alongside the window and looked cautiously across the street. The double main doors of the warehouse were wide open. Through them, to the rear but in plain sight, she could see four oblong and two square wooden boxes of the kind used for transporting quantities of rifles and ammunition. Near by were four large bales less easy to identify.

'There they are!' Darren announced dramatically, exposing himself far more than Belle did. 'Four boxes, twenty-five rifles to the box. Five thousand ·44 rimfire bullets in each of the square boxes. The hats, uniforms, boots and accoutrements are

44

in the bales.'

'Huh huh!' Belle said, still studying the interior of the warehouse. 'They've been there like that ever since they came from the boat?'

'Yes. I've had them under observation all the time.'

'Do they leave the doors open at night?'

'Of course not!' Darren snapped, scanning the beautiful features for traces of the faintly sarcastic undertones he had thought he detected in her voice. 'But I keep watch at night and make patrols around the warehouse at intervals.'

'Mercy!' Belle gasped, understanding the cause of the dark lines under his eyes. 'When do you sleep?'

'During the day. But I've got one of Molloy's men working for me. He's to let me know as soon as anybody comes to collect the consignment.'

'I see,' Belle drawled. Although she would have liked to go further into how Darren had made such a fortunate acquaintance, she decided against it. Her instincts warned that to do so would antagonise him and ruin all hope of willing co-operation. 'So all we need to do is wait for whoever comes to make the collection.'

'That's all,' Darren agreed. 'There wasn't any real need for Unc—them to delay your vacation, Miss Boyd. Not that I don't appreciate your coming to he—to work with me.'

'Why thank you, 'most to death,' Belle purred. 'I hope that I can be useful. Is there any way I could take a closer look at the consignment?'

'*I've* already done *that*!' Darren pointed out.

'Couldn't I take just a little peek, so I can feel I'm doing something worthwhile?'

'You couldn't get in my way. I used a ladder to reach the hayloft's loading door, slipped its fastener and got in through it.'

'Couldn't I do that?' Belle wanted to know. 'With *your* help of course?'

When Belle Boyd put on her most appealing manner, she could charm even a less egoistical and susceptible man than Darren. Wanting to impress her, he felt that a visit to the warehouse would be a big step in the required direction.

'I suppose you could, if you can climb the ladder,' he conceded.

'I think I could do that,' Belle replied, sounding uncertain. 'Isn't there a watchman?'

'No. Don't worry. If there's any trouble, I'll protect you, Miss Boyd.'

At that moment, several men emerged from the warehouse. They swung the big doors shut and one of their number turned. Waving a hand, he crossed the street in the direction of the hotel. Tall, lean, with a tanned, heavily moustached face, he wore similar style clothing to the men he had left—that of a poorly paid worker.

'That's O'Reilly,' Darren commented, indicating the man. 'Now they've closed for the day, he's coming to report.'

'He comes straight over here——' Belle began.

'By the rear entrance,' Darren elaborated. 'It would arouse suspicions if he used the front door.'

'I can see that it might,' Belle conceded. 'Perhaps it would be better if he didn't see me.'

'He's quite trustworthy——!'

'I don't doubt it. But I don't need to tell *you* how much of an advantage it will be if nobody other than ourselves learns I'm involved.'

'That's true,' Darren agreed. 'Perhaps you can hide in the wardrobe?'

'It won't be necessary,' Belle replied. 'I'll leave now, before he arrives, and go back to my hotel. I'll come later this evening and see the warehouse.'

'That would be best,' Darren confirmed, crossing to open the door.

Leaving the room, Belle hurried along the passage. She heard footsteps in the hall below, so went by the head of the stairs to halt at a door. Facing it, she bent her legs, bowed her shoulders and made as if she was searching for the key in her vanity bag. O'Reilly reached the top of the stairs, darted a glance in her direction and went to Darren's door. Letting the man disappear inside, Belle straightened up and descended to the ground floor. Leaving the hotel, she crossed the street and halted so that she could see inside to the foot of the stairs.

Apparently O'Reilly had not brought an extensive report that afternoon. He soon came into view on the stairs. Despite his earlier precaution of making the visit via the rear door, he left through the front entrance. Belle followed him as he strode off along the street.

As she walked, Belle wondered if she might be wasting her time. Perhaps she was allowing first impressions to influence her against Darren. He could have been lucky—or shrewd—

46

enough to find a corruptible member of Molloy's warehouse staff. Yet, for all that, Belle could not throw off her feeling that all was far from being well. Everything seemed to be happening just too conveniently; the boxes being placed in plain view and Darren finding the right man to keep him informed. Belle was suspicious by nature and training. Of an active temperament, she always believed in taking the most direct means of satisfying her curiosity.

Belle had not been following the man for long before she decided that her misgivings might have some foundation. Instead of making for the section of town in which one of his class might be expected to live, O'Reilly directed his steps towards the higher-rent district. Much to her surprise, Belle watched him pass through the portals of the Traveller's Hotel. That was hardly the kind of establishment in which a poorly paid warehouse attendant would live. Yet he was clearly known there. The desk clerk handed over a room-key without question or comment. Allowing O'Reilly to disappear up the stairs, Belle entered and went to the desk.

'Was that workman going near my room?' she inquired. 'If so, I hope he isn't going to make a lot of noise.'

'Workman?' the clerk queried, then smiled. 'You must mean Mr. Sheriff.' He dropped his voice to a confidential whisper. 'It's all right, Miss Winslow, he's not a workman. He's a Pinkerton detective in disguise.'

'*Mercy!*' Belle gasped, sounding suitably impressed. 'Who-all's he after, somebody at the hotel?'

'Certainly not!' gasped the clerk. 'He's heard that the James gang is planning a robbery and is keeping watch for them down by the river.'

'I just hope he catches them,' Belle said and, wanting to avoid having her interest in 'Sheriff' mentioned, went on, 'And I surely hope you-all don't tell him about my foolish mistake. Why, I'd be right mortified if you did.'

'I won't say a word, Miss Winslow,' the clerk promised.

Probably, Belle told herself as she crossed to the dining-room, because he had realised that he might be regarded as having been indiscreet in discussing 'Sheriff's' occupation with another guest.

Selecting a table which would allow her to see O'Reilly—or Sheriff—if he returned downstairs, Belle ordered a meal. She pondered upon the remarkable coincidence—which no author would dare to let happen in his stories—of O'Reilly using her

47

hotel. Then she decided that the man had probably selected it, as she had, for its high standard of comfort and proximity to the docks. One thing was for sure. O'Reilly was no ordinary, if disloyal, warehouse employee. Belle could imagine that Darren's surveillance had aroused somebody's suspicions. So O'Reilly had made his acquaintance and was ensuring that he saw only what the conspirators wanted him to see.

The question, to Belle's way of thinking, was why should they go to all that trouble?

Learning the reason struck the girl as being one of the things which must be done. Perhaps the visit to the warehouse would provide her with the answer.

O'Reilly had not made an appearance by the time Belle had finished her meal. Noticing that the clerk was not behind the desk, she crossed to it and turned the register around. A quick examination told her the number of O'Reilly's room and that he had come to the hotel on the same day that the consignment arrived in Memphis. Replacing the book, Belle went up to the first floor. In passing, she paused to listen at O'Reilly's door and heard him moving about. Then she went to her own quarters.

Deciding that they must deal with O'Reilly the following day, Belle gave thought to her examination of the consignment. She had no intention, except as a last resort, of entering the warehouse by the route which Darren had suggested. However, she meant to conduct the investigation wearing suitable clothing.

Removing her hat and wig. Belle took them to the wardrobe. She placed them inside and brought out the long black cloak which hung there. With that on and the hood raised, she could dispense with the coat and skirt as covering for her male garments.

Having removed her feminine attire and placed it, with the vanity bag and parasol, in the wardrobe, she thrust the Remington Double Derringer into her waistband. Then she donned the cloak and raised its hood. A look in the wardrobe's mirror satisfied her that she could get by in her unconventional attire, especially as night had fallen, and not arouse unwanted interest in her appearance.

Dressed and equipped for the work which lay ahead, Belle prepared to go and do it. Glancing along the passage as she emerged, she saw that the door of O'Reilly's room was opening. A subconscious reflex action caused Belle to retreat into her room and almost close the door. Peering through the crack she had left, she was grateful that she had taken such a precaution. On coming out, O'Reilly proved to have changed his clothes. Now he was dressed more in keeping with a resident at an expensive hotel. Settling a bowler hat on his head, he made for the stairs. His appearance and attitude implied that he was leaving the building rather than merely going down to the dining-room.

'Fortune favours the fair,' Belle mused, allowing O'Reilly to pass out of sight before stepping into the passage. 'Twice in one day. It can't last.'

Belle waited until the man had reached the ground floor before starting down the stairs. Already she had decided to revise her plans. There would be ample time later to follow the original arrangements. In fact, the visit to the warehouse could not be undertaken until after midnight. So she considered that she would be more usefully employed in trying to learn more about O'Reilly.

By the time Belle reached the foyer, her quarry had gone out of the front door. She followed as he strolled along the sidewalk. Using all her skill, she stayed close enough to make sure that she did not lose sight of O'Reilly, yet at a sufficient distance to prevent him detecting her presence. The night was warm and star-lit, but not many people were on the streets. For all that, Belle felt certain the man had not located her. She hoped that he would remain on foot. If he should take a carriage, she might have difficulty in obtaining one in which to continue her surveillance.

Fortune still appeared to be favouring the fair. O'Reilly kept walking, passing into the business and entertainment section of the poorer part of the city. Then he turned down an alley by the Bijou Theatre. If the darkened, deserted aspect of the building was anything to go on, there was no show that night. Belle arrived at the mouth of the alley in time to see him turn at the rear of the theatre. Stepping quietly, she reached and peered around the corner. Unlocking what would probably be the stage door, O'Reilly paused. He struck a match, found and lit a lamp which had been hanging near the door. Going in, he drew the door closed behind him.

Moving even more cautiously, Belle advanced to the door. A faint glow of light showed as she bent to the keyhole. Squinting through it, she watched the man enter one of the row of dressing-rooms. There was no other sign of life in the darkened building. So Belle decided that she would try to take O'Reilly prisoner. If she did, she felt sure that she could induce him to answer questions.

Twisting at the door's handle, she pushed gently. Nothing happened. A cluck of annoyance broke from the girl. Either the lock was one of the new-fangled variety that operated automatically, or O'Reilly had turned and taken away the key on entering.

At least, Belle hoped that it was only the lock which held the door against her push. If O'Reilly had shot the bolts on the inside, she would not be able to effect an entrance at that point.

On the other hand, providing that the lock was of the comparatively uncomplicated, standard variety—as seemed most likely in such an old building—Belle felt certain that she could accomplish something. One of the subjects in which she had taken training, in the South's and the United States' Secret Services, had been how to open locks for which she did not possess the formal key.

Shoving firmly at first the top then the bottom of the door, Belle felt it yield a little on each occasion. That implied it was secured in the centre, at the region of the lock. Wishing that she dare strike a match and make a closer examination, she ran the tip of her right forefinger over the surface of the keyhole.

'It's a lever, I'd say,' she mused. 'Let's hope that I stay lucky and it's been cut for a master-key.'

While Belle had proved a ready learner, when being instructed by an expert in the art of picking open locks, she was aware of her limitations in that line. Given time, she could probably manipulate the mechanism of an ordinary lever-lock. If it should have been equipped with the accessory she mentioned, her chances of success would be considerably improved.

A 'lever' locked was operated by a series of small plates which fitted into the grooves of the bolt and prevented it from sliding. Each of the plates, or levers, had a notch in its end that corresponded with the notches of the key. When the key was turned, the pressure would raise all the levers to their correct positions and permit the bolt to function.

What Belle hoped to find was the addition of a master-key's lever. Set beyond the reach of the ordinary key, the 'master' lever was adjusted to operate all the other plates. It was a device often used in public buildings, allowing the janitor, or other persons in possession of a master-key, to enter several rooms without the necessity of carrying a bunch of individual keys.

Reaching into the V-shaped notch at the front of her left boot with her thumb and the tip of her forefinger, Belle drew a useful little tool from its sheath. It was a piece of thick, stiff wire about four inches in length and shaped like a miniature hockey-stick.

Guiding the implement into the keyhole, Belle tested the interior of the lock. Under her gentle pressure, she felt something give a little. Twisting at the pick, she caused the master-lever to perform its function. There was a faint click and the door moved in response to her push. Before opening it fully, she returned the pick to the sheath in the Hessian boot. That left her hands unencumbered and ready for use in her defence if the need arose. However, she wanted to have complete freedom of movement. So she reached up to unfasten her cloak.

Then a thought struck Belle.

If O'Reilly had locked the door behind him, why had he taken out the key?

Most likely because somebody else was coming and would wish to gain admittance.

The realisation came just too late.

Belle heard a faint sound close behind her. Then a hand caught hold of her left shoulder and swung her around. Something hard crashed into the side of her jaw before she could think of protecting herself. For a moment bright lights seemed to be bursting inside her skull. Then everything went dark and she crumpled limply to the ground.

## CHAPTER SIX

# YOU'RE GOING TO TELL US *EVERYTHING*

'Who the hell is she and where did she come from?' demanded a man's voice, hard, rasping, yet educated Southron in its timbre.

'Don't ask me,' replied a second set of male tones, higher pitched and less definable by accent. 'It's strange, but I've had a feeling all day that somebody was watching me.'

'I know it's not likely, but she could have come here looking for *you*,' suggested the first speaker. 'It's pretty well known that you're playing here tonight.'

'She was following *you*, I tell you,' protested the other man, sounding almost femininely petulant. 'I saw you coming along the street and was just going to call out when I spotted her. There was something in the way she acted that made me keep quiet. Sure enough, she followed you down the alley. And she was just coming in here when I sneaked up and dealt with her.'

'I locked the blasted door behind me!'

'She had got it opened—some way.'

Wishing they would stop, as the words seemed to be pounding like hammer-blows inside her head, Belle Boyd lay listening to the conversation. At first, the voices had seemed to be coming from a long way off; but they were rapidly drawing closer. Everything about her appeared to be sheltering in a swirling cloud of mist. Then a faint light pricked its way through, growing brighter until it started to hurt her eyes. Groaning a little, she tried to shield them from the glare. When she began to raise her right hand, the left stubbornly insisted on going with it for some reason.

Dull pain, throbbing in the region of her jaw, brought Belle to a partial realisation of her predicament. Then a fuller sense of understanding assailed her. Thoughts flooded through her disturbed senses, warning her that her situation might be desperate.

Belle became aware that she was lying on her back upon a hard, bare, wooden floor. Raising her head slightly, she discovered why her hands had functioned in unison. While she had been unconscious, her captors had crossed her right wrist over the left and lashed them firmly together with a gaily coloured silk scarf. There was one bright aspect, her arms were bound at the front and not behind her back. An experiment told her that her legs were still free.

The mists cleared completely and Belle gazed about her. What she saw, by the light of a lamp which stood on a table in what must be a dressing-room of the Bijou Theatre, was not calculated to lessen her forebodings and perturbation. The speakers were standing, gazing down at her. One she identified as O'Reilly—or 'Sheriff'—and he was scowling in a puzzled, menacing manner.

Not quite as tall as his companion, the second man was slender, with a pallid, weakly handsome face. He was dressed tidily, even fussily, in a black frock coat, frilly bosomed and cuffed white silk shirt, multi-coloured cravat, tight white trousers and highly polished town boots. His right hand toyed with a Remington Double Derringer which Belle recognised as being from her waistband.

From studying her captors, Belle completed her examination of the room. It was meagrely furnished with the dressing-table and two chairs. In the left rear corner, her cloak was hanging over a large trunk which bore the inscription, 'DEXTER OPAL. Eccentric Tramp Juggler And Distinguished Comedian'.

'Ah!' said the slender man, his voice high with excitement. 'Our mysterious visitor has awakened.'

'I bet you was worrying in case *you* had to be Prince Charming and kiss her,' O'Reilly answered dryly, then addressed Belle. 'Why did you follow me here?'

'I—I don't know what you mean,' Belle replied, wriggling into a sitting position with her back resting against the wall at the hinged side of the door. 'Wh-Why have you brought me here?'

'She doesn't know, Opal,' O'Reilly mocked.

'It won't work, girlie,' Dexter Opal warned. '*You* know why we brought you here. Now *we* want to know why *you* came. You're going to tell us *everything* we want to know. And it will be a whole lot less painful, if not as much fun for us, if you do it straight away.'

'I—I don't kn-now wh-what you mean,' Belle bluffed; and was called.

'And I hate to be lied to, girlie!' Opal hissed, advancing to drive his right foot viciously in the direction of Belle's body.

Having seen the play of emotion on the juggler's face, the girl had read his intentions. So she responded swiftly and with perfect timing. Flinging herself sideways, she avoided the kick. Grazing her shoulder in passing, Opal's toes impacted against the wall. A tinny screech of pain burst from him. Hopping on his left leg, he grabbed at the right's boot. Then fury distorted his features. Slamming his foot to the floor, he thrust forward the Remington.

'Quit that, damn you!' O'Reilly ordered, catching his companion by the shoulder roughly and jerking him away from the girl. 'She's got to answer some questions for us.'

'I'll make her answer, damn you!' Opal promised almost hysterically, twisting his shoulder from the other's grasp. 'I'll make her beg to answer.'

'Not here, blast it!' O'Reilly fumed, holding his arm across the other's chest and restraining him. 'She could have people looking out for her, Besides which, *they'll* soon be arriving for the meeting.'

'We could have the answers before they get here,' Opal protested, glaring malevolently in Belle's direction.

'I wouldn't want to bet on it,' O'Reilly answered, watching Belle return to a sitting position. 'She's not as scared as she wants us to believe. I'll bet she'd be a hard nut to crack.'

'Just leave me at her,' Opal suggested eagerly. 'I'll soon enough crack her for you.'

'I'll just bet you would, Tiger,' O'Reilly grinned. 'But not here. We'll take her to a cabin I know in the woods and you can go do it after the meeting.'

'You mean you're going to leave her here until then?'

'No. We'll take her there now. It'll be safer that way.'

'How do we do it, *walk*?'

'There's a livery barn along the street,' O'Reilly replied. 'Go fetch a rig and we'll take her in that.'

'You go and fetch it,' Opal snarled, showing his resentment at the other man's disparaging attitude.

'Why me?' O'Reilly challenged.

'Because I've a better reason than you have for being in here, if anybody belonging to this rat-trap comes.'

'There's that to it. Will you be all right until I get back?'

'If you mean, can I handle her?' Opal purred, studying Belle with cold, cruel eyes. 'Just let her try anything on with

54

me and *she'll* soon enough learn the answer.'

'I'll fasten her ankles and gag her be——' O'Reilly offered.

Tensing, Belle prepared to make a desperate fight rather than submit to having her legs secured. During the conversation, she had studied her bonds and believed that—given a suitable opportunity—she could unfasten the knot with her teeth. However, she knew that the men might do a better job and, with her legs bound, she would have no hope of escape.

'I can do that,' Opal assured his companion, solving the problem for Belle. 'You fetch the buggy. We don't have that much time to spare. And, if she has friends who'll be looking for her, the sooner she's away from here the better.'

'You're right,' O'Reilly admitted, reluctantly. 'I'll get back as quickly as I can.'

'You don't sound Irish,' Belle commented, as they heard the man close and lock the stage door. She wanted to delay the gagging as long as possible, in the hope that she might raise the alarm. 'If it comes to that, neither does O'Reilly.'

'Hah!' Opal ejaculated, slapping his thigh triumphantly as if he had made an important discovery. '*You're* working with that fool who's watching the warehouse.'

'Do you know who *he's* working for?' Belle challenged.

If her estimation of Darren's character was correct, the girl felt sure that he could not have resisted trying to impress O'Reilly by disclosing his official status.

'The Secret Service, he says,' Opal replied, confirming Belle's supposition. 'They must be short of men.' He paused and eyed her in a speculative manner. 'You're a Southron, aren't you?'

'Yes. But I'm also in the Secret Service. Your principals won't like it if you kill me——'

'Don't count on it,' the juggler jeered. 'They'd probably call you a traitress.'

'Why?' Belle inquired, genuinely puzzled by the comment.

'That's for me to know and you to find out,' Opal replied, with the air of one who had realised that he was on the verge of being indiscreet. 'Not that you'll get the chance to find anything out.'

Watching the slender man, Belle decided against taking any action at that moment. She wanted to be sure that O'Reilly was out of hearing range before she made her bid to escape. Until then, she meant to do all she could to lull Opal into a sense of false security. She guessed that she could keep him talking and divert his thoughts from completing the binding and gagging.

'Why are *you* involved in this business?' Belle inquired. 'You're not Irish, so it can't be for national reasons. Are you a Catholic?'

'Like hell I am!'

'Then that rules out religious motives. So it's for money——'

'Put your ankles together——'

'If it's for money,' Belle said, obeying. 'I can get you as much—in fact even *more*—than they're paying you.'

'*You* can?' Opal asked, halting as he started to back away.

'Certainly,' Belle confirmed. 'All you have to do is set me free——'

'And trust you to fill my hands with gold?' Opal sneered.

'Why not?' Belle countered. 'I don't want to die. And besides——'

'Yes?' Opal prompted, making no attempt to start tying her up.

'We're determined to break up this crowd you're working for. So we'd pay well for any information you could give us. And even better if you could help to place one of our people in their organisation.'

Clearly Opal was interested in the idea. Belle watched his brows crease and knew that he was turning it over in his mind. Frowning, he closed the dressing-room's door. Much to her delight, he still made no attempt to carry out further bondage.

'Stay where you are!' Opal warned, jerking up the Remington as the girl made as if to rise. 'I don't trust you.'

'But you like my proposition,' Belle guessed.

'It's a stupid idea,' Opal complained. 'How do I explain when Ga—O'Reilly tells them I've let you escape?'

'We'll make sure that he *can't* tell them.'

'You mean *kill* him?'

'That won't trouble you, the way he treats you,' Belle drawled.

'You're right!' Opal spat, mentally recalling all the insults and humiliation he had suffered at O'Reilly's hands.

'I know how you feel,' Belle said sympathetically. 'I like *girls* and I've had some of it.'

'I knew you *were*!' Opal breathed, eyes raking her from head to toe. 'Your hair, those clothes—— Can I trust you? Will your people do as you say?'

'Of course. With fifteen and a half million dollars at stake, they can afford to be generous.'

'Fifteen and a half million——?'

'I see *they* don't trust you enough to tell you *everything*,' Belle smiled. 'They're willing to *use* you, but they despise you because—— Well, that's what they could cost the United States if their plot succeeds. So we can afford to pay you handsomely.'

'Shut up!' Opal hissed, showing that her reference to the money had both puzzled and interested him. 'I want to think this thing out.'

'Go ahead, but think carefully,' Belle advised. 'We're on to that crowd's game. And we're not all as stupid as Mr. Darren *pretends* to be. It's only a matter of time before we lay our hands on *everybody* concerned in it.'

'I said shut up!' Opal snarled, menacing her with the Remington pistol. 'Stay right where you are.'

'Time's running out, but I can wait,' Belle drawled, settling down as if she felt sure that the result was a foregone conclusion. 'Just so long as you've decided *before* O'Reilly comes back.'

Stepping to the rear without taking his eyes from Belle, still gripping the Remington in a threatening manner, Opal hooked his rump daintily on to the edge of the table. Belle could sense the wavering of his attitude. If she guessed correctly, he was debating which line of action would be most advantageous to him.

Should he remain loyal to his employers, or would he be safer and better off if he accepted Belle's offer?

Belle knew that her fate, in fact her very life, hung on the answer.

Almost two minutes dragged by in silence, with Belle allowing Opal to stew in his own juice and draw his own conclusions. She had done all she could to lead him in the right direction. Playing upon his obvious greed, she had also reminded him of the contempt with which O'Reilly—and probably others—had regarded his homosexual tendencies. She had also established a bond with him by pretending to be a lesbian and, as such, understanding his problems.

Now everything rested in Opal's hands. Belle sensed that any further prompting from a woman, even one he assumed to be a lesbian, might turn him from the proposal. On the other hand, her hint that Darren might not be the dupe Opal imagined and the comment on the Secret Service's interest in the organisation were definitely weighing heavily in his considerations.

As clearly as if Belle had read the words on his face, she knew that Opal had reached his decision.

Even as the juggler rose from his seat on the table, the door of the dressing-room opened!

Due to the door swinging inwards, Belle could not see the new arrival from where she was sitting. With a cold, sickening feeling assailing her, she assumed that O'Reilly, or another member of the organisation, had appeared on the scene. Confronted by another conspirator, Opal might decide that discretion was the better part of valour. Especially as he could, if he had decided on the financial benefits of a betrayal, contact another member of the Secret Service without any great difficulty.

Then Belle became aware of how Opal was reacting.

'That didn't ta——' the juggler began, glancing at the doorway. Starting to bring his gaze back in Belle's direction, he snapped it rapidly towards the door once more, in what would one day be called a 'double-take'. 'Wha—Where——!'

The man framed in the doorway was not O'Reilly. Tilted at a jaunty angle, a black stovepipe hat topped a thatch of long-ish, flaming red hair. He was tall, well built. Almost V-shaped rufus brows grew thickly above deep-set eyes, a hooked nose, tight lips and a sharp chin. There was something sinisterly Mephistophelian about him, accentuated by his scarlet-lined black opera cloak, matching broadcloth coat, vest and trousers. His white shirt had wide, hard-starched detachable cuffs, a celluloid collar and a black silk cravat knotted in the manner of a bow-tie.

'Hello, Dexter,' the newcomer greeted. 'They said at your rooming-house that I'd find you here. I've been waiting all day to get a chance to talk with you in private. I suppose you remember me?'

'M-Mephisto!' Opal croaked, staring in fascination at the speaker. 'I—I heard you were d-dead.'

'The report was premature,' the man replied, having glanced about him as if to make sure that they were alone in the theatre. He advanced into the room. 'Although I was close——'

Realising that the newcomer was not O'Reilly, nor—if Opal's reactions were anything to go on—another member of the organisation, Belle twisted on her rump and kicked the door closed. That achieved the desired effect of bringing the man's attention in her direction. At first he seemed to be on the point of defending himself. Then, as his eyes roamed over her and took in her bound wrists, a smile of understanding flickered to his lips.

'What's this, Dexter?' the man inquired sardonically, returning his gaze to the juggler. Taking off his hat with the left hand, he held it so that the right was just inside its mouth. 'Don't tell me you've started playing your little games with *girls* now?'

'What do you want here, Mephisto?' Opal challenged.

'Information,' the man replied. 'I'm looking for good old Simmy Lampart. Where is he?'

'How would I know?' Opal demanded, then went on just a shade too quickly. 'I did hear that he's gone to Mexico.'

'He's not there, and you know it,' Mephisto growled. 'Come on, Dexter, tell me where I can find him and I'll leave you to go on playing bound-and-gagged with the lady.'

'I don't know how true it is,' Opal said, spitting out the words like an alley cat faced by a hound dog. 'But I did hear he's founded a town for outlaws somewhere in the wilds of Texas.'

'So that's what you heard, is it?' Mephisto purred.

'A dancing boy I know met an outlaw called Joey Pinter who'd been there,' Opal elaborated, raising the Derringer to line it on his visitor's chest. 'He said Simmy and Giselle do their magic tricks to entertain the Indians. You know, their sawing-the-woman-in-half routine. Now get going!'

'You're sure it was them?'

'The descriptions fitted them. Now go, I've done all I can for you.'

While the men had been talking, Belle had taken the opportunity to adopt a posture which would permit a great freedom of movement. Easing herself upwards, she halted kneeling on her bent right leg and with her left foot braced against the wall, to be used as a spring that would propel her erect in a hurry when the time came. She also studied the newcomer and drew certain conclusions. That mop of red hair was a wig and his face——

'It's not quite that easy,' Mephisto explained with disarming pleasantness, ignoring the Derringer's ·41 calibre superposed tubes. He dropped the hat and his left hand rose to rub at the underside of his jaw. 'You see, Simmy is another who thinks

I'm dead——'

'So?' Opal challenged.

'So *you* know I'm alive and you always were a blabber-mouth,' Mephisto replied. 'I'd hate for anything to disillusion Simmy about me.'

With that, the man twisted his extended right arm and a bunch of brightly coloured paper flowers materialised—apparently from thin air—in his hand. At the same instant, his left fingers hooked under and seemed to rip all the skin and hair from his head.

Removing what Belle had suspected was a cleverly constructed mask, the man exposed what lay underneath.

There was no face as such!

Only a hideous mass of cratered, seamed, dirty-grey flesh without any real semblance of a nose or lips; but from which glowed deep, burning, hate-filled eyes.

## CHAPTER SEVEN

## YOU'RE NOT MUCH BETTER OFF

Letting out a strangled, horrified gasp, Opal swung his head away from the ghastly sight presented by Mephisto. Down whipped the scar-faced man's left hand. Still clasping the mask and wig—which looked like a grotesque, bloodless scalp removed by an Indian warrior—he struck the top of Opal's extended right wrist with some force. The Remington slipped from the juggler's limp fingers and he involuntarily stumbled back a couple of steps.

Up and across whipped Mephisto's right hand. The lamp's light flickered briefly on something which gave off a metallic gleam amongst the paper blossoms. Their heads passed beneath Opal's chin and jerked sideways. A momentary shocked and pained expression twisted at the juggler's features. Blood gushed thickly from a gash, which laid open his throat almost to the bone, in the wake of the moving flowers. Gagging out strangled, meaningless words, Opal twisted around and stumbled blindly across the room. With hands clawing unavailingly at the terrible, mortal wound, he collapsed against the wall and slid to the floor.

Although the sight of Mephisto's ravaged features, taken with the expression on Opal's stricken face, almost nauseated Belle, she forced herself to remain calm. To give way to panic, or 'go woman'—as the Rio Hondo gun wizard, Dusty Fog,* had once referred to becoming hysterical—might easily prove fatal. She would need every ounce of her courage, and to keep her wits about her, if she hoped to survive.

'Th-Thanks, mister,' she said, staying in her crouching posture and contriving to sound grateful. 'I think he was planning to kill me.'

'Was he?' Mephisto replied, moving forward with the bloody blade of the razor-sharp spear-pointed knife seeming almost incongruous in its surrounding of gore-soddened paper

* Details of Belle's association with Dusty Fog are given in *The Colt and the Sabre*, *The Rebel Spy*, *The Hooded Riders* and *The Bad Bunch*.

flowers. 'Then you're not much better off.'

Belle did not need an explanation of what he was implying. Having seen him commit a cold-blooded murder, she could make an excellent witness for the peace officers who would investigate his crime.

Studiously avoiding looking at Mephisto's face, Belle concentrated upon watching his right hand. He lunged forward, directing his thrust towards her torso. It was the swift, deadly efficient attack of a trained knife fighter.

Instinctively, almost without the need for conscious thought, Belle's *savate* training had supplied a possible solution to her predicament. Thrusting with her left foot and straightening her right knee, she rose swiftly. Using the momentum of her rising, she brought up her left leg and swung it in a circular motion. The inside edge of her left boot struck the man's arm at the elbow before the knife reached her. Such was the power of the kick that it not only deflected the blade, but also caused his upper body to turn away from her.

Lowering her foot, Belle ducked her right shoulder and charged. She rammed into Mephisto's back before he had recovered from her kick, Dropping his mask, wig and weapon, he went reeling away from her. Colliding with the dressing-table, he sent the lamp flying and rebounded at an angle. His progress was halted when he ran up against the corner of Opal's trunk. Falling to the floor, the lamp broke and its fuel burst into flames.

Staggering slightly from the impact, Belle managed to regain control of her movements. Then she made preparations to defend herself even more effectively. Darting to where the Remington pistol lay, she grabbed for it. Having her wrists lashed together did not prevent her from retrieving the weapon; although she moved more clumsily than would have been the case if she was free. Her fingers curled around the Derringer's 'bird's head' handle. Hooking her thumb over the hammer, she eased it back to full cock; a precaution which Opal had failed to take. Holding the weapon, she swivelled, dropping into a crouching position, ready to start shooting.

Having lost his disguised knife, and realising that the girl was not acting in blind panic, Mephisto sought for some other means of protecting himself. His eyes flickered to where the flames were licking up the wall and spreading from the shattered lamp. Snatching up Belle's cloak, he flung it at her. It landed over her head and shoulders, enveloping the Derringer as it slanted in his direction.

Belle flung herself to the wall, fighting to throw off the cloak. Instead of following her, Mephisto bounded to and snatched up his mask, wig and hat. He then darted to the door, ignoring the girl. Jerking it open, he plunged out of the room.

Although she dragged away the cloak, Belle continued to grasp it in her left hand. Following Mephisto from the dressing-room, she found that he was already well on his way to making good his escape. Before she could do anything constructive, he had gone through the stage door and disappeared into the darkness. Belle did not attempt to follow, knowing that she must leave his capture to the local peace officers.

Turning back, she felt the heat of the growing fire beating at her and gave her attention to Opal. One glance, even across the width of the room, told her that he was beyond human help. Nor, with the way the flames were spreading, could she make a search of his property.

Still clutching the cloak, which she knew that she would need if she hoped to return to her hotel unnoticed, Belle quit the dressing-room. She was on her way to the stage door, which Mephisto had left wide open, when a male figure appeared at it. For a moment, she wondered if the scarred man had returned. Then she realised that it was somebody just as dangerous to her well-being.

It was O'Reilly!

What was more, the recognition was mutual!

Letting out a snarling curse, the man sprang forward. His right hand dipped into his jacket pocket and emerged gripping a Colt Cloverleaf House Pistol.*

Encumbered by the cloak, Belle responded in the only way she dared under the circumstances. Raising the Derringer, she found the task easier in that her right hand was supported by the left wrist. Swiftly she took aim, remembering the old Texas' axiom that 'Speed's fine—but accuracy is final', and shot to kill. A ·41 ball spiked between and just over the man's eyes. Spinning around, he let his revolver fall and followed it down.

Running towards the stage door, Belle glanced at O'Reilly and went out. Behind her, the flames were roaring and throwing an eerie red glow from the dressing-room's door. She heard yells of alarm and shouts of 'Fire!' Remembering that her

* Despite its name, the Colt Cloverleaf House Pistol is a revolver,

captors had spoken of other members of the organisation being expected at the theatre, she did not linger in the hope of obtaining assistance to free her hands. Holding the cloak out to one side, she darted as fast as she could towards an alley between two darkened, empty-looking buildings.

Standing in the shadows of the alley, Belle looked about her and strained her ears to detect any hint of Mephisto's presence. Later she might find time to ponder on the reason for his visit to the theatre and wonder if his search for 'good old Simmy Lampart' was connected with the hideous damage that had been inflicted upon his face. She would also remember to notify the appropriate authorities about the 'town for outlaws' which Lampart was alleged to have founded in the wilds of Texas.*

At that moment, however, Belle's only concern with Mephisto was in locating and dealing with him if he should be lurking in the vicinity.

Satisfied that the strange, terribly scarred man had not lingered after fleeing from the theatre, Belle dropped the cloak and tucked the Remington into her waistband. Gratefully, she turned her thoughts to finding the means of escaping from her bonds.

Lifting her wrists, she felt for and gripped the knot with her teeth. The men had improvised, using the silk scarf as being the item most readily available and confident that she could not escape as long as they had kept her under surveillance. Free from such observation, she made short work of the knot and it yielded to her teeth's tugging. Released from the scarf's clutches, she dropped it with a sigh of relief and retrieved her cloak. Donning it and raising the hood, she peered back in the direction from which she had come.

Although a number of people had gathered at the theatre, so far no fire-fighting appliances had arrived. Nor, by the lack of interest displayed in her position, had she been seen as she had taken her departure. Some attempt was being made to deal with the blaze, apparently. Even as Belle watched, two men emerged from the stage door, dragging O'Reilly's lifeless body between them. She wondered what they had made of finding a dead man—shot in the head—inside the burning building.

* The reasons why Mephisto was searching for Simmy Lampart, along with details of 'the town for outlaws' are given in *Hell in the Palo Duro* and *Go Back to Hell*.

64

Which raised the matter of what Belle should do next.

The most obvious answer was for her to notify the police of her part in the affair and give them a description of Mephisto.

Unfortunately, in Belle's line of work, the obvious answer was only rarely acceptable.

If she told the authorities her story, they might possibly be able to find and arrest the hideously marked man. On the other hand, it was such an unlikely story that they might not believe her. In either event, time would be wasted while they checked up on her veracity. General Handiman would not be pleased if word leaked out that Belle Boyd, the Rebel Spy, was employed as a member of the United States' Secret Service.

There was also another, more immediate aspect to consider before she reported to the civic authorities. A proportion of the police in every large city were Irishmen. Which meant that one of them, already involved in the plot, might hear what she had to say and inform his fellow-conspirators.

By returning to the Travellers Hotel immediately, Belle might find the opportunity to search O'Reilly's room. If she should be held by the police and one of them happened to be in league with the conspirators, he could arrange for somebody to anticipate her, visit the dead man's quarters and remove any evidence.

So Belle knew that she must keep quiet for the time being. Perhaps by doing it, she might allow Mephisto to escape. Nothing she had seen of Opal caused her to regret delaying, possibly even ruining, the peace officers' chances of arresting his murderer.

Having reached her conclusions, Belle put them into practice. Wrapping the cloak tightly about her, she stepped from the alley. If anybody outside the theatre noticed her, they did not connect her with the fire. So she returned to the street without being interrupted. Walking along until she saw a one-horse cab, she hailed it and asked to be taken to the Travellers Hotel.

On her arrival at her temporary home, Belle paid off the cab. She entered and crossed the foyer. The desk clerk gave her a cursory glance, then resumed his scrutiny of the newspaper he had been reading. Meeting nobody on the stairs, the girl was delighted to find the first floor's passage equally deserted. She knew the danger of passing up a good opportunity and figured that she had best cash in on it. Although she had not conducted any tests, she felt sure that the hotel's locks would be fitted to handle a master-key. If so, she would find no difficulty in gaining access to O'Reilly's room.

Removing the pick from its sheath in her boot, Belle went to work. Her belief was justified by results. Finding the master-lever, she unfastened the lock and entered the room. Bolting the door, to prevent anybody from coming in and catching her, she made other arrangements for her safety. Crossing to it, she opened the window and placed the rope—secured to a ring in the wall and supplied as a means of escape in case of a fire—ready for tossing out and use if the need arose. Then she increased the flame of the lamp on the dressing-table.

Starting with O'Reilly's working clothes, which were on the end of the bed, Belle went through every pocket. Making certain that she left no trace of her examination, she searched his other garments. There was not so much as a scrap of paper to help her. Nothing in the room hinted that O'Reilly, or Sheriff, belonged to an Irish nationalist movement.

Turning from the clothing, Belle extended her efforts to the room. The dressing-table's drawers and the bed proved to be as unproductive as his garments. Inside the wardrobe were two carpetbags. Taking one of them up, she was surprised by its weight. So she set it on the floor and opened it, to find it held what looked like two lumps of coal. Puzzled, Belle reached for the larger lump. As soon as she touched it, she sensed that it was something a whole lot more dangerous than coal.

One of the problems which had faced the Confederate States all through the War had been how to counteract the strangling efficiency of the Federal Navy's blockade on Southern ports. To this end, several devices had been manufactured and used with various degrees of success. Amongst the most novel had been the 'coal torpedo'.

Simple to produce, effective in operation, the device—it would have been called a booby-trap in later years—had been nothing more than a hollow-cast chunk of iron, filled with gunpowder and shaped like a piece of coal. To further disguise its purpose, it had then been coated with tar and coal dust. The idea behind the deception was that, when left by Confederate agents in Union marine fuel depots, the torpedoes would be taken aboard Yankee warships. When a torpedo was fed into a furnace by a stoker, it exploded and blew up the boilers. Belle knew that at least three Northern vessels had been set on fire and destroyed in such a manner.

What Belle could not understand was why O'Reilly would

have the 'coal torpedoes' in his baggage. Great Britain had the most powerful navy in the world, so they might be intended as a means of dealing with blockading warships. Or they could have some other purpose in the fight to 'liberate' Ireland. Maybe the two examples were being sent to show 'freedom fighters' in the 'ould country' how to produce more of them. Yet Belle thought that the organisation ought to be able to find some better way of transporting the samples.

Slowly the girl turned the 'coal torpedo' over in her hands. It looked as if it had been made some time ago. While it was black, all its original coating of tar and coal dust had been removed. That had left a metallic glint which might be noticeable when compared with the genuine article.

Belle wondered where the 'coal torpedoes' had come from, Possibly they had been part of a consignment overlooked at the end of the War, or kept as mementoes. Irishmen had rendered good and loyal service to the Confederate States and one of them might have had the dangerous items in his possession or have known how to make them. If it came to a point, a man with Northern persuasions might have heard about them and decided to make some for his own purposes.

Realising that she had neither the time nor the inclination for idle conjecture, Belle replaced the 'coal torpedo'. She put the bag back into the wardrobe and ascertained that its companion was empty. Satisfied that the room held nothing of interest, she reduced the lamp's glow. Closing and fastening the window, she went to the door. Opening it, she stepped out ready to act as if she had been making a legal visit. She still had the passage to herself, so she locked the door behind her.

Safely in her own room, Belle removed the cloak. She studied her reflection in the wardrobe's mirror, touching her jaw gingerly and wincing a little. After making such repairs as she felt were necessary to her appearance, she sat on the bed and gave thought to her next line of action.

Once again Belle was faced with the problem of what to do for the best.

Should she stay at the hotel and hope that somebody would come to search O'Reilly's room? Or ought she to go as arranged to examine the consignment in Molloy's warehouse?

If she took the former alternative, she might be able to follow whoever arrived when they left and see what developed. A sound and profitable way of spending the rest of the evening

—provided that somebody came and presupposing that she could follow him after his departure without being detected or otherwise losing him.

Against that, there might not be an attempt to collect O'Reilly's belongings that night. Maybe his companions, or superiors, would not want to take a chance on drawing further attention to him. The police would be interested in him already, more so than was comfortable for the organisation. Adding a further mystery would not be to the conspirators' advantage.

Could the others rely upon O'Reilly not to be in possession of incriminating documents?

Belle was inclined to believe that they might. From what she had seen and deduced, O'Reilly was an intelligent man and might be high in the organisations's chain of command. As such, he would know better than keep incriminating papers in a hotel room. The 'coal torpedoes' would mean little or nothing, and might be ignored as unconventional but innocuous souvenirs. They might puzzle the police but would not be connected with the organisation.

So the girl would gamble on the attempt not being made that night.

A fresh, alarming thought gave added strength to her decision. She had to consider Darren. He might have made a fool of himself, but it was technically still his case. So he had the right to know everything that had happened that evening. There was also another point about him for her to consider.

Not only was he expecting Belle, but his life might be in peril.

Everything depended upon the conclusions drawn by the conspirators regarding O'Reilly's killing. If they decided that Darren had been fooling them and was not their dupe, they could figure on closing his mouth. Despite the prominent manner in which he displayed his gun—or rather because of it—Belle doubted if Darren would be capable of protecting himself against an unexpected attack.

What was even worse from Belle's point of view, she could indirectly contribute to Darren being taken unawares. Hearing a knock at his door and expecting her to arrive, he was likely to open up without first checking who might be at the other side. Belle might dislike Darren, but she had no desire to have his death on her conscience.

Replacing the cloak, Belle hurried down to the foyer and

asked the desk clerk to find her a cab. If he was puzzled by her second departure, the man concealed it very well. Leaving the desk, he carried out her request. While he was gone, Belle wondered if she might confuse a possible visitor to O'Reilly's quarters. She remembered hearing of how a professional gambler of her acquaintance had saved his life by altering the number of his hotel room.* However, she decided against making such an attempt. Probably whoever came would know in which room O'Reilly had been lodging, so would be suspicious if he checked and found an alteration in the register.

Boarding the cab, Belle told its driver to go to the street upon which the warehouse and Darren's hotel were situated. While being carried in the required direction, she felt the uneasy sensation rising again. Somehow, she was certain that there were ramifications to the affair which had not yet fully come to her attention.

* Told in *Cold Deck, Hot Lead*.

## CHAPTER EIGHT

# THE SHIPMENT'S GOING ON SATURDAY

'Hello, Miss Boyd,' Darren greeted, having opened the door without checking who was at it. However, he stood with his right hand concealed and she guessed that it held his revolver. She also figured that the weapon was there merely to impress her with his preparedness. 'I'd almost given you up.'

'I had a little difficulty getting here,' Belle replied, walking by him.

Having left the cab some distance from the hotel, Belle had continued the journey on foot. She had kept a keen watch for anybody who might have had the building under observation, but felt sure that none were present. The hotel did not maintain a permanently manned desk, so she had gone unchallenged on her arrival. At Darren's door, she had paused and steeled herself against the possibility of having reached him too late. It had been a relief when he had opened up to her knock.

Watching Darren twirl the bulky, short-barrelled British Webley Bulldog revolver on his forefinger, as a preliminary to tucking it under his waistband, Belle could hardly hold down her smile. There was no wonder that the Irishman had become suspicious of him. However, he had shown sufficient good sense to dress suitably for the expedition. The clothes he had worn earlier were replaced by a black shirt, matching trousers and Indian moccasins.

'What kind of trouble?' Darren inquired, then remembered his duties as a host. 'Let me take your cloak.'

On removing and handing over the cloak, Belle saw surprise and then grudging approval flicker across Darren's face. He laid the cloak on the bed and indicated a chair at the table.

'Did you see the fire at the Bijou Theatre?' Belle asked, sitting down.

'Is that where it was? I saw the glow and heard the commotion. By the way, O'Reilly said that the shipment's going on Saturday.'

In his eagerness to pass on the choice tit-bit of information, Darren was clearly dismissing the fire at the theatre and Belle's difficulties as of minor consideration. He searched her face for some hint that she was over-awed by his words. Nothing showed. In fact she appeared to be taking it very casually.

'How did you come to meet him?' Belle wanted to know.

'In the saloon along the street,' Darren replied. 'Not that I make a habit of going into saloons when I'm working——'

'It's lucky that you broke your rule. But *how* did you get to know him?'

'Luck, mostly. He was cursing Molloy for a Protestant son-of-a-bi—Well, I could see that he didn't like Molloy. You know how Irish Catholics are where the Protestants are concerned?'

'I've heard about it,' Belle admitted, but the full significance of the words did not register at that moment. She was to remember them later. 'So you made him an offer to spy on Molloy?'

'It took a little longer than that,' Darren protested. 'But that's about how it happened. He's been very useful.'

'I'm sure he has. Where does he live?'

'I couldn't say for sure. Nor far away, most likely.'

'At the Travellers Hotel?'

'That's not likely,' Darren stated. 'It would be too expensive for him.'

'I'd have thought that,' Belle remarked. 'Except that I followed him there after he left you.'

'He must have been delivering a message, or something!' Darren insisted. 'On his pay, he couldn't afford to live there.'

'Not on a warehouse hand's pay, I agree,' Belle drawled. 'But he's been there since the day the consignment reached Memphis. Claiming to be a Pinkerton detective, Sheriff by name.'

'How did the Pink-eyes\* get involved?' Darren asked dazedly, then a glint of understanding showed. 'I suppose they're on to this affair and are trying to show they're more efficient than the Secret Service, as usual.'

Ever since Allan Pinkerton had retired from the Secret Service at the end of the War and had resumed operations with his National Detective Agency, there had been considerable rivalry between the two organisations. Members of the Secret Service believed, possibly without justification, that the Pinkerton family would not be averse to seeing them fail in their appointed duties; and for Congress to be compelled to turn to

\* Pink-Eye: derogatory name for a member of the Pinkerton National Detective Agency.

the National Detective Agency for assistance.

'I'd be surprised if O'Reilly really was a Pink-Eye,' Belle stated. 'That was just an excuse he used at the hotel; so that he could come and go in his working clothes without arousing comment.'

Watching Darren's face start to register alarm and realisation, Belle suddenly felt sorry for him. He was young, inexperienced, but desperately eager to make good. Possibly he had never received any training for the exacting work in which he was engaged. Trying to break her news as gently as possible to him, she went on to describe all that had happened since she had left him.

'You went alone?' Darren growled, when Belle reached the point where she had broken into the theatre.

'Everybody makes mistakes,' Belle answered, with an attitude of apology that she did not feel. 'I believe that I could take him prisoner——'

'You——?'

'I'm an expert at *savate*; and I expected to have the element of surprise in my favour.'

'Yes, but——'

'It *was* a mistake.' Belle conceded. 'But *all* of us make them. Don't *we*?'

'Yours could have gotten you killed,' Darren warned, taking the point.

'It nearly did,' Belle admitted wryly, touching her jaw. Continuing with her story, she concluded by saying, 'Neither Opal nor O'Reilly were Irish.'

'O'Reilly always sounded like a Mick-lander to me,' Darren protested.

'Not when he was speaking to Opal, he was a Southron then,' Belle countered. 'Of course, he would probably have put on an Irish accent for your benefit.'

'How about Opal,' Darren inquired, changing the subject. 'I've seen him on the stage, but he does a dumb act and I've never heard him speak. Where does he fit into all this?'

'That's puzzling me, too. Apparently they were planning to hold a meeting of some kind at the theatre tonight——'

'Not *tonight*. Opal had taken over the Bijou to give a show for Confederate veterans. A *free* show, so there'd be a good attendance.'

'And provide an excellent excuse for a large number of conspirators to get together. Nobody would notice them,

72

attending a free show at a theatre.'

'That's true,' Darren agreed. 'O'Reilly's crowd must have employed Opal to do just as you say. But he's an important performer. Why would he do it?'

'For money, I'd say,' Belle guessed. 'It certainly wasn't through patriotism, or any other high motive. I'd almost persuaded him to set me free and help us against them, for a price when Mephisto walked in.'

'Who is this Mephisto?' Darren asked.

'A professional magician, or something of the kind, I'd reckon. He must have picked the lock, which wouldn't take a genius. But the way he produced the bunch of flowers was no beginner's trick. Opal knew him and seemed surprised to see him, but I don't think he's connected with our business.'

'Or me,' Darren agreed, showing that he was willing to dismiss Mephisto from his thoughts on those grounds.

'What do we do about him?' Belle demanded.

'Who?'

'Mephisto. He murdered Opal in cold blood.'

'For his own private reasons. He's hardly our concern——'

'The hell he isn't!' Belle barked, then felt contrite as she identified the cause of her irritation. 'I'm sorry. My conscience is pricking me. If I'd gone straight to the police——'

'They probably wouldn't have caught him. It's not likely he would have stayed around, with people coming from all sides to the fire,' Darren consoled her. 'Besides, it's possible that Captain O'Shea would be in sympathy with the Irish nationalists, even if he isn't in cahoots with them.'

'That's possible,' Belle sighed. 'In fact, I'd thought of it.'

'Anyway, I think you acted for the best,' Darren declared and put up almost the same reasons that Belle had considered when she was deciding against speaking to the police. 'What you could do is write an anonymous letter, describing this Mephisto and pretending that he killed Opal and O'Reilly while trying to rob the theatre. That way, O'Shea's men will know who to look for and we won't need to become involved.'

'That's what I'll do,' Belle agreed. 'But, if O'Shea's with them, it might make them suspicious. That could be dangerous for you.'

'We'll worry about that when the time comes,' Darren assured her.

'You said that the shipment will be going on Saturday?' Belle prompted, wanting to avoid a demonstration of heroics.

'Yes. They're sending it downriver to New Orleans.'

'Why New Orleans?'

'So it can be put on a ship for Ireland,' Darren replied. He did not add the words, 'of course', but they were there.

'They could do that far more easily in New York, or any of the East Coast ports,' Belle reminded him.

'Which is where we'd expect them to ship from,' Darren countered.

'True,' Belle conceded. 'Only that doesn't explain why O'Reilly should be telling you their plans.'

'I've been paying him for information.'

'How well do you pay him?'

'Huh?'

'Have you been paying him enough for him to have been able to move into the Travellers Hotel?' Belle elaborated.

'Of course I haven't!' Darren snorted indignantly. 'Unc— Mr. Stenhouse keeps a sharp eye on my—all his agents' expenditure. I gave O'Reilly five dollars for each report and increased it to twenty for tonight's information.

'That hardly seems enough money to have made him decide to turn traitor,' Belle admitted, having withheld any mention of the disparaging comments made by Opal concerning Darren's abilities. 'Could they have suspected that you're watching the shipment?'

'I don't see how they could have!'

'And you never let O'Reilly, or anybody else, know that you're a member of the Secret Service?'

'Certainly *not*!' Darren stated vehemently, but his cheeks reddened and he refused to meet her eyes.

'Then it's a mystery,' Belle drawled and let the subject drop.

There was nothing to be gained, other than profitless self-satisfaction, in exposing the young man's inadequacies. Belle knew that she would be working with him, at least until Saturday. Letting him know how badly he had failed would shatter his confidence. It was sure to render him useless for anything that might lie ahead.

Yet, as Belle knew, there were many puzzling aspects to the affair. Time, thought and investigation would supply the answers. Until then, Darren must be prevented from brooding and, if possible, stopped drawing the correct conclusions about how he had been fooled by O'Reilly.

'Is everything ready for our visit to the warehouse?' Belle

74

asked.

'Yes,' Darren replied. 'If you still think it's worth our while going.'

'Why wouldn't it be?'

'Well, we know that the shipment's going. So all we need to do is arrest Molloy and his men.'

'Which you could have done on the day that it arrived,' Belle pointed out.

'It wouldn't have got us anywhere then,' Darren objected.

'Nor will it now,' Belle replied. 'We'd pick up a few men, with little real evidence against them, and the remainder of the organisation will go free to make fresh arrangements.'

'Then what do you suggest?' Darren demanded.

'Do you know how the shipment is going to be carried out?'

'On the *Prairie Belle*——'

'Fortune still favours the fair!' Belle ejaculated.

'Huh?' grunted the puzzled male agent.

'Nothing,' Belle smiled. 'Go on.'

'I don't know any more. Except that it's to be held in Rattigan's warehouse until it's collected, just like here,' Darren responded, then an idea struck him. 'Hey though! If they were suspicious, he might have told me that to mislead me. Now they're counting on me relaxing. Then they'll move it earlier.'

'That's possible,' Belle agreed, having reached a similar conclusion. 'They might even be planning to move it tonight. The sooner we've taken a look at that consignment, the easier I'll be.'

'I've got the ladder, a bull's-eye lantern——'

'We won't need the ladder, given luck,' Belle interrupted. 'It's too early for that. Besides, Mephisto isn't the only one who can pick locks.'

Although he looked a little sceptical, Darren allowed Belle to have her way. Lighting his bull's-eye lantern, he escorted the girl from the hotel and learned some of the basic precautions to take when embarking upon such a mission. Not until Belle had checked on the street did she permit them to emerge. Next, she insisted that they took an indirect route to the warehouse. Reaching its left side door, she breathed a silent prayer that she could manipulate the lock. If she failed, the respect with which Darren was now regarding her would rapidly diminish.

Holding his Webley, the young man kept guard while Belle manipulated her pick. The lock was not equipped with a master-lever, but she managed to align and operate the other plates.

'Neatly done, Miss Boyd!' Darren enthused, as the lock clicked and Belle eased open the door.

'Thank you,' the girl answered, stepping into the gloomy building.

'The boxes are across this way,' Darren advised, opening the front of his lantern as he followed Belle inside. 'I'll——'

'Let me lock the door first!' Belle ordered, closing it hurriedly. 'Somebody just might happen by and try the handle.'

Instead of debating the matter, as would have happened earlier in their acquaintance, Darren yielded to greater experience. Still grasping the Webley in his right hand, he waited until Belle had relocked the door. Then they crossed the room to the consignment.

'There's no hope of opening these,' Belle commented, indicating the firmly nailed lids of the rifles' and ammunition's boxes. She took hold of an oblong box's rope carrying-handle and lifted to test the weight. 'But they seem to be all right.'

'Why shouldn't they be?' Darren demanded.

'No reason at all,' Belle answered, although she could think of at least one very good reason. 'Can you put the light on the bales, please?'

'There's no doubting what's in *them*,' the young man replied, doing as she had requested. He illuminated one of the bales. 'This has uniforms in it. There's a tear in the covering and you can see the buttons on a jacket. If you feel at the next, you can make out the shape of boots. The one with the hats has a rip in it, too. Not a big one, but it lets you see some of the brims. They're tucked one into another, you know.'

'Huh huh!' Belle grunted, bending closer to scrutinise the tear and the brass military buttons on a dark blue background. From them, she made a close study of the bale's edges.

'All of them have been opened and stitched again,' Darren informed her. 'The two men would have had that done so they could examine the contents before making the purchase.'

'Yes,' Belle agreed. 'Shall we go?'

'We may as well,' Darren affirmed, but his attitude stated that he believed they should never have bothered coming. 'What did you expect to find?'

'Not a thing,' Belle sighed and returned towards the door through which they had made their entrance. 'Kill that light!'

'Wha——?' Darren began, but obeyed. 'What is it?'

76

Aware of the necessity for unceasing alertness when on such a mission, Belle had constantly darted glances at the building's various windows. So she had observed a light through the one nearest to the left hand door. People were approaching, one of them carrying a lantern. Faintly, the sound of the words still inaudible, voices reached the intruders' ears. However, Belle did not notice any change in the timbre to suggest that they had seen the faint glow from Darren's bull's-eye lantern.

'What're we going to do?' Darren hissed and Belle could sense that his gun hand was quivering with eagerness.

'Stand one on each side of the door and wait,' Belle replied. 'If they come in, we'll jump them. Don't speak, crack your man on the head with your gun.'

'No shooting?' Darren whispered.

'Only if there's no other way of doing it,' Belle replied. 'There're only two of them, but others might be close by.'

'Or they could just be passing on their way home,' Darren sniffed.

Once again, the young man proved to be a poor judge of a situation. Nearer came the two men and their voices preceded them. By now, Belle and Darren could hear what was being said.

'What do you reckon come off at the theatre, Mick?' one of the pair was saying in deep, local accent.

'Sure and Gaylorne must've been riling that swish* again,' replied the other. He at least sounded Irish. 'Opal never took to it. Maybe they had a fight, the lamp got knocked over and they shot each other.'

'Opal wouldn't've dared start anything,' the first man protested.

'Some of those swishes can get mean, you rile them enough,' Mick insisted. 'Way his body looked when they got the fire out, we'll never know if I'm right.'

'The Frenchman wasn't any too pleased about it. I'm not sorry he'll be going down the river tomorrow. He's a bad bastard when anything crosses him.'

'He got crossed tonight,' Mick commented. 'That fire ruined his meeting.'

'You sound as if that pleases you.'

'It does, Andy-darlin'. We're not ready for anything as open as that yet.'

'I dunno,' Andy replied, halting at the door. 'It wasn't going

* Swish: derogatory name for a male homosexual.

to be like it will in Shreveport.'

'What'll happen there?' Mick inquired. 'Hey! What're you doing?'

'Like Molloy said. Going in to make sure everything's all right.'

'Why bother? That damned knobhead at the hotel couldn't've gotten in. He only made it last time because we left the door in the hay-loft unlocked. Anyway, if he gets in, there's nothing for him to see.'

'Nothing he hasn't already seen,' Andy admitted. 'You know, Mick, there's a feller who's lucky to be alive. When the Frenchman heard he was following the stuff, his first thought was to kill the bastard. as painfully as possible. He'd have done it, too, but for Gaylorne saying we could make use of such a stupid son-of-a-bitch.'

Standing in the darkness, Belle could hear Darren breathing more quickly. Clearly he knew that he was the 'stupid son-of-a-bitch' in question. Maybe he was even aware that, in range-country parlance, a 'knobhead' was an exceptionally stupid, worthless mule. Certainly he must be boiling with rage and mortification at having his faults discussed in such detail. Belle hoped that he would control his temper and not disclose their position prematurely.

There was a faint scrabbling sound close to Belle's hand, then the lock clicked.

Crouching slightly in the stygian blackness, Belle prepared to launch a devastatingly effective *savate* attack upon one of the men as they entered. She hoped that she could rely on Darren to deal with the other. Easing back silently, she avoided being caught in the pool of light which followed the opening of the door.

'Aw, the hell with it, Andy,' Mick said, before either of them had stepped inside. 'Why bother? He couldn't get in and won't, anyway, after Gaylorne's told him we're moving the shipment this Saturday. I see more than enough of this place during the day, without going in on my own time.'

'And me,' Andy admitted, reversing the direction in which the door was moving. 'Let's go have a drink, then head back and say everything's fine. Hey though! I wonder who'll get to go now Gaylorne's dead?'

'So do I,' Mick agreed, while Andy locked the door and removed the key. 'If they was to ask for volunteers, 'tis myself who'd offer. I'd fancy a trip down to New Orleans.'

'So would I,' Andy drawled. 'Even if I did have to finish it riding in Tully Bascoll's boat. Come on. I'll let you buy me a drink.'

'Sure, and 'tis kindness itself you are to me, sir,' Mick replied. 'And I'm thinking it's not the likes of us who'll be getting that ride on the *Prairie Belle*.'

'I'm with you on that,' Andy was saying as they strolled away. 'But it'd sure be a sight to see, when it happens.'

Whatever Mick replied was lost as distance killed the sound of their voices.

## CHAPTER NINE

# YOU LOUSY TRAITOR

Twirling her parasol jauntily, as it rested on her left shoulder, Belle Boyd strolled along the wooden dock towards the *Prairie Belle*. It was Friday afternoon and she was going to renew an acquaintance with an old and trusted friend. She was no longer the 'Miss Winslow', who had a stateroom on the *Elegant Lady* and patronised the expensive Travellers Hotel. In fact, a lady of 'Miss Winslow's' class would probably have drawn aside rather than come into contact with a girl such as Belle appeared to be.

After Andy and Mick had taken their departure from Molloy's warehouse, Belle had faced the task of restoring at least a part of Darren's shattered confidence. Using tact, a little flattery and some good, sound common sense, she had convinced him that things were not so bad as they appeared. While he had made a few mistakes, Belle had insisted that he could redeem himself if he tried. Such had been her powers of persuasion that she had dragged him from the morass of self-criticism into which he was sinking.

Satisfied that, with Belle's guidance, he could make good, Darren had given her some interesting information. Clearly the organisation had wondered if he might have been responsible for the incident at the Bijou Theatre. That had been proven by the fact that they had checked up on him. Although Darren had neglected to mention it earlier, he had had a visitor before Belle had arrived. Dressed in the manner of a professional gambler, the man had claimed he was looking for a high-stake poker game and had come to the wrong address. Fortunately, Darren had been in the process of changing his clothes. So he had answered the door in his stocking-feet, grey trousers, no jacket and a collarless white shirt.

Not only had Darren given Belle a good description of his visitor, but—on meeting her at Stenhouse's hotel suite the following morning—had presented her with a sketch of the 'gambler's' face.

On hearing of Belle's single-handed visit to the Bijou

Theatre, Stenhouse had grudgingly admitted that she had acted in the only way possible under the circumstances. He had been less in favour of the Mephisto aspect of the affair. However, he had finally stated that Belle had been correct in her decisions. Promising that he would arrange delivery for the anonymous information, and try to learn from the police of any further developments, he had hinted that that side of their business was closed.

Referring to the meeting which Belle had heard her captors discussing, Stenhouse had claimed that it was unlikely to have taken place. Nor, in his opinion, would it have been of any great significance. Probably, he had said, it was no more than a means of raising funds to finance the proposed rebellion. Having no evidence to the contrary, Belle had been inclined to agree with Stenhouse.

There had been a variance of opinion regarding O'Reilly's motives in informing Darren of the shipment's departure. Taking the obvious line, Stenhouse had declared that it would be removed secretly before Saturday. Showing more imagination than previously, Darren had suggested that the organisation—having discovered that they were under surveillance by the Secret Service—might be willing to sacrifice the consignment. In doing so, they could be hoping to divert attention from other supplies already in transit or awaiting shipment.

Remembering the conversation which she had overheard at the warehouse, Belle had proposed that O'Reilly had been lying about the means of removal and destination. Perhaps the consignment would be placed on board the *Prairie Belle*, but unloaded at some point before New Orleans. After which, it would be transferred to some other, unsuspected boat to complete the delivery.

Realising the futility of continuing to debate the probabilities, they had turned to deciding what action they should take. For once, Belle had found herself in complete agreement with Stenhouse. There was insufficient evidence to arrest Molloy and his employees. Nor would anything of importance be gained by having the consignment confiscated. The organisation would only obtain more arms and continue their operations. To prevent this, they must lay hands on the leaders and organisers. With that in mind, Stenhouse had ruled that the shipment must be allowed to depart. Then Belle and Darren could follow it and, it was hoped, bring about the desired result.

They had also decided that Darren should, in fact must, continue with his established routine and behave as if he was unaware of O'Reilly's death. So he would have to avoid displaying any interest, or surprise, over his 'informer's' non-appearance until Friday at the earliest.

With the possibility of the shipment being moved before Saturday, it had been considered advisable that Belle should move into a vacant room at Darren's hotel. She would then be able to help him maintain a constant watch on the warehouse. That had meant she was compelled to purchase suitable clothing to let her blend into the neighbourhood.

Before concluding the meeting, they had examined the coverage given in Thursday's copy of the *Memphis Clarion* to the previous night's fire at the Bijou Theatre. There had been a brief sketch of Opal's career; the kind of thing he would probably have given to a reporter on his arrival. Mention had been made of the disappointment experienced by the Confederate veterans, who should have been his guests at the free performance he had arranged for them.

Captain O'Shea of the Memphis Police Department had personally assumed control of the investigation. He had deduced that Opal had been attacked by an unknown man. During the struggle, the lamp in the dressing-room had been broken and set on fire. Although the juggler had followed his assailant and killed the man, he had returned to the blazing room—presumably to save his property—and had been overcome by the smoke. The charred condition of Opal's body, when it had been recovered, had precluded any hope of discovering if he had suffered injuries which had contributed to his death.

There had then followed a comment which might have given Belle a clue if she had been in possession of other facts. Discussing motives for the 'mystery man's' attack on Opal, O'Shea had 'not ruled out the possibility of a pro-Union fanatic resenting the juggler giving a free performance to entertain ex-members of the Confederate States' Navy and Army'.

Having been working west of the Mississippi River for some months, the girl had lost touch with conditions in the Southern States. While Stenhouse might have enlightened her, he had failed to do so. In fact, when she had remarked upon O'Shea's statement, he had dismissed it as ill-advised but unimportant and had said pointedly that it was inadvisable to leave the warehouse unobserved for too great a length of time.

Taking the hint, Belle and Darren had left to continue their duties. The day and night had passed uneventfully and Friday morning had disclosed that the boxes were still in the warehouse. At noon, while Belle kept a watch from her room, Darren had visited the saloon in which he had made O'Reilly's acquaintance. He had been told by a man—who he had suspected was 'Mick', from the night visit to the consignment—that O'Reilly was ill and would not be back at work until Monday morning.

So, as there had been no further developments, Belle had decided to visit the *Prairie Belle*. Unless there had been a drastic change in the crew, she hoped to discover whether or not the consignment would be travelling on the boat.

To conceal her hair, and avoid having to use the inappropriate wig, she wore a cheap white 'spoon bonnet'; which covered her head and looked vaguely like the rear canopy on a Conestoga 'prairie schooner' wagon. Although old-fashioned, it was in keeping with her appearance of being a 'lady of easy virtue'. So was the form-hugging, sleeveless white blouse's extreme décolleté, the cheap, flashy jewellery she sported and the tight, glossy purple skirt which emphasised the contours of her hips.

Passing amongst the inevitable crowd of loafers on the dock, Belle felt sure that she was creating the desired impression. Nor, unless the man she had come to meet had changed his ways considerably, would her visit appear to be out of the ordinary.

Having come in at noon, the *Prairie Belle* was a hive of industry. The passengers had disembarked, but at the bows a steady stream of Negro roustabouts trotted along the stage-planks carrying cargo or returning for further loads. They were urged on by a bull-voiced, burly white mate who exhorted, praised, insulted but never really abused them. In fact, one formed the impression that the roustabouts were enjoying his efforts as much as the listening on-lookers. That figured, for the *Prairie Belle* had always had the reputation of being a happy ship.

Reaching the front of the crowd, twirling her parasol and swinging a cheap vanity bag from her other wrist, Belle saw a familiar face. A tall, well-built, good-looking young Negro, better-dressed than the roustabouts, stood watching them work with the air of one who had already completed his daily grind.

'Hi there, Willie,' Belle greeted, approaching the Negro and hoping that he would not betray her identity. 'Where'd I find Mr. Bludso?'

Before the Negro could reply, Belle sensed that somebody had moved to her side. A hand caught hold of her arm in a firm, hard grip.

'Now what'd a pretty gal like you want with the likes of Jim Bludso?' demanded a hard, tough, but—Belle noticed gratefully—male voice.

Turning her head, the girl looked into a surly, bristle-covered face under a peaked dark blue hat. Her accoster was a big, thickset man, wearing a blue civilian uniform coat, black trousers and heavy Wellington-leg boots. His appearance matched his voice, hard and tough. From his right wrist dangled a length of stout knotted rope, like the 'starter' once used as a means of inflicting punishment by petty officers aboard ships.

'That's my business, bucko,' Belle answered, sounding as coarse as she looked. 'So get your cotton-picking hands off me.'

'I'd do it, was I you, Cap'n Bascoll,' the Negro advised politely.

'Who the hell asked you to bill in, shine-boy?' Bascoll demanded, still holding Belle's arm. 'On the *Stream Queen*, we keeps the niggers in their place. Don't we, Mr. Tyrone?'

The man to whom the words had been directed moved forward. Big, burly, he had a typically Irish cast of features. Dressed in a similar, if cheaper, manner to Bascoll. he had a heavy riding quirt grasped in his right fist.

'That we do, Cap'n,' Tyrone confirmed. 'Same as should be done on the *Prairie Belle*.'

'I ain't looking for fuss with you gentlemen,' Willie said quietly, glancing from the *Stream Queen*'s captain to its mate.

'You ain't knowing your place, either,' Tyrone warned, hefting his quirt and striding forward. 'But we know how to treat uppy niggers on the *Stream Queen*.'

Watching Willie clench his fists, Belle prepared to help him. To do so might draw unwanted attention her way, but she had no intention of allowing him to be assaulted on her behalf. The question was, how to do it without attracting too much notice by virtue of her fighting abilities. Luckily, a 'lady of easy virtue' could be expected to know a few defensive and offensive tricks.

The need for Belle's intervention did not arise.

Before Belle could move, she saw something hurtling through the air from the direction of the cordwood stacked ready to feed the furnaces on the *Prairie Belle*'s main deck. On striking and enfolding Tyrone's face, the missle proved to be a piece of oil-dripping rag. It had been flung, with considerable precision and accuracy, by the man Belle had come to see.

Bare-headed, with crinkly reddish hair. Jim Bludso—senior engineer of the *Prairie Belle*—was ruggedly good looking. He was tall' powerfully built, yet neither slow nor clumsy. Oil was streaked on his face and the muscular arms that protruded from the rolled-up sleeves of his grey flannel shirt. His black trousers were tucked into Wellington-leg boots and a long-bladed Ames Rifleman's knife hung in a sheath at the left side of his wide waist belt.

Vaulting from the main deck to the dock, Bludso sprang forward. Before Tyrone had managed to claw the oily rag fully from his face, the engineer had come within striking distance.

'You lousy traitor, Bludso!' Bascoll bawled, releasing Belle's arm and lunging in the engineer's direction.

Knotting his right hand into a useful-looking fist, Bludso propelled it solidly against the edge of Tyrone's jaw. The mate pitched sideways, dropping the rag and his quirt, before crashing down and rolling over three times on the hard wooden planks of the dock.

Raising the knotted rope's end, Bascoll intended to lay it vicious across Bludso's shoulders. Struck there, the engineer would be momentarily incapacitated. Long enough, certainly, for the captain to deliver a more damaging assault with fist or boot.

The treacherous attack was destined never to be completed. Realising that Bludso might not be able to turn fast enough to cope with his second assailant, Belle took an effective hand. Sliding the parasol through her fingers as she brought it from her shoulder, she grasped its end. Then she reached down, hooking the crook of the handle under Bascoll's rearmost ankle and jerking sharply. Yelling a curse, the captain stumbled. In his efforts to retain his balance, he let the rope's end fly from his fingers.

Turning as fast as a scalded cat, Bludso thrust out his left fist. Hard knuckles collided with Bascoll's nose and halted his advance. A sharp right cross turned it into a retreat. Shooting out first one fist then the other, Bludso drove Bascoll across the dock until the captain was teetering helplessly on the very edge of the planks. Catching hold of the dark blue jacket's breast with his right hand, Bludso restrained Bascoll from tumbling into the water. Then the engineer drew back his left fist.

'Mr. Bludso!' roared a voice from the pilothouse, which perched high on top of the *Prairie Belle*'s upper 'Texas' deck. 'Take your hands off Captain Bascoll immediately!'

'Aye aye, sir!' Bludso replied, having identified the speaker without requiring to look around, and, like any dutiful officer receiving a lawful command from a superior, he obeyed.

Perhaps Bascoll was grateful for the intervention, but it proved to be a mixed blessing. Although Bludso did not deliver another blow to the captain's already bloody and suffering features, he released his grasp on the jacket. Deprived of the engineer's support, Bascoll wailed and plunged almost gracefully backwards into the river.

'Behind you, Massa Jim!' Willie yelled.

Watching Bludso, Belle had not troubled to keep Tyrone under observation. Swinging her gaze in the mate's direction, she decided that Willie's warning was well-founded.

Shaking his head from side to side, Tyrone was in a crouching position like a sprinter waiting to start a race. However, his right hand was less innocently occupied. It was reaching towards the quirt which he had earlier discarded. From what Belle saw, the quirt served a second, more deadly purpose than as a mere inducer of recalcitrant horses, the force of its landing had caused the cap of the handle to separate from the remainder. Attached to the cap, and normally concealed inside the quirt, was a razor-sharp knife's blade.

Belle realised that Bludso could not hope to reach Tyrone and prevent him from picking up the knife. So she felt that, being closer, it was up to her to attend to the mate. With that in mind, she darted towards the man.

Reaching the same conclusion as Belle, Bludso did not attempt to advance. Instead, he sent his right hand flashing across to pluck the Ames knife from its sheath. Up, then down whipped his arm. Showing the same precision and aim as when he had flung the oily rag, he sent the weapon spinning through the air. As if drawn by a magnet, its eleven-and-three-quarters-of-an-inch-long blade guided the needle-sharp spear point into

Tyrone's right forearm.

Letting out a shriek of anguish, the mate forgot his intention of arming himself. Even as he tried to lurch upright, with his left hand grabbing at the hilt of the Ames knife, he found that he had further troubles coming his way.

Hitching up her skirt and wishing that she had decided to wear her elegant, but stoutly made, Hessian boots, Belle let fly with a kick. She found that she had no need to regret adopting footwear more in keeping with the character she was pretending to be. Her cheap high-buttoned shoes proved adequate for the occasion. Catching Tyrone under the chin with all the power of her slender, yet steel-muscled left leg, she caused his head to snap back. He rose at an increased speed for a few inches, then flopped forward limply. Considering the thud with which he landed, he might have counted himself fortunate that he was unconscious before his body and face struck the timbers.

'Hello, Jim boy,' Belle greeted, as the engineer walked towards her. 'Remember lil ole me?'

Already Bludso had been studying her in a calculating, yet not too puzzled manner. Recognition, surprise, then understanding flashed briefly across his face to be replaced by a broad grin.

'I surely do, gal,' the engineer confirmed, then indicated Tyrone with a jerk of his left thumb. 'What's up. Didn't you figure I could handle him?'

'I should have known you could,' Belle admitted truthfully, glancing about her to see if any of the on-lookers were inclined to take up hostilities on the behalf of Bascoll and Tyrone.

Although Belle failed to locate any further assailants, one of the crowd caught her eye. He was tall, dark, handsome and, if his style of clothing was anything to go by, a successful professional gambler.

That fact alone did not interest the girl.

If the sketch produced by Horatio Darren had been accurate, Belle believed that she was looking at the gambler who had visited the young agent's room on the night of the fire at the Bijou Theatre.

## CHAPTER TEN

## ARE THEY AFTER YOU, OR ME?

'You're lucky we weren't in Helena when you came to the *Belle* asking after me,' Jim Bludso remarked, as he and Belle sat at a side table in the almost empty bar-room to which he had escorted her. 'There's a lil red-haired gal there who'd get into a real tizz happened she'd heard you.'

'Knowing you, that could apply in Greenville, Vicksburg, Natchez and all points down to New Orleans; although maybe not always with a red-head,' Belle replied with a smile. 'In fact, I nearly didn't chance coming. I was a long time getting over the bruises from the first time we met.'

Bludso grinned in sympathy. The incident to which Belle referred had taken place during the War, in New Orleans. On an assignment to smash a Union counterfeiting ring which had operated in that city, Belle had required the services of a safe-cracker. Because of an incident involving a woman of Bludso's acquaintance, the girl had found herself in a boxing ring and compelled to fight a professional female pugilist.*

'Mind if I ask why you did chance coming?' Bludso drawled. 'Not that I'm not real pleased to see you again.'

Before answering, Belle glanced quickly around her. Apart from the bartender, idly shooting poker dice with a customer, they had the room to themselves. The two men were far enough away to be unable to overhear any conversation that took place. So Belle knew that she could supply her companion with the answer to his question. That was why they had come to the bar, to talk without the danger of anybody eavesdropping.

A soaking, furious Captain Bascoll had managed to haul himself from the river. His appearance on the dock had coincided with the arrival of a sergeant and a patrolman of the Memphis Police Department, which had prevented any further hostilities.

The peace officers had asked questions concerning the cause of the disturbance, learning that the captain and the mate of

* Told in *The Rebel Spy*.

88

the *Stream Queen* had been the aggressors. On being asked if he wished to prefer charges, Bludso had refused to do so. Accepting the decision, the sergeant had suggested that the two parties stayed aboard their respective vessels and saved their feuding until they were long gone out of his jurisdiction.

Due to being occupied in acting as a witness on Bludso's behalf, Belle had lost sight of the gambler who had attracted her notice amongst the crowd. That had meant she would be unable to satisfy her curiosity about him. So she had accepted Bludso's offer to go and talk 'old times' over a drink. Belle had wondered if it had been made due to the engineer's desire to satisfy his curiosity about her presence on the dock, or concerning her appearance. She had settled on the former reason when Bludso had selected the small bar-room after passing other, better patronised establishments.

'I need your help, Jim,' Belle said frankly.

'You've got it,' Bludso promised without hesitation. 'What can I do?'

'Find out if a certain consignment is being sent down to New Orleans on the *Belle* and, if it is, arrange for me to travel with you.'

'The first's's good's done. Second might take a lil fixing, though. We're likely to be running full. So I might not be able to get you a stateroom, unless you'd be willing to share.'

'I could share,' Belle admitted. 'But it might be better if I was alone.'

'Huh huh!' Bludso grunted. 'We'll go talk to le Verne. He's the clerk and he'll do what he can to help you.'

'I'd rather he didn't know who I am,' Belle hinted.

'It'll be me that he's doing the favour for,' Bludso answered. 'Shall we go and see him?'

'Don't you want to know what it's all about?'

'You want help's enough for me. But I figure you'll tell me as much as you can about it.'

'I will,' Belle agreed. 'By the way. Do you ever run across Madame Lucienne when you're in New Orleans?'

'Near enough every trip,' Bludso replied and nodded as if he was forming a clearer understanding concerning Belle's activities. 'I keep telling her how she's getting too old and fat for *that* game. All it gets me is a hide-blistering. That gal's got an educated tongue.'

The few lingering doubts, which Belle had harboured, faded

away with her appreciation of the meaning behind Bludso's words. If Madame Lucienne had let him know that she was now employed by the United States' Secret Service, Belle could rely upon his discretion and co-operation.

Recollecting Captain Bascoll's comment, accusing Bludso of being a traitor, Belle decided that the engineer's actions during the War were still misunderstood by some Southrons. Yet she would have imagined that, like her own, Bludso's connections with the Confederate States' Secret Service had been made public knowledge. Certainly the term 'traitor' struck her as being most inappropriate.

During the War, the original *Prairie Belle* had been sunk by raiding Yankee gun-boats. The crew had escaped and most of them had enlisted in the Navy of the Confederate States. Just as loyal as his companions, Bludso had elected to remain in New Orleans. Although he had worked for the Yankees, he had also been a very capable, effective member of Madame Lucienne's spy ring in that city.

Concluding that Bascoll might have employed the term to remind the on-lookers of Bludso's supposed treachery during the War—and so to enlist their support or sympathy—Belle put the matter from her thoughts. Holding nothing back, she told the engineer of her current assignment. On hearing that she was dealing with Irish nationalists, Bludso showed what Belle took to be a brief expression of relief. However it had come and gone again before she could be certain of its existence, to leave his face a mask of interest and understanding.

'So it's the Mick-landers you're after,' Bludso drawled quietly at the conclusion of the story.

'Who did you think it might be?' Belle challenged, puzzled by the comment.

'I wasn't sure. You folk handle more'n just spies and trouble-causers, way Lucienne tells it.'

'We do. I've been out West hunting counterfeiters for almost a year. And I'm not after any of your friends who might be doing some smuggling.'

'As if *I'd* know folks who'd do that, for shame,' Bludso grinned, then he became serious. 'Don't these fellers know what could happen if they go through with their game?'

'I doubt if they'd care, if they do,' Belle replied. 'Anyway, I have to try and stop them.'

'What I don't figure is why that O'Reilly bucko told your man they'd be sending the stuff on the *Belle*,' Bludso remarked.

'The way I see it, there are three possibilities,' Belle answered. 'O'Reilly lied about them sending it on the *Belle*. They are sending it, but not to New Orleans. Or O'Reilly told the truth for some reason. I like that one least of all.'

'We can soon enough check if they're sending it on the *Belle*,' Bludso declared, finishing his drink and shoving back his chair. 'Le Verne'll tell us that.'

'Will I hurt the bartender's feelings if I don't drink this?' Belle inquired, indicating her glass. 'One sip was enough for me.'

'I surely wouldn't want to hurt his feelings,' Bludso grinned, taking and sinking the girl's drink. 'After that, even engine oil'll taste good.'

Taking Belle on board the boat by the stern stage-plank, Bludso led her up the crew's stairs to the boiler—or cabin-deck. They went along the promenade and entered the big Gentlemen's Cabin section of the saloon. In the small office, next to a bar sufficiently magnificent in appearance that it would not have disgraced the finest saloon in the land, they found Hervey le Verne hard at work. The clerk of the *Prairie Belle*—he would have been called the purser on a sea-going vessel—was a small, bird-like man who conveyed an air of competence.

Setting down a list of supplies that he had been checking, le Verne looked from Bludso to Belle. On the point of returning his gaze to the engineer, the little clerk gave Belle a quick, but more careful scrutiny.

'Well, Jim,' le Verne said, lifting his eyes from their examination of the girl's hands. 'What can I do for you?'

'Do we have a shipment, four rifle-boxes, two ammunition, and four bales aboard this trip?' Bludso asked.

'Not yet. But we should have before sundown.'

'Where're we taking it?'

'Right through to New Orleans.'

'All the way, huh?' Bludso said.

'I hope so,' le Verne replied, his face impassive and almost disinterested apart from his eyes. 'It's being stowed right for-rard in the hold. That's why it's coming down today.'

'Who's sending it, and where to?' Bludso drawled, asking the question that Belle had wanted without the need for prompting.

'The consignors are the Shamrock Supplies Incorporated,

although I've never heard of them before,' le Verne answered, having checked on the cargo manifest which he plucked from amongst the other papers on his desk. 'The consignee is Rattigan's Warehouse, to await collection. Is that what you want to know?'

'Sure,' Bludso agreed. 'How're we off for cabin space?'

'Not an empty stall,' le Verne declared. 'We've one berth, but that's in a gentlemen's stateroom. There might be a vacancy, Miss——'

'Winslow,' Belle supplied, smiling.

'There might be a vacancy if you wouldn't object to doubling up with another lady, Miss Winslow.'

'We're sure fooling Mr. le Verne, Jim,' Belle remarked. 'Was it my hands?'

'Partly,' the clerk admitted. 'Mainly, though, it's part of my duties to separate those who *are* from those who are merely pretending to be.'

'Old Hervey knows every gambler, tinhorn, thief and conjuneero* on the Big Muddy,' Bludso praised.

'Not *every* one,' the clerk protested good naturedly.

On an impulse, Belle opened her vanity bag. She had placed Darren's sketch into it before leaving the hotel, in the hope that she might see and recognise the gambler. Taking the sketch out, she passed it to the clerk.

'Is this one of those you know?'

'His name's Brunel,' le Verne stated. 'Is there anything wrong with him?'

'Should there be?' Belle countered.

'I've never seen him before today,' the clerk replied. 'But he came this afternoon with a letter from a Mr. Gaylorne, cancelling a booking for a stateroom. Brunel said that he would take it. I agreed. After all, it's not an uncommon thing to happen.'

'Looks like he's coming instead of that O'Reilly bucko, Belle,' Bludso remarked.

'It does,' the girl agreed.

'I won't ask you what this is all about, Miss Winslow,' le Verne said soberly. 'But I feel I'm entitled to know if this man, or the consignment, will in any way endanger the safety of the *Prairie Belle*?'

'There's no reason that it should,' Belle replied. 'It's just that my organisation is very interested in learning where the consignment is going and who receives it.'

* Conjuneero: a confidence trickster.

92

'I see,' le Verne answered. 'Now, with regards to your accommodation——'

'Can you reserve the man's berth, please?' Belle requested. 'I'll have a male companion travelling with me.'

'Certainly, I'll see to it. But how about you? There might not be a lady's vacancy.'

'I could travel as a deck-passenger,' Belle suggested. 'That way, I could keep a closer watch on the consignment.'

'That won't be necessary,' the clerk objected. 'Once it's in the hold, there'll be no way of getting it out before we unload at New Orleans. On top of which, travelling as a deck-passenger isn't suitable for a lady.'

'It sure as hell isn't,' Bludso confirmed thoughtfully.

'*That's* the least of my worries,' Belle smiled. 'Very few of my kin-folks would regard my line of work as being suitable for a lady.'

'We might be able to accommodate you until a stateroom is available,' le Verne offered. 'There'll be one after Helena.'

'I couldn't spend much time on the main deck, if I'm travelling as a stateroom passenger,' Belle pointed out. 'That would draw too much attention to me.'

Neither of the men could dispute Belle's point. The 'deck-passengers' travelled on the main deck, taking whatever accommodation they could devise, as being the cheapest fare. There was no mingling socially between them and the occupants of the boiler deck's staterooms.

'Couldn't the man——' le Verne began.

'Brunel would recognise him,' Belle interrupted. 'That's why he's coming, to keep attention from me. Anyway, he wouldn't look the part as a deck-passenger.'

'There's one way out,' Bludso remarked hesitantly. 'Happen you're willing to chance it, that is.'

'What would it be?' the girl asked.

'Travel down dressed like you are now—and use my cabin.'

'You've only got the one bunk in there, Jim,' le Verne pointed out.

'I can always bed down by the engines,' Bludso countered.

'Would it be out of the ordinary if I did it?' Belle inquired.

'Not especially, except for Jim bedding down by the engines,' le Verne answered. 'Officers in single cabins are allowed to have their wives along. Some of them even bring *their* wives.'

'I'll bet it wouldn't be the first time you've done it, Jim,'

Belle commented with a smile.

'I'm not married,' the engineer protested and looked embarrassed.

'Which doesn't answer my question,' Belle remarked. 'Seriously though, I think it's a good idea. If I'm travelling as your "wife", Jim, I'll be able to come and go with greater freedom than either a deck- or a stateroom passenger.'

'There would still be the matter of where you both sleep,' le Verne warned.

'We'll face up to *that* problem when the time comes,' Belle declared. 'Come on, Jim. We're keeping Mr. le Verne from his work.'

'You'd best tell Captain Yancy what's happening, Jim,' the clerk advised as his visitors turned to depart.

'I'll do just that,' Bludso promised.

Leaving the office, Belle and Bludso passed through the hustle and bustle of the Gentlemen's and Ladies' Cabins. Already passengers were coming aboard and being escorted to their accommodation. Stewards and stewardesses were making everything ready for the journey. So there was considerable coming and going on all sides. When the girl and the engineer reached it, the Texas deck—on which the officers lived—seemed almost peaceful. The captain, both mates, the pilots and their cubs and Jim's trio of junior engineers were all attending to their duties. Passengers were discouraged from visiting the Texas deck in dock, and none were to be seen.

Belle suggested that it might be tactful if they reported to the captain before Bludso showed her to his quarters. Agreeing that to do so would be sound diplomacy, the engineer said that they would need to go up to the pilothouse.

Towering high in the air, the square, multi-windowed pilothouse was positively tranquil after the hurly-burly of the main- and boiler-decks. It was one area of a riverboat that had always fascinated Belle; although not one in which she had ever been encouraged to linger when paying a visit. With the great wheel—half of its twelve feet diameter disappearing into the Texas deck below—bells and bell-ropes, the whistle's cord and a speaking tube which connected with the engine-room, it was regarded as being male domain.

Belle had liked what she had seen of the tall, lean, smartly dressed Captain Yancy when he had joined them on the dock after the fight. There could not have been a greater contrast than between the master of the *Prairie Belle* and the ruffianly

Captain Bascoll. Yancy had been ready to back his engineer to the hilt and had shown that he would stand no nonsense.

Eyeing Belle in a coldly speculative manner, Yancy was nevertheless polite when Bludso introduced her as 'Miss Winslow'. On being asked for a few words in private, the captain had suggested that they should go along the deck. The pilot-house was occupied. On the long bench at its rear, the pilots were discussing conditions farther down the river with two of their opposite numbers from a boat which had just come up.

'If you wish to do so, I won't raise any objections to you sharing Mr. Bludso's cabin,' Yancy declared, after he had heard Belle's reason for making the request and had ascertained that Brunel's presence would not endanger his boat and passengers. 'But I'm afraid that I won't be able to offer you a place at my table.'

'Of course not.' Belle smiled. 'People would be suspicious if you did.'

While the captain of a riverboat might allow his officers to travel in company with women other than their wives, he could not acknowledge the fact openly. So, although he guessed that Belle was of a social status that might expect the hospitality of his table, he had known that he could not give it.

'One thing more, Miss Winslow,' Yancy remarked. 'If there should be the slightest hint of danger to the *Belle*——'

'I'll tell you straight away,' the girl assured him. 'But I don't think there will be.'

'Neither do I,' Yancy said. 'If I did, I wouldn't have given you permission to go ahead.'

Returning to the Texas deck, Bludso opened the door of his cabin and let Belle precede him into it. She looked around at what would be her base of operations for the next few days. There was a homely, yet masculine air about the room. Its furnishings were comfortable and adequate to the needs of a man like Bludso. There was a locker, a washstand, a small writing-table and chair, a chest and a narrow bunk.

'What's that?' Belle inquired, indicating a feminine hat-box in the centre of the bunk.

'A hat I've bought for that lil red-headed gal in Helena,' Bludso explained, walked forward. 'Take a look and tell me if it'll go with her hair.'

'How gallant!' Belle sniffed, following on his heels. 'Only a bachelor would dare to ask his "wife's" opinion about a hat he's bought for a lady-friend.'

Something at the extreme lower edge of the girl's range of vision attracted her attention. It was a small splash of bright colour, contrasting vividly with the bare white planks of the deck. While she was speaking, she lowered her gaze to take a closer look. The ends of two blue satin ribbons lay on the floor, extending a little way from beneath the bunk.

'My father 'n' grand-pappy both were lifelong bachelors and they allus taught me to stay the same,' Bludso grinned. Placing the base of the box on the palm of his left hand, he started to lift the lid with his right in a perfect parody of a snooty milliner exposing her latest Parisian creation. 'This hat——'

An alarm signal blasted its ways through Belle's entire being!

Jumping forward, the girl thrust with the tip of her parasol to knock the box from Bludso's palm. It flew from beneath the lid, landing on the centre of the bunk and tipping sideways. Bludso's startled exclamation almost drowned a sudden, sharp, violent hissing which was emanating from inside the box.

Almost, but not quite!

Hearing the sound, Belle and Bludso had had a fair notion of what might be making it even before the box emitted its contents. That still did not prevent its appearance from handing them one hell of a surprise and shock.

Something that looked like a four feet length of rope, as thick as a man's wrist, slid on to the bunk. Except that no piece of rope had ever been plaited with dull brownish, wrinkled skin, sporting an evil spade-shaped head, and endowed with the power to writhe and move under its own volition.

Instead of sliding to the deck, the big Eastern cottonmouth went into its fighting coil on the bed. Vibrating its tail like a rattlesnake, only without the accompanying warning sound, it threw back its head. Opening its mouth to show off the long, curved, poison-dripping fangs and darting, restless, forked tongue, it also exposed the snow-white interior which gave its species their name. All in all, it made a frightening sight as it poised ready to attack.

Involuntarily, Belle and Bludso stepped away from the bunk. Their movements brought the furious snake's attention to them. Fortunately, neither was incapacitated by shock to such an extent that they were unable to respond.

As swiftly as Bludso sent his right hand flying towards the

Ames knife, Belle moved even faster. Her left hand closed on and tugged sharply at the body of the parasol. Separating from the lower half, the handle displayed its clandestine second function.

Swinging her right hand outwards horizontally, Belle reversed its direction with a snapping motion of the wrist. Attached to a short steel rod, a small ball of the same metal slid into view. These were followed by a twelve inch length of powerful coil spring, into which they had been telescoped within the handle. Whipping through the air in an arc, the spring propelled the ball faster than the human eye could follow. Emitting a sickening 'thwack!', the ball impacted against the cottonmouth's head. With its deadly skull reduced to a harmless bloody pulp, the snake's body was hurled across the bunk to strike against the cabin's wall.

Shuddering violently, Belle spun on her heel to avoid watching the death throes of the hideous creature. At her side, Bludso was giving off a flow of invetive that was violently profane in content, but understandable under the circumstances. He, or Belle, had been very, *very*, close to death.

Several seconds went by before either of them regained his, or her, composure. Yet neither spoke until Belle had retrieved and reassembled her parasol and Bludso had returned the knife to its sheath.

'No,' Belle finally said, still not looking at the bunk. 'I don't think it would go with her hair.'

'This one might,' Bludso drawled, bending and drawing the hat—the ribbons of which had probably saved his life—from under the bunk. 'Only somebody's changed it since I fetched it on board.'

'I didn't think you'd done it as a joke,' Belle admitted.

'Riled up like it was, that cottonmouth would've killed whoever was nearest to it when it come out of the box.' Bludso said quietly. 'Thing being, Belle, are they after you, or me?'

'You, I'd say,' Belle replied. 'They couldn't know that I'd be coming here with you, even if they suspected me.'

'You're right on that,' Bludso growled. 'Let me take this blasted thing and heave it into the river. Then we'll go and start asking folks how it got in here.'

## CHAPTER ELEVEN

# THE COAL TORPEDO!

'I suppose you're happy now you've got the *Stream Queen* behind us,' Belle Boyd remarked to Jim Bludso, as they stood at the rear of the engineering section of the *Prairie Belle*'s main deck and looked back along the river.

'Shucks, no,' the engineer replied. 'It was only a matter of time before we passed her. That hogged-up scow's no match for the *Belle*. She might have pulled out Friday evening, but I knew we'd be leaving her behind before we hit the Baton Royale Glide.'

'Do you think that they left the cottonmouth in your cabin, Jim?' Belle inquired, watching the lights and red glow from the *Stream Queen's* twin high, flaring-topped, smoke- and sparks-vomiting smoke-stacks.

'I wouldn't put anything past Bascoll, or Tyrone,' Bludso growled. 'Except that I don't know how they managed to do it, or have it done.'

On being informed of the attempted murder, Captain Yancy had insisted that the police be notified. He knew the temper of his engineer and had had no desire for Bludso to commence an independent, unofficial inquiry; especially as the most obvious suspects had appeared to be Bascoll and Tyrone.

Despite all their efforts, the police had not been able to discover who had placed the snake in Bludso's cabin. On being questioned, Bascoll and Tyrone had presented unshakable alibis. The possibility of them hiring another person to make the attempt had not been overlooked, but could not be proven.

There had been a considerable number of people coming and going on the *Prairie Belle*, due to the preparations for departure. With so many strangers aboard, none of the crew had noticed any suspicious person or persons lurking around. The simple lock on Bludso's door could have been picked easily and, with all the officers fully engaged by their various duties, the would-be killer had had ample opportunity to do it. Once in the cabin, he had probably selected the hat box as the most suitable hiding place for the cottonmouth snake, the Police had concluded that he had hoped Bludso would not open the box until the *Prairie Belle* was on its way downriver.

Although the police had been aware that Bascoll could have organised the attempt, they had known that proving it would be difficult. So, wishing to avert the possibility of open warfare between the two boats, they had allowed the *Stream Queen* to leave at its scheduled time of departure on Friday night.

Much as Belle would have liked to take an active part in the investigation, she had had her own duties to perform. So she had left it in the hands of the police. Returning to the small hotel opposite Molloy's warehouse, she had compared notes with Darren on their activities. She had found that her efforts in securing a berth for him had been needless. Showing more initiative than Belle would have credited him with possessing. Stenhouse had already booked accommodation for all of them. Learning that Stenhouse would be going along had not filled her with delight, However, she could hardly have blamed him for arranging their transportation. Having been uncertain whether Bludso would be aboard the *Prairie Belle*, she had not mentioned her hopes in that direction when discussing plans with Stenhouse.

Working separately, Belle and Darren had continued to keep the consignment under observation. They had never let it out of their sight until it was delivered to the docks and disappeared into the *Prairie Belle*'s hold. While the young man had kept watch, to guard against a last-minute change of destination, Belle had collected her belongings from the hotel and transferred them to Bludso's cabin. She had not known whether Stenhouse would approve, but was not worried on that score. Travelling as the engineer's 'wife' would allow her greater freedom than if she was occupying the stateroom. With her property aboard, she had relieved Darren so that he could collect his.

That evening, in a carefully arranged, casual-seeming meeting, Darren had given Belle the latest developments. Clearly Stenhouse had been busy and the results of his enterprise had not been entirely worthless. Calling upon Captain O'Shea in his official capacity, he had obtained information concerning the investigation into the Bijou Theatre's incident. Apparently the police had given little credence to Belle's anonymous letter, for they had been making no special efforts to locate and arrest Mephisto. They had, however, collected the dead man's property from the Travellers Hotel and contacted the nearest Pinkerton's field office to ask if 'Sheriff' had been a member of the National Detective Agency. Belle had been willing to bet that the answer would be negative.

One puzzling factor had emerged from Stenhouse's visit to O'Shea. He had been allowed to examine O'Reilly's effects. The 'coal torpedoes' were no longer in the carpetbag.

That had been a source of some speculation between Belle and Darren. Obviously, O'Reilly's companions had removed the 'torpedoes' rather than allow them to fall into the hands of the police. Also, the organisation would not want to lose the weapons if they were to serve as models for future missiles.

Brunel had come on board shortly before the boat's departure. For all the interest he had displayed in the consignment, he might have been nothing more than a professional gambler making a trip. At no time had he gone ashore during the journey. Nor had he displayed more than a casual interest in any other passenger. While he had introduced himself to Darren, using the 'mistake' he had made at the hotel as his excuse, he had not attempted to develop a closer acquaintance with the view to obtaining information.

After watching Brunel for a few days, Belle and Darren had come to the conclusion that he was merely supervising the delivery and, in all probability, travelling alone.

Belle had been amused, but not perturbed by Stenhouse's reaction to her choice of accommodation. Admitting that her pose of being Bludso's 'wife' had its advantages, he had been concerned about her doing so reflecting badly upon the good name of the United States' Secret Service. The girl might have explained that his fears were groundless. Although she and Bludso had occupied the cabin every night, nothing sexual was happening outside of Stenhouse's imagination. By a careful arrangement of timing, their undressing and dressing was carried out with as much privacy as possible. While Belle occupied the bunk, Bludso had bedded down on the floor.

Once satisfied that Brunel did not suspect her, Belle had reverted to wearing the Hessian boots and riding breeches under her shirt and had donned a somewhat more decorous blouse.

The journey had been uneventful and pleasant. As Jim Bludso's 'wife', Belle could come and go as she pleased with one exception. Her presence in the Ladies' Cabin had not been encouraged. That did not worry her, for she was accepted in the gentlemen's section of the boiler-deck's huge, stateroom-lined saloon and her visits to the main deck had aroused no comment.

To help pass the time, Belle had fallen into the habit of joining Bludso on the main deck every evening. There she had seen much of interest which she had previously taken for granted. She had also become aware of why a riverboat's engineer was regarded as being as important to the vessel's well-being as the captain or the pilot.

Not only did Bludso have to supervise the ceaseless work of his Negro stokers, who were commanded by Willie, but he was also responsible for manipulating the controls. Responding to instructions, via the pilothouse's voice-pipe, he kept the two enormous side wheels turning at the required speeds for propelling or manoeuvring the *Prairie Belle*'s vast bulk.

From Bludso and Willie, Belle had learned the simple code by which the riverboat engineers lived. Always tend to and care for the engines; heed the pilot's bell and instructions; never let the boat be passed by another.

Attempting to uphold the last condition had been the cause of many a disaster. Boilers had exploded, because they had been subjected to excessive pressures and strains. In the excitement of the races, boats had been run aground or had struck snags—fallen trees carried by the current until sinking one end into the river's bed—although that had been the pilots' faults rather than the engineers'.

Even without racing, the danger of fire was always very real upon the riverboats. Due to the vessel's specialised requirements, it had to have its superstructure constructed as lightly as possible. In addition to making use of the thinnest available timbers, every top-class boat had to be well painted and carry much decorative carving and fretwork which rendered it highly inflammable.

To further save weight, the boats were powered by engines working at high pressures of at least 120 lb. per square inch; using standard types of locomotive boilers fed by a general service pump known as the 'doctor'. The small, rapidly steaming boilers—each vessel carried sufficient to power the paddle-wheels—were wood-burners and required a large grate-area to ensure complete combustion. This could not be obtained, so the chimney stacks vomitted out sparks, flames and glowing embers amongst the clouds of black smoke. The sun-dried nature of the vessel's timbers needed little encouragement to catch fire.

'We ain't never had a fire on the *Belle*,' Willie had told the girl on the night before they had reached her old home town of Baton Royale. 'And I sure enough hopes we never does.'

'I should think so,' Belle had replied. 'It would be terrible.'

'Massa Jim always allows that if it happens, he'll hold her nozzle again' the bank while everybody gets ashore.' Willie went on.

'He's just about cussed enough to do it,' Belle had praised, visualising what would happen to Bludso if he should ever be compelled to keep his promise.

On arriving in Baton Royale, Belle had found the *Stream Queen* at the landing stage. Despite having reached the town ahead of the *Prairie Belle*, the other boat had not taken its departure when the *Belle* had cast off.

There had been considerable delight amongst the crew of the *Prairie Belle* at finding themselves ahead of their hated rivals. When Belle had inquired about the reason for the *Stream Queen*'s delay, she had been treated to a variety of possible motives. One had been that Bascoll did not dare take his ramshackle old bucket through the Baton Royale Glide after night-fall.

Of all the reasons, that had been the one which struck Belle as the least likely. A mile below Baton Royale, some freak of the terrain caused the river to flow fast and deep with hardly any shallows. On either side, the shoreline fell away steeply from the man-made levee bank into at least ten feet of water. Although the current would thrust a boat along at a fair speed, the area was not regarded as being particularly dangerous. So she had concluded that the crew's summation was founded more on contempt for Bascoll's abilities than upon actual fact.

'Did it hurt you, seeing Baton Royale again?' Bludso inquired, turning his back on the *Stream Queen*.

'A little,' Belle admitted. 'But I couldn't see where my home used to be from the landing and I didn't want to go ashore in case somebody recognised me.'

'Is that why you've stayed on board at all the other halts?' Bludso asked with a grin.

'*You* know it's not,' Belle replied. 'If I'd landed, I'd probably have wound up fighting off one of my many rivals.'

'Shucks, there ain't that many of them,' Bludso protested. 'It just seems that way.'

'I'm sure it does,' Belle smiled 'Did your red-haired friend like her hat?'

'She sure did,' Bludso confirmed, then his face lost its smile. 'Damn it, Belle, it *had* to be Bascoll—— But I don't see how they managed to set it up in the time.'

'Or me,' Belle said soberly. 'Have you any other enemies?'

'None's'd go that far,' Bludso replied.

Motives for the attempted killing had been discussed many times during the journey, but were doomed to be forgotten that night. Underfoot, Belle could sense that a force almost as powerful as the *Prairie Belle*'s paddle-wheels was gripping the hull and carrying them forward. Even more aware of the change, Bludso walked in the direction of the controls. Until they had passed through the Glide, he would be constantly on the alert for the pilot's instructions.

Walking at Bludso's side, Belle looked along the lamp-lit deck. Negro stokers were feeding cordwood into the yawning, glowing mouths of the furnaces, but they did not hold her attention. Up by the forward boiler, Willie was speaking to the gambler, Brunel. Even as Belle watched, the white man swung away from the Negro and walked—hurried would have been a better word—towards the stairs leading to the boiler-deck.

'What did Brunel want down here?' the girl asked.

'That's what I'm wondering,' Bludso replied. Then, as Willie came up ready to support him in the passage through the Glide, he repeated Belle's question.

'Allowed he'd spilled ink all over his carpetbag and spoiled most of his clothes,' the Negro answered. 'So he'd bundled 'em up and fetched 'em down to get shut of 'em. I was too late to stop him pitching them in.'

'The coal torpedoes!' Belle shrieked.

All in a single flash of intuition, the girl had seen the answers to many of her assignment's puzzling aspects.

At last she knew why O'Reilly had spoken the truth to Darren about the consignment's departure. She also understood why he had been carrying the 'coal torpedoes' in his carpetbag and for the organisation taking the chance of robbing the hotel to retrieve them. Brunel's lack of activity had also been explained. So had the references made by Andy and Mick outside the warehouse, with regard to *finishing* the trip on Bascoll's boat.

Everything was suddenly, frighteningly, almost unbelievably

clear!

Regrettably, Belle's understanding had come just too late!

With a thunderous roar and a sheet of raging flame, the forward boiler exploded. Blazing chunks of wood flew in all directions. The furnace's stoker screamed briefly but hideously as the sheet of leaping fire engulfed him. Such was the force of the detonation that the *Prairie Belle*'s massive bulk heaved ponderously. Its starboard paddle-wheel lifted clear of the water, spinning wildly and hurling spray; then it regained an even keel.

Thrown off balance, Belle was flung against the control panel. Bludso's weight collided with her and sandwiched her against the board. Winded and unconscious, she slid to the deck as he lurched away. The incident had one benefit. Cushioned by Belle's slender body, Bludso suffered no injury and retained the use of his faculties.

With the effects of the explosion felt throughout the boat, pandemonium reigned. Seeing the fire growing rapidly, the deck passengers, roustabouts and stokers who had not been flung overboard hurled themselves into the river. Their actions were understandable, for they could see the full threat of the conflagration.

On the boiler-deck, glassware and crockery cascaded to ruins on the floor. Men and women went sprawling in all directions. Screams, shouts, crashes and moans filled the air. Lamps left their hangers and rained down to create further fires.

Clinging to the hand-grips of the wheel, the pilot had managed to avoid deserting his post. Ignoring his visitors, who had been tumbled from the bench at the rear of the pilot-house, he followed the instructions laid down by Captain Yancy for such an emergency. Without needing to check, he knew which was the nearer bank. So, catching his balance, he swung hard on the wheel. Heeling slightly as the push of the current caught her, the *Prairie Belle* responded to the helm and started to turn. The pilot hoped that Jim Bludso was at the engine's controls. Without him, the boat would not be able to fight the pressure of the river and complete its turn towards the shore.

On the main deck, Bludso shook his head and sprang to the controls. Like the pilot, he had learned the proposed drill to be followed in the event of a fire. No instructions had come from the pilothouse, but the engineer knew what he must do. Being closest to the port bank, they would head in that direction. So Bludso reduced the revolutions of the left side wheel. He knew that merely directing the bows against the levee would not be sufficient. The boat would have to be held in position for long enough to present the passengers with an opportunity of escaping. So the wheels must be kept turning— and that could only be done from the engineer's control panel.

Bludso knew just how slight his chances of getting clear in time would be, but he did not let that lessen his resolve to continue doing his duty.

'Willie!' the engineer called, trying to see through the flames. 'Are you all right?'

'Shook is all,' answered the Negro. 'What can I do for you?'

'Get Belle ashore.'

'I can't leave you-all, Massa Jim!'

'You can. There's no sense in us both staying. And I want to know that somebody'll be around to tell the truth about the explosion.'

'But——!' Willie groaned.

'Do like I tell you!' Bludso roared. 'You've never failed me afore, old friend.'

'I'll do like you says,' Willie promised, bending to lift the unconscious girl from the deck.

'Another thing,' Bludso put in. 'Before you go, take my old Ames Knife—and when you lay hands on that bastard Brunel, use it for me.'

CHAPTER TWELVE

# THERE'S NO WAY YOU CAN STOP ME

'Brunel escaped from the *Prairie Belle*,' Belle Boyd told General Handiman as they sat in Stenhouse's hotel suite at New Orleans. 'Darren saw him on shore, but we lost contact with him after that.'

'He wasn't aboard the *Stream Queen* when she arrived,' the head of the Secret Service replied. 'I had Lieutenant St. Andre of the New Orleans' Police Department* make a search as soon as it docked.'

Belle was once more the elegant, fashionable lady, dressed in an outfit which she had purchased in Baton Royale. Yet her face showed signs of grief and of the deep strain she had been under. She had had little rest since the night of the *Prairie Belle*'s fire.

Carried on to the levee by Willie, the girl had recovered consciousness in time to see the end of the drama.

Due to Jim Bludso's gallant act of self-sacrifice, the blazing boat's bows had been held against the river's bank while all its other occupants had fled. The engineer had stuck to his post until the end, going through what must have been hell as the flames raged higher and the heat had become unendurable in its intensity. Boiler after boiler had exploded, ripping the once magnificent vessel to pieces. Knowing that he had no hope of surviving, Jim Bludso had carried out his promise at the cost of his own life.

Learning what had happened from Willie, Belle had immediately started to search for Brunel. Darren had seen the gambler on the levee, but they could find no trace of him there or in the town of Baton Royale. Remembering Andy's comment about having to finish the ride to New Orleans on Bascoll's boat, Belle had insisted that Stenhouse telegraph to Madame Lucienne and ask for her to arrange to have the gambler arrested when the *Stream Queen* arrived. Carrying out Belle's instructions, Stenhouse had also asked that accom-

* Details of Lieutenant St. Andre's career are given in *The Bull-whip Breed*.

106

modation be arranged for himself and his two agents.

Taking the first available boat, Belle, Willie, Darren and Stenhouse had journeyed down to New Orleans. They had been met at the dock by Madame Lucienne's Negress maid, bringing a letter from her employer. In it had been instructions as to the hotel at which she had arranged for the two men and Belle to stay. To Belle's delight, Lucienne had also sent along her trunk. Learning where he could contact Belle, Willie had set off alone and in search of the man who had been responsible for his friend's death. Before they had separated, Belle had obtained the Negro's promise that he would inform her as soon as he had located Brunel. She had also asked that, if possible, Brunel should not be harmed before she was on hand. It was her intention to try to take the man alive and induce him to answer her questions.

On the point of going to visit Madame Lucienne, as a start in her hunt for Brunel, Belle had been summoned to Stenhouse's suite. Darren, who had delivered the message, had agreed to go to Lucienne's fashionable and exclusive dress shop immediately. There he would tell the woman everything that had happened and save any further waste of time. Much to her surprise, Belle had found that General Handiman was with the co-ordinator.

While going through her story for Handiman's benefit, Belle had seen him show a hint of puzzlement on more than one occasion—particularly when she mentioned a point that had not struck her as being consistent with the other facts. At the same time, Stenhouse had displayed a growing alarm and apprehension.

'Anyway,' Stenhouse remarked, exhibiting an air of relief which did not ring true. 'At least the consignment will never reach Ireland.'

'I wouldn't be too sure of that,' Belle replied.

Big, heavily built, Handiman looked more like a prosperous businessman or planter than the head of the United States' Secret Service. He glanced at Belle in a speculative manner as she spoke.

'Why is that, Miss Boyd?' he asked.

'There's no way they could recover the rifles,' Stenhouse went on. 'Even assuming that any could have survived the explosions. The river——'

'I know all that!' Belle interrupted. 'And I'm sure the

Irishmen planned everything so we'd be led to such a conclusion.'

'Go on, please,' Handiman requested, waving Stenhouse to remain silent.

'It all fits,' Belle obliged. 'They knew that we were on to their game and wanted to throw us off the track. So, somewhere or other, they transferred the rifles and ammunition to other containers. Then they let the bales and weighted boxes go on the *Prairie Belle*, making sure that Darren knew about it. O'Reilly, or whatever his name was, should have accompanied the shipment. When he was killed, Brunel took his place. They planned to wreck the boat in an area where, even if we wanted to check, it would be impossible to do so. The Baton Royale Glide was the finest place for their purpose.'

'The uniforms, boots and hats were on the boat,' Stenhouse reminded her.

'What use would the Irish nationalists have for them?' Belle answered. 'The rifles would be useful, but they wouldn't need uniforms. And leaving the bales intact, making sure that Darren could see and identify the contents, did much to divert attention from the possibility of the boxes not containing rifles and ammunition.'

'They've gone to a lot of trouble, just for a hundred rifles,' Handiman remarked. 'Of course, that many repeaters might go a long way in winning Ireland back for the Pope.'

'How's that?' Belle inquired, a vague recollection of something she had been told struggling to burst through her memory.

'Didn't you know?' Handiman smiled. 'I'm assured, by an Irish waiter in my Washington club, that is what they're trying to do.'

'Then it's not likely that an Irish Protestant would be helping them?'

'I'd say it's highly *unlikely*, Miss Boyd,' Handiman corrected. 'Why do you ask?'

'Because Darren said that O'Reilly had agreed to work for him out of dislike for Molloy,' Belle answered.

'And——?' Handiman prompted.

'According to O'Reilly, Molloy was a "Protestant son-of-a-bitch",' the girl elaborated. 'He is also one of the few Irishmen involved in the affair. "O'Reilly" and Opal certainly weren't. Nor were Brunel and Bascoll. And I heard mention of somebody they called "the Frenchman" as one of the leaders.'

'The two men who made the purchase were French——'
Stenhouse began.

'Who spoke with such obvious Irish accents that they
aroused suspicion,' Belle put in. 'I've little respect for nationalist agitators of any kind, but I don't believe they would be *that*
stupid.'

'You think that somebody other than Irish nationalists
might be involved, Miss Boyd?' Handiman inquired, darting a
cold glare at the co-ordinator who was showing increasing
alarm.

'It's possible, though I can't think who,' the girl replied.
'Everything points to them being Irish. Perhaps too obviously.
Men with French names and Irish accents would be sure to
start us thinking on the required lines. Using Molloy's—an
Irishman's—warehouse kept us thinking that way. So did
"O'Reilly" adopting a brogue when he was dealing with
Darren. And giving a typical Irishman's excuse, religious
bigotry, for betraying his employer. Even the name they had
given to the consignors of the shipment, the "Shamrock Sup-
plies Incorporated" would help keep us thinking they were
Irish.'

'I'm inclined to agree with you,' Handiman declared.

'Thank you,' Belle answered. 'Perhaps you can tell me who,
other than the Irish, they might be.'

'You mean that you haven't told her?' Handiman growled,
staring at his worried-looking male subordinate.

'Well, sir,' Stenhouse began hesitantly. 'You see—That
is——'

'What haven't I been told?' Belle demanded suspiciously.

'There are men in the South formenting discontent and
advocating that the Southern States should secede from the
Union,' Handiman elaborated. 'According to our reports, they
are hoping to stir up an armed rebellion.'

'The Ku Klux Klan?' Belle asked.

'They've practically disbanded now that the worst excesses
of Reconstruction have been ended,' Handiman replied. 'It's
possible that some of the Klan's more radical members are
involved, but we've no proof of that. In fact, we've no concrete
evidence of their existence, other than fairly reliable rumours.'

'And did Mr. Stenhouse know of these rumours?' Belle said
icily.

'Well—Er—Yes,' Stenhouse spluttered. 'I had heard of
them.'

'Then why didn't you mention them to me?' the girl blazed. 'If I'd known, it might have opened up a whole new line of thought.'

'I didn't think that it had any connection——,' Stenhouse commenced.

'The hell you didn't!' Belle shouted, springing from her chair with such velocity that it went flying backwards across the room. 'You didn't *trust* me enough to mention it, if it might involve Southrons. I'm the Rebel Spy.'

'That's nothing to do with——!' Stenhouse yelped, also rising and registering alarm before the girl's barely controlled fury.

'You're a rotten, stinking liar, Stenhouse!' Belle yelled, tensing as if to fling herself in a savage attack at the cringing, pallid man. 'You didn't mind General Handiman bringing me into it to cover your nephew's inadequacies, as long as only Irish nationalists were involved——'

'Really, General Handiman!' Stenhouse spluttered. 'This is intolerable——'

'What happened to Jim Bludso and the *Prairie Belle* was intolerable too!' the girl thundered, making an almost visible mental effort to restrain herself from taking violent physical action.

'That's enough, both of you!' Handiman barked, slapping a big hand hard on the top of the table. 'Bickering between ourselves——'

'*Bickering!*' Belle spat out the word viciously. 'God! If I'd only known——!'

'You'd have seen everything in a flash, *Colonel* Boyd?' Handiman challenged, for the first time using the rank which Belle had been given to enhance her official standing and to help when dealing with military or civil authorities.

'Perhaps not,' the girl admitted. 'But I might have suspected——'

'There are *some* who might say that you ought to have suspected what was going to happen as soon as you heard that the "coal torpedoes" had been stolen from "O'Reilly's" carpetbag,' Handiman pointed out, glaring the other man into silence and anticipating his comment. 'It's all too easy to say what one should, or could, or ought to have done, after the event.'

'It is,' Belle conceded, 'but, if I *had* been told——'

'*Perhaps* things would have been different'. Handiman finished for her. 'Nobody could have conceived that they would take such an extreme step, endangering hundreds of lives, to destroy a fake cargo and throw us off their trail.'

'I believe that they were counting on a large loss of life, so that we wouldn't believe they would have done such a thing,' Belle said bitterly. 'That's why they had the snake left in Jim Bludso's cabin. They'd heard of his claim that, if the *Prairie Belle* caught fire, he would hold the bows against the bank until everybody got ashore. That wouldn't have suited their ends. So they wanted him out of the way.'

'Which you can see now, *after* the event,' Handiman pointed out gently. 'Our present concern is not to lay the blame, but to decide on what action we must take against these people.'

'I'm going after whoever's responsible,' Belle declared.

'Even if they are Southrons?' asked the co-ordinator, stung into indiscretion by the challenging glare which the girl had directed his way.

'*Mister!*' Belle hissed. 'I swore the oath of allegiance to the Union before I joined the Secret Service. Since then *I've* been in the field, carrying out dangerous assignments, not sitting behind a desk co-ordinating. There has never been any question against my loyalty. If that doesn't satisfy you, I'll resign right now.'

'It satisfies *me*,' Handiman stated and gave added strength to the words by crossing the room to collect the girl's chair.

'Apart from realising that no good could come from another attempt at secession,' Belle went on, sitting down. 'I've personal reasons for getting them, whoever they are.'

'Personal reasons?' queried Handiman.

'When I went to Jim Bludso for help, he agreed to give it without even asking what I wanted. Despite the fact that he suspected what I was doing and how helping me could be dangerous. Helping me caused his death. That's all the reason I need for avenging him. There's no way you can stop me going after them.'

'You can't conduct a private vendetta, no matter what was between you——' Stenhouse put in.

'Don't you even finish *that*!' Belle warned the co-ordinator. 'Even if Jim and I *had* bedded down together every night, it wouldn't have been any of your damned concern. But we didn't, although we slept in the same cabin. To satisfy your filthy little mind, Jim slept on the floor.'

'I—I——!' Stenhouse spluttered.

'There's no need for you to go on, Colonel Boyd,' Handiman announced, cutting off the other man's protests. 'Your morals are not being questioned and neither is your loyalty.'

'Do you concur, Mr. Co-ordinator?' Belle challenged.

'I agree with General Handiman,' Stenhouse confirmed, with humility. 'Although I want to go on record as saying that you misinterpreted the comment I was going to make. I apologise, ma'am.'

'Then I accept your apology, sir,' Belle replied. 'What do we know about these Southron agitators?'

'Very little, beyond the fact that they do exist and have been very busy,' Handiman replied. 'Nothing important, or too dangerous, but active. So far, they have restricted their efforts to making inflammatory speeches, or appeals for funds——'

'The fund-raising was one of the reasons I didn't take them more seriously,' Stenhouse announced, in hopeful self-exculpation. 'I believed that they were no more than a bunch of confidence tricksters, duping the unwary.'

'And, as long as they were only doing it to Southrons, that was all right,' Belle drawled sardonically.

'No!' Stenhouse yelped. 'Of course not. It just didn't seem to come under our jurisdiction.

'Madame Lucienne thought that it could become serious,' Handiman injected, directing a cold glare of remonstration at Belle. 'That's why I'm down here. As soon as I saw in which direction the consignment was heading, I wondered if we might have been deliberately misled by the purchasers.'

'One hundred repeating rifles wouldn't be a big factor in helping the South to secede,' Belle remarked. 'But it would be a start. It might even appeal to the agitators' sense of humour to know that the first weapons of the new conflict had been purchased from a regiment that had been organised to fight us.'

'That's part of it,' Handiman guessed. 'Mainly, though, the purchase of so many arms would arouse interest. So they selected a way that would mislead us, if news of it should leak out.'

'What do we do now?' Stenhouse inquired.

'Any ideas on *that*, Colonel Boyd?' Handiman requested.

'Not until I've seen Lucienne,' the girl admitted, then a thought struck her. 'Where is the *Stream Queen* now?'

'She went north again on the morning after she arrived,' Handiman replied. 'There was no legal reason for holding her. I had her stopped and searched before she reached Baton

Rouge. Brunel wasn't on board.'

'Then he must be in the city,' Belle breathed.

'That's likely,' Handiman agreed. 'We can't cover every exit, but we're watching those he's most likely to use if he wants to leave. And we've men alerted to watch for him all through Louisiana.'

Belle was less impressed by the information than Stenhouse seemed to be. There were too many ways by which Brunel could have escaped from New Orleans. Nor would the watchers, armed with no more than descriptions, be guaranteed to identify him. In a few days, they could be supplied with copies of Darren's excellent sketch but by that time it might be too late.

'Lord!' the girl said fervently. 'Let him still be in New Orleans. If he is, Willie might find him.'

'*Willie?*' Handiman questioned.

'Jim Bludso's Negro stoker.' the girl elaborated. 'If there's nothing more, General, I'll be going.'

'What if you can't find Brunel?' Stenhouse asked as she stood up.

'One of the men at the warehouse said that something was going to happen in Shreveport,' Belle replied. 'If I don't find him, I'll go and make another start from there.'

'This time you can count on *every* co-operation,' Handiman assured her.

'Thank you for *that*,' Belle answered and walked out of the room.

Leaving the suite, Belle went out of the hotel and found a cab. While riding to Madame Lucienne's establishment, she started to think about the latest developments.

If she had only known about the Southron agitators!

That damned fool, Stenhouse, and his mistrust——

Yet there had been cause—if unjust and unfounded—for it. During the War, Belle had been a very successful spy and had given loyal, devoted service to the Confederate cause. She could hardly blame a man like the co-ordinator for being wary where Southron interests were concerned. In his place, she might have experienced similar misgivings.

For all that, if Stenhouse had been frank with her, she might have connected the 'coal torpedoes' with the shipment and the *Prairie Belle*. She had been aware of the possibility that they were on a wild-goose chase. Possibly she would have anticipated a means by which the Secret Service could be thrown completely off the trail. The purpose of 'coal torpedoes' was primarily to blow up and destroy ships. They would have an extremely limited use in the 'liberation' of Ireland. And, more to the point, they offered a solution that would be only too obvious to a Southron mind.

Of course, as General Handiman had said, it was hellishly easy to be wise *after* the event.

Who could have foreseen how the agitators would be so disdainful of human lives that they would deliberately wreck the riverboat?

Forcing herself to become calm, for she found her body shaking and trembling with the fury of her emotions, Belle settled more firmly on the seat. She accepted that she would gain nothing by mulling feverishly over the past. That could not be changed, whether it had been right or wrong. What mattered was the future. So she gave her thoughts to what lay ahead.

Nothing that Belle might have imagined could have equalled the shock of the next development.

Leaving and paying off the cab, the girl looked at the darkened display windows of Lucienne's shop. The drapes had been drawn at the windows of the living quarters, but a glimmer of lamp's light showed through. So Belle went to the right hand alley, knowing that there was a side entrance which she could use. Turning the corner, she came face to face with Darren.

Such was the shock and horror on the young man's face that Belle slammed to a halt and felt a terrible sensation of foreboding. He hardly seemed to recognise her as she blocked his path.

'What is it?' Belle gasped.

'Must—get—doctor!' Darren croaked.

At that moment Belle became aware that the side door was open.

'Lucienne!' she ejaculated.

'D-Don't go up!' the man warned, catching her left bicep as she started to brush by him.

Wrenching her arm free, Belle ran along the alley and entered the building. The Negro maid sprawled in the hall, dead, with her throat cut from ear to ear. Sobbing in anxiety, Belle raced up the stairs. Although she had known that something must be terribly wrong, she was unprepared for exactly what met her gaze.

Completely naked, her arms and ankles lashed to the posts, Lucienne was spread-eagled upon the bed. Her plump body bore numerous horrible abrasions, as if whole chunks of flesh had been plucked from it. A further horror was that each nipple had been ripped from its breast. There was a gag in her mouth. Despite the bloody stab-wound in her stomach, the movement of the bosom and feeble struggles showed that she was alive.

Slowly Lucienne's head turned towards the door. Her eyes opened. Showing the torments she must be suffering, they held recognition too. Flinging herself across the room, Belle jerked free the gag with shaking hands.

'Who did it?' the girl demanded.

'Paul de Bracy,' Lucienne moaned, slurring her words yet making them audible. 'One de Bracy called "the Frenchman" —and Alvin Brunel.'

## CHAPTER THIRTEEN

## YOU'LL NEVER MAKE ME TALK

Swinging his silver-capped walking-stick jauntily, Paul de Bracy strolled from the house in which he was supposed to have remained hidden until arrangements could be made for him to join Alvin Brunel and leave New Orleans. The time was ten o'clock on the evening after he had helped to deal with the traitress Madame Lucienne. Against his orders, and in the face of common sense, he was going to visit a lady of his acquaintance.

Tall, slim, very handsome, every inch the proud, haughty Creole dandy, de Bracy was a recent enlistment in the ranks of the Brotherhood For Southron Freedom. However, he believed that his social standing—reduced as it might have been by the War—automatically rated him worthy of a high place in the organisation. That was, indirectly, why he was acting in such a reckless manner.

If only the Frenchman—how he hated that name—had not been so all-fired uppy and had phrased his words as helpful advice to a social equal, instead of snapping them out like orders, de Bracy would have been more inclined to comply. In which case, he would have ignored the message, delivered by a tall, burly Negro, inviting him to go to Marie Larondel's apartment and resume their intermittent, yet enjoyable amatory association.

Fancying himself as a veritable lady-killer and God's answer to every woman's dreams, de Bracy had not paused to ponder on the means by which Marie had learned of his present whereabouts. He had been brooding too heavily upon the Frenchman's assumption of superiority and had seen Marie's offer only as a way to regain his injured self-respect. Not only was her apartment more to his taste than his present accommodation, in a small, middle-rent district house, but by going there he would assert his independence and demonstrate a complete rejection of the Frenchman's self-appointed authority.

Not only had de Bracy objected to being given orders, but

he felt that the Frenchman's summation of the situation was wrong. Certainly, from what de Bracy could gather, things had not gone entirely to plan higher up the Mississippi River. However, he believed that the main object of the exercise had been achieved. The fake cargo had been destroyed, as planned, and—he felt sure—its going would have thrown the Secret Service off the genuine shipment's trail. Only the—to de Bracy —unimportant side elements had misfired.

The cottonmouth snake which Brunel had contrived to conceal in Jim Bludso's cabin had failed to do its work. So had an attempt by Bascoll and Tyrone to cripple him in a fight. In de Bracy's opinion, there had been too much emphasis placed on removing the engineer of the *Prairie Belle*. Apparently the Frenchman and other senior members of the Brotherhood had been impressed by Bludso's often-repeated vow that, in case of fire, he would stay at his post and hold the boat against the shore so that the passengers could escape. They had said, if he should succeed in doing this, there was a chance that an investigation of the remains would reveal that the arms and ammunition had not been on board. De Bracy considered that their selection of a point for the wrecking, along the Baton Royale Glide, would have rendered such an investigation impossible even if the boat went down by the bank. He did not know it, but there had been another reason for the attempted assassination.*

In one way, Bludso staying alive had probably rendered Brunel's work less risky. Instead of having to leap into the water and swim for the shore, he had been able to land dryshod and get aboard the *Stream Queen*; which had halted at the foot of the Glide to collect him and such other passengers who had been willing to purchase a passage to New Orleans.

Fortunately, as it had proved, Brunel had kept his wits

* In view of his work with the Confederate States' Secret Service during the War, Bludso had been invited to attend a meeting and join the Brotherhood. He had declined to enlist, but had sworn an oath that he would never reveal the existence of the organisation. The Frenchman had insisted that they could not rely upon Bludso remaining silent, so he must be eliminated.

That Bludso meant to keep his word is certain. Although he had guessed Belle's mission concerned the Brotherhood, he had not spoken of it. If Belle had been aware of the facts, she would have understood the correct meaning of Bascoll calling Bludso a traitor.

about him. The Secret Service agent, Darren, had seen him on the levee. More than that, Darren had apparently connected him with the destruction of the boat and telegraphed to New Orleans to arrange for him to be arrested. Alert for the possibility, Brunel had left the boat five miles clear of New Orleans. He had sent a message to the Frenchman, by Bascoll, and de Bracy had been assigned the task of collecting him.

During the ride to town, Brunel had bitterly cursed himself for not having followed the line of action planned by 'O'Reilly': keeping out of Darren's sight on the *Prairie Belle*, then killing and dumping the agent overboard at the first opportunity. By failing to do so, Brunel had been compelled to remain in New Orleans while the Frenchman had set off to take part in some enterprise at Shreveport. Much as de Bracy would have liked to go along, the Frenchman had imperiously ordered him to stay in New Orleans.

Not that de Bracy had regretted the separation from the Frenchman. There was something cold-blooded and sadistic about him which repelled the young Creole. De Bracy thought that he was tough, but he had been almost sickened by the way in which the Frenchman had treated Madame Lucienne. Not that he had opposed her being killed, for she had come too close to the Brotherhood for comfort, or safety.

According to the Frenchman, somebody had been informing on their activities to Madame Lucienne and she was now a member of the Yankee Secret Service. So he, de Bracy and Brunel had set off to discover the identity of the informer and to silence the woman.

Arriving at the shop just as Madame Lucienne had been about to close, they had overpowered her. Knocking her out, they had locked the front door and taken her upstairs. Under the Frenchman's guidance, they had stripped her and lashed her to the bed. They had just brought her back to consciousness when there had been a sound downstairs. While the Frenchman had gone to investigate, de Bracy—whom Lucienne had recognised—had given her a warning of her danger. He had not used the Frenchman's real name, but she had clearly recognised his pseudonym. For all that, and despite being told that the Frenchman had slit her maid's throat, she had refused to answer their questions.

Gagged, so that she could not scream, Lucienne had been put through purgatory as the Frenchman clutched, twisted and tore at her flesh with the jaws of a powerful pair of pincers he had brought along. Give the old woman her due, she had taken everything the Frenchman had done without yielding. Goaded to fury by his failure, he had finally hurled the pincers down and, drawing a knife, stabbed her in the stomach. Nor would he allow Brunel to finish her off, insisting that they should allow her to die in agony. Knowing the Frenchman's temper when crossed or opposed in his desires, Brunel and de Bracy had acceded to his demands. Letting themselves out of and locking the front door, they had departed in the belief that Lucienne would be dead long before anybody missed her and investigated.

Apparently that hope had been justified. The local newspapers had not announced that the two murders had been discovered. Nor had there been any mention of Brunel's part in the destruction of the *Prairie Belle*, which appeared to be dismissed as another riverboat disaster. So de Bracy was under the opinion that the Frenchman had been alarmed for nothing. Or perhaps he was motivated by a desire to lessen the share of the honours and acclaim to be gained in the success of whatever was planned in Shreveport.

De Bracy's thought-train was interrupted by the sight of a carriage halted at the edge of the sidewalk. Turning from where she had been crouching over a huddled shape seated against the front wheel, a slender, shapely, fashionably dressed young woman approached him. In a rougher part of the city, on such a deserted street, de Bracy might have been more alert and cautious. However, the woman's appearance and the respectable aspect of the neighbourhood, lulled him into a sense of false security.

'Can I help you, ma'am?' de Bracy inquired, doffing his hat.

'Why I just hope you can, sir,' the woman replied, her voice cultured and well-educated. 'My coachman has fallen asleep and I do believe he's been drinking. Could you help me rouse him?'

'I think I can,' de Bracy confirmed and went to kick the seated figure with his toe. 'Wake up, damn——'

The Creole had not replaced his hat, which proved to have been a regrettable oversight on his part. Belle Boyd produced a short rubber billy from her vanity bag, took aim, and swung it. Caught at the base of the skull, de Bracy's knees buckled and he sprawled unconscious across Darren's legs.

'I hope this is him, Belle,' Darren remarked, rolling the limp body from his legs and rising to his feet.

'It is,' the girl replied. 'Willie knows him from delivering the message and signalled when he came out. Here's Willie now. Let's get de Bracy into the carriage. This isn't the best neighbourhood in which to carry out a kidnapping.'

Having left Belle to do what she could for the stricken, dying woman, Darren had gone to fetch a doctor and the police. Lucienne had known that she had no hope of remaining alive, so she had been determined to help Belle locate her attackers. Showing how every word was taking an effort of will and causing her untold agony, she had told the girl where she had concealed her reports on the Brotherhood For Southron Freedom. She had, however, lapsed into unconsciousness before she could describe her assailants.

Without waiting for Darren to return, Belle had removed the knob from the left upper bed post and extracted the papers it held. With Lucienne on her way to a hospital, although the doctor had stated there was no hope of saving her life, the agents had left the police in charge of the shop. Leaving Darren to return and report to General Handiman, Belle had followed the ambulance. While waiting in the hope that her friend might recover and give more details, Belle had read the reports.

There had been little new added to the girl's sum of knowledge. Lucienne had listed the names of several members, but warned that—to the best of her knowledge—they were not the leaders of the Brotherhood. There was a comment on the organisation's activities and a note that there would be a meeting of a different, more significant nature, held in Shreveport. Wise in her work, Lucienne had been alert to the possibility of the reports falling into the wrong hands. So she had avoided leaving any clue to the identity of her informer. Belle had guessed that the name would have been passed on to her verbally when she and Lucienne had come together.

Lucienne had died without recovering consciousness. However, Lieutenant St. Andre—who had been assigned to the case—had promised every co-operation in locating the men responsible for her death. He had also promised to keep the story out of the newspapers and had succeeded in doing so. However, he had pointed out the difficulties in finding the three men. To the best of his knowledge, none of them had criminal records. That would make his work doubly difficult. He had known de Bracy, but not intimately. Using the Creole as a starting point, St. Andre had commenced his investigations. He would, he had warned, be working under the handicap of the necessity to prevent any warning of his Department's interest being passed to de Bracy.

Appreciating the difficulties faced by the police, Belle had been relieved to find another means of locating de Bracy.

In some way, which he described scantily as 'having got the word', Willie had learned of Lucienne's death and where to find Belle. Already he had started a widespread and capable net moving in search of Brunel, but without results. Given another name to work on, he had promised to do what he could.

Being employed in various capacities at all levels of society, Negroes were almost ubiquitous in New Orleans. They became party to their employers' affairs and frequently were in possession of what should have been stoutly and strictly kept secrets. What one Negro knew, he would usually pass on to another.

By eight o'clock on the evening after Lucienne's death, Willie had not only known where de Bracy was in hiding, but had learned a number of personal and confidential details about his private life. On hearing about his association with an actress, Marie Larondel, Belle had selected a means by which they might induce him to leave the house and fall into their hands. She wished to capture him without his host—who was on Lucienne's list of the Brotherhood, being aware of his predicament. So she, Willie and Darren had made their arrangements. The Negro had delivered the fake message, not only to lure de Bracy out but to make certain they collected the right man.

Lifting the unconscious Creole between them, Willie and Darren thrust him aboard the carriage. Then the Negro clambered on to the box, while Belle and Darren climbed inside. To make sure that de Bracy did not recover and create a disturbance, Belle had brought along a bottle of chloroform. By using it when he showed signs of returning to consciousness, she kept him silent during the journey to the place she had selected for his interrogation.

Aided by cold water dashed into his face, and the acrid, biting fumes of the smelling-salts which Belle held under his nose, de Bracy recovered from the effects of the blow and the chloroform. Moaning, he tried to sit up. Finding himself unable to do so, he twisted and tugged at the ropes which bound his wrists and ankles.

Conscious thought returned through his throbbing head and despite the nausea caused by the chloroform. He realised that he was lying on a bed and bound, with a gag in his mouth, in the same way they had treated Madame Lucienne.

*Exactly* in the same way!

Throwing his head from side to side in his struggles to free himself, he caught sight of his naked body in the dressing-table's mirror. Not only was he bound identically, but he was in Madame Lucienne's bedroom.

And he was not alone!

Standing at the foot of the bed, looking as mean as all hell, the Negro who had delivered the message from Marie glowered at de Bracy with loathing.

To the prisoner's right, looking a mite pale but grimly determined, was a tall young white man.

At the left of the bed, a slender, beautiful girl dressed in unconventionally male attire, opened and closed the jaws of a pair of powerful pincers. With a shudder, de Bracy identified them as the identical implements used by the Frenchman. They had been hurled aside and forgotten when he had stabbed Lucienne.

'He's awake, Belle,' Darren remarked. 'Can you understand me, de Bracy? Nod your head if you can.'

'Take the gag out,' Belle ordered, after the prisoner had given his assent to being able to understand. 'Now he knows how Lucienne must have felt, we'll make a start.'

'Our people are controlling the street,' Darren commented, crossing to look out of the window. 'They're signalling that everything's clear and we don't need to worry about his screams being heard.'

Watching the shock and fright displayed by de Bracy, Belle knew that they would make him answer their questions. That was the reason for bringing him to Madame Lucienne's room, where he had seen the woman tortured and would better recollect how she had suffered. Causing him to be stripped naked was a part of the process, as the conversation had been. Sweat poured down his face as Willie inserted the point of the Ames knife and severed the handkerchief gag.

'Wha-What do you want?' de Bracy demanded, trying to sound a whole lot braver than he felt.

'Information,' Belle answered, clicking the jaws of the pincers in an anticipatory manner. 'About Brunel, the Frenchman and the Brotherhood For Southron Freedom.'

'I—I don't know what you me——'

Before de Bracy could go further, cold steel was thrust against the inside of his right thigh. Even as he realised what was going to happen, and tried to jerk his limb away, the pincers closed upon his flesh. Sudden, searing, numbing pain ripped into him. It was so shocking in its intensity that he could not as much as cry out in agony. In vain he tried to wrench himself free, but the ropes held him immobile.

After what had seemed like an eternity to the suffering man, although it was only a few seconds, the girl relaxed her hold.

'That's not true,' Belle chided. 'Lucienne was still alive when we found her and she named you.'

'I told the Frenchman to fin——!' de Bracy began.

'Go on!' Belle ordered.

'You'll never make me talk!' de Bracy screeched. 'So do your—Agh!'

Again he felt the steel jaws take hold of him. This time it was closer to his groin and the pain increased in severity. A moan of anguish burbled from his lips and perspiration flooded from his pores until his whole body glistened with moisture.

'I wouldn't count on it,' Belle drawled as she removed the pincers.

'I don't know, Belle,' Darren put in, looking shaken but remembering his cue and prearranged speech. 'They must have been sure we couldn't break him, or they wouldn't have let us know where he was.'

'They expected us to kill him,' Belle corrected. 'Not to take him prisoner. The letter said that he was armed and a dead shot.'

'Wha—How—What letter?' de Bracy gasped, drawing the required conclusions.

'The letter telling us where to find you,' Darren explained. 'Your good and loyal friends sold you out.'

'The-They wouldn't!' the prisoner stated, but his voice lacked conviction.

'Who else could have told us where to find you?' Belle demanded. '*And* about Marie Larondel?'

That was the point which de Bracy had been considering ever since he had recovered. Apart from Brunel, the French-man and the people with whom he had been hiding, his whereabouts had been a secret. Yet the Secret Service agents—he assumed correctly that was the status of his captors—had

123

not only found him, but had known of a means by which to lure him from the safety of the house. Such information could only have come from another member of the Brotherhood.

'They even said that it was you who tortured and knifed Lucienne,' Belle commented, watching de Bracy's every emotion. 'That was to make sure we'd hate you enough to kill you on sight.'

'That's what they wanted,' Darren continued, while the prisoner showed increasing signs of anger and strain. 'They knew we'd never rest until we caught whoever was responsible, so they decided to make you a sacrifice. After all, you'd brought all this trouble on them by killing——'

'I didn't kill her!' de Bracy screeched. 'That was the Frenchman. He cut the maid's throat, too.'

'We'll need more than your word for that,' Belle remarked. 'Where is he, so that we can learn the truth?'

'He—He's left for Shreveport,' de Bracy answered despondently. 'But Brunel's in town. At the Hotel de Grace, calling himself "Browning".'

'And the Frenchman's gone to Shreveport?' Belle drawled, working the jaws of the pincers briskly.

'Ye-Yes!' de Bracy yelled, fear of further torment causing him to struggle violently. 'There's an important meeting there! It's true! I swear it's——'

Suddenly, in the heat of his tirade, the prisoner's face contorted and his body jerked as if in violent agony. His words ended in an incoherent gobble and blood gushed from his mouth. Not only blood. A lump of flesh spat from between his lips and landed on the edge of the bed.

'Wha-What——?' Darren gasped.

'Oh my God!' Belle ejaculated. 'He's bitten through his tongue!'

## CHAPTER FOURTEEN

# I JUST COULDN'T HOLD BACK

Everything was quiet and peaceful as Belle Boyd, Lieutenant St. Andre and Willie entered the Hotel de Grace. A modestly priced establishment, it catered mainly for the family trade and people of a staid, sober nature. By twelve o'clock any night, the majority of its patrons were already in bed and the building silent.

Protesting that there 'wasn't nobody about to let rooms', a Negro porter had opened the front door to St. Andre's knock. Studying the detective's badge of office—for he was not wearing uniform—the porter had allowed the party to enter. The reception desk had no attendant, so Belle crossed to it and obtained the required information from the register.

'Number thirteen,' she told the handsome, smartly-dressed young peace officer. 'That's unlucky for somebody.'

'Let's hope it ain't for none of us,' Willie commented, fingering the hilt of Jim Bludso's Ames knife.

Knowing that there would be no hope of obtaining further information from de Bracy that night, if at all, Belle had decided not to waste time on him. She had left him in Darren's and Willie's care, to be dressed and to be given such medical aid as they could manage, while she had gone out to make arrangements for his removal to a hospital. On her return, she had suggested that Darren continued to watch over de Bracy, leaving the arrest of Brunel to herself. It said much for the respect in which Darren now held the Rebel Spy that he had agreed; with one reservation. She must not make the attempt alone. Willie had insisted that he should accompany Belle. She had agreed, but had declared that they must also have official backing.

Finding Lieutenant St. Andre at his bachelor apartment, after inquiring after him at Police Headquarters, Belle had been entirely frank about her activities of the night. She had been pleasantly surprised at his response to her story. Already aware of the gravity of the situation—and having known, respected and liked Madame Lucienne for many years—he had merely commented that he hoped the Secret Service would not make a habit of such behaviour in his jurisdictional area. Then he had asked how he could help his visitors.

General Handiman had ordered Belle and Darren to handle the affair without—if it was possible—allowing word of it to become known to the public. If it could be done, he wanted to end the Brotherhood For Southron Freedom quietly. That way, he would avoid presenting the South with martyrs and reminders of the past; or providing material which Northern radicals could use as propoganda against the ex-Confederate States.

Belle had requested that St. Andre alone of the police should accompany her and Willie to the Hotel de Grace. A very smart peace officer, the lieutenant had understood, and approved of, General Handiman's motives. So he had agreed to handle things as Belle had required.

'How do we take him?' Belle whispered, as they stopped at the door of Room Thirteen.

'Burst in and shove a gun against his head before he's fully awake,' St. Andre suggested, drawing a Colt Peacemaker from under his jacket. 'He wouldn't open the door, or give up without a fight, if we give him the chance to do otherwise.'

'Let me get rid of this skirt,' Belle requested, unfastening the garment which she had donned before leaving Madame Lucienne's apartment. She stepped out of it, leaving her paletot jacket on. Then she drew the pick from its sheath and went on, 'I may be able to open the lock.'

Inserting the end of the pick, Belle felt it come into contact with an obstruction. She pushed gingerly, causing the key to move through the lock. It fell out and clinked softly as it hit the floor. Instantly Belle froze, alert for any hint that the sound had disturbed the man sleeping in the room. Nothing happened and she assumed that the faint noise had been insufficient to waken Brunel. So she tested for and located the master-lever.

'You'd make a good hotel thief,' St. Andre praised *sotto voce*, as the lock clicked. 'Now it's my turn.'

Although she was wearing the gunbelt and the Dance rode in its low cavalry-twist draw holster, Belle did not argue the point. From the way he handled the Colt, St. Andre was more than competent in its use. So she stepped aside, leaving him unimpeded as he took her place at the door.

Cocking his Colt, St. Andre turned the handle. Flinging the

door wide open, he sprang into the un-illuminated room—and came *very* close to getting killed.

Always a light sleeper, Brunel had been even more so since his escape from the levee at the Baton Royale Glide. He had known that the Secret Service and the police were hunting for him, which had not tended to lend itself to a deep, untroubled slumber.

When the key had fallen, its collision with the floor had wakened him. He had not stirred, but his every faculty had been working to assess the danger. From the other faint noises, including the unmistakable 'click-click-click' of a Colt's hammer being drawn to full cock, he had concluded that somebody was planning to enter his room. It might be no more than a thief, but Brunel felt disinclined to take the chance that it was anything so innocuous. Unlike de Bracy, he had not been misled by the lack of comment in the newspapers. The police and the Secret Service would be using every means available to them in an effort to trace him. Once they had found him, they would be unwilling to risk letting him escape or make a fight. Besides which, there was no reason why a thief would cock a gun at his door. If a robbery was planned, the thief would have tried a more easily accessible room and have held his weapon ready for use ever since entering the building.

Slipping the Starr Navy revolver from under his pillow, Brunel prepared to deal with the intruders. To his way of thinking, it was the ideal weapon for his purposes. Unlike the gun held by the intruder, the Starr had a double-action mechanism. It did not require cocking manually before it could fire, squeezing the trigger performed that function.

Raising the Starr, Brunel lined it along the bed, through the darkness, in the direction of the door. His right forefinger depressed the trigger gently, sensing the rearwards movement of the hammer and halting it before reaching the point where it would be liberated to return to its original position.

Two things combined to save St. Andre that night.

On opening the door, the detective plunged through it at an angle which was calculated to carry him out of the line of fire if the suspect was ready for him. That alone would not have sufficed to keep him alive. As he prepared to enter, he had allowed the light from the passage's lamps to flood in ahead of him.

The sudden glare, coming on top of complete darkness, dazzled Brunel at exactly the right second. Involuntarily, and only slightly, he flinched just as he completed the withdrawal of the trigger. Down lashed the hammer, to impact on the cylinder's uppermost percussion cap. A tiny spurt of flame passed into the powder charge in the chamber and the gun roared. Muzzle-blast blazed brilliantly ahead of Brunel, reducing his vision still further, but he heard a sharp cry of pain and knew that his lead had struck its mark.

Caught high in the left shoulder, with his left foot off the ground, St. Andre was spun around. Pain and shock caused him to yell out. Then he collided with Belle as she followed him.

Brunel had not been under the sheets, but was lying fully dressed on top of them. Swinging his feet sideways, he bounded off the bed to land facing the door. He squinted against the glare and could see well enough to lay his sights at the two figures on the threshold.

Entangled with the bewildered peace officer, Belle could not raise and use the Dance in an attempt to protect them. She felt herself and St. Andre shoved violently aside, Leaping by them, Willie hurled himself across the room. Staggering, Belle saw the light glinting on the blade of the Ames knife held low in the Negro's right hand. Then Brunel's revolver cracked. As its bullet did not come anywhere near her, or strike another part of the room, Belle knew that Willie had been hit.

Twice more the Starr spat lead, but the ·36 calibre bullets lacked the power to halt the charging Negro in his tracks. Around and upwards licked the Ames knife, with all the rage-induced strength of Willie's powerful body behind it. Brunel started to scream as the spear-point found his lower belly. The sound ended in a strangled sob, for the blade had ripped his stomach open to the base of the breast-bone. Stumbling back against the wall, he went down with Willie following him. Again and again the Ames knife tore through flesh. Any one of the blows would have been fatal.

Slowly the Negro lurched to his feet. The knife was red with blood from point to guard, hanging loosely in his big right fist. As Belle darted towards him, he staggered and held himself upright against the wall.

'I—I'm real sorry, Miss Belle,' Willie apologised weakly as she supported him and helped him to the bed. 'I just couldn't hold back when I saw him and recollected what he'd done to Massa Jim.

'That's all right, Willie,' the girl replied. 'You saved our lives. And a man like Brunel wouldn't have talked, no matter what we'd done to him. Lie back until I can get help for you.'

'I—I reckon I killed that feller,' Willie groaned, complying with her suggestion. 'And you wanted 'special' to have him took alive.'

'That's all right,' Belle assured him gently. 'I'm not sorry he's dead.'

Which was true enough in one respect, Belle told herself. However, Brunel's death had deprived her of a means of learning what the Frenchman looked like. And he, of all the Brotherhood, was the man she wanted most badly to apprehend.

Voices rose and doors slammed as people, disturbed by the shooting, came from their rooms. Repeating her advice to Willie, Belle turned and went to join St. Andre. Holding his left hand to his wounded shoulder, the detective was telling the first of the awakened guests that he was a peace officer.

'Everything's under control,' St. Andre went on. 'But we need a doctor.'

'I'm one!' announced a night-shirted, burly man. 'Let me get my bag and I'll be right with you.'

Heavy footsteps pounded on the stairs. Followed by a uniformed patrolman, General Handiman hurried along the passage.

'Darren got word to me that Brunel was here and you'd come after him,' the General announced, seeing the surprise on Belle's face as he appeared in the doorway. Wanting to keep her presence a secret, if possible, he waved her to stay back beyond the range of vision of the onlookers in the passage. 'Did you get him?'

'He's in here, by the wall,' the girl replied. 'Dead.'

'You'd best put this on again,' Handiman remarked, picking up the discarded skirt and handing it into the room. 'Then keep out of sight until I can get rid of these people.'

Showing brisk efficiency and considerable diplomacy, the General set to work at his self-appointed task. First he calmed the crowd, telling them that a notorious train- and bank-robber had been trailed to the hotel. The man had resisted arrest, so was shot down by the peace officers. Then Handiman apologised on behalf of the New Orleans Police Department for the hotel's guests having their sleep disturbed and requested that they should return to their rooms.

Something about the General's attitude, respectful, apologetic, yet warning that he would brook no interference, had caused the men and women to accede to his wishes. Before the doctor had returned, the passage was empty except for Handiman, the patrolman and the manager. From the latter, the General had obtained permission to make use of an empty room on the same floor. Then, dismissing the man with further apologies, he had escorted Belle to it. So smoothly had he acted that not even the doctor had been granted a clear view of the girl.

'What happened?' Handiman asked, having lit the room's lamp and closed the door to ensure their privacy.

'We caught de Bracy, just as we planned, and made him talk. Then I came here with Lieutenant St. Andre and Willie. Either Brunel was suspicious and had stayed awake, or he was a light sleeper. Whichever it was he shot St. Andre as we burst in and would maybe have killed us both if Willie hadn't tackled him. Willie was shot and hurt badly.'

'The doctor will tend to him. Count on St. Andre to see to that. How much have you learned?'

'Not a lot. Only where to find Brunel. And that the Frenchman has left New Orleans. He's going to Shreveport. According to de Bracy, the Brotherhood For Southron Freedom are going to hold a special, important meeting there. Of course, he may have been lying.'

'Do *you* think he was?' Handiman wanted to know.

'He was a very frightened man,' Belle replied. 'And he spoke the truth about where we would find Brunel. If it was any other town but Shreveport, 'I'd be certain he hadn't lied.'

'Why the doubts about Shreveport?'

'*You* know what's happening up there between the Army and the civilian population. With a man like that Colonel Szigo in command, its not likely the Brotherhood would dare to make any public demonstration.'

'Maybe they believe that would be the best town to make it in,' Handiman suggested. 'Lucienne told me they haven't been having any great, or lasting success in stirring up the population so far. Oh, they pull in the usual rabble of malcontents and loafers. But the majority of the population don't see any sense in trying to secede again. There's not a lot of bitterness against the Union since Reconstruction has tailed off and folks are starting to get prosperous.'

'So they want a town where there's real bitterness in which

to make their grandstand play?' Belle drawled. 'It's possible, but it could be as risky as all hell. Szigo would be only too pleased to put down a Rebel rebellion, if all I've heard of him is true.'

'Well——' Handiman said, unwilling to make an open criticism of another serving officer.

'He's an embittered man,' the girl elaborated. 'Lieutenant Colonel is only his brevet rank. He knows that, at any time, he can be replaced with a substantive officer and be reduced to the rank and pay of captain. A man like that would leap at a chance to come to the attention of Washington, by *any* means. And there aren't so many means of doing it in the East. All the glory's being won out West.'

'You seem to know plenty about Szigo,' Handiman commented, neither confirming nor denying the statement. 'Anyway, he's being replaced.'

'Replaced?'

'We're not exactly deaf, blind or stupid in Washington. Despite anything you agents in the field may believe, we do have some idea of what's going on around us. Like you, we've heard of what's happening in Shreveport and a full colonel, Manderley I believe it will be, is being sent to relieve him. With orders to make peace with the civil population.'

'I only hope that he arrives in time!' Belle declared fervently. 'The Brotherhood have proved that they don't give a damn about shedding innocent blood. With those hundred Henry repeaters, they could raise hell around Shreveport and it would spread all along the Red River—and beyond.'

'You're right,' Handiman conceded. 'So, in the morning, I'm going to have all the people named by Lucienne visited and questioned.'

'From what she said, few of them are deeply involved in the Brotherhood.'

'That's why I'm only having them visited. I've found that people who go in for joining these impressively named clandestine organisations soon drop out again when they find it's not so secret after all.'

'You might pick up a few details,' Belle admitted, then looked at Handiman in a calculating manner. 'You won't need me for it, will you, sir?'

'Have you something else in mind?'

'The Frenchman has gone to Shreveport——'

'And you want to go after him?'

131

'I intend to kill him,' Belle stated calmly.

Studying the beautiful face as he listened to the flat, impersonal words, Handiman felt as if an icy hand had touched his spine. That had not been a mere empty figure of speech. The Rebel Spy meant to do exactly what she had said.

'He'll be amongst friends——' the General warned.

'That won't stop me.'

'Some of them might be men you served with in the War——'

'Any friendship, or loyalty, I might have felt for them ended on the night of the *Prairie Belle*,' Belle answered. 'General, I don't want my country ripped apart by another civil war. God! The last was bad enough. Next time, if it happens, it will be to a finish. They have to be stopped.'

'I trust you, Colonel Boyd,' Handiman assured her. 'But the Frenchman——'

'He's caused the deaths of two good friends,' Belle interrupted. 'So I'm going to avenge them—And if I have to smash the Brotherhood to do it, so much the better for everybody's sake.'

Again there was no bombast, nor hysterical, unintended female threats; just a plain statement of facts.

Handiman found himself blessing the providence which had persuaded him to show good sense and hire Belle Boyd after the War had ended. With such a woman on their side, the Brotherhood For Southron Freedom would have been an even more terrible menace to the peace of the nation.

Yet, such was his faith in the Rebel Spy, the General—whose post as head of the Secret Service was not calculated to leave him with exaggerated faith in human nature and honesty—did not for a moment question her loyalty, or doubt that she would remain true to the oath of allegiance she had sworn to the Union.

'Go to Shreveport,' Handiman confirmed. 'You have your identification documents?'

'In the secret pocket on my gunbelt,' Belle replied.

'I'll give you letters of introduction to Manderley and Szigo, telling whichever's in command to give you every co-operation. You outrank Szigo, but my name will make sure that he appreciates that fact.'

'Thank you, sir.'

'Have you any plans for dealing with the situation?'

'None,' Belle admitted. 'I'll wait and see what develops. Or if it has developed, carry on from there. If I arrive before it happens, my uncle will do all he can to help me stop it. He's Colonel Alburgh Winslow.'

'A sensible and influential man,' Handiman praised. 'In fact, he, his newspaper and his group of moderate friends have done much to avert serious trouble between the Army and the town's people.'

'He'll keep right on doing it, come what may,' Belle promised and glanced at the door as somebody knocked. 'Shall I?'

'I will,' Handiman corrected, opening up to admit St. Andre.

'It's only a flesh wound,' the detective assured Belle when she had inquired about his injury. 'But Willie's hurt bad. He's asking to see you, Belle.'

'I'll go right away,' Belle said, coming to her feet. 'Is he alone?'

'The doctor's still with him, but he's an Army surgeon and won't talk,' St. Andre replied. 'My man's keeping the passage clear. By the way, I searched Brunel's belongings.'

'Is there anything of interest?' Handiman asked.

'I found this sheet of paper in his wallet,' St. Andre answered, producing and handing it over. 'It may not mean anything. All it gives is a name. "Sabot the Mysterious, last performance. Shreveport." He's a really good magician, I've seen his perfor——'

'At Memphis, they were going to hold a meeting in a theatre,' Belle interrupted. 'How soon can I start for Shreveport?'

'The *Elegant Lady* leaves at dawn,' St. Andre supplied the information. 'You could ride her to Baton Rouge, or Natchez, and get another boat to Shreveport. There's pretty sure to be one waiting to make a connection with the *Lady*.'

'That's what I'll do,' Belle declared. 'As soon as I've seen Willie, I'll go and gather my belongings. You'll see that Willie——'

'*I'll* attend to it, Miss Boyd,' St. Andre promised. 'He saved my life, too.'

'Miss Belle?' Willie groaned, as the girl went to his bed. 'You's going to Shreveport after the Frenchman?'

'Yes, Willie,' the girl agreed.

'Do me a lil favour.'

'Anything.'

133

'Take Massa Jim's ole Ames knife along,' Willie requested, gesturing weakly to the weapon on the dressing-table. 'When you gets to where the ole *Belle* was sunk, throw it in so's he knows I done got that Brunel feller.'

## CHAPTER FIFTEEN

## YOU SHOULDN'T HAVE HIT HER

*Belle Boyd had carried out Willie's request on her way north along the Mississippi River and had arrived in Shreveport in time to witness the Brotherhood For Southron Freedom's special meeting. Unable to decide what lay behind the interruption to Sabot the Mysterious' final performance, she was returning on foot to the theatre with the intention of satisfying her curiosity.*

Feeling certain that his presence was not suspected by the 'gal wearing pants', Hermy watched her disappear into an alley without any undue alarm. He saw nothing suspicious in her action. Shreveport had long since left behind the days when even an armed *man* could walk the streets without arousing curiosity. A girl, dressed in such an unconventional manner, would draw attention without the revolver hanging holstered on her right thigh. If she was headed to the theatre for some clandestine purpose, she would wish to avoid being the source of interest or comment.

Reaching the mouth of the alley, Hermy could neither see nor hear the girl in its deeply shadowed length. So he hurried forward, wanting to know which way she had gone. At the rear end, he stepped cautiously out and looked in the direction she would have taken if she was going back to the theatre. Still being unable to locate her, he scowled and wondered if he had been mistaken about having seen her entering the alley.

That question was answered promptly; although not in a manner he would have wished it to happen.

'To arms! To arms, in Dixie!' said a feminine voice from behind him.

Letting out a startled, profane ejaculation, Hermy started to turn and sent his hand under his cloak-coat in search of a weapon.

Having detected Hermy following her, Belle had decided that she must throw him off her track. However, he might have been merely a casual, disinterested pedestrian and taking the same direction by coincidence. Or he could have been a peace officer, made suspicious by her male attire and the gunbelt. In either case, she had no desire to assault him.

Taking cover behind the corner of the building farthest from the theatre, the girl had awaited developments. Everything had depended upon how the man reacted to her disappearance. Once she had seen that, she had settled upon her own line of action. It was simple, effective—and very much to the point.

The fact that the man had approached so cautiously had not been sufficient in itself to prove he belonged to the Brotherhood and had guessed her purpose. A peace officer, following an armed suspect, would have displayed a similar caution. However, Hermy's actions on arriving at the end of the alley had struck her as significant. When he had turned immediately to look in the direction which she would have taken on her way to the theatre, she had been satisfied that he was following her on behalf of the organisation.

Although Belle held her Dance, she did not use it as a firearm. To have done as would have made a noise and attracted unwanted interest in her actions.

Instead, the girl launched a *savate* attack with all the power and precision she could muster. The area was so dark that she could not make out details of the man's clothing and appearance, other than that he was big enough to be more than she could handle in a fight. So she hoped to render him helpless, without allowing him to defend himself.

Belle's boot drove upwards, between Hermy's spread-apart thighs and caught him full in the groin with nauseating force. Unmentionable, unendurable agony ground its way through his whole being. He started to fold over, knees buckling and hands clutching at the stricken region. His troubles had not yet ended.

The girl did not rely upon the kick to disable the man. There was too much at stake for her to chance him recovering prematurely. So she swung the Dance. As it was an open-frame revolver, like the 1860 Army Colt, she knew better than to strike with the barrel. Instead she flung the base of the butt savagely against the back of Hermy's close-cropped skull. Down he went, like a steer under a butcher's pole-axe.

Without waiting to establish the extent of her victim's injuries, Belle holstered the Dance, She did not particularly care if the man was alive or dead. One thing she knew. There was nothing more to fear from him at that moment—nor for some time to come. Satisfied on that score, she strode away in the direction the unconscious man had been looking.

On drawing near the theatre, following the back alleys, Belle could see no traces of the evening's dramatic events. Despite their enthusiastic response to the speech-making, and subsequent excitement, the crowd had not lingered in the hope of further developments. Perhaps, once out in the cool night's air and removed from the symbols of their patriotic fervour, they had had second thoughts about their reawakened loyalty to the Confederate cause. Or they might have scattered to spread the news of what had happened. Belle hoped that it was the former contingency that had brought about the dispersal of the audience.

Whatever the reason, the building and its immediate surroundings were devoid of human life. That was just how Belle had hoped to find it. She noticed that half a dozen horses were standing fastened to the hitching rail behind the theatre and decided that her return had been justified.

Keeping away from the animals, for she did not want them to raise an alarm at her presence, Belle passed along the dark alley by the theatre. She was approaching the flight of stone steps which led up to the stage door when it opened.

Two long, silent strides carried Belle to the wall at the level side of the steps. There she crouched in the deep darkness, clear of the pool of light which was coming through the door. Heavy boots thudded close above her head and men started to emerge from the theatre.

'Vic!' called a voice which she recognised as that of Sabot the Mysterious, mingling with the sound of hurrying, lightly shod feet.

'What's wrong?' demanded the leading figure, bringing his companions to a halt.

Again Belle believed that she should know the voice, but failed to place it. Hoping for a clue, she remained in her position and stood as if turned to stone. Relying upon her dark clothing to help keep her concealed, she drew the Dance. Holding its white handle before her, she turned to face the wall. It was a trick she had learned from Big Sam Ysabel during the final hunt for Tollinger and Barmain.

'Selima's not in her dressing-room,' Sabot replied. 'She's changed into her street clothes and's taken off.'

'Where to?' growled the man Belle assumed to be 'Vic'.

'I'm damned if I know. Maybe back to the rooming-house. But, the way you laid into her when you came off the stage, she might have decided to run out on us. You shouldn't have hit her that way.'

'So let the stupid whore go! She damned near gave the whole snap away, the way she carried on out there tonight. Damn it! She didn't even pretend to be worried when we came on to the stage.'

'I warned you that she wasn't very smart,' Sabot protested, in a self-exculpatory tone.

'Can you trust her, is more to the point,' Vic stated.

'How do you mean?' the magician inquired.

'Would she inform on us?'

'I'm damned if I know what she'd do, pot-boiling mad like she was over you slapping her around. De Richelieu didn't help, either, saying she deserved it and worse. She's a hot-tempered bitch at the best of times.'

'God damn it!' Vic raged. 'If I thought that she aimed to——'

'Somebody had best go and fetch her back,' Sabot interrupted. 'I can keep her under control. And I'll need her for the act when I reach Texas.'

'Can't you train another girl?' Vic challenged. 'One with a few brains this time.'

'I could do that easily enough, if I could find the right kind of girl,' the magician confirmed. 'But leaving Selima behind won't make her feel any better disposed towards us. So she's got to be fetched back.'

'What about the rest of our plans?' Vic asked.

'I'd say let them ride until we know what she's got in mind,' Sabot counselled. 'Get after her and bring her to me, then go on to Winslow's, is what I'd advise.'

'You're right,' Vic admitted grudgingly. 'That's what we'll do.'

'How about those two fellers who've gone to keep watch on him?' Sabot put in. 'They're expecting you to get there soon.'

'Matt's steady enough,' Vic replied. 'He'll stay put until we get there and stop that other bastard doing anything stupid. Once we've got her, or made sure she can't talk, we'll go ahead with the plan. What will you be doing?'

'Following de Richelieu's orders,' Sabot replied coldly. 'Heading for the river and the *Texarkana Belle*. If I've gone when you come back, send her after me, will you?'

'I'll do that,' Vic promised. 'We'd best not all go. Andy, you and Mick come with me, the rest stay on here.'

A muttered rumble of agreement rose. Then some of the feet started moving. Three men came through the door and walked down the steps. Apparently Sabot did not want them to remain for long in view of the street. Almost as soon as they had emerged, he closed the door.

With the light blotted out and the darkness returned to the alley, Belle chanced looking over her shoulder. The men went by, without noticing her crouching in the deepest shadows. However, the lack of light proved to be a mixed blessing. While the trio failed to locate her, she could not see any of their faces. All she managed to do was pick out certain significant details of their attire.

Something under six foot in height, with a good but not heavy build, the man in the lead—Belle assumed he was 'Vic' —wore what could only be an Army *kepi* on his head. Given that much of a clue, she identified his outer garment as a cavalry officer's long cloak-coat; from beneath the hem of which thrust the scabbard of a sabre that must be hanging on the slings of his waist-belt. He had on regulation white gauntlets, she could see, and shining riding boots.

Taller than their companion, or officer, the other two had on Burnside campaign hats, enlisted men's cloak-coats and riding boots, although neither of them was armed with a sabre.

Peering through the gloom, Belle watched the trio depart. The man she believed to be 'Vic' seemed vaguely familiar. He strolled along with the cocky military swagger that was often the gait of an arrogant young officer. Trudging slightly to his rear, the other pair had the bearing of soldiers. They passed around the corner of the building. Leather creaked soon after and Belle heard the sound of horses moving away.

'Now what would soldiers be doing in there?' Belle mused as she retraced her steps along the alley. 'Uncle Alburgh said that the town was off limits to them tonight.'

Could Szigo have learned of the Brotherhood's visit and laid a trap for them at the theatre?

That was not likely. Besides which, Szigo was no longer in command.

Why were the men, whoever they might be, so interested in her uncle that they had some of their number watching his home?

Then Belle remembered General Handiman's comment about Winslow and the other moderate, influential citizens—her uncle's companions at the theatre that night, in fact—having prevented trouble between the civilian population and the soldiers.

'So that's the plan!' Belle gasped.

The three men had already ridden out of sight. Running to the horses which remained at the rail, Belle unfastened one's reins. She swung into the saddle, finding that it was of the military McClellan type. That proved little. Many such rigs were in civilian hands, being cheap and reasonably serviceable. Hoping that she would not be seen, she started the horse moving at a fast trot.

Traversing the town, Belle guided her borrowed mount along the darkened almost deserted street towards Winslow's mansion. A big, bulky figure leaned against the gates to the property and peered in her direction. Then he turned and hurried into the garden. From his size and bulk, Belle knew that he was not one of her uncle's servants. In addition, she had noticed the shape of his hat and detected the glint of metal buttons on distinctive clothing.

There had been something furtive about his actions that was calculated to arouse her suspicions. Mainly, though, her interest had stemmed from the fact that he was an enlisted man of the United States' cavalry—or dressed like one.

Even as her mind was assimilating the details of the man's appearance, and drawing conclusions from his presence, she rode by an empty buggy. It was parked unattended near the sidewalk before the commencement of Winslow's property. Glancing at it in passing, she noticed a civilian cloak lying on the seat.

A vehicle of that kind had passed shortly after she had caused her uncle's carriage to be halted. At the time, she had thought nothing of it other than to automatically make a note of its occupants' appearance. They had been a pair of big, burly, bare-headed men wearing either long overcoats or cloaks, despite the warmth of the evening.

The man who had followed her and had been left unconscious would have fitted that description!

Draping the one-piece reins on the horse's neck, Belle slid from the saddle without causing it to slow down from its walking gait. She could not see through the thick hedge which surrounded her uncle's garden, but felt that she might turn the lack of vision to her advantage. A gentle slap on the rump encouraged the horse to keep going. Winslow's stable would provide her with any further transportation she might require and she was not concerned with where the animal went now that it had served its purpose.

Allowing the horse to disappear along the street, Belle walked silently to the garden's gates and entered. There was no sign of the man, but a number of decorative bushes offered him a selection of hiding-places. Giving no hint that she was aware of his presence, she strolled along the wide gravel path towards the front of the big, Colonial-style mansion.

Having no desire to be seen, and perhaps challenged, by the approaching rider, Matt had taken up his place of conceal-ment behind a bush not far from the open gates. Vic's party would not arrive singly, so the rider could not be one of the Brotherhood. One disadvantage to the cover he had selected was that he could not see the street. However, he had no difficulty in hearing the horse's hoof-beats and knew that it was going straight by.

On the point of emerging, Matt saw a slender, boyish figure walking through the gates. At first he felt puzzled, wondering why the newcomer would be visiting Winslow at such a late hour. Then realisation came with the impact of a kick in the stomach.

That was no boy, but a slim girl wearing male clothing!

Matt recollected how Hermy had claimed to have seen a 'gal wearing pants' emerge from Winslow's carriage. At the time, Matt had been suspicious of his companion's veracity. He had believed that Hermy was lying, as an excuse to quit the poten-tially dangerous business upon which they were engaged. So he had accepted Hermy's story and given the order for 'her' to be followed. He had not expected to see his companion again and had felt that it was good riddance.

From all appearances, Hermy had been telling the truth. That he should have mentioned a girl wearing riding breeches and for one to turn up at Winslow's house went beyond the bounds of pure coincidence. Hermy had seen the girl, but she must have eluded him in some way. That would not have been a difficult task, in Matt's opinion. He had formed a very low impression of his companion's intelligence and abilities.

Well, the man concluded as he crept from behind the bush, she would find Matt Cilstow a much more difficult proposition than the dull-witted Hermy.

Moving cautiously across Winslow's well-barbered lawn, Matt kept to his victim's rear as he converged with her. He realised that his progress would be anything but noiseless once he set foot upon the gravel of the path. So he intended to get as close as possible before doing it.

One thing was in Matt's favour, or so he told himself. The girl was unaware of his presence.

With that thought in mind, Matt stepped on to the path. He had gauged his distance perfectly. Before the girl could take fright from hearing his footsteps, and turn or try to draw her revolver, he was close enough to make his move. Encircling her from the rear with his brawny arms, he pinioned her elbows against her sides. He intended to crush her savagely, driving the air from her lungs and rendering her incapable of crying for help. Having taken that precaution, he would fling her down so that she could be completely subdued. Then, carried away to some secluded spot, she could be induced to answer questions.

All of which might have worked, but for one small, yet vitally significant detail. Belle was far from being as unsuspecting of her peril as Matt had fondly imagined. Moreover, by using some of the techniques which she had learned from Dusty Fog, to augment her *savate*, she had hopes which ran parallel to her assailant's intentions.

Instead of trying to pull away, as Matt expected and was ready to prevent, Belle seemed to wilt in his grasp. She also contracted her torso as far as possible and hugged inwards with her trapped arms. Having decided how she would react, the man was disconcerted by her refusal to behave in the expected manner.

Clenching her left fist, Belle ground its knuckles vigorously against the back of Matt's right hand. At the same time, she stamped the heel of her right foot against the edge of his left instep. The double pangs of pain caused him to separate his hands before the fingers interlocked. Instantly Belle rammed her rump into him, gaining a little more room to manoeuvre. Bending at the waist, she reached between her legs in an attempt to catch hold of his left ankle.

At which point, her counter started to go wrong.

Before she could lay hands on his leg—with the intention of jerking it upwards, sitting on his knee and toppling him backwards with considerable force, Matt's hands had clamped on to her shoulders and snatched her upright.

'Smart whore, huh?' the man gritted, moving his fingers until they coiled about her throat and his thumbs pressed forward on the nape of her neck. 'Well, I'm too smart for you.'

Already Belle had commenced a line of action calculated to refute Matt's claim to possessing greater intelligence. Once again, she failed to respond in the way her attacker had anticipated.

Despite the crushing, choking pressure being exerted upon her wind-pipe, Belle did not attempt to tear her neck free by brute force. To do so against her captor's strength would have been futile. Instead, she tilted her torso towards him. Her right leg raised and bent, then flung back its foot to spike the heel hard on to his right knee-cap.

Matt let out a sharp intake of breath and relaxed his pressure a trifle. Instantly Belle's hands whipped up and over her head to grab his thick wrists. Using her left foot as a pivot, she swivelled her body sharply to the right. Snatching the man's loosened fingers from her neck, she elevated his left arm and jerked his right underneath it. Swiftly forcing his left elbow on to the right arm, she invested all her weight and strength into a forwards and downwards thrusting heave. Thrown off balance, Matt's feet rose into the air. His Burnside hat tumbled off as he sailed over in a near perfect somersault.

Too near, in fact!

Belle released her hold once she had got him into the air. Staggering with the force she had put into the effort, she saw that he had contrived to land on his feet instead of alighting hard on the base of his spine. However, he stumbled and seemed to be in danger of falling flat on his face.

Wanting to incapacitate her assailant, Belle fought to regain her equilibrium. Doing so took her four running strides. In control of her movements, she swung around and darted in his direction. Too late she observed that he too had recovered from the effects of the throw.

Obligingly, if inadvertently, Belle ran into range. Swinging towards her, Matt whipped his left arm up and across. The back of his hand collided with her cheek. Bright lights burst in front of her eyes. Gasping in pain and half blinded by the tears it caused, she went spinning helplessly across the path. Catching her left toe against her right ankle as she reached the lawn, she tripped. Her horse-riding instincts helped her to soften the impact of the fall. For all that, she landed hard and rolled over three times before coming to a halt, supine, dazed and winded, on the grass.

Spitting out threats of violence, Matt thumbed open his holster and started to draw his revolver. He had decided against trying to take that hell-cat a prisoner and intended to close her mouth permanently.

Belle saw what the man planned to do, but was too befuddled to make a move in her own defence. Out came the revolver, slanting in her direction. A shot rang out; but it was the flat crack of a rifle and from farther away than her attacker's weapon. With the top of his head seeming to erupt like a burst sack of flour, the man was flung sideways and to the ground.

Lights showed at the doors of the mansion. Grasping a rifle, Winslow sprinted along the path, followed by Hector carrying a lantern.

'Are you all right, Belle?' Winslow demanded.

'I've felt better,' he girl admitted. 'But it could have been worse. How did you——?'

'I've been watching him hanging about at the gate ever since Hector said that he'd followed us home,' Winslow explained. 'When he attacked you, I got my Winchester lined and stopped him as soon as you were out of my line of fire. He's a soldier!'

'It looks that way,' Belle admitted, standing up and approaching the body. 'Bring the light here, please Hector.'

Bending closer, Belle studied the buttons on the blue jacket. At first glance, they looked like the standard issue. There were, however, two noticeable differences. Each button had the usual spread-eagle and three-pointed shield insignia, but instead of the 'A', 'C' or 'I', by which the wearer's branch of service— Artillery, Cavalry or Infantry—was revealed, it bore the letter 'D'. And while ordinary buttons displayed no further adornment, the ones worn by her attacker carried an inscription.

'*Ad Astra Per Aspera*,' Belle read out.

'That's the state motto of Kansas,' Winslow interpreted.

'And the "D" means "Dragoon". He must have belonged to some Kansan militia outfit and kept the buttons on his jacket.'

'I don't think he served in the Blue,' Belle contradicted. 'Can you have two horses saddled, Uncle Alburgh? You and I have to go out. Pray God we're in time. If we're not, there'll be murder done tonight and we'll be on our way to another civil war comes morning.'

## CHAPTER SIXTEEN

## SHE'S DONE FOR, VIC!

Although the sergeant of the guard looked with a hint of incredulity from Belle to the identification card she had shown him and back again, he did not attempt to question the validity of the document.

'You want me to send a man with you, ma'—col—ma——?' the non-com inquired, uncertain of how he should address the visitor.

'Is that Headquarters?' Belle asked, indicating the large, well-lit mansion ahead of her.

'Yes'm,' the sergeant confirmed. 'You'll find the colonel up on the first floor, in the officers' club. I'll have a man——'

'I can find it,' Belle assured him and started her horse moving.

'You reckon that paper she showed us's real, serge?' the sentry wanted to know as Belle rode away.

'I dunno,' admitted the non-com. 'What I *do* know is that happen it is for real, I didn't want to stop her. That gal's not like the other. She's a lady. And talking of Selima, where the hell's Brody?'

'Maybe the new colonel's got him up there in officers' country for a drink 'n' a talk, friendly-like,' grinned the sentry. 'This here's a no good chore, serge. There's too many folk coming tonight.'

'It's to be expected,' commented the sergeant. 'With the change of command and all.'

If Belle had heard the reference to Selima, she might have been very interested. As it was, she rode the mount borrowed from her uncle towards the hitching rail by the porch of the mansion.

Having explained her theory to Winslow, Belle had left him to take care of certain precautions. Then she had mounted the horse which he had selected and set off for the Army post. She prayed that she might be in time to set the soldiers into motion. Given luck, anyway, she had spoiled the devilish scheme which the Brotherhood For Southron Freedom had planned to implement in Shreveport.

Leaving her horse alongside two others which were tethered to the hitching rail, Belle slipped off the cloak which she had donned at Winslow's house. She had worn the garment to avoid attracting attention during the ride to the post, but the night was too warm for it to be comfortable. So she draped it over her saddle, secured the horse and ascended the steps to the porch. Crossing it, she tried the front doors. They opened and she stepped into the dimly illuminated main hall.

Hearing Belle enter, a man turned from where he had been standing at the door of one of the rooms which led from the hall. Stiffening slightly, he threw a glance at the door. Then he walked towards the girl. He advanced with a somewhat arrogant gait. His whole bearing hinted that he belonged in the building, but that he doubted whether the newcomer did.

Something about the man caught Belle's eye and started thoughts leaping in her head. Under six foot in height, he had a sturdy, yet not exceptional build and a handsome, but hard, face. An officer's *kepi* sat at a rakish angle on his head and his uniform was that of a cavalry captain. Going by his white gauntlets and the sabre dangling from the slings of his weapon belt—balanced by the holster at his right side—he was performing some military duty rather than relaxing after a day's work.

The duty could not be officer-of-the-day, Belle realised. That was the province of first, or second, lieutenants, not captains.

'Good evening,' the officer greeted, with coldly polite formality, while still some distance from the girl. 'Can I help you?'

Was he speaking louder than necessary? Belle mused. Or did he always adopt that carrying tone of voice?

Even as she pondered on those points, Belle realised that the captain had spoken with more than a hint of a Southron accent. What was more, she felt sure that she had heard a similar style of speaking already that night. She observed that he was starting to draw off his right gauntlet——

And the flap of his holster was open!

Taken at its face value, the latter was not an important detail. Considering the other items which Belle had noticed, it might be highly significant.

There were Southrons serving as officers in the United States' Army; men who had felt that their loyalties lay in preserving

147

the Union, or who had been disenchanted with the Confederate States' way of life. So the accent was not out of place.

However, Belle's study of the captain had led her to class him as a bow-necked, parade ground martinet who would take great pride in his personal appearance. Such a man would only allow the flap of his holster to be unfastened if he was expecting to need the revolver it carried. There could be no such need, or expectancy, at the Headquarters building of an Army post, unless——

Thinking back to her second visit to the theatre, Belle remembered the conversation she had overheard between Sabot the Mysterious and the man he had called 'Vic'. It had had to do with the possibility of the magician's assistant informing the authorities of their activities. 'Vic' had promised to find her. What was more, he had been wearing the uniform of an officer in the United States' Cavalry. The cloak-coat and the darkness had combined to prevent her from discovering his rank, but she had seen the sabre he was wearing.

At the time, Belle had been puzzled by seeing the weapon. In most cases, a sabre merely served as a symbol of authority when performing some duty.

A duty like arresting men guilty of treason!

That would be a task assigned to a captain!

Before Belle could take her thoughts any further, somebody opened the door at which the captain had been standing. A tall, burly corporal stepped out in a furtive manner. Raw scratches showed on his cheeks and hands, as if he had been raked by a cat's claws——

Except that the bloody furrows were spaced at wider intervals than any domestic cat's talons would spread.

'She's done for, Vic,' the corporal said as he appeared. 'Lord, did she——'

On hearing the words, a hot flush of anger played over the officer's features. He saw a flicker of understanding cross the girl's face and sensed that, somehow or other, she realised he had no right to be in the building. If so, his 'corporal's' stupidly incautious words would have been proof for her that something was radically wrong.

There was only one thing for 'Vic' to do.

Snapping his right hand back to the already unfastened holster, the captain started to draw his revolver. The move was made with some speed and hinted that he was well used to the kind of rig in which the United States' Army insisted that its

148

personnel carried their side-arms.

Everything was suddenly plain to Belle. By some trick of accoustics, Vic's voice had been distorted at the theatre. So she had failed to recognise it when he had addressed her on her arrival. Yet she now realised why it had sounded vaguely familiar. The first time she had heard it was on the stage of the theatre. Unless she was badly mistaken, 'Vic' had been the second of the spokesmen.

Pure instinct caused the girl to respond to the menace. Already her right hand had turned and was wrapping its fingers about the smooth ivory grips of the Dance. Throwing herself sideways, she swept the gun from leather. Its hammer went back under her thumb and she swung the barrel into alignment as she had done so many times in practice.

Even as Vic's revolver cleared the cumbersome holster's lip, flame licked from the barrel of Belle's Dance. Aimed by instinctive alignment, the ·36 ball ploughed into 'Vic's' forehead. Releasing his revolver unfired, the captain pivoted almost gracefully and sprawled headlong to the floor.

Realising that he had made a mistake, the corporal was equally aware of the danger to himself. He saw his companion shot down and was all too aware of the slender girl's skill in handling her gun. It was a standard of ability to which he could not aspire. So he did not make any attempt to do so. Jumping back into the room, he jerked the door closed behind him.

Darting across the hall, ignoring the shouts which rang out from the floor above, Belle heard the man's feet crossing the room. Then glass shattered and the footsteps faded away. Belle knew what the sound implied. So she did not offer to enter the room. Turning, she ran along the passage to the front door.

Starting to go through, the girl discovered that the man had moved swiftly after leaping through the window of the room. He had also taken the opportunity to arm himself; a fact of which Belle was rapidly made aware.

Having sprinted to the front of the building, the corporal had been on the point of freeing his horse when he had heard Belle approaching the front entrance. He also heard the sentry yelling for the sergeant of the guard, but treated it as of secondary importance. That blasted girl not only dressed like a man, she could shoot like one. So she was a greater potential danger than the soldiers of the guard. They might hesitate before opening fire upon a man they took to be a corporal. At least, they would most likely delay for long enough to let him ride them down and burst through the gates to safety.

First, however, the girl must be dealt with.

Thrusting forward his Army Colt, the corporal snapped off a shot in Belle's direction. He fired fast and without making sure of his aim; never a combination conducive to accuracy.

Lead impacted on the frame of the door in front of the Rebel Spy. Jerking back involuntarily, she paused to review the situation. Hearing sounds which told her the man was mounting his horse, she made her second attempt to effect an exit. Going through the door in a rolling dive, she halted on her left side at the edge of the porch. Clasping the Dance's butt in both hands, she looked swiftly along the barrel at the corporal's rage-distorted face.

Then Belle changed her point of aim. A living, if wounded, prisoner could satisfy her curiosity on a number of points. Chiefly, given the correct inducements, he could describe the Frenchman and instruct Belle on the source of her hatred's appearance.

So the girl lowered the Dance's barrel, until it pointed at the corporal's right shoulder. Controlling his restless horse, he was trying to throw down on her. She refused to let that fluster her, or change her intention.

The Dance barked, but Belle believed that she had heard a second, more distant detonation. Aimed truly, her bullet entered the blue jacket in an ideal position to break his clavicle. The light load of a Navy-calibre* revolver might lack stopping power, as had been proven when Brunel had shot Willie, but Belle was confident that the corporal could not ride far while suffering from such an injury.

As Belle's bullet found its mark and entered, something burst violently out of the corporal's chest in a spray of blood, splintered bones and pulverised flesh. His body jerked uncontrollably and blood gushed from a far vaster wound than the

---

* The Navy had not selected the calibre of ·36 because—as many soldiers boasted it was easier to kill a sailor than a soldier. A revolver of that calibre could be made light enough—two pounds, ten ounces in the Colt Navy Model of 1851, as opposed to the four pounds, one ounce weight of the same Company's Model 1848 Dragon—for a man, who would be on foot and indulging in strenuous activities, to spend long periods wearing it holstered at his belt. The ·44 'Army' calibre handguns had been intended primarily for use by Dragoons and other mounted men.

Navy's ball could have made. Shying violently, his horse flung him from the saddle. Falling on to the mount 'Vic' had used, he was pitched from its rump and to the ground.

Coming to her feet, Belle sprang from the porch. While approaching the writhing shape, she saw the sergeant turning and addressing the sentry. The latter lowered his smoking carbine and attempted to offer some explanation. Ignoring him, the sergeant urged the remainder of the guard to increase their speed and led them on the double towards the house.

Although Belle held her Dance ready for use, she saw that she would not require it. Before she reached the stricken corporal, his body gave a final convulsive shudder and went limp. Lowering the hammer to rest on the safety notch between two of the percussion caps, she returned the Dance to its holster. Without considering how the action might be interpreted, she turned to go back into the mansion.

The sergeant of the guard did not know what had happened inside the building, having only the evidence of his eyes to go on. What he could see looked highly suspicious and dangerous to his rank. A long-serving soldier, he was inclined to take the side of the shot 'corporal' for want of better evidence. If the sentry—who had fired without orders—had killed another member of the U.S. Cavalry, the sergeant would be held responsible. So he intended to hold on to the only witness, who might also be a guilty party.

'Hold it right there, lady!' the sergeant bellowed, making the command in such a manner that she could not use it against him if the rank on her identification card should be genuine.

Wisely, Belle complied. She guessed that the sergeant had reached an erroneous conclusion regarding her actions. Although the corporal's horse had bolted on being relieved of his weight, two more animals were fighting their reins at the hitching rail. So the non-com suspected that she could be contemplating mounting one and making a dash for safety.

The arrival of the guard, glowering suspiciously in the light of the lanterns two of them carried, coincided with the appearance of three officers at the front door.

'What's happening?' demanded the burly, bearded colonel in the lead.

'I'm damned if I know, sir,' the sergeant of the guard admitted. 'That two-bar come running like his arse was on fire, just after we heard a window busted. He jumped on his hoss, then this ga—lady come out shooting.'

'He'd shot at her first,' protested the sentry, wishing to absolve himself of blame for his spontaneous action. 'And was set to do it again.'

'That's right, sir. He did,' conceded the non-com. He was still uncertain of Belle's standing in the affair and aimed to take no chances.

'Who is this man?' asked the major who had been last of the trio to emerge, studying the dead 'corporal' in the light of the lanterns. 'I don't seem to recognise him.'

'He come in with the captain's'd brought the dispatches for Colonel Szigo, sir,' the sergeant explained.

'Dispatches?' grunted the lanky, miserable lieutenant colonel, making his first comment. '*Dispatches?* I've seen no damned captain——'

'But he came maybe ten minutes back, sir,' the sergeant protested. 'He said I didn't need to send nobody with him, 'cause him and the corporal knew their way. Then the sentry told me the gal was coming and they rode up here while I was turning to look.'

'Which girl?' asked Colonel Manderley and indicated Belle. 'This one?'

'No, sir,' corrected the non-com. 'It was Selima, that magical feller's gal. She come asking to see Colonel Szigo. Wouldn't say what she wanted, 'cepting that it was important. Looked like she'd been getting slapped around by somebody and she was madder'n a boiled owl. So I told Brody to fetch her up here.'

'She never arrived, either,' the major growled. 'Just what the hell is going on here?'

'I think I can explain,' Belle put in. 'But you'd better have somebody look in that open room along the hall first. You'll find the girl in there, and your soldier. I hope that he's still alive, but I'm sure she isn't.'

'Do it, Major!' Manderley ordered, eyeing Belle with interest and appraisal. After the officer had departed, he went on, 'I think explanations are in order, young lady.'

'Shall we go inside?' the girl suggested. 'I would prefer to talk in private, if that's all right with you.'

'Come with me, please,' Manderley consented. 'Sergeant, leave the body until the officer of the day comes and searches it.'

Clearly the major had not wasted a second in carrying out his orders. As Manderley and Szigo followed Belle into the hall, he appeared at the door of the room. Other officers were gathered and one was kneeling alongside 'Vic's' body.

'There's a dead girl in here,' the major declared. 'She's been strangled. Brody's here, too, unconscious. Get inside and do what you can, Doctor.'

'Excuse me, sir,' said the officer, rising from his examination of 'Vic'. 'I know this man. But he shouldn't be wearing that uniform.'

'How do you mean?' Szigo demanded irritably.

'His name is Victor Brandt, sir,' the officer elaborated. 'He was a lieutenant in the Fourth Cavalry when I was with them. But he was busted out of the Army when some soft-shell* politicians reported that he was abusing and mistreating the enlisted men.'

Until she heard the 'captain's' name, Belle had wondered if he might be the Frenchman. She had felt sure that he was the second of the spokesmen; which had suggested that he was a senior member of the Brotherhood. When he had spoken to Sabot at the stage door, it had been in hard, imperious tones that might have been indicative of a hasty temper. From the conversation, it had been he who punished Selima for her unsatisfactory behaviour on the stage.

Against that, Belle had heard another name mentioned. 'De Richelieu' was definitely of French origin. Its owner had clearly approved of 'Vic's' chastisement of Selima, implying that he had been the first spokesman. He might also have been the Frenchman, and had held back from dealing with the girl because he had known that he could not hold his temper within reasonable bounds.

'Victor Brandt' was certainly not a French name. Nor did it seem likely that a man with the Frenchman's warped pleasure in inflicting pain would have left the disposal of a traitress to another member of the Brotherhood. So Belle decided that her quest had not yet ended. She would have to seek elsewhere before she could avenge the deaths of Madame Lucienne and Jim Bludso.

* Soft-shell: a crusading liberal-intellectual.

## CHAPTER SEVENTEEN

# I'M NOT SORRY SABOT ESCAPED

'They've all got clean away, Miss Boyd,' Colonel Manderley announced grimly as the girl entered his office at one thirty in the morning. 'My men raided the theatre, but it was deserted. By that time, the *Texarkana Belle* had left and they didn't even get Sabot.'

'How about my uncle and his friends?' Belle demanded anxiously.

'They're safe. If the thing was planned as you suspected, they didn't carry it out. Probably because Brandt wasn't there to lead the others.'

'Yes. They're weren't likely to have two "officers". Your men didn't locate the arms, I suppose?'

'Not yet. I've got them scouring the woods around the city. It's possible the Brotherhood have them hidden somewhere in Shreveport, I suppose.'

'I doubt that,' Belle objected. 'It's my belief that they wouldn't want to take a chance on losing their weapons. So they'll have held them somewhere that would allow them to be moved to safety if anything went wrong. Either out in the woods, or along the river.'

'That's how I see it,' Manderley admitted. 'I hope we do find them. A hundred repeaters, even old Henrys, in the hands of men like the Brotherhood isn't something I care to contemplate.'

Having invited Belle to accompany him and Szigo into his office, Manderley had checked her documents. He had read Handiman's letter of introduction, then asked the girl how he might best be able to help her. Making her suggestions, she had told the officers about the Brotherhood's activities. Szigo had not been pleased to learn that he had been duped, but he had been wise enough to keep his opinions to himself.

Although much of Belle's summation had been speculative, she had come close to the truth in her explanation of the night's events.

Having stirred up considerable ill-feeling against the Union, amongst the audience at the free show, the Brotherhood had planned to keep tempers at boiling point. If their next move had worked, it would have probably resulted in open conflict between the citizens and the soldiers.

Disguised as members of the United States' Army, in uniforms taken from the Dragoons' equipment bales, Brandt's party were to have 'arrested' Winslow and his companions for their part in the treasonable activities at the theatre. With them all collected, they would have been murdered. Not only would their deaths—apparently at the hands of men under Szigo's command—have inflamed the town's people with a desire for revenge, it would have removed the restraining influence which Winslow and the others might have exerted.

A man like Szigo could have been relied upon to add further fuel to the fires of hatred by his attitude. Probably he would have refused to even investigate the accusations. Faced with what he would have been only too pleased to call an open rebellion, he would strike back. There would have been fighting, with Southrons and soldiers killed.

Such an incident could not have been kept out of the newspapers. Once the story got out, it would spread like a brushfire. Agitators in both the North and the South would pounce on to it. Perhaps it would not lead immediately to a second secession, but the seeds would have been sown. The Brotherhood would have made sure that they developed and blossomed into an open break from the Union.

The plan had started to go wrong when Brandt had punished Selima. Bitter at the treatment, she had been determined to take her revenge. Leaving the theatre, she had visited the rooming-house in which she was boarding. After collecting her portable belongings, she had set out to lay her information. That had presented her with a problem. She wanted to benefit financially from her treachery and had wondered who might best suit her needs. Knowing little about the Brotherhood, other than that its members claimed to be well-supported in their activities, she had decided against consulting the local civilian authorities. They might have been in league with her employers. So she had elected to take her news to the Army. She had known Szigo and other officers, which would ensure that they granted her an interview.

What the girl had not known was that her departure had been discovered. Brandt and the two soldiers had gone to the rooming-house and learned that she had already left. Guessing which way she would go, Brandt had sent Mick to the theatre with orders not to start the plan until he returned. Then he and Andy had made for the post, hoping to find her before she arrived. Missing her, due to taking a more direct route, they had been interviewing the sergeant of the guard when they had seen her coming. So they had made their way to the Headquarters building and lain in wait for her. Her arrival with an escort had presented no problems. Brody had been clubbed insensible as he entered and the girl silenced. At Brandt's suggestion, Andy had taken Selima into the room and dealt with her. A 'captain', even one who was not a regular member of the garrison, would have been less likely to have his presence in the building questioned. So he had left the silencing to his companion while he kept watch.

When Brandt had not returned, Sabot the Mysterious had taken it upon himself to cancel the rest of the plan. Dismissing the men and sending a warning to de Richelieu, who was waiting with the arms at a farm five miles from Shreveport, the magician had made his departure as planned on the *Texarkana Belle*. Assuming that the horse which Belle had taken had pulled free its reins and wandered off, the conspirators had attached no greater significance to its disappearance. Most of them, indeed, had been so eager to make good their escapes that they had not given the matter a second thought. Before the Army had commenced its search, the Brotherhood For Southron Freedom were well on their way to safety.

While being very eager to capture the agitators, Manderley had also been aware of how delicate the situation was. He had approved of Szigo's decision to place the town off limits that night, so did not want to alarm the population—or permit accusations of failure to keep his word—by sending a large armed force in search of the Brotherhood. Compromising, he had sent a dozen picked men under the command of his most trustworthy officer; a major who had never approved of Szigo's handling of the civilian population. Reinforcements had stood to arms, ready to follow the patrol if there should have been any shooting. The major had returned from his abortive mission and reported to Manderley. Having sent to the room where Belle was catching some badly needed sleep, the colonel had brought her up to date with the events of the night.

'We found that feller you told us about,' Manderley went on. 'He was still unconscious and the doctor says his skull is fractured. So he might not remember anything when, or if, he recovers. That must have been a hell of a crack you gave him.'

'It seemed like a good thing to do at the time,' Belle answered. 'I hope that he can talk, though.'

'Yes. It might help us to locate the others,' Manderley growled. 'Damn it, ma'—Colonel Boyd, if you'd——'

'I've been thinking the same thing, Colonel,' the girl answered, without sounding apologetic. 'But I acted as I thought best at the time. Everything at the theatre pointed to Sabot being in cahoots with the intruders. It was too much of a coincidence that he would have selected a trick that fitted their requirements so perfectly. To say nothing of it being highly unlikely that they could have substituted their portraits for whatever he had hidden behind the curtain. Then there had been Selima's behaviour. She acted as if nothing was wrong. It caused her death in the end, poor little fool. On top of it all, the orchestra had been ready to play "*Dixie*" at just the right moment.'

'None of which would have been remembered, or considered, if they'd succeeded in their plan,' Manderley admitted.

'It wouldn't,' Belle agreed. 'I went back to the theatre to see if there was any way I could prove what I suspected. Then, when I realised what they must be planning, I had to warn Uncle Alburgh and his friends. He sent word to them and I came here as quickly as I could.'

'I'm not blaming you, Colonel,' Manderley stated. 'There's few enough would have realised what was being planned.'

'Thank you, sir. Do you think that your men will find the arms?'

'It's not likely. The Brotherhood must have become suspicious when Brandt didn't return. If so, they won't have lingered in this neck of the woods. If I make too big a fuss, searching for them, it's going to arouse a lot of comment. The truth about what's happened could get out, and neither of us wants *that*.'

'Nor do our superiors,' Belle commented wryly. 'We're safe as far as the civilian population is concerned. Uncle Alburgh will have his newspaper pass off the business at the theatre as a stupid, ill-advised, but unimportant piece of foolishness. Handled that way, people will have forgotten it by the end of the week. But not if the truth gets out. Yankee radicals will make a big thing of it and the Brotherhood will suggest that the Army really intended to arrest and murder Uncle Alburgh as an example to other Southrons not to attend treasonable assemblies.'

'You're right,' Manderley conceded.

'I'm not sorry Sabot escaped,' Belle remarked.

'Why not?'

'Aren't there two Navy steam-launches here in Shreveport?'

'Yes. They come under my command and are used for policing the river.'

'One of them could easily take me to Mooringsport,' Belle said thoughtfully.

'Not before the *Texarkana Belle* arrives,' Manderley warned. 'I had thought of sending one of them after her to arrest Sabot.'

'I'm pleased that you didn't,' Belle drawled. 'With luck, and a little planning, he's going to take me to the rest of the Brotherhood—and the Frenchman.'

How Belle Boyd followed the Brotherhood For Southron Freedom in search of the Frenchman is told in *The South Will Rise Again*.

## J. T.'S LADIES RIDE AGAIN

BY J. T. EDSON

Big, beautiful, high-spirited – and as quick on the draw as they are at outwitting a criminal.

Woman deputy Alice Fayde of the Rockabye County Sheriff's Office in Texas; Amanda 'Blonde Genuis' Tweedle; Rita Yarborough of Company Z, Texas Rangers; Calamity Jane and the lady outlaw, Belle Starr, all prove that when danger threatens, J.T.'s Ladies are as tough and resilient as any of the legendary heroes of the West.

0 552 13341 8


## RAPIDO CLINT STRIKES BACK

BY J. T. EDSON

**Nobody noticed the little Texan till the trouble began . . .**

It was a typical country-house party, though perhaps a touch more decorous than most – perhaps even a tiny bit dull. Then suddenly all hell broke loose. The host was found murdered and the house was bristling with hard men whose methods of extracting information were anything but polite.

But nobody bothered about Rapido. And Rapido kept pretty much to himself. In fact the slow-moving, slow-talking Texan seemed remarkably ill-named. That is until danger threatened, and the quiet man, transformed into a deadly fighting machine, treated the English to a showdown worthy of *Gunfight at the OK Corral*.

0 552 13623 9

## J. T. EDSON OMNIBUS VOLUME 1

Of all the characters created by J. T. Edson, Dusty Fog –
that small, softly spoken hero who strikes when least
expected – is surely the most famous, the most popular.

Here, for the first time, are three Dusty Fog stories in one
volume. *You're in Command Now, Mr Fog: Kill Dusty Fog!:
The Devil Gun* all deal with Dusty Fog's exploits during the
Civil War.

0 552 13602 6


## J. T. EDSON OMNIBUS VOLUME 2

The Ysabel Kid is one of J.T. Edson's most vibrant and
colourful characters. Half Comanche, half Irish, the Kid was
raised as a Comanche brave. From his Irish father he learned
superb rifle skill, and from Dusty Fog he learned how to be a
fighting man on the OD Connected Ranch. Dressed in black,
riding his white stallion, the Ysabel Kid is a character no one
can ever forget.

Here are three stories, all featuring the Ysabel Kid –
COMMANCHE
SIDEWINDER
OLD MOCCASINS ON THE TRAIL

0 552 13603 4

# J. T. EDSON OMNIBUS VOLUME 3

Waco is one of J.T. Edson's youngest characters. Wild, brave, and sometimes inexperienced, Waco has the best teachers in the West. For characters like Dusty Fog, Mark Counter, and the Ysabel Kid have all taken a hand in training Waco to be as fearless and skilled as they are themselves. The three stories in this volume feature Waco, holding his own with the most dangerous characters in the West.

Three Waco Stories
**TRIGGER FAST**
**THE MAKING OF A LAWMAN**
**WACO'S DEBT**

0 552 13604 2

# J.T. EDSON OMNIBUS VOLUME 4

Mark Counter, six-foot-three, big, blond and dangerous, is certainly the most handsome character ever created by J. T. Edson. From the top of his low-brimmed Stetson to the soles of his cowhide boots, he is one-hundred-per-cent a fighting man.

Here are three stories of the Floating Outfit, all featuring Mark Counter –

TROUBLED RANGE
THE WILDCATS
RANGELAND HERCULES

0 552 13605 0

# J. T. EDSON OMNIBUS VOLUME 5

Life was wild and dangerous in the West – particularly in the Trail End towns where violence and corruption ruled and the only law was that of a gun. Dusty Fog and his friends, quiet, tough, and as quick on the draw as any gun slinger, were the only people able to cope with taming the West. When they moved in the citizens of the Trail End towns knew that the law had arrived, and the best Lawman in the West – Dusty Fog.

Three Lawman stories featuring Dusty Fog –

QUIET TOWN
THE TOWN TAMERS
THE SMALL TEXAN

0 552 13606 9

# J. T. EDSON OMNIBUS VOLUME 6

The big cattle-drives across the land were hard, long, and beset with dangers. They bred tough men in a tough land and the Trail Boss and his crew worked hard and played hard. Ole Devil Hardin's legendary Floating Outfit were one of the best trail herd crews around – quick on action, fearless in dangerous situations, and ready to cope with anything and everything.

Three Trail Herd stories featuring characters from the legendary Floating Outfit

FROM HIDE AND HORN
TRAIL BOSS
GUN WIZARD

0 552 13607 7

# J. T. EDSON TITLES AVAILABLE
# FROM CORGI BOOKS

| | | | |
|---|---|---|---|
| ☐ | 13602 6 | **EDSON OMNIBUS VOLUME 1** | £3.99 |
| ☐ | 13603 4 | **EDSON OMNIBUS VOLUME 2** | £3.99 |
| ☐ | 13604 2 | **EDSON OMNIBUS VOLUME 3** | £3.99 |
| ☐ | 13605 0 | **EDSON OMNIBUS VOLUME 4** | £3.99 |
| ☐ | 13606 9 | **EDSON OMNIBUS VOLUME 5** | £3.99 |
| ☐ | 13607 7 | **EDSON OMNIBUS VOLUME 6** | £3.99 |
| ☐ | 13608 5 | **EDSON OMNIBUS VOLUME 7** | £3.99 |
| ☐ | 13541 0 | **MARK COUNTER'S KIN** | £2.50 |
| ☐ | 13341 8 | **J.T.'S LADIES RIDE AGAIN** | £2.50 |
| ☐ | 13623 9 | **RAPIDO CLINT STRIKES BACK** | £2.99 |